The Red Cupboard

Stephen T Gilbert

This book is a work of fiction.
The characters, incidents, and dialogue are all products of the author's imagination.
Any resemblance to any actual events or persons, living or dead, are purely
coincidental.

ISBN: 1981167404

ISBN-13: 978-1981167401

DEDICATION

This book is dedicated to Vivian Oscher. She is my Mindy. The Red Cupboard sits in her living room, and prompted this story.

CHAPTER 1

Blind dates can be dicey. Sometimes they lead to wonderful adventures. And then there was the time when I got up to pay the bill only to find my date missing when I returned to the table. I checked the restaurant, and then glanced out the window, just in time to see her scurrying around the corner. Evidently she'd had enough of my sparkling wit. On the other hand it saved an awkward goodbye. All I could do was laugh.

Mindy and I were on a blind date, sort of. We'd been set up by a mutual friend, and had been emailing back and forth for several weeks just to find a time when we could match our busy schedules. So I suppose it was still a first date, but it didn't really feel that way, since we'd really gotten to know each other over the previous weeks. All that was left was the face to face encounter.

The day finally arrived, and I showed up at her house, flowers in hand. We had lunch at a nice seafood place overlooking the ocean, went for a long walk on the beach, and now were sitting on Mindy's bright red sofa, trying to get to know one another. All in all, the day was going well. After all, she hadn't skipped out when I went to pay the bill. And she did invite me back to her place.

I suppose this would be a good time to mention that Mindy's condo is a little different from mine. In fact, my initial reaction upon stepping into her living room was overload. I'm kind of a minimalist. Mindy, not so much. Her room reflected not only all of the travel she'd done, but also the gifts she'd received from her many friends. And it was all very, very colorful. On the other hand, it helped with conversation starters, like, "Gee, that's an interesting life sized voodoo mask staring at me. How did you happen to get that?" What I left out was, "And why in the world would you ever have anything that spooky inside your house!"

But enough about my phobias. Like I said, we were just sitting and talking.

"Do you ski?" she asked.

I reflected on the lunatic idea of racing down a steep slope at breakneck speed on a couple of sticks and decided to deflect. "No. I never have, but I like the forest, and snowy hikes can be beautiful." I reached for a glass of wine. It was a refreshing white, and perfect for a hot summer day. I sipped and turned to her again. "Have you ever gone for a winter walk along a mountain stream? I think maybe that's why I've never skied. You lose some of the solitude that you find just walking through the forest on a fresh bed of snow."

"Maybe," she replied with a smile, "but there's something to be said for sliding down the hill, wind in your hair, carefree…"

"I suppose." I looked around the room, seeking a new topic. "Where did you find this furniture?" I asked.

"Do you like it?"

"It is unique," I said, "almost more art than function." I gestured toward one of two tall cabinets. "That one, for example, do you keep things inside?"

She rose and went to the cabinet, her wavy red hair trailing down her slender back. She looked back at me as she opened the door revealing an assortment of wine glasses along with an array of figurines. "Of course. This and that."

The casing of the piece was lacquered shiny black on the outside and turquoise inside. The two drawers were bold green and bright yellow and the door she'd opened was sky blue. It wasn't just the colors of the furniture that attracted my attention. The case itself was structured in the shape of a swirling 'S,' about six feet tall, and wound up along the wall like some kind of surrealistic vine.

"I was at an art exhibit at Fort Mason, up in San Francisco, and I met a furniture designer. I gave him some suggestions and he built these. They just seemed to want to come home with me."

"Well they're certainly unique," I raised my glass. "You've hardly touched your wine," I said. "Don't you like it?"

She smiled. "To tell the truth, I'd forgotten it was there."

She lifted her glass and took a small mouthful. "Ah, light with a hint of grapefruit and melon. A delightful Sauvignon Blanc."

I laughed. "Pardon me," I said, properly rebuked. I leaned back on the sofa and looked expectantly in her direction.

She flashed me a subtle grin, and then settled on the other end of the couch, legs tucked under her catlike, still holding the wine glass in one hand while she adjusted her t-shirt over her bare knees with the other. "Would you like something to eat?"

I demurred. She looked so settled and comfortable on the couch that I could hardly ask her to get up. We talked about skiing, and hiking, and art. Presently, I noticed another case in the corner. It had the bold red cabinet of the others, but was small, more of an end table than anything else. I hadn't noticed it before, probably because it was nestled between two black leather chairs. The top twisted like the others, in the shape of a sideways 'S,' matching the sides. Only the bottom was flat where it merged into the carpet. A piece of fused glass rode the top, balanced precariously like a surfer challenging a wave. And on top of the glass was a tall plant with large glossy green leaves that served as a perfect background for clusters of white star shaped flowers. I pointed to the plant, "What's that called?"

She looked at the plant, "It's one of my favorites," she said, "a Voacanga Africana."

"Really," I replied. "I don't think I've ever seen a plant like that before. Do you mind my asking where you got it?"

She laughed. "Well I don't know," she said. "Can you be trusted not to turn me in?"

I must have looked confused, because she laughed again, and then whispered conspiratorially, "I brought it back from Africa. I don't think I was supposed to."

"Really?" Now she had my attention. "Why not?"

"Well I hear that you can buy them here, if they're properly imported. I've never checked." She looked longingly at the plant. "I put that one in my luggage." She paused and took a sip of wine. "It's a medicinal plant."

"Even more interesting. What are its uses?"

"Well I don't think that the traditional imports have any potency, but this one came from Senegal, and it's full strength. It's a mild stimulant, and an analgesic. It's also a fairly potent hallucinogenic."

"Interesting." I walked over to the plant and looked more closely at the flowers. "How big does it get?" I asked.

She laughed again and I looked back at her. "Much bigger than that. In the jungle it'll grow to thirty feet. But not in my little pot."

"Huh." I stepped back and looked over at her, and then back at the plant. "So what do you keep in your funny little red cupboard under the hallucinogenic plant?" I watched her, expecting to see her laugh, but she just furrowed her brow.

"You know, I don't think I've ever opened it. I brought it home and was so busy setting up the others that I just pushed this one against the wall and set the plant on top."

"Never?"

"No, not that I recall. This one's a little different. I inherited an ugly old case from my grandfather." She smiled shyly. "I must have been feeling sentimental, because in retrospect it didn't make any sense."

"What's that?"

"Well I actually had the cabinet maker build this using the other one for a frame. I call it 'grandpa's cupboard.'" She chuckled. "I suppose he'd roll over in his grave if he saw what I've done with it!"

I looked back at the cabinet, intrigued now. "Do you mind if I…"

She finished for me, "Open it?"

I nodded.

Now she did laugh, detecting my curiosity. "Sure," she said. "Go ahead."

I knelt down, pushed my face through one of the white floral clusters, and then gently pulled the knob on the red door. It resisted at first, and then popped open. The inside was painted a glossy turquoise blue, and though it was dark, I could see that it was completely empty. I turned back to see that she'd come up next to me. I backed away so that she could look.

Putting one hand on my shoulder, she leaned in. "It's so smooth," she said as she ran her hand across the turquoise interior. "The wood is almost soft, like it's a living thing." She turned toward me and my eyes caught the blue in hers, just a couple of inches away.

8

Nervously, I put my hand inside alongside hers, just touching. "You're right," I whispered, "almost too soft to be wood."

Still running her hand along the bottom of the cabinet, she dropped her eyes and nodded slowly. "Almost sensual…" she started, and then looked back at me, "Well that's interesting."

"What's that?"

She took my hand and placed it into the back right corner of the cabinet. "It's almost like someone's carved a pattern back here."

I felt around the dark corner until I found a small circle carved in the wood. "Huh," I said. I ran my fingers over it and then tapped it, gently at first and then a little harder. With a soft click, a small button popped up. Startled, I backed away and placing her hand on the button, rose to my knees.

She held her hand there for another moment, before leaning back to join me, shoulder to shoulder. "Why would that be there?" she asked.

I shook my head. It was clearly the base piece of the cabinet. There couldn't be anything under it. And yet…

"Do you suppose it opens in some way?" I grinned conspiratorially, "Maybe it has some kind of false bottom where you can hide your valuables."

She frowned at me. "Maybe. I'm surprised the cabinet maker never mentioned it when I picked it up."

"And you never opened it."

"No. I never did."

We knelt there for another minute or so, pondering the knob before I finally said, "Well it's your cabinet. Are you going to open it or are you going to leave that for me?" Then I winked at her, "Or will we leave it as a mystery?"

She started to lean forward and then rocked back. "Uh, you found it. Go ahead."

I reached my hand back into the cabinet and felt along the bottom until I touched the small turquoise knob. I pulled gently and the bottom rotated easily up along invisible hinges on the opposite wall. I knelt back up and looked at her. "Interesting," I said and grinned, "Spooky."

She rolled her eyes at me. "Are you going to look inside or will I to have to?"

Properly chastised and challenged, I nodded my head. "I will."

I bent forward again, and put my entire head into the cabinet. I had expected to see a thin piece of lacquered wood underneath the hatch. Barring that, I figured it would open to reveal the carpet. "Uh, Mindy, I think you should look at this."

"So what is it?" she asked.

I pulled my head out and knelt beside her again. I looked directly at her, "Why don't you tell me?"

She rolled her eyes and said, "Fine." Then she leaned forward and reached into the empty space. Surprised, she looked back at me. "It feels rough, like the original wood. All of the rest is so smooth and soft. Do you suppose he found the latch?"

I shook my head. "Hard to tell."

She continued to run her hands carefully around the base of the cabinet until she pulled back with a start. Looking at me, she said, "There's something back in the corner. Something soft."

I laughed. "Mysterious! Scary!"

That seemed to break the mood and she punched me playfully on the shoulder. "Did you see it? There's definitely something there in the corner."

"Probably some kind of nest. Do you have a flashlight?"

"What, you can tease me but won't reach your own hand in there?" She rose and shaking her head went into the kitchen. "And here I thought you were brave."

I laughed again. "Brave yes. But I don't stick my hands into places I can't see. Bring the flashlight and I'll take a look."

She padded back on stocking feet and handed me a small penlight. "This is it?" I asked.

She rolled her eyes again and said mockingly, "You're stalling. Scared of a little nest?"

Chuckling nervously, I took the light and shone it into the cabinet. Surprisingly, it threw a strong beam into the small space. Leaning forward, I slid it under the false bottom and then stretched out so that I could see into the back corner. "I don't think it's a nest," I said as I reached warily back. "It's…" Suddenly I yelped and snatched my hand back. "Watch out!"

Mindy scrambled back so quickly she nearly knocked over the coffee table with the wine glasses. Grabbing one, she saved it.

The other rattled, and then settled back onto the coaster. Only then did she look at me. "You okay?"

Nodding gravely and clutching my hand, I said, "I think so. There's something back in that corner."

She looked cautiously at the open cabinet and then took my hand. "Let me see." Stroking it softly, she said, "I don't see marks and I don't feel anything."

She continued to explore my hand intently and finally I said, "Right there, on the pad of my index finger." She explored it and then looked up into my eyes, a worried expression on her face. "There's nothing there."

Her hand was still in mine, so I reached over with my other and held it gently. "Perhaps if you give it a kiss?"

She looked back down at my hands, now encasing hers, and then back up into my eyes. "Do you really think that would help?" she asked demurely.

Her face was inches from mine, and I could see the sparkle in her eyes. Nodding solemnly, I whispered, "I'm certain of it."

She turned back to my hand. "Well, if you think it will help." She pulled my left hand away, and taking my right, raised it to her lips. "The tip of your index finger?"

I nodded. "Yes."

"All right," she said softly and then wrapped her lips around the end of my finger. For an instant, the feel was entirely sensuous, and then I felt her teeth come together against the soft flesh. At first, she seemed to nuzzle the finger, but the pressure increased until suddenly she gave me a sharp bite.

"Ow!" I yelled as I yanked my finger back. There was no blood, but I could clearly see a bite mark on the slippery end of my finger. "Why'd you do that?"

She snorted at me and reached over for her glass of wine, "Perhaps if you kiss it," she mocked.

"But," I was flustered and she could see it.

She gave me a suspicious look. "No marks; no redness; not even any sensitivity when I touched it." Then she looked up into my eyes. "Perhaps if you kiss it, he says with a smirk on his face. Perhaps if you kiss it." Then she smiled and said demurely, "Well you got your kiss, and a little more. Now the pain might be real!"

I laughed. "Am I that transparent?"

"Well," she smiled, "I wasn't born yesterday." She patted my hand and said, "Does it still need a kiss?"

I looked at her and chuckled. "Can I trust you just to kiss it?"

She took my hand and lifted it to her lips and delivered a gentle peck, and then looked me in the face. "As much as I can trust you not to pretend to be hurt."

Now I laughed deeply. "Touché," I said and shook her hand firmly. "Now about that cabinet."

"Yes," she said, "about that cabinet."

I crawled over and took up the flashlight from the carpet. Peering inside, I could definitely see some kind of bundle in the back corner. I reached in cautiously and pried it loose.

Mindy was there by my side when I rose to a kneeling position. "What is it?" she asked.

I handed it to her. The bundle was roughly the size of a brick, but lighter, wrapped in faded calico cloth and tied off with a narrow pink ribbon.

She cocked her head to one side and then rose, motioning me to the couch. She sat, as if in a trance, focused entirely on the small cloth bundle in her hands. Her feet seemed to settle under her on the soft fabric automatically and then she looked up at me with a puzzled look on her face. "I…" she started, and then stopped, as if searching for words. "Do you suppose…" she began, and then dropped her eyes back to the cloth. "This is silly," she finally got out. "I don't know what to think."

I sat across from her on the sofa and reached out, taking her hand in mine. "Are you alright?"

She shook her head, as if coming out of her trance. "Of course. I just wonder how long this," she nodded down at the package again, "has been in there." Then she looked up at me again and the puzzled look returned. "Hmmm."

I squeezed her hand and then let it go. "How about a refill on that wine?"

"Just what I need," she said, smiling. "And then maybe a peek inside." She nodded toward the bundle again. "Oh, was there anything else in the cabinet?"

I shook my head. "I'll check again later, but I don't think so." I poured a little more of the white wine into each of our glasses and then settled the bottle back onto its coaster. I raised my glass. "To mysteries," I toasted.

She grinned and then touched my glass with hers. "To mysteries," she replied softly.

CHAPTER 2

We sat for several minutes, the package nestled comfortably on the sofa between us. Periodically, one of the other of us would gaze at it and start to speak, but we always seemed to catch our words before they could emerge. So the package sat, an enigma, offering no clues.

Finally, Mindy set down her wineglass and said, "Well I'm too curious to just leave it there." She picked up the small bundle and cautiously touched the ribbon. "Feel this," she said, reaching for my hand. "Do you think it's silk?"

I ran my fingers along the ribbon and nodded, "Feels like it."

"Interesting." Carefully, she untied the ribbon and let it fall to the sides of the package and then began to pull the calico cloth away from the contents.

By now I'd moved right next to her, our bodies nestled together as we both focused on her hands. As the cloth fell away, I glimpsed a stamp, and realized that we were looking at a bundle of letters, carefully saved and wrapped in a protective cloth bundle. I whistled softly. "So old," I said.

She nodded distractedly as she pulled back the last fold of calico. "I wonder who wrote them." She picked one up and looked at the address. "It's so faint." She lifted it and then leaned to the side and turned on a small accent lamp.

"You said that the table belonged to your grandfather. Do you suppose they were his?" I asked.

"I don't know," she said distractedly. "They could be."

Peering intently, she lifted the envelope closer so that she could read the address. She squinted for a while and then shook her head with a smile. "Perhaps your eyes are better than mine. Would you like to try?"

I leaned down until my head was nearly touching hers and stared intently. "You're right, it's very faint. It looks like it says 'Mrs. Catherine Lewis Woodward,'" I read down, "43 Lakeshore Avenue, Bradford, Pennsylvania. There's no zip code." I looked up at her, "Any idea who that might have been?"

She shook her head, and then started. "I have a family tree upstairs. My mother started it several years before she died." She tilted her head to one side. "I think it's in a box of her things in the office closet." She jumped up and reached out her hand, "Come on, let's go find it."

She took my hand and led me to the stairs. I'd never been up before, and took in the pictures of family, along with her shots of African scenes, both wildlife and landscapes. Forgetting that I was holding her hand, I stopped in front of one small daguerreotype of a young woman. "Who's that?" I asked. Mindy stopped abruptly, looking down at my hand. Then she smiled, "That's my great grandmother. She was just a girl then. I never met her, but understand that she was quite a woman."

"Really," I said, "She looks a little like you, around the eyes, the little twist of a smile." I looked up at her and back at the picture. "Surprising," I said.

She stood by my side now, one step higher, and we looked at the picture, still hand in hand. "I never saw it," she said wistfully, "but then I never met her. She died many years before I was born." She reached out and touched the woman's brow absently, "Maybe. My father thought so anyway. He said that's why he named me after her."

"Really," I smiled. "Mindy?"

She shook her head, "Marie. My middle name."

"Well she's a beautiful woman. And somehow mysterious at the same time." I looked back at the picture. "Your father was right." I took her hand back, and then looked into her eyes. "Sorry for the distraction...Marie...Shall we see to that family tree?"

Grinning, she squeezed my hand and pulled me up the stairs.

The office was at the end of the hall, and once we entered, I could see why she'd been hesitant about finding anything there. Her desk was an antique upright model, with a drop leaf writing surface, exactly the opposite style from what I'd seen downstairs. That and two side tables were covered with books, papers, and knickknacks, leaving just enough room for a small laptop computer. Against the wall was a small sofa, probably a hide-a-bed, equally burdened with stuff. She looked back at me and held up a warning hand. "Don't even say it. I know it's a mess and someday I'll clean it."

I grinned sheepishly and looked toward the ceiling. Laughing, she opened the glass side bookcase on the desk and still talking with her back turned to me, said, "Actually it's pretty well organized. This was my grandfather's desk, and that little cabinet used to sit next to it. I can remember him putting his mail on the cabinet, then sitting right here to pay his bills. I liked that image of him so much that I've kept it up." She turned to face me. "Well, except for the cabinet. I put my mail on the kitchen table and then bring it up here later." She turned back to the desk and took a small wooden box out of the bottom of the bookcase and put it on top of a pile of papers on the drop leaf. "I think it's in here."

I stepped next to her and looked down. The box was the size of a shoebox, and the top was ornately carved, showing an eagle in flight. Mindy went on, "He gave this to my mother when she was a girl. I understand that he carved it himself from a single piece of oak. He was very talented that way."

I studied the box and could see that indeed, the grain from the bottom and the top matched perfectly. "It's beautiful," I said.

She looked back at me and smiled. "It is." She removed a number of papers along with a handful of cheap costume jewelry. "Ah, here it is." She pulled out an old piece of paper. The edges were brown and frayed, and it had obviously been folded and unfolded many times.

Then she looked up with a grin and said, "Come on. The light's better downstairs." She took a step and then hesitated and gave me a warning look. "And there's also a place to sit, right? Better not say it."

I laughed and held up my hands up in front of me. "I'd never say that!"

She wagged a smiling finger at me and said, "but you were thinking it, right?" Then she giggled and turned for the door.

CHAPTER 3

We settled back on the couch, nestled together like two little kids with an exciting discovery, and after another sip of wine, she spread out the family tree.

Much of it, particularly the recent bars, had been filled in with names, years, and occupations, but many gaps remained. Mindy turned to me. "Since it was in Grandpa's cabinet, I'll start with his line." She put a finger on her name, and then moved back to her mother, "Melissa Stevens, teacher," she said. And then moving up the tree, "Joseph Stevens, my grandfather, a railroad engineer." She moved higher, "Then there's Marie, my great grandmother. She was a doctor, very rare for a woman in those days." Her finger traced up yet again and she smiled, "and her mother, Catherine Lewis." She scanned the document and then turned to me. She's the only Catherine I can see here, so it's probably her. Do you suppose this is Catherine Lewis Woodward?"

I looked over the rest of the line, "I don't see any other Woodwards. She may be. Do you have any information on her husband?"

She scanned the paper and shook her head. "She's the only Catherine listed. It doesn't even say that she was married, let alone to a Woodward. I wonder why. Her parents are here, Arnold and Jeanie Lewis, but no husband. Do you suppose the letters were hers?" She turned to me with a puzzled grimace. "Strange."

I smiled and looked at her. "Well, what next?"

"Don't be silly," she laughed, "Let's read a letter."

Carefully, we spread the fragile documents out in front of us on the coffee table. We quickly realized that while several of the letters were written to Catherine Woodward at the Pennsylvania address others were written to a Joel Woodward in Sonora, and later Murphys, and San Andreas, California. Still others had no mailing address beyond the name Joel Woodward. The oldest one had been written in the spring of 1850, and postmarked in Philadelphia. The last was written to Joel in the fall of 1854. We organized them, and Mindy picked up the first, and then put it down when her hands started to tremble. "How silly. Suddenly I'm as nervous as a schoolgirl." She looked into my eyes and said, "How about if you read the letters from him. I'll read hers."

I nodded and took the letter.

April 6, 1850

My dearest Catherine,

Although it's only been a few weeks, my heart quakes at the thought of leaving you behind. I can still see you standing there, in that beautiful glen where we spent our final night, waving tearfully at me as I struggled to fight back my own tears. May you forgive me for the hardships I have left with you.

I can't thank you enough for the locket. I wear it around my neck on a leather thong for safekeeping. Many a night I've opened it just to gaze at your picture. It reminds me of how badly I wish to be reunited with you.

My horse was fast and sure, and we outdistanced all pursuit. Oh I saw them from time to time, but as I traveled further away, I was able to leave them behind. I slept in a series of wood sheds and barns, saving money for my journey. I found that if I arrived after sunset and left well before sunrise, I could avoid any farmers, angry at finding a stranger sharing their hayloft.

I was able to find passage to California shortly after arriving in Philadelphia. The ship leaves early tomorrow, and I and a few other hearty souls have managed to secure berths. They're small, but they'll do. There are no women, and I am led to believe that the hardships will be too great for gentle souls.

We shall stop in Charleston, and I will write you again then. For now, you remain foremost in my thoughts.

Your loving companion,

Joel

I looked at Mindy and said, "It seems to raise more questions than it answers." We had already found a letter postmarked from Charleston when we sorted them, and I reached out to take it.

Mindy put her hand softly over mine and whispered, "No. Not today. I'd like to think about this other letter for a while."

"But," I started and she squeezed my hand.

"Not today. Later."

I nodded, "All right." I settled back into the sofa and she straightened too. Taking a chance, I draped one arm over her shoulder. She looked up at me, smiled, and then settled closer. It seemed the time was right, so I brushed her forehead with a kiss and then leaned back.

After a moment, she asked, "Why do you suppose that they stayed in the glen?"

"I don't know. How old do you think they were? I wasn't really looking at dates of birth on the family tree. Were they there?" I thought a moment. "Correct that. I didn't notice a birth date on the family tree for her, and he's not listed at all."

She smiled up at me. "So many questions. Might they have just met? Did they spend the night together? He was clearly smitten with her. I wonder what happened."

"She gave him a locket with her picture in it, so there must have been some kind of mutual attraction."

She nodded. "Quite a gift. Photography was pretty new back then." She paused for a moment, thinking as I rubbed the back of her neck. "Hmm. That's nice. You suppose it's a photograph, or maybe a drawing or a painting?"

"Daguerreotype?"

She looked at me, seemingly lost in thought. "A photo from 1850. Wouldn't that be something."

"Well it sounds like he was going off to the gold rush." I looked down at her and she nodded her head. "If we read another letter, it might tell us more."

Mindy laughed. "You're incorrigible. I said no. Not today." She slowed and added softly, "Let's focus on us instead."

I looked down and fell into her eyes. Kissing her on the forehead, I said, "Now that sounds like a good idea."

CHAPTER 4

Over the next week, I thought occasionally about the letter we'd read, but work kept me busy and I didn't see Mindy again until the following weekend. We met for dinner in a small bistro in Santa Cruz. They were known for their Spanish Tapas, and I had been anxious to try it. To be quite honest, as I walked down the sidewalk toward the place, my thoughts were more on their renowned braised lamb shanks than on a pair of long dead lovers.

The day was warm, with a breeze just strong enough to cause the leaves of the elm trees that shadowed the street to flutter. I noticed a bench in front of the restaurant and after looking for Mindy inside, decided to sit and wait for her. I suppose that those living in the area became immune to the smell of the ocean air, but I had driven over the mountains that evening, and found the salt air mixed with the jasmine in the window baskets enchanting. As I waited, I closed my eyes and inhaled deeply, pleased to experience such a peaceful evening.

I suppose I must have drifted off, because the next thing I knew, someone was patting me gently on the shoulder. I opened my eyes, squinted against the brightness, and smiled when I saw the setting sun haloed around Mindy's glowing red hair. "Hey sleepyhead, you ready for dinner?"

I smiled and slid to the side. "Join me," I said. It's delightful out here."

She paused a minute, and then sat, balancing on the edge of the bench. Reaching over, she kissed me on the cheek, and then said,

"So what time's our reservation?"

I looked at my watch. "We've got a few minutes. I made it for 7:30. It's just quarter past now." I raised my arm at the sun dipping toward the ocean. The sky was just starting to glow, and I could tell that the streaks of cloud cover would capture that sunlight as it went down, leaving us with a glorious sunset. "On second thought, let's check in now. Maybe we can get the table in the window so that we can watch the sunset."

Mindy nodded and stood, offering her hand. I took it, thought of pulling her into my lap, and then decided better to rise. As we walked into the restaurant, I could see that the couple in the window table was in fact starting to leave. I smiled at the hostess and nodded toward the table. "We'd like to sit there if possible. We have a reservation for 7:30."

She smiled, took my name, and said, "I'll see what I can do. It'll be a few minutes before it's cleared."

Meantime, Mindy had taken a copy of the menu and was skimming through it. "Have you eaten here before?" she asked.

I shook my head. "A friend told me it was good. He recommended the lamb, said that was a specialty." She scowled, and I recalled that she didn't care for lamb. I laughed, "but you can try something else if you'd prefer."

She pointed to an item on the menu. "This rock cod looks good." I looked over her shoulder as she added, "It says it's served over a bed of local vegetables. I think I'll try that."

Just then the hostess called our name and directed us toward the window table. As soon as we settled, she asked if she could bring us anything to drink. I ordered a split of Tempranillo, and returned to the menu. "So we're getting lamb and rock cod," I said. "What else?"

Over the next few minutes, we discussed several other items on the menu, placed our order, and tasted the fruity wine. The sun was still hovering above the horizon, but the sky was glowing nicely when Mindy pulled out her purse and said, "I've brought the next letter. I thought maybe we should read it together, since you found them and all."

I smiled. "Have you read it yet?"

She shook her head. "No, I was waiting for you. And…well I wasn't sure we should read them for a while. That first one was so personal. It felt almost like we were invading something private in a way."

I nodded. I had felt the same way. "What changed your mind?"

Shrugging her shoulders, she looked down at the letter in her purse. "She saved them. She must have intended for someone to read them or she wouldn't have saved them."

"Or maybe she just never got around to throwing them away and then it was too late."

"No," she shook her head determinedly this time. "She wanted them to be read. Somehow, I can just feel it." As she was about to take out the letter, our first Tapas arrived and she smiled, putting her purse by her side on the seat. "After dinner."

"After dinner," I agreed. "After all, they've waited this long." Mindy had picked up a spoon and began dishing delicate pieces of rock cod onto her plate. She offered some to me and I held out my plate. I then put a little bit of aromatic lamb onto my plate and offered some to her. She shook her head reached for a crab cake. "Later?" I asked.

Scowling, she said, "We'll see."

§§§§

Dinner was excellent. All of the tapas were artfully prepared and creatively cooked to bring out delightful if subtle flavors. Mindy had finally broken down and tasted the lamb, and even admitted that she might be willing to try it again. The sunset was all that it had promised, with the sky bursting into a bright rainbow of colors that lit the white walls in the restaurant through our window. We finished the meal with a cup of coffee, and as I swirled the last of mine, I asked, "About that letter. Is it time to read it yet?"

She smiled. "I was just waiting for you to ask." Reaching into her purse, she pulled out a plastic bag. "I put it in here to protect it. The paper has become so delicate."

I nodded and watched her carefully remove the letter and spread it on the table. Once open, she offered it over to me. "It's from Joel. Would you?" she asked.

I nodded solemnly, pleased to be entrusted with this family relic. Taking the paper carefully, I noted that it was heavier than the original. The phrase 'industrial' came to my mind, as if this was more the type of paper one might use in business, while the first had been a stationary. Possibly this was all that had been available aboard the ship, I thought. I smoothed it out in front of me and began to read,

April 22, 1850
Charleston

My darling Catherine,
We arrived in Charleston early yesterday morning. I've had a difficult time finding paper, and finally managed to purchase some from the steward. He has many things for sale, and I am sure that he makes a tidy income off of the passengers during each voyage. No doubt his prices will only go up as we move farther from home. I shall take a little of my savings and buy some essentials before we sail again.
Our trip south was uneventful save for a frightful storm off the coast of North Carolina. Although it lasted only a few hours according to my pocket watch, it seemed an eternity. The wind shrieked through the rigging constantly creating a sound almost like cats fighting in the night. At one point, I had to leave this confining cabin behind, so went up on deck. We were canted nearly forty five degrees, and I was immediately soaked first by the rain that battered down upon us, and then by the waves breaking against the hull and throwing up frightful sheets of water. At one point I lost my footing and was washed across the deck. I was afraid that I might be thrown into the sea and lost forever, but at the last minute, I struck the far rail and managed to wrap my arms around a stout stanchion. I held there for what seemed hours, but in fact was only a few minutes, until the winds abated and the ship righted. Without wasting a moment, I immediately scrambled to my feet and returned to the relative safety below decks.
I am embarrassed to tell you that I tore a large hole in the seat of my trousers, probably when I slid across the deck. You can imagine the teasing I have taken from the other passengers. I have never been adept with a needle and thread, but I am learning by necessity, and even you might be proud of my handiwork.
The port of Charleston is a fascinating place, but I am glad that you are not here, as it is no place for a lady. The men are rough and ill tempered and use language that causes even me to blush. Still, it is an intriguing place. Each street seems to have a bar that is coarser than the others, with music, and gambling, and liquor, and of course, the worst sort of women. The captain has warned us to travel only in groups and to stay out of the bars. Just in case that

warning was not enough, one of the crewmen was brought back aboard this morning by the local constable. It seemed that he had been robbed and frightfully beaten. He will heal, but will likely carry a nasty scar on his cheek for the rest of his life.

I have made a few friends among the passengers. They, like me, are headed for the goldfields of California. Unlike me though, they left voluntarily and have the option of returning some day, just as I hope that someday, once things blow over, I might return to you. Jonathan is an upright young man, approximately my age and build. He grew up on a farm in New York and is off to California for the adventure, not even caring really whether he even finds gold. Samuel comes from Philadelphia. He is a giant of a man, and a few years older than I, but as gentle as a kitten. He is secretive about his past, and I suspect that there is some problem there. Fortunately, neither of them drinks, and none of us has a desire to frequent the bars.

We have found that if we walk inland several blocks, we get into a more respectable section of town where we can do our shopping. I have not spent much, preferring to hold on to my limited savings for this long journey, but I did purchase another set of trousers along with a shaving mug and razor. Since I left in such a hurry, I was unable to get those from home. My beard grows slowly, but after three weeks, had started to itch and I felt the need to shave. I daresay you would not have recognized me.

We are sharing the cabin and there is just enough room to stand on the floor. Our bunks are stacked, one on top of the other, so that if one was to sit up too suddenly, he might get a nasty crack on the head. According to the steward, this was once an officer's cabin, and there used to be only one bunk, with drawers below and a cabinet above. Those were removed to allow for two more passengers, and now the officers also share accommodations.

We shall be in Charleston for another day, re-provisioning and will stop next in St. Agustine, in Florida. I am told that it will only be a few days sail, so I will write you again from there.

I miss you dreadfully and think often of your soft voice and gentle touch, the sunlight in your hair, and the way my heart lit up when you smiled at me. At night I dream of you, lying in the green stillness of the glen, your arms reached out to me, beseeching me to join you. If only I could…

I remain,
Your faithful suitor,

Joel

I quietly lay the letter on the table and reached for a sip of coffee. It was cold, and I let it be. Mindy looked at me, but she too was quiet. Finally, she said, "Was there any more?"

I shook my head. "No, that was all." I lifted the letter. The writing had been finely spaced and covered both sides of the coarse paper.

"So we still don't know why he left."

"No." I rubbed my chin and pushed back my glasses. "We don't." I thought for a moment and then added, "He mentions the glen in both letters. Do you suppose that it has something to do with that?"

She had been putting the letter back into her purse and looked up at me. "I don't know. It seems that he was forced to leave. Certainly if they had spent the night there…"

I nodded. "Her family would not have approved."

"Not in 1850." She grimaced. "Not at all."

"Still," I wondered, "Why California? Why the hurry to get so far away?" I gestured toward her purse. "It seems that nearly all of the letters were written by him."

Now Mindy surprised me. "Not at all," she said. "I went through and organized them yesterday. Certainly many of them were written by him, but she wrote quite a few as well."

"Did you look at them?"

"You mean, did I read them?"

I smiled. "Yes. Did you read them?"

Mindy reached out and patted my hand. "No. Nor do I intend to read any more tonight. There is one from St. Petersburg, and one of hers that's dated before he lands there."

"Really? I wonder how she got it back."

"It has no postmark and no address. I'm not sure that it was never mailed." Mindy squeezed my hand. "It was a lovely dinner. And I have a nice bottle of port waiting on ice at home. Since it's no longer 1850, and I doubt that we would cause a scandal, would you like to join me?"

I signaled the waiter for the check.

CHAPTER 5

I didn't see Mindy again over the next few weeks. I had business travel that kept me on the east coast with a client for most of that time. We kept touch by phone though, so I knew that she had decided to take the letters in sequence, and intended to read Catherine's letter next. The fact that it had never been mailed didn't matter. She wanted to work with them as they were written.

I reclined my seat for the flight back from Washington to San Francisco, and reflected that I would be accomplishing in just a few hours what had likely taken Joel weeks if not months to do. Here I was, sitting in relative comfort, a glass of sparkling water close at hand, listening to Mozart through my headphones. How had his trip differed?

As the jet raced above the clouds, I drifted into a dreamy state, flowing with my music. I became Joel, imagining his difficulties. Did he attempt the crossing at the Isthmus of Panama? Had he ventured around the tip of South America? Both were perilous journeys and many had died making either passage. For that matter, why had he chosen to travel by ship, when an easier course might have been an overland trip? There were so many questions unanswered and I wondered if the letters would shed light on those and other matters.

I let my mind wander, imaging ocean storms, jungle perils, and the fear, excitement, and wonder that must have coursed through his thoughts during his months of travel.

§§§§

Mindy planned a picnic at Point Lobos, just south of Carmel. Never having been there, I'd come prepared for hiking as well as a quick dip in the cold surf. The weather was glorious, a sunny but breezy, perfect day by the ocean. She'd insisted that I slather sunscreen on my face, and after hiking for a while I was glad. The sun burned down but the wind kept it cool enough that I was surprised to see that my arms were reddening where I'd rolled up my sleeves.

We hiked along the coast for about a mile until we came to a lookout above a sheltered cove where we peered out over the beach. The water was a startling turquoise color, and the gentle waves merely caressed the white sand of the beach. I could see several sea lions sunbathing just above the water's edge. I turned to her and she said simply, "It's calving season." She pointed. "Do you see the little one, right there next to a larger one?"

We were over a hundred feet away, but it was clear to see that there were several smaller sea lions there. I noticed another pair in the water, playing among the kelp beds. Periodically, one would bark out, as if calling for others to come out to enjoy the fine swimming.

"Point Lobos," she said. When the Spanish first came here, they heard the barking and thought that there were wolves here. They named it Point Lobos, or Wolf Point. It was a combination of sea lions and harbor seals feeling frisky in the water and talking with one another."

She took my hand and before I could say anything, led me further down the trail. Looking back, she said, "We can't go down to this beach. It's closed for calving now, but I wanted to show it to you. It seemed appropriate somehow, that we come here today before reading the next letter."

I cocked my head in confusion, but followed her. She walked along the trail for a while, and then took a side branch toward the beach. "But I thought we couldn't go down," I began.

"We're not. I just thought…" Her voice tapered off sadly as she walked around a slight bend in the trail. Just ahead, and a little off the trail, was a bench. She walked around to the front and sat, and then looked back at me and motioned me to join her, so I did.

The view was magnificent. The bench was placed just so that it would look out along the inlet, starting with the white of the sand, through the light green of the water that lapped at the shore, and progressively turned darker and bluer as it flowed out toward the ocean. The cliffs rose abruptly from the sand on either side. I was surprised to see that a colony of cormorants had made their nests along the walls. I pointed and she simply nodded sedately, and then turned back to the ocean. Sensing that she wanted some time to take in the view, I sat quietly and looked out over the inlet.

A few minutes passed, and Mindy turned to me. Her face appeared to be as peaceful as I had ever seen it. She smiled softly, her eyes glistening as if with tears, and said, "This is a very special place for me. My mother found this spot during one of our hikes here. We watched the birds, and the lobos, and just enjoyed the serenity. It's a great place to recharge your batteries." She paused and looked back at the sea. I was about to interrupt when she continued, "It seemed important that we bring Catherine's letter here. She's family. When my mother died, I bought this bench in her honor and sprinkled some of her ashes down below. I come here when I'm confused, or depressed, and it soothes me. It's like I can feel her presence reaching out to me, helping me to focus on what's important."

She leaned back against me and I put my arm around her, pulling her close. She lay her head on my shoulder and we sat that way for a long time, quietly gazing out at the sea.

Finally, she reached out and squeezed my knee, and then rose. I stood with her. I hadn't noticed the white handkerchief before, but now I smiled when I saw her lean over to polish the brass plaque on the bench. She picked out a few grains of sand and some other debris, and then smiled at me. The tears were gone, and her face was suffused with contentment. She stepped back and took my hand, and we both looked down. The plaque read, "May this bench comfort all who sit here. In loving memory of Melissa Stevens."

We hiked back to the main trail and down about a mile to a rocky cove with a wide beach. A steep staircase led down through the brush, and we climbed carefully down. Once at the beach, Mindy led me to a sheltered spot at the base of the cliff. "I thought this would be a good place for our picnic. It's out of the wind."

"It looks good to me," I sighed. I shrugged off my daypack

and flexed my shoulders.

Mindy reached inside hers and pulled out a light blanket that she spread out on the sand. "I packed yours with lunch and a bottle of wine, along with a few bottles of water."

I smiled. "Well now I know what's been bumping against my back." I looked inside the pack and saw a bottle of Chardonnay along with plastic containers of vegetables and a tub of chicken. "Perfect beach picnic fare," I grinned. "And I've worked up an appetite."

When I unpacked, I discovered that I'd also been carrying two plastic plates and a pair of wine glasses. I set them out on the blanket while Mindy prepared lunch.

Evidently we were both hungry, as we ate silently for several minutes. Finally I tipped my wine glass toward Mindy in a toast. "Thank you for showing me that very special spot. I agree with your mother. It's beautiful, relaxing…it's a wonderful spot. I'm honored that you took me there."

She smiled softly and touched my glass with her own. "Mom," she said.

We ate and then packed the plates and all of the garbage back into my backpack along with the water. The wine bottle was nearly empty, so I lifted it and looked at Mindy. She nodded, "Sure, we might as well finish it." We'd sprawled out on the blanket, enjoying the warmth of the sun. Slowly, Mindy sat up, stretched her arms, and then reached into the bottom of her backpack. She pulled out a letter, again protected in a plastic bag. Offering it to me, she said, "Will you do the honors?"

I started to take the letter, but then hesitated. "I don't think so. She wrote this one. I think it should have a feminine voice. Isn't that what you suggested earlier?" Mindy inclined her head in agreement and pulled her hand back. She unwrapped the letter and I could see that the paper was different, lighter, and somehow daintier than the others. I sat close to her and looked at the script. It was written in a beautiful, flowing hand, one much more practiced than I'd read with Joel. "You can tell it's written by a woman."

Mindy nodded, "My great, great grandmother." She settled back on the blanket, opened the letter reverently, and began to read.

April 26, 1850
Bradford, Pennsylvania

My dear Joel,
Can it be that it's been a month since I last saw you? I wonder as I write this, where you are and what you are doing. And I pray as I do every day, that you are safe from harm.

My brothers were gone looking for you for nearly a week. They finally returned, frustrated and angry, but confident that you were gone. I was furious with them, but they would not listen to me. Even Robert, who has often taken my side in the past, refused to hear me. You were gone, and that was all that mattered to them. They seemed to feel that they had saved the family honor by chasing you away.

And yet I cannot believe that our love was dishonorable. I went with you because I wanted to; because I needed to; because you mean the world to me.

I know that they will open and defile any letter that I might receive from you, so each day I go into town. Oh, I have many different excuses, but I need to be the one who checks the mail first. And every day, I have returned, having completed my errands, but without word from you.

So when I got your letter today, well I am not sure my feet touched the ground all the way home. Oh, I put on a stoic expression when I came into the house, but inside my heart was singing, and I could hardly wait until bedtime so that I could go to my room and read what you had to say.

You called me your dearest Catherine.

But you are sailing for California. Is it a real place? It seems so impossibly far away. How long will it take you to get there? Send for me and I well follow you.

Ah, but how can I even send this letter. I know not where you are, nor even where you will be. I cannot wait for your ship to reach Charleston, so that you can write again. Until then, I will hide these letters where they will be safe from prying eyes. And tonight I will dream of you.

Your loving bride,

Catherine

Mindy, folded the letter and returned it to the envelope and the plastic bag. Only when she looked back at me did I notice the tears glistening in her eyes. She reached up with one hand and wiped them, and then smiled. "Well," she said, "she was certainly smitten."

"I'd say so." I thought for a moment. "So her brothers chased him away. I wonder why."

"I don't know. She doesn't say." She looked at me conspiratorially, "Maybe we'll find out in one of the other letters."

I frowned. "She said they thought they were protecting the family honor. Could they have been having an affair?"

"It's possible," she said, "but in the end she called herself 'your loving bride.'" Why would they have chased away her husband?"

We packed up in silence, and hiked back up to the main trail. The sun was lowering in the west, and we were about three miles from the car. Mindy set a brisk pace and I followed, wondering what we might find in the next letter.

CHAPTER 6

"This is the hard part," I said, reaching back my hand. "It's slippery, so you'll have to be careful." I reached out cautiously with my left foot onto the big boulder, and then feeling secure, settled my weight on it. The trail along the side of the creek had eroded, and was blocked by a mudslide, most likely caused by the unusually wet weather we'd experienced in the spring. Nonetheless, I was determined to hike up to the waterfall.

I looked back. "Are you okay?" I asked.

Mindy scowled at me. "I'm wet, and I think I turned my ankle back there, but other than that, I'm fine."

"Well in that case…" I started, but I could see that I'd lost her attention. She was staring off to the side, midway up the hillside. I started to ask what she was looking at when she squeezed my hand and gave me a look that silenced me. Slowly, I followed her gaze. I couldn't see anything but the hillside. "What?"

She gently shook her head, then ever so slowly lifted her hand to point toward an opening in the rocks, about thirty feet above us. I stared, but still couldn't see anything. I was about to speak when I detected a slight movement at the base of the rocks. I craned my neck and stared. Presently, there was another movement, and I was able to focus. What had appeared to be brush and scree slowly transformed into a face and a nose. Periodically, ever so slightly, the animal would twitch its ear, giving me the movement that I'd noticed before. As I continued to watch, I detected another movement, another ear twitch, and a second face.

Mindy squeezed my hand, and then ever so slowly, backed up so that she could sit on one of the dry boulders that edged the creek. I followed and soon we were both sitting, watching the faces up the bank. She turned to me and whispered so silently that I could barely hear her over the trickling of the stream, "They're tiny. They look like fox pups. Do you suppose that's their den?"

"I think so," I replied, afraid to make any noise. I can see two. Are there more?"

"Four, I think."

I stared at them and gradually made out a nose, and then another body behind the first two. Try as I might, I couldn't see the fourth.

And there we sat, for the next half hour, staring at them as they stared at us. Presently, our patience paid off, as one of the pups rose and yawned, and then started to scratch at a flea. It was such a natural behavior that we could tell that he'd obviously lost interest in us, or maybe we'd simply become part of the scenery. He yawned again, and then bored, reached over and bit one of the other pup's tails. The other pup yelped softly, and turned to defend himself. I smiled, and could tell from the pressure on my hand that Mindy too was enjoying a chance to spy on nature. What had begun as one fox biting the tail of another was soon a free for all, with fox pups tumbling in their den, attacking siblings and lost in the joy of play. Periodically, one would glance in our direction, but as long as we stayed perfectly still, they would quickly rejoin the play.

While we sat there, I detected another movement out of the corner of my eye and turned my head just enough to see an adult fox move cautiously toward the den. She was carrying something in her jaws that appeared to be a rodent, and just as she came out into the open, she spotted us and froze. We continued to sit silently, hardly daring to breathe, until she began to move again, carefully walking toward the den, never taking her eyes off of us. When she reached the entrance, one of the pups came bounding toward her, and reached for the catch. She growled softly, causing him to stop and sit, watching her warily. She put her catch down, and I could see what looked like a gopher. Then with one last look at us, she knelt down to feast. The pups joined her, and they all fed, occasionally looking warily in our direction.

Mindy and I continued to watch them, sitting silently on the damp rock, communicating only with light hand squeezes. Presently, one of the pups stood and yawned, and then disappeared into the den. After a while, the others followed, leaving their mother in the entrance to guard against intruders. I leaned toward Mindy and said softly, "I think it's time to go."

"I agree," she whispered. "I'll follow you."

I stood slowly, and turning my back to the den, resumed my careful walk through the slippery rocks. After a minute or so, I looked back. The mother fox was still there, guarding her pups. She'd accepted that we posed no danger, but was cautious nonetheless.

A few minutes, and about a hundred feet later, we rounded a bend and could see, just ahead of us, Castle Rock Falls. Though not a large waterfall, I'd always been impressed by it. There was a platform at the top, overlooking the falls, and we could see a group of hikers up there, about seventy-five feet above us, looking down. I raised my hand to wave, and one of them nodded his head and returned my salute, then turned his gaze out to the vista. We continued up to the base of the fall, until we were able to sit on two reasonably dry boulders, just out of reach of the tumbling water.

I took off my backpack and Mindy shrugged hers off as well. "That was amazing," she said. "I felt like they almost accepted us."

"Almost," I nodded. "I imagine that mom could tell that we couldn't get up there. Still, she was pretty wary. And the pups," I laughed. "They just wanted to play."

"Still," she sighed, "I've never seen anything like that." Then she looked around. "What an amazing place. I'd heard of the falls, and the rocks, but didn't know you could get down here. It's so different!"

I shrugged. "Well, it's not like we stayed on the trail the whole way. It's a pretty rugged hike to get down here, but it's worth it." I started to pull off my shirt and she frowned at me. "I'm hot and grimy," I said. "I want to cool down." Then I jumped up and scrambled over the rocks to the back of the fall. Once there, I poked my head into the cool water as it cascaded down the face of the cliff. Leaning out, I called, "Care to join me?"

Mindy rose and shook her head, but walked carefully to the back of the fall. "You're crazy," she yelled above the noise of the tumbling water."

I smiled. "Crazy but cooling off. Go ahead, stick your head in. It's great!"

Taking my hand, she climbed up behind the fall and then reached in her hands, cupping the water to wash her face. I shook my head. "Go ahead, like this!" I leaned forward, dousing my upper body with water. When I straightened up again, I smiled at her, water coursing off my head. "As hot as it is today, you'll dry off before we get back to the car."

Mindy looked at the fall again, then taking my hand, leaned into the waterfall. The torrent hit the crown of her head, then as she pushed further in, covered her entire head and began to trickle down her back. Pulling back, she sputtered and wiped her face, trying to get the water out of her eyes. "Once more," I said. You're just wet enough to turn that dust into mud." She looked at me, scowled, and then plunged her head back into the fall. This time she stayed under for a good fifteen seconds, shaking her head back and forth, and when she emerged, her entire upper body was soaking and her golden curls were plastered to her forehead.

She reached again for her eyes, and I caught her hands in mine, and then gently smoothed her hair back and wiped the water from her forehead. As I worked, she looked up at me, and I lowered my mouth to hers and wrapped my arms around her back. She accepted me eagerly, pulling hungrily on my shoulders. It was a long, tender kiss, and when it ended I gave her a wet hug and said, "I told you that you'd like it here.

We made our way back to where we'd left the backpacks hand in hand. Once there, we leaned back on a big flat rock, and closing our eyes, turned our faces into the sun. After a few minutes, she started to laugh. Curious, I turned toward her. Her hair was smeared across her forehead, with one sodden lock curling across her cheek. Her blouse was drenched, and she was twisting the shirttails in an attempt to rid herself of some of the excess water. Strangely, she had never looked more attractive.

"What?" I asked.

She just laughed again, louder this time, and reached up and prodded my chest with her finger.

I was clueless, so she just deepened her laugh, and then said, "I was just thinking of the lengths you've gone to see me in a wet t-shirt!"

"Ah," I smiled. Then I took the time to very deliberately work my eyes down front of her blouse. "And a very nice wet t-shirt at that!"

Laughing, she pushed me away and started to stand. "How about lunch?"

CHAPTER 7

Later that day, as we were driving back from the park, Mindy reached over and patted my knee and said, "You know what I miss?"

I glanced over at her. The mountain road was windy, and I wanted to focus on my driving. Nonetheless, I was curious. "No," I said. "Should I?"

She took a deep breath and continued, "I miss my dad's old Ford. He had a great 1960 Ford convertible. We'd put the top down and just luxuriate in the feel of the wind whipping around us. A road like this would have been perfect." She mused silently for a moment and then added, "Now you get a little of the pine scent, but in the old Ford, you'd get the smell of the trees, the crispness of a fall day, and the breeze streaming your hair straight back." She sighed and squeezed my knee, and then leaned back.

"I could open the moon roof if you like," I offered.

She just shook her head.

"Not the same. In that old convertible, the wind wrapped around you and you somehow became part of the road."

I reached over and took her hand for a moment and then said, "I remember driving some of those old cars. They were no fun on windy roads like this. To say they handled poorly would almost be complimentary!" I chuckled. "They guzzled gas; they smoked; and they didn't turn worth a darn. Good muscle though." I patted her hand. "I'd rather be driving this one, especially here."

"There was one other thing," she said softly.

Glancing at her, I could see that she had a far away look on her face. "Oh yeah? And what was that?"

She smiled. "Bench seats."

All I could do was nod. "Good point."

§§§§

Mindy insisted on showering when we got back. "I just need to wash off the sweat and the creek." As she ran up the stairs, she shouted behind her, "You can use the shower downstairs. There're towels in the cabinet."

Taking the hint, I cleaned up. I had to admit that I felt a little more acceptable when I finished. I'd anticipated getting wet, so had brought a change of clothes, and it was nice to get out of the stiff jeans I'd worn on the hike. I was waiting on the red sofa, looking at a photography book when she came down.

She noticed me out of the corner of her eye, "Would you like a glass of wine?" she asked.

Absently, I nodded, and then vocalized. "Yes. That sounds good."

She poured a nice light chardonnay, and came back into the living room. "Do you like those photos," she asked.

I looked up. "They're very good. They seem to capture the wildness of Big Sur."

She smiled. "It's always been one of my favorite books." She put down the wine glasses and then took the book from me. Opening it up about mid-way through, she pointed to a photograph. "My brother took this one." It was a seascape that showed the surf pounding against a rocky coast. He'd caught it at sunset, and splashes of spray had flown up to be backlit in a rainbow of wild abandon.

"It's amazing," I said. "So…" I paused, trying to find the words, "It almost looks like a primitive ocean." Then I thought. "Your brother the accountant? Where did he learn to take pictures like this?"

She smiled, "His hobby. Actually, he majored in art, but there wasn't any money in it, so he got his masters in economics." She looked back at the picture. "Still, sometimes I wonder what he might have become…"

She leaned against me and I inhaled. The scent of her

shampoo was intoxicating and I buried my nose in her clean hair. "Wonderful," I said. "Think I'll just stay like this all night."

She giggled. "Time enough for that later." Opening a small folder, she continued, "Your turn to read."

As she pulled out the old envelope, I could see that it was different. Joel's scribbled writing had faded over the years. I reached over and took it gently. I carefully removed the old paper and inhaled abruptly. The paper was covered with cursive that went from left to right, and more that flowed from top to bottom. They overlapped, but if I concentrated, I found that I could read both scripts. "How interesting! I've heard of this but I've never seen it before."

She had cuddled up close, distracting me with her head on my shoulder, so that she could see the paper. "Why did they do that?"

I smiled, "It was the cost and availability of paper. They'd re-use it, or just write horizontally and then vertically. If you concentrate, it's still legible. Obviously, Joel was trying to save some money."

"So what does it say," she purred.

April 27, 1850
St. Augustine

My Darling,
We arrived in St. Augustine yesterday and plan to leave for Havana tomorrow, our first stop outside of the United States. I cannot help but admit to you that I am a little nervous. They speak Spanish there, you know, so I am not sure at all how we will communicate. The captain claims to speak a little of the tongue. He has been there several times before, so I suppose he knows his way around. Still, it is a little daunting to think that I will be at the mercy of him and the crew. We have been told of unruly passengers being beaten and left ashore there. You need not worry about me though. I have been the picture of propriety.
Jonathan and Samuel and I have become fast friends. In fact, we have formed a kind of informal partnership and plan to go into the gold mining business together. I have heard that this is common in the goldfields of California, as one man can only mine a small claim whereas three can work that much more, increasing everyone's opportunity to find gold. At least, that is what I have been told. Anyway, it will be good to have friends there, and to work with two such

wholesome fellows as these will certainly be a pleasure.

We managed to find a small second hand store in St. Augustine, where I was able to purchase several sheets of good paper for just a penny. I am carefully monitoring my spending, as I have heard too many horror stories of the steep prices in the gold fields, and of miners who fell into hardship due to lack of funds. I am not above finding work if it comes to it, but will try to use frugality first, so that I have time to work my claim. Anyway, I was able to find this paper. Evidently it had been used before. I read the previous letter, but it did not interest me, as it dealt primarily with the financial accounting of a cotton farmer. He seemed to be struggling to pay his loan to a northern bank. Please excuse the rough language. I have tried to erase much of it, but some may still be legible to your delicate eyes.

St. Augustine is a tiny hamlet compared to Charleston. I can see why people referred to that grand city as the queen of the south. Once we ventured beyond the dockyards, we found the streets to be wide, and the buildings magnificent. Many had fine balconies that overlooked the harbor. And the flowers! I could not help but think of your and your love of beauty as I walked through the streets of that town, inhaling their heady scent. Perhaps one day, if I am lucky in the fields, we shall be able to build a fine home like those. St. Augustine on the other hand is a mean place. Few of the structures are painted, and the streets are dirt, or after one of the frequent rains, mud. Only the main street through town is cobbled, and that poorly. Even our little village in Pennsylvania is grand in comparison.

I dream of you every night, and miss you terribly. It has been over a month now since I last held your hand, or pressed my lips to yours, or smelled the sweet scent of your hair. It is hard for me to imagine how long we will be separated.

I wonder if your brothers are still chasing me, or if they have given up. And how long will it take them to forgive me, for now I am beginning to understand how deeply I must have offended them.

But my motives were pure, and I did what I did out of my adoration of you. I relive that night in the glen every night. Laughing with you. Holding you. Making our vows of eternal love. My dreams of you are ever pure and loving. Still, I have had time to reflect, and in that time I have tried to think like a brother, protecting my sister, and I can begin to understand their anger. Your father was a fine man, one that I always admired. He was an honest employer, and a good friend, and I miss his council. I wonder if he would have given his blessing to us. Alas, because of the accident, we will never know. And as you know, it was like I lost my mother too when he died. Has she resumed speaking at all? Oh, I am getting maudlin. I have clearly had too much time to think on this trip. Still, when I look back I have to believe that our shared grief brought us together. I had always been aware of you, but we had spent little time together before his accident. That such joy could originate from such sorrow. God truly does work in mysterious ways.

It is growing dark, and we sail in the morning. I will need to rush into town to post this letter at first light. Know that you are foremost in my thoughts and my dreams and my heart and that as I fall asleep every night, I hold your picture in my hand.

Loving you,

Joel

Mindy was cuddled up against me when I finished reading. She sighed, and I wondered if she had fallen asleep. Looking down, I could see that her eyes were open, but had a far away look. I bent down and kissed the top of her head. "You okay?"

She nodded silently and continued to lean into my shoulder. I put the letter on my lap and reached my arms around her, holding her for a time, leaning my head onto hers. After several minutes, she straightened up and said, "I'll be right back. I'm going to get the family tree." She untangled herself from me and walked thoughtfully up the stairs.

I picked up the letter and reread it. I could trace Joel's path down the eastern seaboard now. I wondered what Havana would be like. I knew that in 1850, it was like Charleston, one of the grand cities of the western hemisphere, but it was certainly a Spanish city, and would be a foreign experience in many ways for a country boy from Pennsylvania.

Mindy came down with the family tree and spread it out on the coffee table. She took her finger, much as before, and traced her family line from her mother to her grandmother, and then to her great grandmother Marie, and finally to Catherine. "And here are her parents, Arnold and Jeanie Lewis. Hmm. Isn't that interesting." I looked. Her index finger had stopped on Arnold's name, or more clearly, on his dates of birth and death. "Jeanie lived until 1857, but Arnold died in 1849. He was only 51 years old. I wonder what happened."

CHAPTER 8

Several days later, I found myself sitting in my office, computer humming away, a pile of projects in my inbox, and appointments stacked up all afternoon. Work should have commanded my attention, but I had been daydreaming.

I knew a little about Florida in the 1850's, but almost nothing about Cuba. Was it even Cuba then? Did it have a different name? I knew that it was had been Spanish colony, and that Havana was the largest city, and presumably the capital, but little else. What must it have been like for Joel, a young man from a small Pennsylvania village to suddenly find himself hundreds of miles away, in an unknown country, where he didn't understand the culture or speak the language? Was there much commerce back and forth between the United States and Cuba? I remembered reading somewhere that Alexander Hamilton had lived in the West Indies as a child and young man, but was pretty certain that most people stayed close to their homes back then, rarely traveling far away, unless to move to a new area.

My dreaming was interrupted when my secretary poked her head in the door. "Mr. Overton," she said quietly, "Your 2:00 is here."

"Thank you," I replied and shook my head to clear the musing. "Show him in."

Later that evening, I met with Mindy for dinner. We'd chosen a small Mexican place on the water in Capitola. Our table offered a fine view of the river, and the kayakers paddling back and forth. Mindy had picked up her menu, taken a quick look, and then put it down on the table. I opened, and then immediately closed mine. "This is your place," I said, "What do you recommend?"

"Anything with prawns."

I looked back into the menu. Under the fajitas part of the menu, I saw a prawn fajita for two. "Fajitas?"

She nodded and brushed back a strand of red hair that had fallen down onto her forehead. I'd noticed that something had changed, but hadn't placed it until just then. "You've changed your hairstyle," I commented. "It looks very nice." I hesitated, looking at her face. Something was familiar in the new style, but I couldn't place it.

She chuckled. "You're wondering where you've seen it before."

Nodding, I continued to look at her hair. "I am. What am I missing?"

Her shoulders shook as she laughed out loud. "It'll come to you." I pursed my lips and wrinkled my brow. She laughed again.

Finally, I shook my head. "Must be a senior moment. I know I've seen that, but I can't place it." Just then the waiter arrived to take our orders, and saved me from more embarrassment. We ordered the fajitas and margaritas, and then settled back to watch the tranquil scene on the water.

"I've always thought that kayaking would be good exercise," she said suddenly. "Have you ever tried it?"

I nodded slowly, watching as a family paddled together, talked for awhile, and then turned upriver. Two children, a boy and a girl aged about six or eight, sat in the front seats of the kayaks while their parents paddled from the rear. I was pretty sure that the children's efforts to paddle were more hindrance than help, but they were laughing and having fun, occasionally taking the opportunity to use their paddles to splash one another. I answered. "I've done a little bit of kayaking, not much." Looking back at Mindy, I added, "It is good exercise, at least if my sore arms meant anything the next day. I suppose it's like anything else. The more you get out, the better shape you're in, and the easier it becomes." I reached out and patted her hand across the table. "Fun though! And a great excuse to be on the water. Would you like to try it some day? I would guess that we can rent kayaks somewhere along the beach."

"One kayak," she said with a sparkle in her eye and squeezed my hand. "You paddle. I'll enjoy the ride." Then she mused, "I've got a waterproof housing for my camera. I'll take the pictures. It'll be fun to get up close to some of the nesting areas along the shore and see the birds."

"Got it," I said. Still holding her hand, I turned back to the window. The family was disappearing out of view up the river. There were a variety of gulls and other birds wandering the shore or flying overhead. While we watched, a pelican dove into the water and emerged with a small fish in its beak. I turned back to Mindy. "That'll work."

Just then the waiter returned with our margaritas, and I pulled back my hand so that I could raise my glass. "To kayaking," I said. The glass was frosted from the cold blended beverage inside, and the salt offset the sour lime taste perfectly. I opened my eyes wider as I looked across at Mindy. "This is good! They've got something different in here."

She nodded quietly and took a sip, and then put her glass down on the coaster in front of her. I could see her swirling the beverage around in her mouth. "I always go slow with a margarita," she said, "don't need a brain freeze."

"Ah. Good idea."

Finally, she swallowed and then said, "I brought the next letter. It's written by Joel, postmarked from Havana." She offered the old envelope across the table to me. "Would you like to read it?"

Excited, I nodded. And then I had it. Her hair was styled just enough like Marie's to look the same, yet modern. I turned to her. "Marie."

She was momentarily confused, and then laughed. "Like it?"

"I can definitely see the family resemblance now. Very nice." I looked down at her hand, "So, have you looked at the letter yet?"

She shook her head. "No. It seems that we're on this adventure together. I wanted to wait for you. Somehow,..." She paused wistfully, "for some reason, I'm enjoying slowing the pace and reading just a bit at a time, and then imagining what's coming next." She smiled and shook the envelope. "Ready?"

I reached across and took the envelope, enjoying and

extending the contact of my hand with hers. Then I pulled it away and looked down at the paper in my hand. Catherine's name was clear on the envelope, along with the postmark from Havana. In the upper left hand corner, I could read Joel's name through a smudge. I opened the envelope and took out a single brittle sheet of paper, covered with a tiny but very neatly written script. Carefully spreading it in front of me, I began to read.

May 3, 1850
Havana

My darling,
I hope that this letter reaches you. I left it with the harbormaster, along with an outrageous sum for his service. I hope that my trust in him was not misplaced. When I asked, the captain said that this is the customary way of sending a letter from Havana. Again, I can only hope to be successful in getting it to you.
We arrived in Havana three days ago. I was able to get off the ship and explore some yesterday and again today with Jonathan and Samuel. It would seem that the primary export here is sugar. I never imagined that I would ever see so much! Ship after ship fill the docks, most filling their holds with canvas bags of the stuff. I think of the cost of a small package of sugar at home and am amazed. It is truly a treasure! There are stacks and stacks of bags scattered on the wharves, and around each stack, a sticky mess of the sugar that has spilled out. I purchased a small quantity in a general store this morning and sprinkled a little on the letter. If I thought that I could get it to you, I would send more by post. In the meantime, I will imagine you wetting your finger and dipping it into the envelope to taste the sugar that so recently rested in my hand. It shall be almost like I have placed my own finger to those lips that I remember so fondly.
When we stopped in Charleston, I was struck by the number of blacks in the community. It was so different from Pennsylvania, or at least rural Pennsylvania. Nearly all of them were slaves, and most were treated almost as beasts of burden, carrying their master's possessions ahead of them. Some were shopping, and it was clear that they were household slaves, assigned to cooking or cleaning. It is very different here. Nearly everyone I see on the docks is black. Of course, the supervisors along the wharves are white, as would be expected. They can be seen running about with paper manifests, checking off the bales of sugar that are loaded onto the ships. But the laborers, and again I am certain that they are slaves, as many of them bear the crisscross pattern of a whipping

across their bare backs, are uniformly black. They seem to speak Spanish, but in a different dialect than the whites, though they communicate well enough. And they are driven hard. Just now, looking out across the deck, I can see several men loading fifty pound bags of sugar onto each shoulder, and then carrying them up the gangways and into the holds of the ships, only to return seconds later for another load. It is almost like watching a stream of black ants, marching in a line, carrying enormous bundles for a cruel master.

I remember a few months ago...has it only been that long? It seems like forever since I have seen you...Anyway, I remember Reverend Jacobs talking about the plight of the negro, and urging us to join him in advocating the abolition of slavery in our own United States. To be honest, I was more interested in you than in his message, but evidently some of it found a space in my memory. Watching these poor men working here from dawn until dusk, I have reflected upon the good reverend's message. I am sure that my family was probably too poor to own slaves, and I know that your father was opposed to the concept of one man owning another. He called it an abomination that in a society that professes freedoms as ours does, one man could hold the power of life or death over another simply because of the color of his skin. I have generally tried to hold my tongue when speaking with the other passengers, but yesterday at supper, after witnessing one of the laborers brutally abused by his overseer, I commented that no man should be allowed to treat another in that way. I was stunned by the response I got from the other passengers. Only a few agreed with me. Even many of my colleagues from the north were quick to point out that blacks lacked the power of reason, and consequently the only way to correct them when they did something wrong, or to keep them under control was with a whip. I tried to argue that it was clear to me that the blacks possessed a mind every bit as ours, and you would have thought that I had blasphemed. One called me an abolitionist and spoke the word with a particularly offensive epithet. Only a few supported me, but their convictions were equally strong and finally the captain ordered us to speak of something else, afraid that we would come to blows there in the dining salon. I have spoken with some of the others today, and their responses have been curt. I fear that I have made some enemies among my fellow passengers. Still, when I look out at the docks at the brutal lives that the men out there must lead...

I hope that I have not offended your sensitive nature. As you can tell, I have been deeply affected by what I have seen here.

Well, onto more pleasant topics. Havana is a beautiful city. Obviously, the sugar trade is lucrative, as the buildings here are magnificent. They tell me that many of the buildings are over one hundred years old, yet they look as new as if they were built yesterday, their stone and stucco covered with a fresh coat of white paint. I do get a feeling for the age of the community, as the cobbles in the streets have been well worn by innumerable carriages carrying important merchants about the city. Samuel has engaged a hackney to take us out of the city tomorrow. We will be here for several days, and he is anxious to see more of the countryside. I am hoping to see a sugar plantation, and I understand that the rain forests are particularly beautiful, covered as they are year round with a wide array of flowers. We will be spending the night out and returning the following day. It should be a grand adventure.

You are in my thoughts constantly, and I dream of the day that we will be united once again. I will write again before leaving Havana.

With my undying love,

Joel

Thoughtfully, I folded the letter and returned it to the envelope, which I then handed back to Mindy. Neither of us spoke for a minute or two, until she broke the silence, "It would appear that Joel might have been an abolitionist."

I nodded slowly. I had been looking out the window again, my mind awash with the images raised by his words. I could see the pier from where we sat, and imagined nineteenth century sailing ships tied up there, carrying a California cargo of hides and tallow. Were the California natives treated any better? I know that they weren't called slaves, but still, I could almost see a horde of brown bodies carrying their own burdens up onto the pier, returning again and again for progressively heavier loads.

I blinked my eyes to clear the vision, and turned toward Mindy. "I'm glad. I think that I would have liked to have shared a beer with him."

She smiled and raised her glass. "Now there's an interesting thought."

CHAPTER 9

Our meals were delivered with all of the fanfare that one expects with fajitas. The sizzling platter had been placed on a wooden tray, and the waiter admonished us several times to be careful. "This is very hot!"

We ordered a combination of flour and corn tortillas, and I motioned to Mindy to select one so that she could prepare her meal. She took out one steaming flour tortilla, and then carefully spooned some rice and beans into it. Following that, she added prawns, onions, and red and green peppers. Finally, she finished it off with salsa and sour cream. It looked delicious. She must have seen the hunger in my eyes, because she reached over and pushed the tortilla toward me. Leaning forward, I took a bite and closed my eyes. She was right. The prawns were magnificent. Not only were they plump and juicy, they had also been treated with some kind of mild pepper sauce so that they carried just a hint of spice into my senses. "Mmm," I sighed. "I'm sold. From now on, I'll eat nothing but prawn fajitas."

She had taken a small bite and was grinning back at me, clearly enjoying the mixture of flavors. "I told you."

"And I trusted you."

"As you should always," she replied with a sly smile.

I nodded. "As I should always," I agreed, and then devoted my attention to the fajitas.

§§§§

Later that evening, we walked back to Mindy's place. I'd suggested that we walk along the coast before heading inland, and she readily agreed. I noticed a staircase leading up the cliff, and a promontory above. "What's up there?" I asked.

She followed my gaze and said, "It's a small park. Would you like to see it?"

I nodded and took her hand. We approached the stairs and started to climb. At first the going was easy, and we laughed as we chatted. Eventually, we began to breathe more heavily and had to concentrate on the stairs. We passed landing after landing as the stairs wound their way up the face of the cliff. Finally, I stepped out onto the grass beyond the staircase, and dropped my hands to my knees, panting and trying to suck in enough oxygen to still my heart. After a moment, I stood straight and looked at the silently laughing Mindy. "How high was that," I asked.

It's about two hundred feet," she responded.

My eyes widened. "And you let an old man like me do that after dinner? It's a wonder we didn't both have heart attacks!"

She chuckled at me. "You'll live." Then she spread her arms and gestured to the view.

Still breathing heavily, I followed her arms. She was right. The view was spectacular. The sun was low in the sky, and had begun to impart a rosy glow to the patchy cirrus clouds above. We were high enough that the sparkle of the water was almost too bright to look upon. Aside from the few clouds, the sky was clear and I could see the hazy outline of the hills behind Monterey on the other side of the bay. A fog bank sat well offshore, waiting permission to creep in and cover us in a cool Santa Cruz evening.

"This is amazing. I'm in awe."

"A local favorite," she replied. "Shall we?" She pointed to a bench that offered a commanding view of the bay. "It's a great place to watch the sunset." Taking my hand, she guided me to the bench. We sat and she nestled against me, sharing my warmth in the cooling evening air.

We rested quietly, gazing out into the Pacific Ocean for quite a while, neither of us feeling the need to speak. The sun sank slowly, and it wasn't long until it touched the distant surface of the ocean, opening up a glorious pool of liquid fire that seemed to flow all the way from the edge of the horizon across the water, and into our laps, warming us with its dying rays. I reached my arm around Mindy and kissed the top of her head, marveling at the strawberry reflection of the sun off her hair.

She purred and kissed my cheek, huddling closer. Turning forward again, we watched the sun settle gently in the distance. The glow on the ocean had reflected onto the clouds above, giving the whole world a vivid orange glow. While we watched, the sun dwindled to a quiet speck on the horizon, and the color left the clouds nearest us and retreated across the ocean leaving a rainbow of reds and purples and finally deep ocean blues beyond.

I took a deep breath and sighed. "It's more than worth every one of those two hundred steps."

Mindy nodded and looked up, her eyes seeking mine. Lifting her chin, I settled my lips onto hers. Our kiss was long and tender, and spoke softly of the dying light of the day. Finally, Mindy reached down and nuzzled her lips against my neck. I shivered as she danced her tongue across my nerve endings and hugged her tight to me. She playfully nipped me and then reached up to pull my face down to hers again. She kissed me lightly this time, leaving me wanting more, and then backed away. I was about to speak when she pressed her forefinger to my lips and said, "I think this would be a good place to read Catherine's letter."

May 22, 1850
Bradford, Pennsylvania

Dear Joel,

You cannot imagine my excitement when I received your letter from Havana yesterday. I had grown accustomed to disappointment, not having heard from you in some weeks. As before, I hid the letter, and then waited until nightfall to open it and savor the contents.

Slavery is so unusual in our little village that it is hard to imagine your description. I know that the Coopers used to have Sarah to help them with the housework and the cooking, and remember that a few of the farmers owned a save or two who worked alongside them in the fields. What you have described though is not just amazing to imagine, but unsettling. From what I have seen here, the slaves are treated almost like members of the family. I never heard of one whipped, though I suppose it may have happened. And to think of scores of them working to load ships! The thought is more than a little unsettling. I am glad not to have witnessed it myself as I feel I would have been quite frightened.

I have continued my crusade to try and gain my brothers' acceptance of you. I believe that Robert is beginning to come around, but the others remain skeptical. I wish that they could see that our love is pure, and that you are a good man. Even Robert though, continues to describe you as a simple apprentice, and worse, one who has abandoned his station. Why can they not accept you as the man I love? I would open my home and spread my arms in welcome to any woman they chose to bring in, but they remain so angry with you.

Yesterday Jonas commented about how I was well rid of you and it was all I could do to contain myself and not tell him that he should hold his tongue and not speak of my husband in such a way. I know we promised not to mention our marriage until you can return, but I find it increasingly difficult to hold my peace. I believe that I shall travel to Corydon and speak with the reverend, to seek his advice both about the marriage and another matter that has me concerned. I am thankful that he was willing to marry us quietly, but am beginning to wonder whether it is time to tell the family of our vows. It is a long trip though. I have thought of contacting my friend Mary Alice and seeing whether I can spend the night with her and her husband. I am certain that my brothers would never permit me to be gone overnight without an escort, but perhaps I can convince Robert to travel with me. He has a few friends in town, and while he is meeting with them, I should be able to meet with the reverend. Surely he would not be concerned if I visited the church to pray, and he would be unlikely to want to join me.

I miss you more every day. How I wish that I could hold you. I long for the comfort that I always felt in your arms. Be safe, and hurry back to me.

Your loving wife,

Catherine

The last of the sunset shone dull lavender in the distant sky as Mindy quietly refolded the letter. She settled in closer and huddled into me against the chill. Lost in our own thoughts, we sat for a few more minutes before she pulled away and slipped the letter into her backpack. "I'm starting to get cold. Time to go home."

I nodded and rose. Reaching for her hand, I pulled her to her feet, and then leaned down and kissed her softly on the forehead. "You're right," I whispered. I turned for the stairs but she stopped me.

"There's another route," she said, "straight through the back of the park. It's a little faster." She looked toward a copse of trees some hundred feet back from the cliff face. I could see a trail winding through them and make out scattered lights beyond the narrow forest. "Right through there." She started forward, and then reached back her hand. I settled mine into hers and we walked slowly out of the park, still lost in thought.

As we approached the hill up to her home, Mindy finally spoke, thinking aloud. "I guess we know now that they were married, but why would they have wanted to keep the marriage a secret?" She looked at me and I waited for her to continue her musing. She walked a few more steps and then went on, "I was looking at the family tree a couple of days ago, particularly her section. Catherine was quite a bit younger than her brothers. She was born in 1833, but Philip, her next younger sibling, was born in 1825, and Tom all the way back in 1818. She must have been a surprise."

"And probably well protected by her older brothers," I added.

She smiled. "Most likely."

As we approached her house, she bunched her eyebrows in thought. "I wonder how old Joel was. It seems that they weren't far apart in age, and I get the impression that he was pretty well into his apprenticeship."

"There's no mention of him anywhere that I saw."

She shook her head. "No. It's like he didn't exist. I suppose that we could try and track down his family. If we were to look at birth records for Bradford, they'd probably list something for Joel Woodward."

"If he was born there."

"Right. If he was born there."

"I'd guess that he was in his late teens, maybe twenty."

She nodded. "And as an apprentice, probably living with the family. That would be how he got to know Catherine."

"So they would both have been much younger than any of her brothers." I reflected. "They would have seen him as a boy, untrained, largely unskilled, and certainly not good enough for their sister."

We had arrived at her home and she led me inside, turning on the lights and adjusting the thermostat. "Brrr," she shivered and started up the stairs. "I'm going to get a sweater."

I started to say something and then bit my tongue. It was probably still 72 degrees in the house, but she did have difficulty keeping warm, and mentioning it wouldn't win me any favors.

I was looking at one of the African masks hanging on the wall when she called down, "Make yourself at home. There's an open bottle of wine in the fridge. I'll be right down."

By the time Mindy got downstairs, I had poured some cabernet into two small glasses and was reading a magazine. She'd changed into a robe and a pair of fuzzy blue slippers. Looking over at me on the red sofa, she said, "Would you like anything to eat?"

I waved her off. "No, dinner was perfect. I'm not hungry at all."

"Okay," she said and went into the kitchen.

When she returned, she had put a few pieces of bittersweet dark chocolate onto a plate. She set it on the coffee table, and then sat next to me on the couch. She lifted one piece of chocolate to her lips and as she made eye contact with me, stroked it sensuously with her tongue. "Mmm. This is so good." She reached for her glass and continued, "and it goes so well with the wine."

I reached for a piece of the chocolate and she playfully slapped my hand. Surprised, I pulled it back and she laughed at me. "You said you weren't hungry!"

"I…but…"

She laughed and then leaned into me and reaching her hand behind my head, pulled me down to her. "Try it this way," she said, and pressed her lips to mine, opening her mouth and swirling the remains of the chocolate along the tip of my tongue. Pulling back, she asked huskily, "You like?"

Afraid my voice would betray me, I simply nodded and reached over to continue the kiss. We started slowly, savoring the flavor of the chocolate on her lips. As our passion grew, I reached one arm around her and began to stroke her golden curls. Presently, she sighed and leaned back against the couch, breaking contact. I followed. She leaned her face into mine, brushed a kiss against my lips, and said, "I was thinking of getting up early and having breakfast at the bakery, that is if you don't have to get home tonight."

I smiled and continued to stroke her hair. "I think that fits very well with my schedule." I kissed her long and gently and then pulled away. "May I have a piece of chocolate now?"

She giggled and brushed her fingers against my cheek. "I suppose."

CHAPTER 10

I held the door as Mindy entered the restaurant. The smell of fresh baked bread and pastries greeted us even in the parking lot, but it was almost overwhelming once we stepped inside. We'd come in along the deli side, and Mindy pushed her way through to the bakery where there was a number dispenser. I could see another wing where two baristas were busy serving a variety of coffee drinks. To the side, several patrons sat with their coffee and their pastries on an airy, enclosed patio, either in groups or alone with books and papers. I scanned the restaurant again and marveled, "It's huge! I thought we were going to a simple bakery."

She smiled and squeezed my hand, pulling me forward. "Carly's is one of my favorite spots." She grabbed a number 103, and then turned to the counter. Several other customers crowded the glass, exclaiming over the variety of delicacies on display. "What would you like?"

I took my time, and finally settled on a larger looking pastry. "What's that?" I pointed.

"It's a crocodile. They're very good. I buy them every once in awhile and take them into work. I'm surprised that they have any. They quite often run out by the time I get here."

One of the attendants called, "102," and she pulled me closer to the counter. I could see a woman wrapping an assortment of croissants into a pink box and directing the patron to the cashier. When she called out "103," Mindy raised her hand and proffered her ticket.

"Right here."

The woman came over and smiled at us. "What can I get you?"

Mindy pointed at the last crocodile and said, "We'll take the crocodile, for here."

While she wrapped the pastry, I leaned in close to Mindy and said, "I'll get the coffee. Anything special you'd like?"

She shook her head. "Just coffee. A little milk and sweetener."

I nodded and made my way to the other counter. In the time it took me to pay, pour the coffee, and then doctor hers, Mindy had found a table with a nice view of the street. The fog hadn't burned off, so the morning was still chilly, but she'd selected a table next to the hearth, where a pleasant fire crackled warmth throughout the patio. I put down the coffees and took a chair by her side. "Is this okay?" I asked.

She lifted the cup to her lips and drank. "Perfect."

I noticed that the pink box in front of her was wrapped with a white ribbon, tied in a bow. "Do they always do that for an inside order?" I asked.

"I asked them to. The crocodile is far too big for two of us. We'll need to take most of it home."

I looked seriously at her and shrugged my shoulders. "I don't know. Between last night's hike back to your place and everything else, I worked up quite an appetite."

She giggled and punched me gently on the arm. "It's pretty big. Then with a dramatic flair, she undid the ribbon and opened the box. The first thing I noticed was the size. She was right. It was huge, much larger than it had looked in the display case. The second thing was the aroma. Whether they'd heated it while I went for coffee or whether it was still warm from the oven earlier didn't matter. I could see steam rising from the crust, filling the air with the tangy scents of cinnamon and apple and fresh bread.

I inhaled deeply, closed my eyes, and sighed with contentment. "Heavenly,"

She cut two pieces and I used my fork to cut off a small corner of one. If anything, it tasted better than it smelled.

We ate quietly for a while, until Mindy reached for her purse and said, "The next letter is also from Catherine. Would you like to read it here?"

I thought for a moment. The bakery was a very busy place, quiet enough on the patio for breakfast, but a little too hectic for the reflection we'd been devoting to the letters. "Didn't you say there was a park not too far from here? How about if we walk over there? I'll carry the crocodile, and maybe we can nibble while we read."

She nodded and took a sip of coffee. "Okay."

June 6, 1850
Bradford, Pennsylvania

Darling Joel,

How I wish you were here. Have you left Havana? Where do you go next? And will you be able to write to me again? You seem to be getting hopelessly further away, and there is nothing that I can do to draw you back to me. You cannot imagine how I need you now, your touch, your smell, and the way that you have always had of comforting me when I am frightened.

Robert agreed to take me to Corydon. We were able to spend two nights with Mary Alice and just returned yesterday. It was an awful trip. The town was in absolute chaos when we got there. I was able to speak with Mary Alice, but she could be of so little help.

I had thought that Reverend Peterson was such a kind man, and never would have doubted his honesty, but evidently I was very wrong. It seems so fantastic that it is as if I have been dreaming.

How can this have happened? How could he have taken in you, me, everyone? My head is spinning and I am not sure where to turn.

I am sorry. I have been rambling. Here it is. It seems that a few members of the reverend's church were upset that the reverend was not following the correct procedures for some of his ministry. They complained to Reverend Jacobs, who forwarded their complaint to a group of church elders in Philadelphia. It has taken some time, a few months, but the church elders finally came to Corydon to investigate and when they arrived...It is almost too terrible to write down. How could this have happened? After all we did to be careful. Reverend Peterson was never ordained into the service of the church. His degrees were forgeries, and his talk just that, talk. He is a fraud. And since he was not a proper reverend, our marriage is not valid!

I tried to find out all that I could from Mary Alice, and eventually confided in her, and told her the details of our marriage and your flight. She was stunned but respected our need for secrecy, given your status as an apprentice and the refusal of my brothers to sanction such a union. She wished though, that I had told her earlier, and now so do I.

Evidently Mr. Peterson has disappeared. They suspect he has run to the west to perpetrate his fraud in some other small town. When they looked for the records of his ministry they found nothing. He recorded nothing. No baptisms. No funerals No marriages. Since there is no record of our ever having married, it is as if we never were. Many of the residents are furious, and the church investigator, a minister himself, has started to rebuild an official written record. He has invited the people of the town to see him so that he can formalize the records by repeating the services if needed. I asked about our wedding and he told me that without you present there is nothing he can do. So suddenly I have gone from being a wife, planning my future while missing my husband, to being a single woman again. I have no idea what to do.

If only you were here, we could straighten this out and no one would need to know. But you are not. You are hopelessly far away, and getting farther every minute. There is nothing I can do myself.

I have considered discussing this with Robert. I feel so alone, and need to speak with someone. Mary Alice has been a good friend, but she is far away, and I cannot discuss this with her easily. Mother would be a logical choice, but she still grieves father, and goes for days unable to even acknowledge that I exist. I can think of no one else. And yet I am so frightened, for I do not know how he will react when I give him the news that we were, are not, should be married.

And when I tell him that I fear that I may be with child…

Oh how I wish you were here, for I need you so much.

Catherine

Mindy folded the letter slowly and carefully without raising her eyes. She started to speak, and then stopped and inserted the fragile paper back into the envelope.

I reached over and rested my hand gently on hers, surprised to find that she was trembling. "Are you alright?" I asked.

She lifted her hand and brushed a single shining tear from her cheek. "No." She sighed deeply and shook her head, as if clearing some cobwebs. "I'm just trying to imagine how she must have felt, and I can only begin to understand how different the world was in 1850." She stood and walked away from the bench, looking into the brush along the side of the trail, as if seeking something but seeing nothing. I could tell from her movements that her body was tense, as if from anger. Finally, she turned back and looking straight through me, said, "I don't know how she must have felt. If it had happened to me, I'd be furious, but I'd know that all could be set right again." She paused and looked down, kicking at the dirt. After a minute or so, she focused on me. "Our culture is so different. A young girl who's pregnant out of wedlock? It happens and there's no real stigma for the girl or the child. And if the records were a problem now, Joel could communicate his wishes to Catherine or to a minister from just about anywhere in the world." She exhaled, as if purging her soul. "But then, 1850. This would have been absolutely disastrous for her reputation, and her child's, for that matter. My god, we're talking about shaming her entire family. It would have been terrifying." She paused for a moment, and then added angrily, "And yet she did everything right. It's so unfair!"

I had been listening and following her reflections. Even from a male perspective, I could see that this was a young girl in serious trouble, and a piece of me wanted to be able to help. But all we could do was look back, read the letters, and wonder at how she'd managed to survive such a calamity.

We stayed where we were for several minutes more, lost in our own thoughts. Finally, Mindy said, "I think I'd like to go home now." I rose and held out my hand. She took it carelessly, as if barely aware that I was there, and we made our way slowly and silently up the hill.

CHAPTER 11

"And I was able to find a little information about her father. Evidently he was a farmer who also made some money as a surveyor."

I looked at the stack of papers that Mindy had brought. I was impressed. "When did you find the time to research all of this?"

She laughed. "Thank goodness for the internet. "I looked up Bradford, and found Bradford County. From there I was able to search census records, church documents, even some early newspaper articles. I searched for both Arnold Lewis and just for Lewis. As I learned more, I was able to include that in my search."

She had laid out a file folder filled with odd papers on the coffee table. In addition to a variety of records relating to Arnold, Jeannie, and Catherine, she'd also found listings of other children and grandchildren. "How about Joel?"

She shook her head. "Nothing. It's like he never even existed. I'm wondering if he just drifted into town, got a job as an apprentice with Arnold, and then later drifted away, but never got his name listed anywhere."

"Well, if you keep looking, you might find something."

"I hope so." She reached into a stack of papers. "I do have a newspaper article from 1851. Look at this. It mentions the troubles caused by young men going off to the gold fields."

I picked up the article. Though the copy paper was new, I could tell that the original copy from the internet had been old and frayed. "This is amazing!" I said. "And it came from Bradford?"

She nodded, and then pointing to the article, continued on, "See, it mentions the names of a few young men who left for California, but no mention of Joel."

"Well it is a year later. Do you suppose there was an earlier article with his name in it?"

She shook her head. "No. I looked. I'm not sure that the paper was publishing until late in 1850. It may have missed him."

"Hmm." I browsed the article. "It must have been similar then. It's interesting anyway. Listen to this. "This reporter is convinced that the departure of young men to the goldfields of California can not but hurt the local economy. Some of the more responsible citizens have decried the lack of labor this harvest season. When one sees fruit rotting on the trees, and grain uncut in the fields, one can only regret the irresponsible attitude of today's youth. While it is easy for me to understand the lure of gold, I must also wonder what might have happened if the families of James Robertson and Isiah Cooper had spent more time focusing on values in the church and less time frequenting taverns!"

Mindy chuckled. "So even then the adults felt that the kids needed a little more responsibility."

I grinned. "Evidently. I guess some things never change. I'm glad I'm not living at a time when the local newspaper could call you out for visiting the pub!" I quickly scanned the rest of the article. "There's more, but nothing relating to your family that I can see."

"I was able to find a few articles. It appears that Catherine's brothers stayed in Bradford, or at least that they managed to slip out without notice. I suppose I could branch out in my search and try to find out what became of them." She reached for the article, and I surrendered it to her. As she put it back into the folder, she commented. "Anyway, it's interesting even if I haven't found anything more. I do know a lot more about the times and the attitudes then."

"I suppose," I replied, and then changed the subject. "So what would you like for dinner?"

"I thought we'd eat in." She rose and stretched. "I made some turkey burgers." Walking toward the kitchen, she continued over her shoulder. "Will you light the barbecue? I'll get them out."

"No problem," I answered as I stood. I looked down at the

folder, wishing that I could take the time to study the information there, but hearing the refrigerator open, knew that would have to wait. "Do you have matches?"

She peeked around the corner and tossed me a box of wooden kitchen matches. "Remember it can be temperamental. Try not to burn your eyebrows this time."

"They weren't burned," I insisted. "Just a little singed."

"Whatever." She smirked and turned back to the refrigerator.

I opened the barbecue and turned on the gas at the tank, and then cautious of her warning, lit a match and placed it on the coals, just above the gas jet. I opened the valve, and the barbecue lit as soon as the gas hit the fire. No explosion, no whoosh of flame. Perfect. It wasn't that I was worried, but I still backed away. "You're fire's lit. Are the burgers ready?"

She poked her head out the door. "That was fast." Then she looked at my face. All I wore was a grin, so she said, "No problems?"

"Of course not. Burgers?"

Shaking her head, she handed me the plate and a spatula. They looked a little pale, but I figured that was the turkey. Occasionally I could see something yellow poking out. Pineapple? Cheese?

§§§§

As it turned out, it was those and mango. They were turkey burgers stuffed with a variety of ingredients, and served with a green salad and wine, they made a very good meal. Later, while I dried the dishes, I asked, "So whose letter is next?"

She polished the salad bowl, careful to clean the raised cheetah perched on the side. "I've pulled out one from each. Joel has written from Havana and Catherine from Bradford. Anxious?"

I was putting away the silverware, my back to her, so just said, "I wonder how long he stayed in Cuba and what they did while they were there."

"Only one way to find out," she said as she sailed past me into the living room. She sat on the red sofa and patted the seat beside her. "Joel's is the next one. Your turn to read."

She handed me the letter and I looked at the date. "But it says May ninth. I thought you were looking at them in order."

"I am," she answered. "Look at the envelope. It's written on the ninth, but wasn't postmarked in the United States until the 30th. I suppose that the harbormaster held it for some reason. Anyway, she probably didn't receive it until June or July."

I conceded her logic and settled back on the couch. Between the burgers and the wine, I was feeling pretty mellow. "You sure you want to read it right now?"

She looked at me innocently. "What else would we do?"

Smiling, I said, "I can think of a few things."

"You're right," she said and bounced off the couch. She walked toward the stairs and as she started to climb, looked back at me suggestively.

I rose and walked toward her thinking, "I don't have to be asked twice."

Then she giggled and said, "That's okay, you stay there. I've got a couple of puzzles upstairs. I'll bring one down."

Shaking my head, I went back to the couch and sat. "She's playing me," I thought. Then I began to laugh. At least I was having fun. Picking up the letter, I began to read, taking my time to make meaning from the tiny horizontal script hidden in the vertical writing. I'd finished about half of the first page when she came back downstairs whistling. She had a puzzle under her arm and a huge grin on her face.

"Shall I set this up on the dining room table? It's chocolate bars. It's kind of fun."

I just stared at her. Finally, I said, "You are a devil woman."

Looking naively back at me, she said, "Me? I thought you were looking for other things to do. I have cards if you don't want to work on the puzzle. Shall I get them?"

By this time, I'd taken her arm, and pulling her toward me, took the puzzle and put it carefully down on one of her black leather chairs. I lowered my arms and locked them behind her back, holding her loosely around the waist. "You know what I meant."

She batted her eyebrows as she looked up at me. "No puzzles?" When I shook my head, she said, "No cards?" I shook my head again and she grinned and said, "I have a fun dice game. Pushing against me, she said, "Shall I get it?"

I held her tight, and moved my head very slowly from side to side. "No dice," I whispered.

"Ah," she sighed and lifted her face to mine again. "In that case…"

I ran my hands up her back and stroked her softly up and down, then continuing up, cradled her chin in my palms, and lifted her lips to mine. Our kiss was slow and gentle, but grew in heat as we lingered. Finally I stopped and she laid her head against my chest, her arms hugging my back. I held her there for a long moment savoring the feel of her body against mine. Finally, I kissed her again, lightly this time, and inclined my head toward the stairs. She nodded, and then took my hand and led me up.

§§§§

Later that evening, as she snuggled next to me in bed, I opened Joel's next letter.

May 9, 1850
Havana

My darling,
Catherine, Cuba is an endlessly fascinating country. Although the hackney fell through, Samuel still found us transportation out of the city. We rented three horses and made our way up one of the few roads that traverse this countryside. Our first stop, just a short way out of the main town, was the Rodriguez Sugar Plantation. The plantation itself is an enormous farm, several times the size of ours. I was told that it comprised over four thousand acres of fine farmland. Although they grew a variety of tropical fruits and vegetables, their main business was sugar. The cane covered the hillsides like a green blanket that swayed in the breeze. It is very much like grass, but like no grass that you or I will ever see. The cane plants themselves are huge. We walked through one field where the tops of the leaves swayed over our heads, and the bottoms had the thickness of small saplings. They cut them with machetes, long sharp knives that go right through those thick stalks as if they really are grass. They then extract the sugar from the cuttings. It was quite a fascinating process to watch, though I was again dismayed by the treatment of the dozens of slaves we saw working the fields. It is brutal, backbreaking work and as I understand it, performed under the hot sun every day of the year.
Anyway, after a filling lunch with the Rodriguez family in their main house, we were on our way. They suggested that we travel along the road to a

small village, some ten miles further along. Mr. Rodriguez gave us a letter of introduction and told us to forward it to Juan Garcia, a friend of his in the village.

The climb was hard and slow, as the road, as they called it, was scarcely more than a path. I wished we'd kept one of the machetes, as we were constantly brushing the low hanging branches out of our faces. Finally though, after a few hours of hard travel, we came to the small clearing that comprised all of the tiny village of Nazareno. In some ways, it was not terribly different from a small town in Pennsylvania. The village centered around a square, similar to our town squares. It was essentially a park, though also used as a marketplace. At one end rose the village church, much like the churches one might see at home, though of course it was Catholic. Opposite the church was a small town hall comprising of a mayor's office and a small police headquarters. Homes of the more prominent citizens and a few shops surrounded the square. Smaller, meaner buildings sprawled back for another street or two on either side. While the church was a beautiful building of polished white stone, only a few of the others were painted or showed any real maintenance at all. Many looked as if they might fall at any moment.

I carried our letter of introduction to Mr. Garcia, who turned out to be the mayor, and a man like Mr. Rodriguez, who spoke passable English. He welcomed us and asked about Jose Rodriguez, and we sang the man's praises. He then offered us the use of his jail for our stay in the village. I can tell you that we were a little taken aback, but when he assured us that he would keep the cell door unlocked, we decided that it might be a good place to get out of the weather.

Ah, the weather. Catherine, you don't know how I long for home, not just because of you, though that is my primary reason for wanting to be back, but also to escape the endless heat of this island. We have been told the weather here is constant throughout the year, hot and humid, with frequent afternoon rainstorms. Seeing as how we had climbed high into the mountains, I asked Mr. Garcia if it snowed in the winter there. He just laughed at me and pointed out that they never have snow, and that today would be considered a mild day. I made up my mind not to seek my fortune in sugar cane right then and there!

Later that evening, after the day cooled a bit, we were able to participate in a most interesting parade. The young women of the village came out in fine dresses and began walking around the village square. Gradually, the young men of the village, also wearing their finest, who had been congregating in small groups around the outside of the square, began to join them, to talk, or laugh, or simply to walk in companionable silence. Mr. Garcia explained to us that this was a formal form of courtship. We watched for a while, and the rules became clear.

Every member of the family came into the square that evening, even the oldest grandmothers and the babes in arms. The young people who paraded were well chaperoned by the family members, but still had an opportunity to meet with one another. As we watched, we saw more than one boy drop away from one of the girls after receiving a disapproving look from a man on the outside who must have been her father, or in some cases, an older brother. Mr. Garcia explained that most of the marriages in the village began with these innocent meetings on Saturday nights.

It was fascinating to watch, but when he urged us to participate in the paseo, or parade, I wasn't sure what to do. Samuel and Jonathan jumped at the chance, and joined in the walk. I tried to explain that I was married, but he sent me out anyway, telling me that it was only a paseo, and that I would not be unfaithful to you by walking. I did, but I have to tell you, I was not comfortable and after one circuit of the square and a few unsuccessful attempts at conversation, I returned to his side. Samuel is evidently quite a ladies man, and though I am sure that language was a formidable barrier, seemed to have a wonderful time with a few of the girls. I pulled him out of the paseo after a while, after noticing that he was arousing the ire of a number of the older men in the village. Not knowing the rules, I felt it best that we not unwittingly anger some girl's father.

We slept that night in the jail, and the beds were surprisingly comfortable. Samuel, as big as he is, snored terribly, but after the long day on horseback, I slept soundly, comforted by dreams of you.

I miss you terribly, and think of how much more I would enjoy this journey if I were making it with you. As we have traveled through the jungles in this country, I have frequently seen flowers and imagined them braided into your golden hair. Gilding the lily, I suppose, for you are so lovely as you are, but still I know how you love beauty, and how you would delight to see the flowers that cover this exotic land.

We sail tomorrow for Panama. I understand that the overland passage is short but difficult. You need not worry though, for I shall be very careful, and my friends and I have formed a strong pact and will be looking out for one another.

And now I must run to deliver this letter to the harbormaster. He told me that he had already sent the first a few days ago and that any others will follow later.

Your adoring husband,

Joel

I folded the letter and handed it to Mindy. She placed it carefully back in the envelope and said, "It's kind of newsy. He spent most of his time describing what he did or saw."

"I suppose that he's off into his adventure now," I commented. "It must be very strange spending this much time traveling to get somewhere."

"Still, he seemed so devoted to her in the earlier letters but now…"

I shrugged my shoulders. "They've been apart for what now, almost two months? And how long were they actually together. They only mention the one night."

"He lived in her father's home. I'm sure that they spent time together there. And he obviously got the attention of her brothers."

"True, but I suppose that his whole life is focused on this trip now. He seems to be a purposeful man, hoping to find gold so that he can return to her."

She looked at me and said sadly, "I don't think he will."

I shook my head. "No. I don't either. If he had, I think that they would have married and left some trace other than these letters."

She stood and walked toward the kitchen. "How sad. They seem so much in love."

I nodded silently. As she was about to round the corner, she turned her face to me, "I'm going to pour a glass of wine. Would you like some? I have one of Catherine's letters here as well, and I think we should read it next."

"That sounds good," I called to her, "The Chardonnay from dinner?"

"Unless you'd like something else. There's more on the rack next to the couch."

I had picked up the other letter and was taking it gingerly out of the envelope. "The chardonnay sounds good," I said absently as I looked down at Catherine's fine handwriting. "Shall I start reading?"

She poked her head around the corner. "I thought I was Catherine. I'll be there in a minute."

I put the letter down on the coffee table, but couldn't get her first line out of my mind. Written as clear as day, it said, "I am being sent to Pittsburgh."

CHAPTER 12

Mindy brought back the wine, along with some sliced strawberries.

"This is a nice surprise," I smiled up at her as she set the plate on the coffee table.

"Well I know you like berries, and they looked so good in the market."

I reached for one and popped it into my mouth, savoring the slightly tart flavor. "They're good." I raised my wineglass. "To the chef," I toasted.

"They're just strawberries. Nothing special about them."

"Oh, I mean the whole dinner. The burgers were great. I'd never have thought of putting pineapple and mango into them, but that worked really well, and the salad with all the little goodies, that was very good too." I waved to the strawberries, "and one of my favorite desserts!"

She rolled her eyes, but still managed a light "Thank you. I slaved over a hot stove all day."

"I could tell." I touched her glass with mine, and was rewarded with a soft ringing sound. "Anyway, to you." We drank, and as she put down her glass, I offered her a strawberry. When she opened her mouth, I put it on her tongue, and then before she could react, covered it with my mouth in a gentle kiss. "Mmm, delicious," I breathed.

She pushed me playfully away. "Behave. We've got Catherine's letter to read."

I leaned over and took up the letter from the table, offering it to her.

She took it, and then leaned in for a quick kiss. "Thank you. Let's see." She spread the letter and began to read.

June 13, 1850
Bradford

My darling Joel,
I am being sent to Pittsburgh. They think that I will be better off with Aunt Ruth there. Afraid that I will shame the family, I suppose. Tom will be taking me tomorrow. They seem to have agreed that as the oldest, it is his responsibility to care for the wayward sister.

Oh, they are all so terribly angry, and mother's gone even deeper into her depression. She hardly speaks at all. I suppose at least with Aunt Ruth, I will have someone to talk with, though she is likely to be just as angry as my brothers.

I told them about the marriage yesterday, and about Pastor Peterson, who is not really a pastor, and so we are really not married, and oh what a mess. They were all so terribly angry, wondering how I could have snuck around their backs like this, and how could I not have told them about something as important as a marriage, and how could I possibly think that you would be welcomed into the family.

At that I finally got mad myself. What was wrong with you, I asked them. You were working hard to learn the surveying business, and besides, you treated me like a lady, something that they certainly have never done. Well you would have thought that I had blasphemed in the house. I have never heard such an uproar. Mother left and went out to the barn, to your old quarters, I suppose, just to get away from the yelling. They hardly noticed. Finally, Tom quieted them down and took control of the situation.

He asked where you were, making sure that I understood that he would tolerate no lying on my part. I did not exactly lie, but I did not tell him about your letters either. I told him that you had gone to Philadelphia to catch a ship to California. Well that ignited a new barrage from the others until Tom quieted them again. When, he wondered, did you plan to return? I'm afraid that was more than I could take, because I really do not know when or even if you will return. I tried to hold on to a brave face, but could not keep the tears from flowing down my cheeks. Robert responded immediately with his handkerchief, and even Tom seemed to soften at that.

It took me several minutes to regain my composure, and during that time, Robert attended to me, his arm around my shoulder, while Tom just stood and looked, and then paced the room. The others held their peace, but I could tell that they were waiting to interject something else. Finally, William started to say something but Tom quieted him with a wave of his hand. Then he asked the strangest question, and it caused me to start to cry again. He wanted to know why I had not been willing to discuss this with him, to tell him that I wanted to marry. He asked whether I doubted that he and the others loved me enough to want me to be happy.

I didn't know what to say, and I could not stop crying. I was so confused, and he seemed more hurt than angry, and I certainly had not wanted to hurt anyone. It was a long time before anyone spoke again, but finally I regained control of my emotions. I could barely speak, but I managed to whisper out that there was more.

Tom just nodded his head, and then Robert looked up at me in surprise and actually rose as if he could not bear to be near me. And that was when Tom asked me why I was telling them now, and I told him that I suspected that I was pregnant, and he just continued to nod, as if he had known all along and that this was his problem now. And I am not sure that I cared. It has been a heavy burden these past weeks.

Tom told Robert to take me up to bed, and he did, and I cried some more, and he did not know what to say, so he just stood by the door awkwardly while I sobbed on my bed. Finally I settled down, and he sat down on the edge of the bed and held me for a while. It helped, but all the time he held me, I could feel his disappointment, and I wished that I was in your arms instead of his. I suppose that I fell asleep then, because when I woke I was under the covers in my bed, but still wearing my dress.

Tom announced the decision the next morning. They had decided while I slept to send me to Pittsburgh to live with Aunt Ruth. They would tell the neighbors that she was unwell and I had gone to take care of her and would be gone for several months. When the baby was born, I would turn the child over to the local orphanage, and return home. It would be as if nothing had ever happened.

I was too tired and too confused to argue. I agreed. And so I am being sent to Pittsburgh. I have no idea what to expect, and no reason to believe that they will be able to hide my shame from the community here. I am not even certain that I wish to hide your child, since we did believe that we were married, and I lay only with you, and only the one time.

It is very confusing. I am packing today, and I will leave tomorrow. I have asked the postmistress to forward my mail to the post office there, and I do hope that she will. I need to hear from you, if only to retain my sanity.

I pray every night that you will come back to me. You are my love, and my dreams for the future.

Catherine

Mindy put the letter down, and reached up to wipe tears from her eyes. Her voice had cracked several times as she read, but she'd continued on, unwilling to stop. I used a tissue to wipe her eyes, and then wrapped my arms around her and held her for several minutes until she too had calmed.

"It's so sad," she said. "And she was so young. She must have been terrified."

I nodded. "It would probably take a few days to get to Pittsburgh from there back then. I can't imagine how hard it would be for her."

She mused, "Pregnant, her marriage snatched away from her, her husband gone, and a feeling that she's shamed her family. I'd want to turn to someone, but it seems that she has nobody there. She's mentioned her mother a couple of times, but it's almost as if the woman's catatonic. I wonder what could have happened to her, and what could keep her from helping her daughter at this time. It doesn't make sense."

"I wish I knew what the accident was. It must have affected them both." I looked at her. "It killed him, but she must have been injured as well, and it's as if they've grown accustomed to it."

"Well, by 1850, he'd been dead for three years. Do you suppose she had some kind of head injury?"

I shook my head. "Could be, or a stroke. Maybe she's just suffering from depression. Either would explain how she just couldn't communicate with the others. It's hard to tell."

She rose. "I think I'm going to do a little more research into my family. I'm anxious to read the next letter, but think I need to let this one simmer for a while." Then looking at me, she tilted her wine glass, "Would you like more?"

I shook my head. "I have a long drive tonight. I need a clear head."

She grinned, "Oh, so that's how it is. Love 'em and leave 'em."

"Don't you have to work in the morning?"

She tilted her wine glass toward me as if in a toast, "and couldn't you get to work from here?"

"Ummm."

CHAPTER 13

Work kept us both busy over the next few weeks and aside from a couple of quick meals snatched here and there, we really were unable to spend any time together. Finally, we hit upon a long weekend that worked for both of us, so I booked a bed and breakfast in Murphys.

I picked Mindy up at her place on Friday morning. Santa Cruz was covered with a thick blanket of its typical summer fog, and she was dressed warmly in a flannel shirt and thick fleece jacket.

"You're going to be hot when we get to the valley," I kidded her.

"Maybe," she replied. "I'll take my chances."

I just laughed. "You ready? It should take us about three hours to get there. I was thinking of stopping at Ramon's for lunch on the way up. It's just a little western bar about midway across the valley."

"Ramon's?" She looked at me. "A bar?"

"That's pretty much it. It's kind of a dump, but they do have good food, and it's a fun place to go. Plus it's right on the way." I looked over at her and smiled. "You'll see."

She nodded skeptically. "Okay."

We had driven for about an hour, making small talk when Mindy said, "I brought a couple of letters."

I looked across the car at her. "That sounds good. I've been wondering what happened to them. Did you preview them?"

She shook her head seriously. "You know I didn't. I wanted to read them with you. It seems that we're in this adventure together."

We were driving through an agricultural area. The corn on

the right side of the car stood swaying in the breeze, nearly six feet tall, with silk caps glowing in the morning light. Old walnut trees stood in stately rows on the left. "I always liked driving through these orchards in the summer," I said, "I can remember being a child, playing in the orchard on a hot summer day." She glanced across at me and I continued. "My grandparents owned some property and grew apricots down in Merced. It was so hot in the summertime, that when I'd open the back door it would almost feel like I'd walked into a wall of heat. But the orchard," I mused, "the orchard was like our secret place. The shade spread over everything, dropping the temperature at least ten degrees. It might still be 95 out, but compared to the sun, it was really pleasant." I smiled. "Good memories."

She turned her head and looked out the window for a while as we drove on in silence. Several miles later, she said, "I'm almost afraid to read the next letter, and it's because I don't know what to expect. For some reason, I keep hoping that they're okay. And then I think of how foolish I am to even think that. After all, regardless of what happened, they've both been dead for over 100 years. Silly I suppose, but still, I worry about her."

"I don't know," I squeezed her hand. We've got a few years on us, and can look at her as a child moving into adulthood for the first time. I think I'd be disappointed if you didn't feel empathy for her. Her situation today would be frightening. Then..."

"I know." She looked out her window again. "A part of me wants to help." Then she giggled. "Isn't that silly."

I was still holding her hand, and I gave it another gentle squeeze. "Your empathy is one of the things I like about you."

Just a few minutes later, we came to the first buildings. The sign that introduced the town was old and simple, and had not had attention in several years. Where the paint remained, it said simply, "Welcome to Farmington."

I parked the car under a big oak tree on a side street and we got out. It was nearly noon, and the sun was out in full force. Mindy had taken off her coat in the car, and now she stripped off the flannel shirt, leaving just the t-shirt underneath. "Layers," she said with a smirk. "Always dress in layers and you'll never be cold."

I laughed and took her hand. Ramon's was right around the corner, and looked like it had last seen paint sometime before the welcome sign had first been thought of. She looked at me skeptically and I said, "It's not much to look at, but the food's good."

Rolling her eyes, she said, "Whatever you say."

Once inside, we decided to split a cheeseburger. It came as advertised, grilled medium rare, and served with a bun, lettuce, pickles, and onions on the side. We'd seen them slice the potatoes for French fries, so knew that they were real, not something out of a bag. Mindy took her half, loading it up with catsup and mustard. One bite and she was smiling.

"See, I told you."

"You were right. It's good. There's something in the meat. I'm not sure what it is."

"And you'll never know. They marinate it in some kind of sauce, but call it their secret recipe. I've asked. No luck."

She looked around. "Who'd have guessed that this place had good food?"

I followed her eyes. The walls were made of old barn wood, the operative word being old. They'd been decorated with a number of brands over the years, some recent and some looking pretty ancient. I suppose that they heated the branding irons on the grill. Beer posters and neon advertisements and ranching tools were hung haphazardly around the room. Displayed prominently up by the bar were two posters. One promoted the schedule of the local high school football team and the other showed game dates for the 49ers football team, both three years old. I guess they wanted the pictures.

I washed a bite down with some iced tea and then asked if she'd wondered about Joel.

"Not as much," she offered. "He seems to be off on his adventure in Cuba."

"I did some reading about the Panama passage to California. Except for the transit of the isthmus itself, it was a much easier and faster trip than either the overland route or the trip around the horn. That land passage though was pretty treacherous."

She sipped her tea and looked at me. "How so?"

"Well it was only ten miles from Atlantic to Pacific, but it was pretty heavy jungle and I would guess that they probably had to walk at least twice that far to get through the mountains. Add to that the constant rainfall, poisonous snakes, disease, and the occasional jaguar, and it must have been a pretty dangerous trip."

"And now it's so easy. Take a boat through the canal and you're done."

"Or drive. I imagine there are roads running east to west."

She laughed. "Or even west to east!"

We chatted companionably for the rest of the journey up to the mountains. Just outside of Copperopolis, the road started to wind up into the foothills. In the distance, we could see the snowy caps on the Sierra Nevada.

CHAPTER 14

At one time, Murphys was a rough and tumble gold rush town. Now it's a small tourist village. True, there is the Murphys museum, and the buildings are mostly the original stone, and several of the houses have plaques showing who lived there, but most of the businesses are now restaurants, wineries, boutiques, and galleries. The old Murphys is largely gone. Even Murphys pokey has been turned into a tourist experience. The door is latched open so that visitors can enter the tiny stone building, but nobody can get locked in. Hardly the requirement for a jail!

We had dinner that night in the oldest restaurant in town, the Murphys Hotel. The business actually dates back to the gold rush, and many of the pictures on the walls celebrate its past. The food was less traditional. My fettuccini alfredo was good and the house salad featured pine nuts, dried cranberries and hearts of palm. Somehow, I couldn't imagine a dusty old gold miner hiking out of the hills for a dish of pasta served with a designer salad.

I commented on this to Mindy, and she was anything but sympathetic. She rolled her eyes and said something about how I should be glad not to be eating gamey pan fried beefsteak done in the style of old shoe leather. I couldn't disagree.

We strolled through town after dinner, window-shopping, wine tasting, and eventually buying a bottle of zinfandel to take back to our room.

I was surprised by the bed and breakfast. The owners did their best to mix modern comfort with nineteenth century decor.

The rooms were furnished with antiques with quilts on the beds, and old pictures and paintings on every wall. The only thing missing seemed to be the chamber pot, which was just as well. One beautiful old dresser had a white marble top with a small placard explaining how to access the internet, an interesting juxtaposition. At any rate, the room was surprisingly large, with a king sized four poster bed as well as a comfortable sitting area.

While Mindy changed for bed, I opened the wine and put it along with two wine glasses on the table by the window. I'd purchased some wine chocolates on a lark, and put a tin of those next to the wine.

I then settled back and picked up a history of the gold country that I'd found in the book basket on the floor. I'd been reading for a while when she emerged from the bathroom. She was wearing a green Chinese silk robe, decorated with a variety of flowers and surprisingly, one rather large dragon. She came over to me and sat on the other chair, followed by a floral scent.

"Mmm," I said. "You smell wonderful."

"It's the bath gel. Sweet Pea. It was in the toiletries packet on the counter." She leaned closer, "You like?"

I closed my eyes and inhaled deeply. "Mmm. I like!" Then I jumped up and headed toward the bathroom. "You smell so good and I'm probably a little ripe right now. I'll be right back."

"There's a good masculine scent in there too," she suggested, "I left it on the counter for you."

"Are you saying I need a shower?"

She wrinkled her nose. "It depends on what else you might want to do tonight."

"Gotcha. I'll be right back."

I was quick. There was indeed a masculine bath gel, though I wondered as I used it what was wrong with plain old soap. Still, I went to work on the dirt, and when I pictured Mindy waiting out there in the silk robe, I scrubbed a little faster.

§§§§

Mindy was pouring the wine when I returned to the sitting area. I hadn't thought to purchase a silk robe, so was dressed more simply, in a clean t-shirt and shorts. No doubt, we made a dashing couple.

I sat opposite her and she lifted her glass, "To a relaxing weekend."

Clinking her glass, I responded, "And to you."

"And to Catherine." She reached into her purse and pulled out a small bundle of letters. "I've brought four. The first three are from Catherine, so I guess that I'll do most of the reading this weekend." She sorted and selected the first one.

June 22, 1850

My darling Joel,

I have been with Aunt Ruth for a week now, and we are finally settling into a routine. Tom brought me up here. It was a long, difficult trip. No, the trip was not that difficult. The roads were adequate, and though the wagon bumped quite a bit, it was not terribly uncomfortable. We stayed along the way with farmers he knew, who were happy to see us. So the trip was not that hard. It was the conversation, or lack of conversation I suppose, that was hard.

Tom was good enough to me, and I know that he was trying to be helpful, but still, I can tell that he has been badly shaken, and as hurt as I have ever seen him.

I was glad to get to Ruth's place. I think that Tom was too. He spent one night, ensured that I was in place, and left with very little fanfare the next morning. We both promised to write, though I am not sure that I will hear much from him. I think he is glad to be rid of a troublesome sister.

Ruth is an amazing woman. She is in constant motion, with a personality to match. I did not know much about her, and am learning more every day. Evidently she has been married twice and buried both husbands. Even more interesting, the men were best friends, though she did wait ten years after Harry died before marrying Frank.

Anyway, she lives on the savings she accrued from her first husband's business. He owned a small factory that manufactured buttons for clothing. I guess he sold them throughout the northeast to the mills. When he died, she took over the business and proved to be quite the saleslady, more than doubling their revenues. She sold out to one of her competitors a few years ago, but still gets a monthly check from them, and stays involved in the planning if not the daily management. Coming from a small family farm, I had no idea that we had a relative like this. And to think that a woman could be so successful in business. The very thought of it is foreign to anything I had expected. Of course,

Pittsburgh is a big city.

I have met a few of her closer friends. She has decided that if I am to live in her home, I will have to have contact with the neighbors, otherwise people will begin to wonder what is happening. She has even assured me that the women understand my situation and will keep my secret. She seems to run with a very progressive crowd. One of them went on one day about how she thought that it was not right that women were denied the vote. I had never heard such talk. Why would women even want to vote? You must think that this is crazy talk!

It seems so strange that my condition, as they call it, should even be a secret. After all, we were married. It is so frustrating at times.

Anyway, I have moved into the house, and am getting along well with Ruth. I think that she enjoys having company, but we will see if she gets tired of me as the months stretch out. I enjoy her companionship more than I had anticipated.

I miss you terribly and wonder where you are. In the last letter that I received, you were about to leave Cuba on your way west. You said that your next stop would be Panama. Oh do be careful. I know so little about that part of the world. I can only imagine how dangerous a jungle must be, and to think of you walking for miles through there. I pray every night that God will keep you safe.

You are never far from my thoughts. I wish that you were here to share in this joyous event. To marry me again. To be my husband as I wish to be your wife.

Thinking of you always,

Catherine

We had been sipping the zinfandel as Mindy read, and I only realized when she finished that the glasses were empty. I reached over and tilted the bottle toward her glass. "More?" I asked.

She nodded. "Just a little."

I poured about half a glass for each of us and returned the bottle to the coaster. "For some reason, I feel that she's better off now with her aunt than she was before."

Mindy nodded slowly, "She's gotten somebody to talk to." Then she cocked her head to one side, "I hadn't thought about this while I was reading, but I wonder if this wasn't her aunt, but maybe a great aunt. After all, if she'd buried two husbands, and run a business, and then retired, she was probably older than Mindy's parents."

"You could be right. It's too bad we don't have the family tree here. That would be something to check out."

She smiled. "You give me too little credit. I made a copy. It's in my bag." She rose and walked over to her suitcase, the silk swishing sensuously. When she returned, she noted the lecherous smile on my lips and slapped me playfully on the arm. "Don't get sidetracked. We're looking up my relatives right now."

Chagrined, I sat back in my chair and smiled at her. "Moi?"

"Yes," she giggled. "You. There'll be plenty of time for playing around later." Then she smoothed out the robe and settled into the chair. "I suspected we might need this."

She proffered the paper and leaned toward me. I inhaled deeply, enchanted by the scent of sweet pea. "Mmm," I sighed, and then looked at her scowl. "Ah yes. A great copy."

She took my right index finger and very deliberately placed it on Catherine's name on the paper. "Here's Catherine," she said brusquely. She leaned her head into mine. "And if we trace back, we find her parents, Arnold and Jeanie Lewis. Arnold was born in 1799, and Jeanie in 1802. So she'd have been just sixteen when Tom was born. Young. Old Arnold was robbing the cradle!"

I nodded. "Yeah, at all of nineteen himself." I looked back at the chart. "All I see next to his name is a list of siblings with dates. There isn't much more. I guess whoever made this up was more interested in the direct line than in branching out." I paused. "I suppose that makes sense. Think of the hundreds of names there'd be here if it tracked everyone."

"I don't see a Ruth there." I moved my finger up the tree. "Lets see. What if I move to Jeanie?"

Suddenly Mindy cried out. "Look. Here. Ruth Smithson Hamilton, married to Harry Winston and later Frank Hamilton." She looked up at me, her eyes gleaming. She traced the lineage. "She was Jeanie's aunt, so that would have made her Catherine's great aunt on her mother's side." She grinned. "Another name; another family member that I get to know."

I continued reading the chart. "She was born in 1792, so she would have been ten years old when Jeanie was born." I thought for a moment. "And in 1850, she'd have been 58 years old. She could well have been retired by then, but young enough to still have input into the business. How interesting."

I looked at Mindy, fully engaged in her family history now. "You said you brought four letters?"

She nodded. "Shall we read the next?"

"Up to you. Whose is it?"

She picked up the old envelope. It was a pale pink color, and contained Catherine's delicate handwriting. "Another of hers." She began to read.

June 27, 1850

Dearest Joel,

Oh, how I long to hear from you! Are you safe? Have you made a successful passage to Panama? Are you hiking through that frightening jungle even as I write?

I miss you more than I thought possible. But there is little that I can do about that now, is there. I need to focus on the future. It is so hard though. I think of you holding our child, and then wonder if that will ever happen, and I cry a little. So I convince myself that you will be back someday soon, and that we will all be together as a family. You, me, and our baby.

Ruth is an angel. As frightened as I was when Tom told me I was being taken to Pittsburgh, I now realize that he made the right decision. We sat over tea on the front porch the other day, and she told me stories about the days when she lived on the farm with my family. I had no memory of that, but then I was just a baby.

Evidently, she moved in with us for a while after Harry died. She said that she did not know whether she wanted to go on living! I look at this strong woman, one who was the mistress of a thriving business, and I am amazed. She was a housewife. She had no connection to the business at all. She quilted with her ladies group, supervised the household servants, and wished for children. Sadly, God never blessed her with any. When Harry died, she said, it was as if her whole reason for living had been taken from her. So she moved to the farm from Pittsburgh and lived there for several months.

It worked out well for everyone. I was born during that time, and my mother was very weak, so Aunt Ruth cared for me. How strange, that my first caregiver was a woman I hardly knew. And to meet her again now when I'm about to have a child. Anyway, caring for a baby during my mother's convalescence was just what Ruth needed. She had time to heal and think about how to handle her future, and I needed her attention as much as she needed mine.

Evidently, there was talk about her staying on to take care of all of us. I had not known my mother was so ill. She nearly died bearing me. Why nobody told me about that I do not know.

She told me stories about the family that I never knew. My brothers (she insists upon calling them the rascals) were older of course, and she took it upon herself to raise them. "That Tom, he was a proper rascal," she said. "I had him cut himself a willow switch more than once!" Tom? My responsible big brother? The one who is always so serious? How amazing. I can not even imagine him as a boy, but then I was so much younger. He was almost a man when I was born. And I can not imagine him not being somber. I have to smile, nay almost giggle when I think of Ruth having at him with a switch. Oh how I wish I had been there, but then I suppose I was.

She told me of one time when he and one of his friends decided to build a fort in the old apple tree in front of the house. I guess they erected a platform some ten feet up in the tree. They had a rope ladder to climb up there, and for a while everything went just fine. Then one day, they got into a fight with Robert and two others. Some of the apples had fallen, and Robert grabbed one and threw it at Tom, hitting him square in the forehead and nearly knocking him out of the tree. Well Tom and James, his friend, had to respond but they had no downed fruit, so they started to strip the ripe apples off of the tree. By the time they were done, all of the boys were bruised, and the tree was pretty well stripped of ruined fruit. From what she says, five boys cut switches, and then lined up for their punishment, heads down. After they were done, backsides still smarting, she made them gather up all of the apples, and bruised as they were, cut them into slices so that she could make pies. I would so have liked to have seen my brothers laid out like that, waiting for their punishment. I will have to ask Robert if he remembers that. Better yet, I think I will ask Tom the next time he acts all high and mighty!

Anyway, after a few months, mother had her strength back, and Ruth was over the worst of her grief, so she took off for Pittsburgh and took over the business from Harry's managers. It is funny though, whenever she gets startled to this day, she's likely to call out, "Oh Harry!" and reach out, as if to take his arm. Even though it's been many years, and she remarried Frank, I think it is Harry who is still in her heart.

Would you listen to how I have carried on. I have reread the letter. How silly. Still, I am starting to smile more now. Ruth has been good for me. She is a no nonsense woman, just like Tom is a no nonsense man, but she can laugh at herself in ways that Tom never has. And she makes me laugh, and I did not know how much I needed that.

I wish you were here. The baby is growing, and my belly is beginning to swell just a little bit. Or so it seems to me.
Missing you,
Catherine

Mindy finished the letter and carefully folded it before sliding it back into the ancient envelope. We'd moved to the bed to cuddle while she read, and now she rested her head on my shoulder. "I think I'm going to like Aunt Ruth," she sighed.

I nodded, lost in thought. "Me too." I hugged Mindy close and stroked her hair. Her golden curls glowed softly in the lamplight, and I kissed the top of her head. She purred and snuggled in closer, and I caressed her head, her face, and her shoulders. We stayed like that for a long time, drifting through Catherine's letter.

CHAPTER 15

We spent the next morning scouring the records of the Murphy's Museum. We found rusty old gold mining tools as well as a large assortment of pictures. The displays had been well organized, and though the museum was quite small, occupying only a tiny store front, it seemed to have been well thought out. One corner had been set up as an old western bar, complete with spittoon, rail, and an assortment of bottles, many filled with amber liquid. I almost felt that if I bellied up to the bar, I could order a shot of whiskey. Most of the smaller items were arranged by era in well worn display cases. I was particularly drawn to one creatively designed window display. A manikin was dressed in a faded red flannel shirt and blue jeans. His feet were in well scuffed boots, but they were disguised somewhat by a plastic insert that was supposed to simulate water in a creek. The creek bed itself, was quite realistic, lined with assorted pebbles, and even some dusty plants. The miner held a pan and seemed to be looking into it for gold. On the bank next to him, were a pick and shovel along with a bed roll, some cooking gear, and two other large gold pans. I lifted one of the pans and tried to imagine myself as a miner, standing in cold water, swirling sand and gravel in the hopes of seeing something sparkle at the bottom. At about that time, one of the docents came over and suggested rather tartly that I put the pan down. Mindy smirked, and I, chagrined, returned the pan to the display.

"Told you," was all she said, before turning back to a display case she had been looking through.

"I was just looking at it." I tried. "It was surprisingly heavy."

Glancing at me, she responded. "I suppose it probably was. Didn't your mother ever tell you to look with your eyes, not your hands?"

I started to respond, then thought better of it. I couldn't really see the point of pursuing an argument that I knew I'd already lost. Still, I didn't regret swirling the pan. It gave me a little of the feel of a miner, and for just a second, I could imagine Joel panning for gold in one of the local creeks. Changing the subject, I said, "I noticed an old journal in the case over there. Did you see that?"

Mindy nodded. "I was wondering if they might have a transcription. It would be an interesting read, but given your experience with the metal pan, I'm sure they're not going to trust you with anything made of paper."

I scowled and she stuck her tongue out at me. Lifting my head, I said, "I think I'll ask."

"You do that," she said. "Good luck."

I walked over to the docent. She was a severe looking woman, wearing a mid-nineteenth century blue calico dress. Her glasses were the only thing modern about her. Even the bun that bound her grey hair seemed to have the dusty patina of age. She was answering a question about early winemaking in the area, and I listened for a moment until she finished. She looked at me, arched her eyebrow, and said saucily, "Is there anything I can do for you sir?"

"As a matter of fact, there is. You see, we're trying to do some research on one of her relatives." I nodded toward Mindy. "He was a gold miner back in 1850, and I'm wondering if you have any suggestions. We noticed the journal there and were thinking that if we read that, we might at least get some of the flavor of the times. Might we be able to look at it?"

I waited as she looked over at the journal. "We'd certainly appreciate it."

"We're not supposed to let anyone touch anything in the museum."

I nodded seriously. "I can understand that. Sorry about the pan. It was surprisingly heavy, wasn't it." I looked up at her eyes and saw them light up. "I know I wasn't supposed to touch it, but it was fascinating to hold it, standing next to the display, imagining that the old miner next to me was my partner, swirling for gold. I even began to wonder what he'd had for breakfast that morning, and how cold the water was." I shook as if to clear the dream from my head. "Anyway, you have quite a museum here."

She looked at me for a moment and then smiled for the first time since we'd entered. "I designed that display, you know."

"Really! It's amazingly realistic. I could almost feel the cold, and holding that pan, I had the strangest urge to dip it into water. I suppose I caught a little of the gold fever." I offered my hand. "Charlie Overton," I said. "You did a great job."

She was tentative as she looked at my hand, as if she felt that she might be warranted in distrusting me. Finally, she reached out and placed her hand in mine. Her touch was feather light, but in that moment, she decided to trust me. "Melissa Adams. What's the name of her relative?"

"Joel," I stated excitedly. I turned to Mindy and waved her over. "Joel Woodward. He might have been in this area sometime in 1850 or 1851. We don't know."

She nodded. "We've compiled a listing of many of the old miners who worked this area." She looked over at Mindy. "You have to understand though, that they were highly transitory. It's entirely possible that someone was here for a month or two but never left any trace of his presence." She walked to the back corner of the museum, behind the bar. "Come on back here. I'll see what I can find."

I looked at Mindy, shrugged my shoulders, and nodded. "Let's give it a try."

Carefully, we made our way behind the bar and walked back into the 21st century. The central piece in the small office behind the curtain was a desktop computer. I noticed two hard drives on the bookcase up above the desk, nestled in between an assortment of technology books. Ms. Adams sat at a rolling office chair and wheeled up to the desk. Almost as an afterthought, she motioned Mindy to an antique hardwood chair next to the desk. I remained standing.

"What was his name again," she asked.

Mindy spoke up for the first time, somewhat uncertainly. "Um, Joel. Joel Woodward. I believe he was my great, great grandfather."

Ms. Adams nodded abruptly, and then opened a database

program. She typed his name into a search field and turned back to Mindy. "Like I said, there may be no record even if he was here. We'll see." She turned back to the computer.

Without turning back to us, she said, "I have several hits for Joel, and a couple for Woodward, but none for the two names together."

I looked over her shoulder and could see that the database was organized in a columnar format, last name, first name, years, age, place of birth, occupation, address. Most of the entries were blank even where a name existed. Two entries were just, 'Joel,' with nothing else. One was for Samuel Woodward and the other had just a last name. I leaned over. Pointing toward the Joel in one column and the Woodward in another, I asked, "Do you suppose that those might be the same person?"

She just shrugged her shoulders. "Could be." She looked back. "The records are so thin. As you might understand, the miners really weren't interested in signing in, so to speak. They looked for gold and some found it. Some never came to town and nearly all of them drifted up and down the gold country, hoping for a lucky strike." She shook her head. "I'm sorry I can't tell you more."

Mindy stood, clearly disappointed. "I understand. It was a long time ago..."

"And a pretty wild time," Ms. Adams continued for her. She started to shut the program when I had a thought. "Just one last question. Are there any other fields that we can't see on that page?"

She frowned. "A few, but they're almost entirely blank. Still, I can look." She highlighted Woodward and scrolled across. Everything was blank. She shook her head.

"And how about this Joel, the one with no last name? If you could..."

"All right," she said. She highlighted his name and scrolled. There at the far right, was a column entitled, 'known companions.'

"Look," I pointed. "Samuel!" I looked back at Mindy. "Wasn't that the name of one of his friends?"

Mindy nodded at me, eyes aglow. "He mentioned Samuel and Jonathan in one of his letters." She reached out and placed her hand on Ms. Adams' shoulder. "Can we search Samuel please? I don't have a last name."

Her excitement was infectious, and brought out a smile from

our old docent. "Certainly." Her fingers seemed to dance over the keyboard as she renewed her search. Finally, the screen started to roll. "Oh my!" she exclaimed. "There are so many!"

"Not to worry." I was thinking of ways to narrow the search. "Let's try 'known companions.' Or better yet..." I looked over her head and thought for a second. "Can we search just that column for the name 'Joel?'"

She nodded slowly, thinking. "We should be able to. She scrolled to the next page and highlighted the field, 'known companions.' She then went to the search feature and typed in 'Joel,' and turned back to us. "Ready?" she asked.

Mindy and I both nodded, eyes fixed on the screen. She hit the return key.

Everything disappeared with the exception of one line. In the 'known companions' field, the name 'Joel' was highlighted in yellow. We all stared, almost in disbelief for what seemed a long time. Finally, Mindy whispered, "What year is this?"

Ms. Adams scrolled back and we looked at the date, January, 1852. "Is that what you're looking for?" she asked.

"It's in the time frame. He could have been there." She looked up at me. "What do you think."

I shrugged my shoulders. "It's possible." I looked down at Ms. Adams. "What else do you have about this Samuel?"

She peeked through the curtain. We could hear lots of talk coming from the front, as if a large group had just come in. "I probably need to get back out front. I'll print you a copy." She clicked on the print button and a printer began to whir behind us. "I hope this will help. If you have any more questions, please come back. Weekdays are usually a little bit better. We're not so busy." She pulled three sheets of paper off the printer and handed them to Mindy. "Good luck."

Mindy took the paper in one hand and Ms. Adams' arm in the other. "I can't thank you enough. You've been amazing." She turned to me. "I can hardly believe this. Do you suppose it's possible?"

We made our way out through the bar to the front door. Suddenly, I stopped. "I'll meet you outside."

I walked quickly back to the counter where Ms. Adams was engaged with another couple. "Excuse me," I said to the man who was talking. "This will just take a moment." Turning to Ms. Adams, I said, "I'm sorry. I'm sure you have a donation bin, but I haven't seen it. We'd like to leave something for your help."

She smiled. "It's over there. The metal box on the end of the bar. Thank you." Turning back to her other guest, she continued, "Actually, the Murphy's Hotel has a wonderful selection of old pictures. You should look there as well."

I noticed a rusty box bolted to the end of the bar and secured with a sturdy if ancient padlock. A slot had been cut in the top and a card informed the visitor that donations were welcome. I slipped several bills into the box and then turned to leave. Mindy stood right behind me, fumbling for money in her purse.

"Ah," I said. "Already taken care of." I wrapped my arm around her shoulder and pulled her toward me. "Great minds do indeed think alike."

As we exited the museum, I inhaled the fresh country air. "How about some lunch?" I asked.

CHAPTER 16

We chose a restaurant down the street that advertised "Authentic Gold Rush Food." I had no idea what that might mean, but it seemed intriguing. When I suggested we try it, Mindy just rolled her eyes and sighed, "I can always get a salad."

We chose seats by the window, where we could watch the tourists browse by on the sidewalk outside. The gallery across the street had quite a sale going, with water colors by local artists displayed on the outside easels. Some were quite good, but I was pretty certain that others might have been produced by children in the local elementary school. The waitress arrived promptly with water, including the traditional gold rush slice of lemon.

Opening my menu, I glanced briefly at the offerings. "See anything that looks good?"

Mindy ignored me for a while, and then said, "I'm not really hungry enough for a full meal. Would you like to split something?"

I looked back at the menu. "Sure," I said cautiously. "You choose."

She looked at me seriously. "Well in that case, the hummus burger looks pretty good, and it comes with a side of eggplant salad."

I gritted my teeth. "If that's what you want." I looked at some of the other offerings that I'm sure never graced gold rush menus. I'd seen someone working on a thick Reuben sandwich when we walked in. The burgers smelled heavenly, thickly slathered with barbecue sauce. And then there was the club sandwich. Walking up the street, we'd commented on the smell of bacon. I sighed and closed the menu.

Looking back at Mindy, I could see that the reflection of the sun in the mirror beside us had caught the red highlights in her hair perfectly, turning them into golden threads. I smiled. I may be eating hummus, but I was with the most enchanting woman in the place. I sighed again and said, "So hummus and eggplant it'll be. Sounds yummy."

Mindy stared at me for a moment, neither one of us willing to break the stony looks on our faces. Finally, she burst into laughter.

"What?" I asked innocently.

She just laughed and waved me off.

"Well?"

She shook her head and then started to speak. "The look on your face..." And again she was overwhelmed with peals of laughter. "I...I..."

We'd both been leaning forward, in the pose of lovers sharing secrets at the table. Now I stretched back and made a point of looking out the window. That just brought on a new paroxysm of laughter. I crossed my arms and stared out the window, determined not to look at Mindy, and equally determined not to crack a smile in response to that infectious giggling across the table.

Finally, she subsided enough that I felt safe in looking at her. "Are you quite done?"

She'd just taken a drink of water, and now erupted again, spraying water across the table. And finally, I lost it though I tried hard to contain myself, pursing my lips together with increasing force until I was sure I'd strain every muscle in my face. I burst out with great peals of laughter, shaking my head as I looked and pointed at the spatters of water all over the table. This set Mindy off again. Which set me off again. After what seemed forever, we both seemed to regain control, and though furtive looks at one another brought out additional chuckles, they lessened to the point that I was brave enough to take a sip of water from my own glass. That seemed to help to calm me down and I said, "So the hummus burger with the side eggplant salad."

She nodded, pleasure dancing in her eyes, afraid to speak.

"Sounds delightful," I added. "Now if you'll excuse me, I think I'll clean up the table. Someone seems to have spilled their water." I took my napkin and wiped up the droplets while Mindy watched across from me, occasionally stifling a new outburst.

Just as I finished, the waitress came to our table, and pulling a pencil from her hair, said, "And now what can I get you for lunch?"

Mindy started to speak and I held up my hand, quieting her. "We'd like to share a sandwich if we can."

The waitress nodded, and I continued. "We'd like a blue cheese burger with a side of barbecue sauce."

She nodded, "And to drink?"

I smiled. "Two Miners' ice teas." I glanced over at Mindy who was again stifling a giggle. "Oh, and can we have a small eggplant salad?"

When the waitress left, wondering no doubt what all of the commotion was about, I leaned across the table, and taking Mindy's hand, said, "Will that be okay?"

She nodded sweetly and then looked at me seriously, "I hope you enjoy the salad, because suddenly I'm feeling much hungrier and I do intend to eat most of that burger."

I just looked up at the ceiling. I thought I'd gotten her but it was like she'd planned the whole order all along. I'd been had. "Fair enough," I said with a chuckle.

The rest of lunch passed calmly, or as calmly as I would have expected with Mindy. The burger was surprisingly good, and she was true to her word, sneaking a little more than half. I've never been a great fan of eggplant, something that she knew clearly, but had to admit that the salad was tasty, helped no doubt by a wonderful black cherry balsamic dressing. When at last we leaned back, sated, the meal was gone. We'd even used the sourdough bun to wipe up the remaining barbecue sauce, so that the plates were nearly clean enough to be used again.

"Good?" she asked.

I nodded.

"I noticed that you seemed to like the salad. Maybe we should have gotten the hummus burger and salad."

I just shook my head. "Maybe for dinner."

She smiled and reached into her purse. "Shall we check out the spreadsheet?"

Extracting the papers, she unfolded them while I cleared the table. Then, spreading them out, she drew a single line with her index finger, so that we could read the key on the top along with Samuel's data. She looked up at me and frowned. "There's not much."

I tapped the side of my head and leaned toward her in my best Sherlock Holmes imitation. "On the contrary, my dear, there's more than meets the eye. Considering we went into the museum on a lark, never planning to even ask for anything, this is fascinating. If nothing else, it may confirm the letters. There was a Samuel who hung around with a Joel, and they spent at least a little time in Murphys."

She cocked her head to the side. "In 1852."

"Right," I said. "In 1852. January. Then I shivered. You suppose they were living in a tent? It must have been freezing!"

"I thought about that. Does it snow here?"

"Occasionally. We could probably look for an old almanac, maybe online, find out what the weather was like in 1852." I shook my head and looked out the window for a few seconds before turning back. "They were here."

She corrected me. "Or someone named Samuel was here with someone named Joel."

"Right."

"I wonder what happened to Jonathan?"

I looked back at her. "You're right. Joel said he'd made two friends." I paused for a few seconds, thinking. "We'll be here tomorrow, and it's Monday so it won't be as busy. You want to check the museum again?"

She shook her head. "No. The name's too common. Look what happened with Samuel. And if he wasn't listed with Samuel, there's no reason to think that Samuel would be cross referenced with him. I do have something else though."

I looked at her, curious. "What?"

She smiled. "I didn't think that you'd noticed, but I did." She took out another sheet of paper, but kept it folded. "Ms. Adams was pretty good at manipulating that spreadsheet. She focused in on the name Samuel, and then eliminated everything before that when we started looking for Joel. Since there was no listing for Joel, we had no reason to ask for Samuel, but here it is."

She unfolded the sheet of paper and I saw at once what had been missing. "Watkins," I said softly. "His last name was Watkins."

Mindy nodded.

Lost in thought, I stood and held out my hand for her. She

rose and we left the restaurant silently. When we got to the sidewalk, Mindy said, "Let's take a look in the old cemetery. Just a hunch. Maybe there's a Watkins there."

"Or a Joel," I added.

She shivered. "I hope not."

CHAPTER 17

We spent most of the afternoon in the cemetery, and never made it into the gift shops or galleries. There were a surprising number of headstones, and we read every one of them, lifting some of the fallen ones out of the dirt and scraping off the front only to find that they stood for some other old pioneer. At one point, Mindy cried out from across the row to me. I hurried over to look, but though she'd uncovered an S. Watkins, the dates were wrong. The stone appeared old, but the man had been born in 1860, dying of "misadventure" in 1887. We found no trace of a Joel.

After a light dinner, we returned to the room. As soon as we entered, Mindy dropped her purse on one of the chairs and announced, "I feel like I'm wearing half of the dirt from that cemetery. I'm going to take a shower." With that, she pranced off to the bathroom. I heard the water running just a moment later and asked at the door, "Do you need any help?"

She laughed. "I need to clean, nothing else."

Chagrined, I muttered, "Okay." I went to the other chair and sat down with my book.

A few seconds later, her head poked out. "Maybe later though."

Well that certainly lightened my mood. I nodded eagerly. "I'll be waiting."

Though she'd returned to the bathroom, the door stood open and I could hear her clearly, "You can have the shower when I'm done. You smell a little gamey after digging up those old headstones."

I sat down again, properly chastised, not knowing whether to be insulted or excited. So I was gamey, but maybe later. An interesting combination.

§§§§

That evening, as we cuddled in the bed, Mindy said, "I still have two letters. Shall we read the next?"

I nodded. She was laying with her head on my shoulder and I'd been twirling one of her curls and wasn't really sure I wanted a letter to take from the mood. Still, I was curious, and we could always read entwined, so I said, "Shall I get it or will you?"

She rose, and in the dim light I could make out the glisten of the moonlight on her naked back. My senses were still filled with the heady aroma of her scent mixed with the sweet pea lotion provided by the bed and breakfast, so I reached for her, suggesting that maybe we should read later.

She glanced over her shoulder at my questing arms and snorted. Shaking her head, she said, "What are you, nineteen? I thought men were supposed to lose their urge as they got older."

"It's all your fault," I said seriously. "If you weren't so beautiful..."

She smiled and straightened up. "You are very sweet, but I have the letter."

I contented myself with her comments earlier. "Maybe later," and reached out, holding up the covers open for her. As she snuggled next to me, I put my arms around her and sought her mouth. She gave me a quick kiss and said, "You read this one."

I kissed her one last time on the forehead, and whispered, "Joel?" She nodded.

As it turned out, it wasn't Joel, though the handwriting was similar. The letter had been posted from Panama City, on the west coast of the crossing. And it was written by Samuel.

July, 1, 1850

Dear Catherine,
I am writing this letter on behalf of Joel. He has been quite insistent

that I write and let you know that he is well.

We spent nearly a week crossing the Isthmus of Panama. It was a brutal passage, and one that we were wholly unprepared for. I had heard that it would be the most difficult part of our journey, but that understated the rigors.

Panama is at the same time, a land of incredible beauty and unbelievable hardship. We spent almost the entire time in a seemingly trackless jungle. The heat and humidity made light of any of my prior experiences on a miserable summer day in Philadelphia. On top of that, it seemed that everywhere we turned was a new danger. We learned the names of several poisonous snakes, some of whom slithered at our feet while others hung from the trees, looking for unwary prey. I myself, reached up to push a liana out of my way on one occasion only to have it writhe in my hands. I quickly flung it into the brush, so have no idea what it was, other than unnerving. I must tell you that it was Joel who came to my side quickly and helped calm me. Even the frogs, as fantastically colorful as they are, are dangerous. In fact, we learned that the poison in the skin of some is used by the natives to make a deadly potion which is then smeared on the points of their arrows and darts and used to kill monkeys in the trees.

The beauty though, is overwhelming. Everywhere we looked through the dense foliage, were flowers in all of their majestic colors and shapes.

Joel spoke of you constantly, and wished on more than one occasion that he could have brought one of the orchids to you, saying that it would pale in comparison to your beauty. I must say that Jonathan and I tired of hearing your praises, having left girls of our own back home. But he would not stop. I know that many of the men in our crew are leaving their old lives behind. Indeed, I intend to make a new life in California, gold or no gold, and never plan to return to Pennsylvania. Joel though, speaks only of his desire to return to you. You will no doubt be happy to know that he is smitten.

You probably wonder why I am writing this letter on his behalf. Many of our crew fell sick as we approached the Pacific Ocean. Joel was one of the more severely stricken. He has been delirious off and on for the past several days, suffering from severe cramping and fever. Jonathan and I carried him into town on a litter and immediately sought the help of a Spanish doctor. The man was an old drunk, longing to return his home in Madrid, and I doubted his competence, but he was all there was. He called the illness Yellow Fever, and indeed, Joel's skin had turned a jaundiced yellow color. He prescribed bed rest, along with a potion that we've been administering several times each day. I'm not sure whether Joel is benefitting from the potion or from time, but he is one of the lucky ones who does seem to be getting better. He is able to speak again, and begged me to write this letter, as he is too weak to lift the pen.

And so I have. We missed the ship to California, for they would not allow the sick passage for fear of infecting others. I am told that there will be another within the next couple of weeks, so we are waiting for that. Given the progress that he has already made, I trust that Joel will be well enough to travel by then.

He sends you his love, and wants you to know that you are in his thoughts every moment of every day.

Your servant,

Samuel Watkins

I think we both caught the name at the same time and again, I whispered it softly. "Watkins, so he was here."

Mindy nodded softly and snuggled in closer. She was silent for a long time and I began to wonder if she'd fallen asleep. Finally, she whispered, "It would seem that he survived the Yellow Fever. How frightening for her though. Half a world away; unable to get to him; unable to help; terrified." She seemed to muse for a while and then added, "He wants to get back. Do you suppose he ever did?"

CHAPTER 18

I woke early the next morning. The yellow wallpaper glowed softly under the early influence of the sun, reflecting back just enough that I could make out the furnishings in the room. I yawned, stretched, and looked at the clock, and then lay back, wondering whether I should try to return to the land of dreams.

I lay still, thinking of Samuel Watkins who maybe had come to this town, and possibly even to this site, back in 1852. I wondered if the Joel with him had been Joel Woodward, the man with a tie to the woman who still slept next to me, a man whose very breath was related to the soft exhalation that I could feel on the hairs of my arm. Hmmm. Interesting thought.

The sun continued its incremental journey up into the sky as I lay, still bathed in the warmth of the covers, to the point where I could make out details in the room. I closed my eyes one last time, savored the softness of the body pressed against me, and then carefully disengaged and slipped out of bed. Mindy sighed softly, and slid a little further onto my side of the bed, capturing the lingering heat I'd left behind.

I dressed quickly, and then leaving a brief note on the dresser, carefully opened the door. The hallway was dim and quiet. Most guests, no doubt, still dreaming. I made my way to the lobby, where the smell of brewing coffee completed my awakening. I nodded to the owner, and he asked how I'd slept.

"Very well," I smiled at him and indicated the coffee. "Have you got a cup of that ready?"

"In a few minutes. I just put it on." He busied himself at the sideboard, laying out scones and jam and cereal. I could see the stream of black coffee dripping into the pot to one side, and settled onto an antique red velvet sofa to wait. The newspaper had been delivered, and I picked up a copy. I was surprised to note that it was the Gold Country Times, published locally in Murphys. It had a few obligatory articles that headlined from Sacramento, or Washington, or San Francisco, but most of the news originated in Murphys and the surrounding countryside. I perused the headlines, and settled into an article about modern day prospecting in the gold country. I was surprised to discover that there was still gold to be found in panning the local creeks. Admittedly, there wasn't much, but the fact that it was still seeping out of the mountains was interesting. I stored the thought away, and moved on to another article. A minute or two later, I heard a voice at my elbow.

"Sir?" I looked up. The owner stood there with a cup and saucer, steaming with hot coffee. "Did I remember correctly from yesterday that you like your coffee black?"

"Um, yes, thank you." I reached out and took the offered cup.

"Can I bring you a pastry?" he continued, motioning toward the sideboard, now brimming with food.

I raised my hand, palm outward. "No. Just coffee for now. Thanks."

He retreated and I returned to the newspaper, occasionally sipping some of the hot black beverage. I smiled at the thought of drinking my coffee from a china cup, and resting that cup onto a matching saucer. This clearly wasn't restaurant quality dishware. He and his wife, most likely his wife, had picked with care to find something that matched the rustic elegance of the gold country. Somehow, it felt different to drink my coffee from a china cup and saucer, instead of a mug or as I had so often, from a paper cup, and to be sitting on an antique horsehair sofa as I did so. Ah well. It was a different kind of getaway. Putting the cup down, I grinned and snapped open the newspaper.

Some time later, I decided it was time to get outside. I glanced at my watch. It was still only 7:15, so I thanked my host, and opened the front door. It was surprisingly chilly outside, considering the heat of the previous day. I thought briefly of returning to the room for a jacket, and then decided against it. The day would warm up as the sun rose, and I didn't want to disturb Mindy.

I've always been fascinated by the machinations of a town that's just waking up. We'd noticed the day before that the commercial portion of the town really was centered on Main Street, and beyond that, almost nothing. Walking along, I whistled softly to myself. I could see residents coming out, picking up the paper to read over their morning coffee as I had, or hopping into their cars for a commute to work. The downtown was virtually empty, but then I'd noticed the day before that most businesses didn't open up until 9:00. I turned up a side road and walked for a while, until I came to a dead end, and then turned back toward town. I was about two blocks from downtown when I passed by a small church. The door was open, so I decided to go in.

Though not terribly religious, I've always enjoyed churches. I suppose that a part of it is curiosity and another part, the sense of peace that one finds sitting in a pew in a church when no service is going on.

I found a spot and sat, noticing that I was not alone. Two others were there. One, an older woman, sat in the front row, clutching what appeared to be a prayer book, and mumbling softly to herself. A man worked at the front, cleaning an arrangement of flowers, some of which appeared a little spent in the early morning light. Despite his blue jeans, his clerical collar told me that he was likely the pastor of this small country church, and I guessed him to be in his fifties, near my age. At one point, he looked at me and I inclined my head in a silent greeting. He nodded as well, and then walked through a door at the back of the church.

The building was obviously old, covered with layer upon layer of white paint over greying wood. The floors had been polished by the footsteps of a century worth of worshipers to a smooth if dull finish. Narrow stained glass windows graced the walls, letting in a dim but colorful light in the early morning. This part of the town was heavily forested with large oaks and pines, and I suppose those blocked much of the sunlight even in the afternoon. The choir loft was directly over my head, reached by climbing a spiral staircase.

I sat back, closed my eyes, and let my mind wander, trying to imagine myself, an old western miner, sitting here, conversing with God. I didn't know Joel's religion. Protestant of some sort, I presumed from the comments about the pastor. Was he religious? Did he become so during his experience here? What kinds of thoughts might have passed through his head when he entered this or some other similar church? The letters, thought they opened our eyes to his journey, really told us very little.

Presently, I stood, and softly made my way out the door. The sunlight was bright after the dimness of the church, and I stood in the doorway for a moment, shading my eyes. As I started to turn toward the street, I made out the pastor, sweeping the walkway that ran around the church. "Good morning," I called.

He nodded his head without stopping his work. "Good morning to you too." He was brushing leaves off of the stones of the walkway into the bushes on either side. As I watched, he picked up a small twig that had fallen and tossed it back under a tree. "I have to clear this every morning, especially if we've had any kind of wind. I wouldn't want anyone to trip and fall." Then he looked up at me. "What brings you to church today?"

"I just love old churches," I said. "The calm. The art. The history. Yours is very nice. Small."

He chuckled. "It is small. Ten rows deep with seating for six across." He bent to pull a weed from the pavers. Rising, he tossed the weed onto a compost pile and continued. "We tend to like it that way. I came from the big city and had a big church. Lots of advantages. We had plenty of money, but it was too big. Too..." He paused, thinking of the right word.

"Impersonal?" I inquired.

He grinned. "That's it exactly. I know everyone who attends my church here." Then he looked me in the eye. "Well, nearly everyone. I don't know you." He reached out his hand. "Jim Adams. I've been pastor here for the past six years."

I took his hand and shook. He had the firm, confident grip of a man who is comfortable with strangers. "Charlie Overton." I looked up at the church, its lines rising up skyward to a white steeple. "It's a beautiful building. How long has it been here?"

"More than my six years, that's for sure," he laughed. "Come on over here. I'll show you the cornerstone. He set aside his broom and we walked around the back. Most of the perimeter of the church was planted in flower beds, but one corner was bare. He approached a large stone and crouched down. I leaned in next to him. "There you are," he said. "1869. It's one of the older buildings still standing here in Murphys. Most of the others from this era either burned down in one of the big fires, or were pulled out in favor of something bigger or more permanent."

I looked at the stone. A few names had been engraved beneath the date, two Murphy's, and an handful of others. No Watkins or Woodward. I rose and he followed. Looking around me, I could see that the surprisingly large back yard was as well kept as the front. "This must be a big job," I said. "You're pastor, gardener, maintenance man..."

"Oh not hardly," he laughed. "I do some. A lot some days, but this is the work of the congregation." He raised his arm and pointed out some of the features of the yard. "That little copse of trees over there was planted some eighty years ago by one of the old families here in town. As I recall, one of the town fathers put the bench in there in memory of his mother." He continued, "And over there." He pointed to what appeared to be a sunken rose garden, overgrown but still flowering. "Old Mrs. Jeffries planted that back in the 40's. She took years working on it, insisting that the flowers glorified God. Funny thing," he mused. "Most rose gardens are a little more orderly, but she wanted this one to be wild, one bush flowing into the next, rose hips and all. God's garden, she called it."

He started walking toward the front again. "I do a lot of the day to day stuff," He retrieved his broom. "The sweeping, that sort of thing, but nearly everything else is done by members of the church. They take care of the garden, the painting, the big jobs." He looked at me with a huge grin on his face. "I can't think of a single member of this church who doesn't do something to make it go, even the kids. Small churches. I think that's where people feel closest to God."

We were standing at the front now, looking out at the street when he said, "So what brings you to Murphys?"

I'd been reflecting on my mother's relationship with the churches in her life. She'd spent her last two decades living in Los Angeles, attending the Crystal Cathedral, one of the largest churches in the country. Still, when I thought about it, I reflected that her favorite had probably been a small Episcopal church in Northern California, not much bigger than this one, where's she and my father frequently socialized with the minister and his wife. Startled, I stammered, "Murphys, Oh, um. I'm with a friend. We came for a long weekend. A getaway from work. Um. She had a relative we think might have come through here back in the 1850's, so we've been poking around a little looking for traces of him."

"Ah, a gold miner."

"That's right."

He looked at me with interest. "What makes you think that he was here?"

I shrugged. "It's an interesting story. We can't be certain, but we did find a packet of letters between her great great grandmother and the man we think was her great great grandfather. One of the envelopes has a Murphys address, so it seems possible."

"You think he was a relative?"

"That's the strange part. He's not mentioned in the family tree. We haven't read all of the letters yet, but it seems likely." I paused. "Anyway, yesterday we ran across the name of one of his companions in the museum. We hadn't expected anything. We just asked out of curiosity." I looked at him. The twinkle in his eye caught my attention.

"Yes?" I asked.

He chuckled. "You must be the people Melissa was talking about. I hear you were playing with one of the mining pans."

I blushed. "Um. You heard about that?"

He laughed. "She scolded you?"

I nodded.

"Well, she's very particular about those displays. Doesn't let anybody touch anything. Me..." He waved toward the church. "Touch it. Get the feel of it. If it helps you to feel closer to God, go ahead."

Suddenly I slapped my forehead. I pointed at him. "Jim Adams!" I turned and pointed toward the museum. "And she's..."

"That's right. Melissa Adams. She's my wife."

I couldn't believe that I hadn't made the connection more quickly. They were similar in age, and had the same last name in a small town. Anyway, I turned to the pastor. "I'm sorry."

"Think nothing of it." He was grinning from ear to ear. "She said you found a name."

"Right," I said. "Watkins. He might have been a partner. Both the first and the last name match, so we're pretty sure he's the right one. And he had a companion named Joel." I hesitated. "That was her great great grandfather's name."

Suddenly, I looked at my watch. It was almost 9:00. "Mindy," I said aloud. "I'd better get going. I left her asleep but wrote a note saying I'd be back by nine."

He nodded sagely. "You'd better go then. You don't want to be late."

I looked back toward town then back at him. "Thank you. I appreciate your time. I've enjoyed our talk."

He reached out his hand. "As have I."

I grasped his hand and shook, then was about to turn when he said, "You know, church records aren't kept at the museum. I might be able to help with your search."

"You have documents from back then?" I asked. "But I thought that the church was built in 1869."

"The building," he replied. "There were two buildings before it, and before that, a tent. The first pastor kept pretty detailed records as well as a daily journal that he passed down to his successors."

"Really!"

"Come for lunch," he said. "Melissa and I get together at one." He turned and pointed to a small white house behind the church. "We'll eat on the patio. That will give me time to look up some of those old books."

I was stunned. "I'll need to talk with Mindy, but I'm sure she'll be thrilled." I hesitated, unsure what to say next. "One o'clock. We'll be here." I tapped my watch. And now I'd really better go."

He waved me away. "You're right. It's never wise to keep a lady waiting. I'll see you then."

I turned and walked back down the street. As I was about to turn the corner, I looked back. The pastor had pulled out an old rusty push mower and was about to cut the grass that ran in two tidy rows along the steps in front of the church. He glanced up as I looked back, waved, and then started to push his mower.

CHAPTER 19

Mindy had showered, dressed, and was sipping from a cup of coffee on the balcony when I returned. I breezed over to the table where she was sitting, bussed her on the cheek, and pulled up a chair.

She looked up from her book. "Did you have a nice morning?" she asked.

I nodded. "I left early. You were asleep. I wandered around town, had a cup of coffee, watched the place wake up. That sort of thing."

"I must have been tired. I didn't even notice you leave."

"I'm glad. I didn't want to disturb you."

Smirking, she said, "No, you'd never try to do that."

"I mean..." I saw the teasing look on her face and crumbled. "Well..."

She laughed and I joined her. "Am I that easy to read?"

She stood and hugged me and I leaned my forehead against hers, all the while appreciating the feel of her soft curves. Finally, she pushed away and said softly, "Always."

"Well I guess you already know what I was doing this morning then." I said as I walked over to the bed and sat.

"Pining for me?" she asked coyly.

"Well aside from that."

"Wishing you were still in bed?"

"Hmm," I mused softly, "and that." I picked up the letter from last night and held it up. "Consider this a clue."

She cocked her head to one side. "The museum doesn't open

until 10:00, does it?"

"That's correct." I patted the letter against my hand.

"Back to the cemetery?"

I shook my head.

She looked at me for a long time, trying to figure out what I'd been up to, and then continued slowly. "You went for a walk. The museum's closed." Furrowing her brow, she looked at me, "Not back to the cemetery. Public records office?"

I shook my head again.

"Then I'm lost."

"Huh," I replied. "Charlie: Am I that easy to read?" I looked at her and rolled my eyes. "Mindy: Always." Now I dropped my head and stared at her over my glasses. "Evidently not."

She laughed and threw a rolled up pair of socks at me.

Affecting a stunned expression, I retorted, "And now she resorts to violence." I shook my head. "Should I tell you or do you want to continue trying to guess?"

She reached over, picked up the socks, and playfully whacked me on the head with them. "You know exactly what I mean. You're easy to read when you want something."

I gave her my most innocent look. "Me?"

"No," she said and then looked at me coyly and batted her eyelashes. "Me."

"Ah."

Mindy went over to her suitcase, put it on the bed, and proceeded to start packing. I walked up behind her and put my arm around her shoulders, giving her a slight squeeze. "You might want to wait on that. I've already checked to see if we can stay for another night."

She turned her head. "What about work?"

"Call them. You're the boss. Take another day."

She twisted her eyes about and looked at me. Then sighing, she sat on the bed and patted the space beside her.

I batted my eyebrows a couple of times, and smiled as I descended toward her.

Chuckling, she said, "No. Not that." She shook her head and repeated, "You are so easy." Then she got serious. "What have you been up to that makes you want to stay another day?"

I sat and slid my hand onto her knee. She slapped it away.

"Well?"

"You have no more guesses?" I looked at her and she glared back at me. "I suppose not." I nodded toward the letter. "I really didn't have any plan to do anything except walk around town this morning, enjoying the chill and the quiet. And that's what I started out with. The stores are still closed, so I wandered several of the side streets. Very pretty, lots of flowers, quite a few quaint little old cottages. It was quite a nice walk..."

"And," she prompted.

"And I ended up at one of the local churches, the one with the tall white steeple, couple of blocks back from Main Street? You remember that? We drove by it the other day." I looked at her inquiringly.

"And," was all she said.

"Well, I went inside, just to look. You know how I like old churches. It's beautifully maintained, peaceful, but tiny."

She took my chin in her hand and turned my face toward her and I could see that she was getting annoyed. "And?"

"And I met the minister. We're invited for lunch. One o'clock." I looked into her eyes and smiled.

She looked at me for a long time. "And because you've been invited to lunch, I'm supposed to blow off work tomorrow?" She frowned. "What am I missing here?"

I beamed at her. "His name's Jim Adams and he's married to Melissa Adams. You remember the docent at the museum?" She nodded slightly and I put my hand back on her knee and squeezed it. "Anyway, the civic records are in the museum, but he has the church records dating back to the old tent church. Evidently the original pastor kept quite a journal. He said he'd look it up and share it with us at lunch." I smiled up at her, victory in my face.

She twisted her mouth into a half grin. "Alright. I'll call work." Then she lifted my hand very deliberately off of her knee and nestled my knuckles against her lips. She nipped slightly and when I tried to pull back, held on. "In the meantime, I was thinking of getting a cappuccino and a croissant in that little bakery up the street. While we're eating, we can decide which gallery to visit first." She tapped me on the nose with her finger. "Anything else will have to wait until tonight."

"Or after lunch?" I said.

At that, she laughed out loud and walked to the closet where she pulled out her jacket. "You are incorrigible. Definitely nineteen! Now come along and let's get some breakfast."

CHAPTER 20

Just before 1:00, we walked across the street to the little white church where I'd met Jim Adams. I noticed a sparkle in the rose window that graced the front of the church, then glancing overhead, checked that the sun was floating in a clear blue sky, well above the horizon where it seemed to have been hovering during my earlier visit. I pointed out the window to Mindy, and she hugged my arm, and then suggested that we explore the church after lunch to check out the stained glass.

We walked around the side on cobble stones, the lawn surrounding them now neatly trimmed. Jim and Melissa's home sat across the back yard, and was set apart from the church property by a rose covered white rail fence. Though the roses on the fence displayed a variety of colors, the vines that hung from the trellis were graced simply with deep red blossoms that scented the air of the passageway.

Jim met us just inside. His collar was still set in place, but he had covered his jeans with an apron that read, "All Hail the Chef" above a cartoon of a man tending a smoky barbecue. He grinned as we approached, "I hope turkey burgers are okay." Waving a spatula toward the grill, he continued, "It's almost hot enough to put them on. I prefer beef myself, but you know how that works." He rolled his eyes toward Melissa, who had just emerged from the house with a pitcher of iced tea.

She smiled, "Well, if it isn't the investigators. Did you find anything at the cemetery? Samuel was it?"

I was about to answer when Mindy spoke up. "Nothing at all, Mrs. Adams. We found any number of possibilities, but when we investigated closer, none quite fit. We even found an S. Watkins, but the dates were wrong. I suppose that's just as well."

"Oh, heavens," she replied. "No need for formality here. Call me Melissa." She grinned and lifted her pitcher. "Ice tea?"

Mindy took a glass and raised it to her, "Thank you."

After pouring four glasses of tea, she motioned us toward a small sitting area under a gnarled oak tree. "Shall we enjoy the shade?"

I nodded enthusiastically and started to follow her, but Mindy looked back ruefully at the sunlight, and then moved one of the chairs so that it sat close enough to talk, but just far enough removed so that she could bathe her shoulders in warmth. Seeing her sitting there caused me to smile, knowing how easily she chilled even on a warm day. Jim joined us a minute later. "I hope you don't mind if I jump up and down a bit, but I'll need to tend those burgers.

"Not at all," I said.

He sat next to his wife in an old wrought iron swing, and inclined his head toward Mindy. "I see you prefer the sun? Feel free to scoot into the shade if you get too hot."

"I will," she replied. "I like the heat. Loosens up the old muscles." Then she looked around. "This is a beautiful spot. Is it all part of the church?"

Jim nodded. Inclining his head toward the white house, he said, "The church provides our home, and it comes with this enormous yard. As I mentioned to Charlie, the folks around here are real good about helping with the upkeep." He spread his arms out to take in the surroundings. "I couldn't ask for a prettier place to live."

I'd followed his gaze, and couldn't disagree. The church sat on the far side of the lot, small but well kept. There was probably at least an acre of open space between the church and the parsonage. We'd seen the creek earlier when we walked around the town, but hadn't realized that it bordered this property as well. Aspens drooped all along the banks, creating a cool retreat on hot days, and oaks, large and small, surrounded much of the rest of the property. I noticed a pair of swings in one tree, and an enclosed area that held a big old sewer pipe along with a children's climbing structure. The horse shoe pit was not far from where we sat. "It looks like the playground for the church."

He laughed. "Playground, picnic area, you name it. We've some musicians in the membership, and they bring out their instruments a couple of times each summer so that we can host an outdoor dance."

Melissa grimaced. "A little dusty for my taste, but people seem to have fun." She noticed that I'd finished my drink and started to rise. "More tea?"

I motioned 'no' with my hand, "I'll wait. I must have been thirsty when we got here. I'm fine now."

"Just let me know," she said. "There's plenty more." She settled back onto the swing, and kicked off her shoes, settling her bare feet under her dress and leaning against her husband. Looking at Mindy, she asked, "So what got you started on this quest to find your relative?"

I looked at Mindy, noting that she too had tucked her feet up onto the big comfortable chair. "It's kind of funny," she said. "It all started with a packet of letters that Charlie found."

Melissa looked at me. "You found them?"

"Well, I think it would be best to say we both found them. You see, Mindy has this red cabinet." I looked in her direction. "It might be best for her to tell you about it."

Mindy paused for a few seconds and then began. "My grandfather died about twenty five years ago. He and I had been very close when I was a little girl and it was hard for me to imagine him getting old and dying. He'd asked everyone in the family to come through and put their names on anything that they wanted." She sighed. "Well he had this old cabinet. It was pretty well worn, but he'd always had it in his living room, and it just felt like it was part of him. Anyway, I put my name on that and he asked me why I wanted it."

She paused for a while, a sad, far away look on her face. Even I was enchanted by the story, never having heard this part. "I told him that it would remind me of him, and I wanted to keep a part of him in my living room. He had a good laugh at that, but I think he was flattered nonetheless. I still remember what he said. He got very serious."

"Then you shall have it," he'd said. "But you need to make me a promise." He bent me down so that we could look at the cabinet together. It was old. Some of the wood was split, and there was a deep scratch that ran across the top. In addition to that, the finish had worn away in several spots, leaving almost a driftwood effect. Altogether, it was an ugly old relic and if it hadn't belonged to him, I might have burned it for firewood. He loved it though. "I've always wanted to rebuild this cabinet," he said, "but never got around to it. Too busy, I suppose. It was in my mother's bedroom when she died, and for some reason, she cherished it just as it is. That's why it's been such a special piece to me. So in honor of her, I'd like you to do what I never did. Refinish it. Make it into a thing of beauty. And most important, make it reflect your personality, something that would make me smile, because, make no mistake about it, I'll be looking down on you."

"Huh," I exhaled. "So that's where the red and the 'S' shaped door came from."

She nodded. "I found a cabinet maker in San Francisco who did amazing work. She and I corresponded for a while and I sent her some photographs of the old cabinet and asked if she could rebuild it. Well," she took a sip of tea while we waited, "she could and she did. And I think it does reflect my personality." Looking up, she nodded her head, "Just like my grandfather wanted."

Melissa asked quietly, "You say it's red?"

I laughed and Mindy turned to me. "You want to describe it? Maybe an outsider will see it differently."

"Sure. If you open the door, you can see traces of the original cabinet. It's been cleaned up and sanded and lacquered with glossy turquoise paint, but it's basically a rectangular box. The outside's what's special. The front and back are flat, but the sides are curved, in something of an 'S' shape, giving it a flowing look. In addition to that, the top's been scooped out and covered with pressed glass." I paused for effect, "Oh, and the whole exterior is painted with a shiny red lacquer. It's about as far from a Victorian antique as you might imagine."

Jim leaned forward. "Interesting. But what's it got to do with the letters?" Then he jumped up. "Hold that thought. I'd better tend those burgers." He ran to the barbecue and opened the top, emitting a cloud of white smoke.

While he was gone, Melissa asked, "So where are you from?"

I looked at Mindy and she looked at me. I could tell that we were both wondering about how they'd feel about hosting lunch at a church for two unmarried people who were obviously traveling together. Mindy answered, "I live near Santa Cruz." She pointed at me. "And Charlie lives in San Jose. We have a mutual friend who introduced us several months ago."

Melissa nodded, completely disregarding our concern, "And what made you decide to come up to the gold country?"

"I've always liked the area," I said and then grinned at Mindy. "I suppose we're taking turns introducing one another to our favorite haunts."

She nodded. "He's camping with me in Big Sur in a couple of weeks." I grimaced and she laughed over her tea. "He's worried that it'll rain, or that wild animals will get into our tent."

Melissa cast me a glance. "I tend to agree with him. I wouldn't want to camp in the rain. It's hard enough to keep clean as it is." Then she shuddered. "And I certainly wouldn't want wild animals in my tent!"

Victorious, I stared over at Mindy. "You see, other people worry about that too!"

She just rolled her eyes, and was about to reply when Melissa continued pointedly to me, "But it's pretty unlikely to rain, and if you're worried about it, take rain gear. And wild animals in tents? Come on." She smiled.

Mindy immediately jumped up, took a few steps over to Melissa, and high-fived her. Then looking at me, stuck out her tongue and returned to her seat. I was too stunned to speak right away.

Just then, Jim came strolling back to the little copse of oak trees where we'd settled. "Did I miss anything?" he asked innocently.

I looked up at him, "Just me being ganged up on by the women."

He laughed. "I've got three daughters. Even the cats are female. Welcome to my life!"

Melissa asked coyly, "Are you complaining?"

He sat next to her, patted her knee, and kissed her on the cheek. "I wouldn't have it any other way." Then he looked back at Mindy. "You were about to tell us about those letters."

Mindy took a deep breath. "Well that's where it gets exciting." She looked across at our new companions. "Charlie was at my house one day, and he was snooping around the cabinet."

"Snooping!" I snorted.

They all laughed and she continued, "Okay, he was checking out the inside. Anyway, he found a button that released a false floor. Inside was the original cabinet, unfinished, rough, and evidently something that the cabinet maker never noticed, because she never mentioned it to me. We found a packet of letters in there."

"Interesting," Jim mused. "Do you suppose your grandfather knew about them?"

"I don't think so. At any rate, he never mentioned them."

"And now you've read the letters and have begun to search for your ancestors."

"Some of them." She looked at me and then back at our hosts. "We've been reading them together. I've organized them by date and we're taking turns."

This piqued Melissa's curiosity. "Taking turns?"

Mindy laughed softly. "I'm not sure how it started, but that's what we've been doing." She looked at me again. "I've been reading Catherine's letters. Charlie reads Joel's." She grinned. "Somehow it seems to make it more," she paused searching for the right phrase, "personal, I suppose. Real."

Jim looked from Mindy to me and back. "It sounds fascinating. So who are Catherine and Joel?"

Mindy continued. "Well Catherine we know. She was my great, great grandmother. I have an old family tree and she appears there. Joel we're less certain of."

"Really," Melissa said. "Why is that?"

"He may have been her husband, but there are some issues, and we don't really know enough about him yet to be sure."

"So this is who you've been looking for," Jim said. "This Joel."

Mindy nodded. "That wasn't really our plan, but it kind of worked out that way."

"I'd love to read one of the letters, if you have one," Melissa added. "And if I could, maybe make a copy for the museum?" She looked at Mindy inquiringly.

Mindy hesitated a bit and Melissa added, "Only if it would be okay with you."

The two women looked across the dirt at one another, and

Mindy relented. "I think I'd like that. We might have found a connection to Joel here. Maybe they should have a presence in the museum."

She reached into her purse and started to bring out the four letters when Jim rose, stopping her, "After lunch. I think those burgers are about ready."

CHAPTER 21

"I've always thought that the best meal is a simple one," Melissa mused as she ladled a small portion of potato salad onto her plate and passed the bowl over to me. "A little meat, some salad, and the ice tea should be plenty."

Jim snorted. "Don't you believe her. This potato salad has won awards at the community picnics. She's constantly tinkering with it."

She looked at her husband. "It's just a salad. Nothing special."

He winked at me. "Nothing?" he asked innocently.

"Not really." She took her fork and speared a piece of potato. "Just a salad."

Mindy tasted hers and smiled. "It's very good." She paused. "There's some aftertaste I can't quite place. Tarragon? No." She looked up at Melissa who took a mouthful of the potato salad, smiled, and chewed.

Chuckling, Jim looked to his wife. "These aren't locals. I'm sure they won't tell anyone here. Why don't you share your recipe."

Melissa gave him a look and then turned to Mindy. "It's not tarragon." She smiled at me. "Did you get enough?"

Jim chortled. "See. She won't even tell me what's in it."

She wiped daintily at the corner of her mouth with a napkin, and then said, "Now how could I claim to use a secret recipe if I told people what it was!" She put the napkin down and turned to Mindy as she reached for her iced tea. "This Joel of yours, he's not on the family tree?"

I smiled and looked at Jim. His wife had deftly changed the topic, as he seemed to predict she would. He was silently chuckling while he ate. We both listened quietly as Mindy explained the supposed marriage and the problem with the false pastor, along with the fact that Catherine's brothers had chased Joel away from the farm. She ended by saying, "So as far as the family history is concerned, it's like he never existed, but at the same time, there's no indication that she ever married, or who Marie's father might have been." She grinned mysteriously, "It's a conundrum."

Jim stared at her for a moment before saying, "Fascinating. I'd still love to read one of those letters." He looked from Mindy to me, "or hear it if you're reading to one another."

I looked at Mindy. She nodded. "Let me help clean up here, and then maybe under the tree?"

§§§§

Once we had settled in the little copse of trees, Mindy extracted a letter from her purse. The day had warmed, and she'd moved her chair a few feet into the shade. "The next letter is from Catherine, so I suppose I'll be the reader." She looked around and unfolded the old paper.

July 29, 1850
Pittsburgh

My darling Joel,
It has been so long since I have heard from you. I am worried and hope that this letter finds you well.

The postman delivered the letter from Samuel just yesterday. How does one contract Yellow Fever? It sounds like such a serious disease. I suppose that by now you are either well, or... I can only believe that you are well. To think otherwise is just too terrible.

Have you resumed your journey to California? Were you able to hire a ship to take you there from Panama? I certainly hope so. There seems in my mind, a sense of safety and progress as long as you are traveling on the ship. Oh, certainly I understand the dangers of a journey at sea, but after what Samuel said about Panama, the ship seems a much more certain way to travel.

I remain in Pittsburgh. You need have no fears there. Aunt Ruth is taking very good care of me. We have been out some. She insisted that I come shopping with her last Tuesday, and then took me to Millard's Emporium, a large general store. I had never seen such a variety of merchandise in one place. I was accustomed to the little store in Bradford. It seemed to have all that we needed, sacks of grains and some spices as well as bolts of cloth, farm tools, and the like. But this emporium just seems to go on forever. Why I had never dreamed of some of the things that they sell there. They had several different types of china dishes. Imagine that. As if simple pewter is not good enough for people! And the shoes and bolts of fancy cloth and even some dresses already made. Ruth told me that there were several thousand people living in Pittsburgh, and when I saw that store, I understood what it meant to be in the big city!

But I have gotten distracted. Ruth took me to the store to buy fabric. She's determined to make me a few new frocks. "To allow room for the baby," she said.

Speaking of that, there is a large standing mirror in my bedroom. I had used it to ensure that my dresses were well pressed but the other day... Well I was curious, so I removed all of my clothing in daylight, something I had rarely done in the past, well at least not since I was a child, and looked at myself. My belly is beginning to swell with the baby. It didn't seem natural, as it has always been so flat in the past, but it is pleasing to know that a part of you is growing within me. I must admit that I wished you had been there, to see me, to feel the swell, to...

Well that kind of thinking will certainly do me no good. You were my husband for only one night, and yet I miss you desperately. The glow in your eyes, the gentleness of your touch, even the feel of your breath upon my skin.

Be safe, husband. Come back to me.

Your loving wife, Catherine

The hoarseness in Mindy's voice betrayed her emotion as she read the last line and we all sat, enchanted, Catherine's words drifting away in the light breeze, each lost in our own thoughts.

Melissa was the first to speak. "There's no doubt that she loved him."

Mindy nodded her head silently, still lost in thought.

"Do you know if he ever returned?"

"We haven't finished the letters, so we can't be certain, but I think we both suspect that he never did."

"Ah," Jim nodded. "From what she said just in that letter, it would appear that he certainly fathered the child."

Mindy looked at him. "It seems so. What we don't know is if the child was my Great Grandmother Marie." Peering out at the rest of us, she continued. "I've wondered whether the child was born healthy, or whether she gave it up for adoption, or whether in fact, she kept the baby. She smiled. "There are several letters left. I suppose we'll find out in time." Then she frowned. "I'm not so sure we'll ever know what happened to Joel, though there are more letters from him, so he did survive his illness.

"But you haven't read them," Melissa pondered.

She shook her head. "It seemed best to take them in order." Then she smiled. "A part of me wants to read them all at once and go from there, but another part is glad to be going slowly, taking them a little at a time, savoring them, reflecting."

"It's almost like we've slowed down time, like we're closer to their schedule," I said.

She continued. "I think that if I was to read them all at once, it would be a kind of intellectual journey, delving into my family's past out of curiosity. And then it would be done. This way," she paused, "this way I'm more emotionally involved." She looked out at us, a puzzled expression on her face, and then added, "It's begun to feel like I'm reading letters from family, people I'm not just related to, but people I care about."

We all sat quietly, savoring her thoughts for a while until Jim broke the mood. "It's an interesting glimpse into that time, isn't it?" He looked around the clearing at each of us. "The description of the store, and the fact that the fancy one in Pittsburgh actually sold dresses pre-made."

Melissa picked up his lead. "Or the china. It was a simpler time. Why indeed would you need a choice if simple pewter would suffice?"

"Even her self-consciousness looking in the mirror," I added.

The two women looked at one another and then simultaneously started to laugh. Mindy reached over and patted me on the knee. "You won't find me spending a lot of time examining my naked body in the mirror!"

Giggling, Melissa said, "Nor I!"

Jim peered over his glasses at her and was about to speak when she smiled back at him. "Especially not when you're in the room."

Our laughter filled the glade, and then as quickly dissolved into silence as each of us returned to the letter that remained so prominent in our minds. After a minute or so, Mindy broke the quiet. "It's hard in some ways and in others so easy to imagine her feelings, and what it must have taken in the nineteenth century to set her hopes and fears so clearly on paper."

I nodded. "She was in the end, a young woman in love."

She smiled at me as she rose, "With a little bit of lust thrown in." Looking at the others, she pulled her chair out into the light. She motioned toward the sun, now hovering midway above the horizon in the west. "Starting to cool off," she said. As she sat again, she looked purposefully at Jim, "Okay, I've shared my letter. Now about those journals..."

CHAPTER 22

Jim took down a dusty leather volume from the shelf above his desk. We had gone into the church office, partly to get out of the chilly breeze, and partly because he was reluctant to take the journals outside. I looked around. The light in the small room, flowing in through a small high window, was satisfactory, even in the late afternoon. He'd dragged in a couple of folding chairs, and we were gathered around a battered card table. His desk in the corner was the only luxury to be seen, and ancient roll top, whose many cubbies were filled with the scraps of papers, envelopes, and other clutter that one might expect in a business office. Seeing me eye the desk, Jim said, "A gift from one of the old congregants back about the time the church was built. Every minister since that time has used that desk." He winked at me. "I understand that there are at least a couple of hidden compartments, but haven't taken the time to find them. Who knows what treasure they might hide." Then he laughed, "Probably old church records. Boring accounts of electric bills and the like."

He got more serious then and referred to the book in his hand. "This is one of the earliest journals, as you can probably tell." He smiled. The volume was in surprisingly good shape, considering its age. The leather cover was cracked and worn, but intact. It appeared that someone had hand stitched the yellowed pages into the binding. He carried it over to the card table and lay it down. "I decided to focus on this one since you said that you were looking around this time."

Opening the book, he began haltingly to read, clearly having some difficulty with the cramped, irregular script. He paused for a moment, evidently trying to figure out a word when Melissa reached across and gestured him to hand her the journal. "Let me." He gave her a questioning look and she continued airily. "I knew all that time teaching writing to third graders would come in handy." She looked up at us and grinned. "Good practice reading the indecipherable."

Mindy looked at her in surprise. "You taught third grade!" she exclaimed.

"That's right. Years ago in Cincinnati and then a little bit here in the gold country."

Laughing, Mindy said, "You and I need to talk later." Seeing Jim's puzzled look, she said, "It seems your wife and I have something in common. I also taught third grade. And I grew up in Cincinnati." She looked back at Melissa. "The best ice cream?"

Melissa laughed. "Well Graeters, or course."

Mindy gave me a haughty look. "Told you!"

Jim burst out into laughter. "You have to put up with this too?" He scanned our faces. "I'm a Ben and Jerry's fan myself."

"Cherry Garcia?" I asked.

He just raised his thumb and nodded. Passing the book over to Melissa, he said, "We'll get to old home week later. For now, let's see what we can find."

Her reading voice was soft but sure. She paused occasionally to make out a word, but her reading had a kind of flow that transported us back to Murphy's in the mid-nineteenth century.

Sunday, January 20, 1852; Another cold day. We had snow last night, and patches lingered on the ground even in the noontime sun. I observed service this morning with only eleven hearty souls. It is difficult to pull them away from their claims even to praise the lord. We gathered around the stove at the front of the church and hoped that the canvas would hold the heat until we could finish. At least it blocked out the wind.

Monday, January 21, 1852; I spent the day clearing the lot for the new church. There is so much to do, but we are fortunate to have the donation of so much land. Took down one old pine and have been working on cutting off the limbs. If I can get some help, I will cut it into rounds and split them when they dry. They should provide a good supply of wood for next winter. One of the Isaac lads helped for an hour in the morning, but then took off to his claim, so I worked alone for the rest of the day. I am thankful though that he helped me to fell the tree. *At least the work has kept me warm. I have decided to reward myself with a bowl of stew at the hotel tonight.*

Tuesday, January 22, 1852; Rained all day. I stayed in the church, reading the good book and writing some long neglected letters. A little warmer by the stove, but damp. Sitting here, I hear the occasional chime as a drop of water splashes into one of the pots. I have found that by placing them under the leakiest seams, I can prevent the floor from turning to mud.

Wednesday, January 23, 1852; The storm let up a little today and I walked into town to post my letters. Johnny Williams, one of the miners working a little creek a few miles to the east, found a small nugget, so he came into town to bank it at the Wells Fargo office and then decided to treat himself to a hearty breakfast and some new equipment. I had stopped by the tavern for a cup of coffee when he came in and bought beer for the house. I must admit that I shared in his good fortune.

Thursday, January 24, 1852; A reminder of what a brutal country this can be. Johnny was beaten and robbed in the hotel last night. Fortunately, he did not have much money left from his find, but whoever attacked him stole all he had along with his new coat and boots. I visited today and offered to help, but it seems the girls have adopted him and he is in good hands. Still, it will take some time for his broken arm to heal. I suppose he is lucky to be alive. I was surprised to find that he came from Northern Kentucky, not too far from my home in Cincinnati. We must have left at about the same time, as he arrived here just after I did in October. Of course, he came in search of gold, while I came to minister to souls.

Friday, January 25, 1852; The sheriff stopped by today. He is raising a posse to go after Johnny's attacker. Evidently one of the girls was awakened by the clamor, and thinks she recognized the man running down the back stairs. He is a drifter who has been hanging out at a camp a little way out Sheep Ranch Road. I deferred. I know that some ministers would have gone along, but as a man of God, I find it hard to condone the violence I know will follow.

Saturday, January 26, 1852; The rain has stopped, and it has gotten cold again. I had left my coat hanging by the door and it was stiff with ice when I awoke this morning. I got the fire going right away and could see the moisture steaming out of it while I worked on my sermon for tomorrow. With Johnny's beating, I have good material. My topic: What benefit it a man if he gains the world but loses his soul in the process.

Sunday, January 27, 1852; Only three came to church today, all women from the hotel. I gave up my sermon, as it was really aimed at the men, but they are out on the posse. Instead, I tried yet again to convince the ladies to shun the evils of prostitution, but to no avail, I suspect. Later in the day, I heard of three newcomers who have established a claim several miles up Murphys' Creek. I will try to make contact with them sometime in the next week.

Monday, January 28, 1852; The weather has turned, thank the Lord. It was probably 50 degrees this afternoon, delightful after the cold. Sheriff Miller returned, with just a few of the posse, the rest having returned to their claims. He dragged in a haggard looking man whose wrists were bound and tied to his saddle. He was wearing torn coveralls and a filthy cotton shirt. His feet were bare, and he wore no coat, that, along with the new boots having been returned to Johnny. He is in the pokey now, awaiting trial. I suspect he will be hanged before the week is out, but will still visit today. The man not only needs comfort for his soul, but will certainly benefit from warm clothes. I have an old trunk full of cast offs that I can loan him for his last few days.

Tuesday, January 29, 1852; The warmer weather has held, and I am grateful for the sake of the prisoner. The poor man has no heat, and dismal prospects. He was tried today and found guilty. He is to hang on Thursday morning. In some ways, I feel sorry for the man. He came to California hoping to find gold, but discovered only a life of hardship, like so many others. Oh, I know that he made the decision to rob Johnny, and probably many others, but it seems that in his heart, he is not a bad man, just a misguided one. I will visit him again tomorrow.

Wednesday, January 30, 1852; I am feeling melancholy despite the continued warm weather. It is probably my visit with Bill Vance, the prisoner. I spoke to the sheriff today about sparing his life, as he seems to be a genuinely good man caught in terrible circumstances. Sheriff Miller seemed to agree with me, and offered to speak with the judge. He did not hold out much hope though, as there is a mood in town to set an example of those who break laws so as to keep them out of Murphys.

Thursday, January 31, 1852; Bill Vance was hanged this morning from an old oak tree in front of the hotel. It was a somber event, and I was heartened to see that nobody seemed happy about it. I held a short service for his soul this afternoon, and then we buried him up on the hill, but only Sheriff Miller, Cindy from the hotel, and I attended. I spoke of some of the things that Vance had told me. A sad end to a life that from what I was told, once held promise.

Friday, February 1, 1852; February already, and another warm day. I was up at first light and traveled up the creek to meet the new miners. They are three unlikely friends who have come as have so many others, to make their fortune. Their leader is a bear of a man, and the only one who gave his name.

He introduced himself as Samuel, from Philadelphia. The others spoke with me briefly, and then returned to their work in the creek. I wonder at the life of men who spend hours in frigid water every day. Their hands are raw with chafing, and some tell me that by the end of the day, they can hardly feel their feet.

"Stop," Mindy cried. "Another reference to Samuel."

"And from Philadelphia, 'a bear of a man.' That sounds like Joel's description of him." I looked over at her. She was beaming with delight.

"He was with two others. Do you suppose one could have been Joel?"

Jim inclined his head. "It's hard to tell. His entries are so short. We'll have to read on to see if there's more."

Eagerly, we all nodded and Melissa resumed.

Saturday, February 2, 1852; Disaster! All of this warm weather has dried out the canvas of my small church. Today, while I was adding a log to the fire, a spark flew out and caught on the back wall. I did not notice it at first, and the wind fanned that spark into a flame. I had been boiling water for coffee, and dashed that at the flame, but it was too late. Fortunately, one of the men in town saw the light from the fire and ran to my rescue. Still, I lost two walls and most of the roof of the tent. I suppose that I should be grateful that there wasn't more damage.

Sunday, February 3, 1852; The lord does indeed work in mysterious ways. The entire complement of women at the hotel arrived in church today, along with several of the men in the community. Evidently, word had spread even before the service that I had been burned out last night, and they started collecting canvas as well as other donations at first light. I tried to conduct a service, but they waved me off, and instead got to work stitching up the canvas into a new tent. My day was filled with laughter and good wishes.

Friday, February 8, 1852; Forgive me for not writing. I have been so busy. The new tent is nearly completed, and I am again warm and snug inside. I have spent the last several nights at the hotel, and the sounds I have heard are certainly enough to make a man of God blush. Still, I am grateful for the support that the community has shown our humble church. Cindy even embroidered a set of daisies into the south west wall. They glow in the evening sun.

Saturday, February 9, 1852; The weather continues warm and dry. I find that I am quite comfortable wearing just my wool sweater when I walk about town. I hope that the weather will continue, but have been told by one of the old timers that we may well have snow again before winter is over. My sermon tomorrow will be about the power of love in a community.

    Sunday, February 10, 1852; To think that such a horrific thing as a fire could work to pull a community together. We had 22 worshipers inside today, and my small church was bursting. We had to pull my meager furnishings outside. After the service, Sheriff Miller came up to me and asked if I needed help clearing the land for the new church. I suppose it was evident that my progress has been slow and tedious. When the land was donated back in 1850, there was an expectation that the church would be built promptly, but Pastor Johannson was so ill, and then he passed away, and I have been busy this winter just getting to know the community. Anyway, Rick Miller offered to help, and when he offered, most of the others voiced their support as well. I can not help but wonder if there is a little guilt over hanging poor Bill Vance. If so, I shall use it. We cleared three trees and stacked the logs for cutting this summer. They should make good wall boards. Even the women joined in, hauling out the smaller branches and cutting them up for tinder. I now have a satisfactory space for building the new church, as well as a clear path into town.

    Thursday, February 14, 1852; Again I must apologize for not writing. I have focused on the new church site. Ben Jacobs over at the general store donated some twine, so I have been staking out corners and planning the construction. It will be a small building, but I would like it to hold up to fifty. Ha, planning for the future. There are not even fifty in the community yet, but someday maybe. It is Saint Valentine's Day and the ladies at the hotel have invited me to supper. I am looking forward to someone else's cooking for a change. Mine is woefully plain.

    Friday, February 15, 1852; It has been drizzling all day which has given me a chance to catch up on my reading and correspondence. The fire is warm and the tent feels snug. It does not even leak any more! Dinner last night was delightful and it was interesting to observe the young women as they are, girls forced into a profession that none care for. I sat next to Cindy.

    Mindy chortled. "Do I sniff a budding romance?"

    I laughed. "The minister and the prostitute. I'm sure it wouldn't be the first time." I looked over at Jim, "What do you think, pastor?"

    "He seems to be a good man. It would seem that he's beginning to see beyond their profession..."

    "As they're seeing beyond his," continued Melissa. She nudged her husband playfully, "It's not always easy to be involved with a man of God."

He started to respond, and then thought better of it. "Shall we continue, or have you all had enough."

"Just a little," Mindy said. She turned to Melissa, "Are you comfortable enough with the handwriting now to be able to scan for their names? Either Samuel or Joel, I think."

Melissa nodded, "I can try. Perhaps if I have no distractions." She thought for a few seconds and said, "Most people are interested in our rose window. Has Jim shown it to you?"

He stood. "Follow me. It actually doesn't date to the original church, but it's still a beauty." He looked out the side window. "And with the sun lower in the west, it should be in its glory now."

We all traipsed out into the church proper, and could see what he meant. The sun was directly behind the window, and it threw a rainbow of colors throughout the room. The wall opposite the window, where a small altar stood, was awash in a kaleidoscope that seemed to touch the senses not just of sight, but of taste and smell and hearing as well. I longed to reach out and run my fingers through the glow of golds and greens and blues and reds.

Mindy felt my same awe, and whispered softly, "It's gorgeous." We stood there transfixed by its beauty until she mused, "I'd have expected a religious motif, but it's a flower garden."

Jim nodded. "I'm sure you've noticed the old houses along Main Street." Mindy and I looked at him curiously and he went on. "Well about three blocks down, there's a winery where Doctor Morton's place used to be. Actually, they use his parlor for the tasting room. Rather inappropriate if you want my opinion, but nobody did." He reflected a moment, then noticing the look on Mindy's face, chuckled and continued. "Ruminating on the past, I fear." He tapped his head, "A problem that comes with the grey hair. Anyway, Doc Morton's wife loved the local wildflowers, and planted her yard full of them. As I understand, there was some consternation in the town."

Mindy cocked her head, "Why?"

"Why indeed," he asked. "Are not all flowers beautiful?" He looked her in the eye. "Evidently there were several formal gardens in the area, and a few of the old biddies complained that weeds from her flowers were spreading to their gardens." He laughed. "It was quite the scandal."

Curious, I asked, "So what happened?"

He shook his head. "So far as I know, nothing. She continued to grow her wildflowers, a 'native garden,' she called it, and they continued to complain."

"But what's this got to do with the window?" asked Mindy.

He raised his finger and pointed at her. "I can tell the teacher in you is still working, keeping the old preacher on task." He took a deep breath and pointed at the glass, "You see the yellow flower up there? Marsh Marigolds, and that red one? Indian Paintbrush."

I nodded, "My mother's favorite flower. She grew up in Wyoming and it grows there as well. I was well trained to identify it in any environment." I hesitated, ready to continue but said instead, "go on."

He didn't seem to notice the interruption, "Anyway, the red bells are Mountain Snowberry, and the iris is Western Blue Flag, and the little white flowers with the yellow interiors are Mariposa Lilies." He stopped and admired the window. "There are more, but those are the main ones."

Mindy turned toward him once again and asked, "So where did the window come from?"

He grinned, "Well now that's the interesting part. Celia Morton lived to a ripe old age. I think she was about ninety when she died. She was a fixture in this town, and a regular participant in everything." He saw Mindy's look and smiled. "Don't get me wrong. That garden caused trouble, no doubt about it. But she did a lot of good in town too."

He turned back to the window. "Those same ladies who complained that her garden was throwing weeds into theirs commissioned and paid for this window to be installed in her memory." He giggled softly and said, "Take a look at this."

Mindy and I followed him to the front door. Just to the right was a bronze plaque. Written on it were the words, "This glass is dedicated to the memory of Celia Morton, who loved beauty in all of its forms. Presented by the Ladies' Auxiliary of Murphys, June 10, 1928."

"It's a treasure," he added quietly.

The three of us stood, transfixed, lost in our own thoughts. I think we'd have stayed longer, admiring the window and the love that had created it, had Melissa not poked her head out the back door, "I found two more entries."

When we returned to the office, I could see that she'd bookmarked two spots in the old journal. One was only a few pages away from the first, but the other mark was near the end of the journal.

Mindy sat next to her so that she could read over her shoulder, "What did you find?"

Opening the book to the first mark, Melissa started to read.

Tuesday, July 16, 1852; Another scorcher. I am sure that the thermometer over at the hotel must read triple digits again today. Ah well. It was a good day to travel, so I made my way up the creek, checking on the miners. Most were happy to see me and took some time to talk. I recognized several who had donated a day to work on the church and thanked them for their support. Had my dinner at about 2:00 at Samuel's camp, the last on this particular loop. They are an efficient bunch, and serious. I have seen them occasionally in town at the Wells Fargo office, but rarely drinking or celebrating like many of the men. Their lunch was spartan, as I might have expected, some hard bread and a little cheese, along with an apple and some coffee, and then back to work. Joel, the young quiet one, was the first back into the creek, but not until he had given me a letter, as he has occasionally before, to mail to his girl back home. I promised to post it on my return and then thanked them for their hospitality. Someday I hope to draw them down to Murphys for a church service. Samuel came once, but I have never seen the others. I left at about 3:00, in order to be back no later than five, as I will be dining with Cindy tonight and need to bathe after a hot, dusty trip. She seems to enjoy working as a seamstress.

She looked up, "Could that be your Joel?"

Mindy nodded thoughtfully, "It's possible. We know he traveled with two other men, and one was named Samuel." She looked back down at the journal. "What's the other entry say?"

Melissa turned to the other marker.

Sunday, December 29, 1852; Today was my last service of the year, and I have to reflect that overall it has been a good year. We'll begin construction on the new church in the spring, as soon as it warms up. It was cold today, and snowed just a little way up into the mountains. We had rain here, but the church was snug and dry, as usual. I was a little disappointed that we had a rather small turnout, but I have found that is often the case in the rain. Most of the ladies from the hotel came, and we talked at some length after the service about their plan to form an auxiliary to organize good deeds throughout the community. They are an interesting group, with personalities entirely different on Sunday than during the week. I suppose we all must make a living. I was pleased to see Samuel Watkins today. He has come occasionally in the past, but his visits have been infrequent. Still, he has become a good friend and I enjoy his company. We ate dinner at the hotel later, and he asked me to pray for his partner. Evidently he was weakened by his journey across Panama and suffers with the cold weather. I promised that I would, reflecting on the funerals I have performed for miners these past few months. It is a hard life they have chosen, too hard for some. On a happier note, I am dining with Cindy again tomorrow. Her stitchery has been so successful that she will be able to take her own room above the general store next month. She talked Mabel Miller into allowing her to cook at their house, and I am looking forward to talking with Rick as well. He too has become a good friend. Interesting that the pastor and the sheriff should have so much in common, but we do seem to tend quite often, to the same part of the community, albeit in different ways. I feel a bit maudlin as I reflect. It has been a difficult year, and the transition from a fairly civilized environment in the east to the wildness here has been a challenge, but I have made new friends and I find that is more important than geography.

Melissa closed the journal as we sat quietly in the lingering light. "That's about all, I'm afraid." She looked at her husband, "Perhaps you have another journal?"

Jim walked over to the bookcase and scanned across the bound leather volumes. He tapped several, reading the handwritten script on the backs. "The next starts in September of 1852. There appears to be a gap."

I nodded. It wasn't surprising that after all these years, some of the history might have disappeared. Actually, it was amazing that we'd stumbled across them at all.

Mindy rose. "I don't know how to thank you. I have to admit that I'm a little concerned about the comment in the last entry, but your help has been more than generous."

"You mean the comment about praying for Samuel's partner," Melissa said. "I wonder about that too."

Nodding, Mindy continued. "It may well have been Joel. He nearly died of Yellow Fever." Then she took a deep breath and let it out in an exhalation of frustration. "The comments are so cryptic. For all we know it's not even the same Samuel." She paused, "Still, I feel a connection somehow..."

I stood and put my arm around her shoulder. "Lots of information to digest. I can't thank you enough." I gave her a squeeze. "We can't thank you enough."

Mindy looked up at me and then across at the Adams. "Well there's one way, would you like to join us for dinner? With all of the talk about my ancestors, it's like you've joined the family." She looked at Jim and Melissa, who gazed at one another, and smiled. "Something simple, I promise."

Melissa laughed, "Well in that case, sure. I don't think we have any commitments, do we?" She looked at her husband and he shook his head. What time? Where?"

Mindy looked at me and I shrugged, "How about 6:30? And for some reason, I have the urge to eat at Murphys Hotel. Shall we meet there?"

CHAPTER 23

Mindy was bubbling with excitement during our drive back to Santa Cruz the following morning. The sun was at our backs, lighting the roadway ahead, and providing that all important nutrient, sunlight, to the crops on the side of the road. Passing through groves of almonds and fields of peppers, we rehashed our unexpected discoveries in Murphys.

"You know," she said contemplatively as we wound through a series of low foothills, "I really do feel that we've found Joel." She paused for a few seconds. "Even if we don't have a last name. Even if we're not sure it was him, somehow I feel that we've made the right connection." She turned to me, a huge grin on her face. "What an amazing coincidence that we happened to run into Jim and Melissa."

"I know," I replied. "It's such an unlikely meeting. It's almost as if it was meant to happen."

She nodded, then lapsed into silence. Neither of us spoke again for several miles. Finally, as we passed through Farmington, she continued as if the conversation hadn't been broken, "So where do we go from here?"

"I was thinking the same thing." I glanced over at her. She was staring straight ahead, but seemed to see nothing of the roadway in front of us. "So far, we've read the letters, and just happened to run into this information in Murphys. We could go back to the letters and leave it at that, or..."

She nodded, still looking out the windshield. "Or we could

look for other traces of either of them." She fell quiet again.

"You did your research on Catherine." I said. "Do you suppose you could find more? Do you have family in Pennsylvania still?"

She thought for a moment. "I probably do. I'm not sure who, but I'm sure I could find them." She looked over at me. "My mother had two sisters and a brother. I know that Aunt Claire died about fifteen years ago. She was married, but her husband passed away when they were young. Killed in Vietnam, as I recall. After that, she lived alone; never remarried. She never did have any children." She tapped her finger on the air, as if trying to recall something. "Then there was Aunt MaryAnne." She paused. I didn't know her very well. She was kind of a free spirit. As I recall, she moved to Paris as a young woman - artist type, fell in with a Frenchman. I never heard much. I think there was some scandal around it but I was just a child at the time. She might have had a baby; maybe that was the scandal; but again, nobody talked about her much, and as I grew older, hardly at all." She looked over at me. "I'm not sure even where to look to find her, assuming that she's still even living." She reflected for a moment, "She was several years older than my mother, so she'd probably be well into her 90's by now."

"How about your uncle," I asked. "Who could you contact for him?"

She thought for a while before answering. "Harold was the baby. I can remember him visiting several times when I was a little girl. He was a favorite uncle, young enough to be playful. He lives in Nebraska." She looked over at me, her face etched with sadness. "But he won't be able to help. The last time I visited, about two years ago, he was in a home. Alzheimers." Softly, she continued. It was so sad. He was so alive, but he couldn't even remember who I was."

She drifted into silence over the next few miles, and I chose not to interrupt her. Finally, she said, "I'll call Sally. She's my cousin, his daughter. She might know something. Maybe he talked to her."

She reached over and squeezed my hand. Let's change the subject. Talk of Harold is depressing!"

I nodded. "Well," I asked, "I saw in the paper that there's a traveling art display coming to San Francisco. Several impressionists.

Would you be interested? Maybe next weekend?"

She smiled, as I knew she would. I'd hit upon two important themes in her life, art and San Francisco. "I'd love it. Sunday? I have plans for Saturday."

"Great. I'll make reservations for dinner too. Maybe the Claremont in Oakland? Have you been there?"

She looked at me curiously. "Isn't that an old theater?"

"No, I laughed. That's the Paramount. The Claremont is one of the grand old resort hotels. You'll like it. Different."

"All right. It's a date." She smiled and squeezed my hand again. "And I'll bring another letter."

Later that afternoon, I dropped Mindy at her place in Santa Cruz, and then with a whistle on my lips and a jaunty step, headed for home. It had been a good weekend getaway, and I was looking forward to the weekend to come.

CHAPTER 24

August 16, 1850
Pittsburgh

Dear Joel,

The baby has started to kick. It is so amazing to think of that tiny life growing inside of me. And to know that it is part you and part me. I smile whenever I feel him, and I am convinced that this baby is your son, a son who will grow up to be just as wonderful as his father.

I say I smile whenever I feel him, but that may not be exactly true. He has a habit of waking up in the middle of the night and moving all around. I do not really care for the kicks then, but I suppose that since I can sleep in, it does not make much difference.

I was eating breakfast with Aunt Ruth the other morning when he just started kicking up a storm. I invited her to place her hand on my belly and she could feel him as well. "A strong, healthy boy," she called him. I can not help but smile and think of you whenever I feel him.

We rode out into the country in Ruth's buggy last weekend. I had not been out of the house much at all since coming here. Not that I am complaining, as she has been so kind. Anyway, we took off, two women alone, and had a grand adventure. We packed a picnic of cold chicken and potato salad along with some wonderfully fresh apples. It was so nice to be out in the sunshine. Ruth knew a family about five miles out, so we stopped at their farm. They are getting ready to harvest their vegetables, so they were very busy, but still took time to eat lunch with us under an old chestnut tree in front of the house. Later, they invited us to come out into the fields and see what they have been working on all year. I love string beans, and they had several acres planted and nearly ready to pick. Even though they were not quite ready, we all pulled off a few and tasted their wonderful flavor.

Later, we joined with Esther in her kitchen. She is canning plums right now. They are a delight, big and plump and juicy. Ruth and I rolled up our sleeves and got right to work. We managed to put up several jars before it was time to go. It was good to feel so useful after sitting at the house over the last several weeks.

Are you in California yet? Are you feeling better? I went to the library and looked up Yellow Fever. There was precious little written about it there, but I was able to find out enough to put a good scare into me. I am so glad that Samuel sent his letter after you started to recover rather than before. Otherwise, I would be so worried.

Come home. Living with Ruth, I am becoming a different woman. In her own quiet way, she is teaching me how to stand up to my brothers. I do not think that is her intention, but I find myself watching how she handles herself, her independence, and her assertiveness. It is so different from what I grew up with where women were definitely expected to honor and obey, to quote a phrase. Will you still love the new me? I hope so. I can definitely honor and obey you, but the new me might disagree from time to time. Come home. I will talk to Tom and ensure that he will welcome you into the family. Come home.

Your loving wife,

Catherine

Mindy and I had selected bench seating side by side in a restaurant high enough in the Oakland hills to oversee the bay, and in the background, the San Francisco Skyline. She leaned her head against my shoulder, the letter still gripped in one hand. "It's interesting that she's written this letter, expressing her newfound personality, but never mailed it. I'd think a part of being a more outspoken woman would be to express herself publicly. Still nobody to mail it to?"

I stroked her hair, lost in thought. We sat there for a while, watching the sun set slowly over San Francisco across the bay. Gradually, we both straightened, and I reached for my wineglass. "To Catherine," I said as I tilted my glass toward Mindy. "To becoming her own woman in Pittsburgh."

She reached for her own glass, and then looking out over the view, said, "and to a glorious sunset."

I reached under the table and squeezed her knee. The sun had slipped lower and now hovered just above the tallest buildings. I held my glass up toward the sun, and marveled at the rosy hue of the cabernet, and then took a sip. "Any luck with your cousin?" I asked.

She shook her head. "I sent her a letter, explaining what we've been doing. I thought it'd be easier than a phone call." She peered over her glass at me. "I'm planning to call next week."

"Ah," I replied, and looked out over the bay.

She giggled then, and I glanced over at her. "I know I said I was just bringing one letter," she said, "but since the next one was from Joel, I decided to bring it too." She reached into her purse. "Interested?"

I nodded eagerly. "Absolutely. I've been wondering all week what might be going on..." I paused, "I mean what was going on with him."

She handed me a square of coarse parchment, folded into fourths, with an address written on the back side. I took the paper and raised my eyebrows, "Paper shortage?"

She nodded subtly. "Evidently."

I unfolded the paper and laid it out flat on the table in front of me. The writing was definitely Joel's. I quickly scanned the document, and drew in my breath. The paper was stained with some kind of brownish liquid that had seeped into the folds. In addition, the ink used was a light brown hue, which had been poorly blotted, and had run in several places, making it difficult to make out some of the writing. Mindy saw the consternation on my face and looked at me questioningly. "I'll do my best," I said, and pointed to some of the more obscure sections of the letter. "Here goes."

August 26, 1850
Panama City

My dear wife,
Please accept my apology for this rough paper. It was all that I could find. I have washed it in the sea to try to bleach out the prior writing, and seem to have been pretty successful. I have had to make my own ink as most of what I brought was spilled in the jungle, and the prices here are so high. I used up the last of it on the letter I sent earlier. One of my shipmates gave me a recipe for

ink, so I hope it works. My thoughts, as ever, are of you.

I hope that you have received my letter of last week by now. As I explained there, we have been waiting for a packet ship from this godforsaken port up the coast to California. It appears that our hopes have been rewarded, as one of the ships that ply these waters sailed into port yesterday. They spent much of the day offloading cargo, and are starting to take on a fresh load, mostly of produce, bananas, coffee, ...

I frowned, unable to make out the words. "Something," I said. Anyway,"

... because they are waiting for another shipment from the interior. So we should be able to depart within the week anyway. I look forward to leaving this port. The heat is oppressive, and the insects harass us constantly. Even a storm at sea would be preferable to this constant draining humidity.

"Something else here. "Michael L...something, from ... something, something, and then,"

consider myself fortunate. I am still weak, but compared to those who have been buried here, my case was minor. I remember little. Evidently I was abed for nearly three weeks, and only really able to speak for the last ...
...tools to pan for gold. He says we should make our purchases in San Francisco if possible as the prices will be very dear once we get to the gold country. I mentioned in my last letter that we will be going to ...

"Oh, this is frustrating," I said. "There're three lines lost here in this fold. It looks like the ink ran and just settled here. It's just a blur."

walk most of the way, but it should not take more than a couple of weeks. There are fewer miners there than there are to the north...

"More staining."

and a stout cradle to sift out the gold. It is a job that will take at least two men, more likely three, so it is good to know that I have got help in Samuel and Jonathan.
...when I try to do too much, but I hope it will get better while I am

aboard the ship. I will certainly need all my strength once I get to ... and after that...

I think of you often and wish that I could hold you in my arms. With all my love,

Joel

Mindy looked over at me, "So much is missing." She reached for the letter and read the same material softly aloud, stumbling over some of the partial words. She raised it to her face and tried to make out more of the writing, but the sun remained just a flowing sliver in the west, and the light was rapidly fading.

"Maybe when we get back inside," I offered.

She took one more look at the letter, and then carefully folded it and slipped it back into her purse. She looked at me, and then shuddered. "It's gotten a little chilly." She reached into her backpack and took out one of the many layers she kept there for emergency warming. Pulling the sweater over her head, she noticed my amused look and stuck her tongue out at me. "It's cold," she scolded.

I signaled for the waiter and he came over. Pointing to the overhead gas heater, I asked if he could light it. He frowned for a moment, and then looked at Mindy. With a light chuckle, he reached for a lighter. Within a minute, we were bathed in warmth, but Mindy kept her sweater. I started to say something about being too hot, but then just ran my hand over her shoulder and stroked the sensitive spot at the back of her neck. "How's that?"

She then leaned against me and mouthed quietly, "Better."

I nodded, reflecting on how easily she chilled and pointed to the west. The sun had dropped beneath the horizon and the sky was transforming into a fiery painting of reds and oranges. Far out to sea, we could see a low purple fog bank creeping its way inexorably toward the shore. We sat quietly huddled together and watched for a long time as the colors slowly lost their brilliance and faded into evening.

Finally, Mindy shuddered almost imperceptibly again, and I knew that it was time to go.

CHAPTER 25

Mindy's attempt to draw more information from her cousin came up empty. Harold had talked some with his daughter about his heritage, but not much, and nothing had been written down. That put us back to the letters, or so I thought.

We decided to meet one Sunday morning at Roasted Beans, a small coffee house that Mindy knew. I'd never been there before. It was a little off the beaten track, midway between Santa Cruz and Monterey, tucked amongst the strawberry fields. The weather was typical for the area, foggy and grey, with enough of an offshore breeze to have us pulling our coats a little tighter as we hurried across what passed as a parking lot into the restaurant. Once inside though, I was pleasantly surprised. A small fire smoldering in the cast iron wood stove in the corner bathed the tiny restaurant in warmth. I looked around as we entered. It was anything but the typical urban coffee house I was accustomed to. Sofas lined two walls. They were old and bore the stains of more than one cup of spilled coffee. Still, they were full, so must have been comfortable. We made our way through a forest of mismatched tables and chairs to the counter. Mindy ordered for us, a cappuccino for me, and a triple espresso low fat caramel latte with chocolate shaved, not sprinkled for her. As she ordered, I closed my eyes, and was tempted to pretend to be with someone else, but the barista didn't miss a beat, even asking at the end if she wanted cinnamon infused or would prefer to sprinkle it on top. She was a sprinkler. Evidently, they were accustomed to customers with highly specific wants.

While we waited, I took the opportunity to look at the walls.

They were painted almost in a replica of Van Gogh's Starry Night, dark blue with stars scattered across the upper levels and a rural scene below, definitely strawberries, from the look of the tiny splashes of red. Most of the eye-level space was covered with a profusion of art for sale. It appeared that this was a favorite hangout for the local artists, some of whom were evidently quite good. I saw the expected array of seascapes and pictures of birds flying over the local yacht harbor, all misted with fog, of course, but was surprised by the variety of abstract paintings and sculptures that graced the place.

Each had a price tag, and, I reflected to myself, most were within my limited price range. I took a firm hold on my coffee when it arrived, to avoid the type of temptation that might empty my wallet before we departed.

After Mindy took her first sip, I started to chuckle, and she gave me a curious look. Tactfully, I reached across with my napkin and wiped her upper lip. "Milk mustache," I said. "Or maybe it's a whipped cream mustache. Good?"

She nodded. "One of the hazards of these drinks, but they're oh so good. Want a taste?"

I shook my head, not being much of a fan of sweetened coffee. Even the cappuccino was a stretch for me, but it was tasty, and I had begun to consider another even after the first sip. "You said you might have something else?"

She nodded and opened her purse. I could see the next letter in a plastic bag on top, and noted that it was in Catherine's hand. She took it out and laid it on the counter, and then went back to her purse. "Sally called and suggested that I contact," she hesitated as she dug, "where is it?" Suddenly she laughed and then closed the bag, opening the zipper on the side. "I forgot. I just slid it in here." She took out a single sheet of paper. "I remember that my grandfather had a couple of brothers, but since he moved to California as a child, I never knew them, or even much about them. Sally did though. It seems that Harold was very close to his uncle Jack, and so Sally got to know Jack's grandchildren. She gave me a list of names of people I've never even met."

"Really?" I eyed the paper. "So these are what, your," I did a quick calculation in my head, "third cousins?"

She nodded, then continued. "But what we have in common is Marie. She was our great grandmother." She looked down at the list, "or in some cases, great great grandmother."

"Have you had a chance to contact them?"

"Not yet. I just talked with her yesterday. Some have phone numbers, but most just have addresses. I figure I'll start writing letters tomorrow." She paused for a moment, and then went on with a grin. "I'd have started calling today, but someone insisted that I meet for coffee. Said he was lonely."

I smiled and raised my cup in a toast. "And I'm very happy that you did." I looked down at the letter on the table. "Are you reading? I see it's Catherine's."

Nodding, she sipped at her coffee, wiped her upper lip, and then put down her cup. "Actually, I've brought two. There's one from Joel as well."

She unfolded the first letter, lay it on the table, and proceeded to read.

September 12, 1850
Pittsburgh

My darling husband,
It seems impossible that I have not written to you in nearly a month. Of course, I have thought of you every day, and I write some in my diary each night, but to not have written a letter in all this time... Well it is a testament to just how busy I have been.

I think I mentioned that Ruth and I purchased some fabric. We have been making dresses, and it seems that no sooner than I finish one, but I need to alter it so that it will be just a little bit larger. They are plain blue calico and I suppose that you would like them. Ruth has helped to pretty them up with a little bit of lace around the collar. It seems a little much, but I must admit that I like the addition.

The baby continues to kick. Sometimes, I will be sitting knitting when I just have to stop and enjoy the sensation of your child inside me. Did you know that I knit? My mother taught me years ago and I find that I have been knitting booties and bonnets and even a tiny sweater. Ruth has brought in some of her friends who are not very secretly working on a pair of quilts for the child's bed.

I am starting to get excited. It is so very strange, this new life I am about to bring into the world. Of course, he will be a wonderful child, with you as his father. I just wish that you could be here for his birth, but suppose that you are probably in California by now. What a long journey!

144

I received your letter from Panama City last week. I am so glad that you are feeling well enough to write. I have been very worried over the past weeks. You are right, the paper was a little bit rough. I had to smile when I saw it though. The fact that you went to such lengths to find writing material just to send me a letter gave me a warm glow that lasted for days. I was impressed that you made your own ink. You are a remarkably resourceful man. You make me proud that you chose me of all the girls you could have had to marry.

I have wonderful news. Ruth received a letter from Tom yesterday. It seems that after the harvest is completed, Robert will be coming to visit me. Oh how I have longed to talk with him. There must have been quite a row between him and Tom when he brought up the visit, as the letter was quite curt. I am not sure that Tom approved, but then Robert is a grown man, and able to make his own decisions. As much as I love Ruth, I miss my family. I mean, the family I grew up with. And Robert especially.

I shall have to ask him about the apple fight. I wonder if he remembers Tom getting switched by Aunt Ruth. Oh I hope he does.

I send you a mountain of love and wish you a safe journey to the gold fields. Be careful and hurry home. Know that your loving wife is waiting here for you.

Love, Catherine

Mindy lay her hand with the letter in it on the table and looked out the window. She started to speak a couple of times, but then stopped. Knowing that she was forming her thoughts, I waited. Finally, she tapped the letter against the table and said, "Chatty this time." She looked at me. "I mean, not as full of longing. Almost," she waited for a while and then repeated, "chatty."

I nodded slowly. "I suppose that's to be expected. She hasn't seen him in half a year, and," I searched for the right words, "they were together for such a short time."

She stared out the window, seeming to look right through me. "And Robert's coming. She seemed happier, not so lonely."

"Well I suppose that's a part of it..." I was about to go on when she raised her hand, stopping me.

"And," she paused, "and..." Then she shook her head.

"What?"

She just shook her head again, and it was clear that she didn't have anything to add. I lifted my cup to drink, but the cappuccino was nearly gone, only the remnants of creamy coffee with clumps of cinnamon remaining cold in the bottom of the cup. I put it down and motioned to hers, "Another?" I started to rise but she just shook her head.

"Not for me thanks. I'm full."

I looked at her empty cup and started to chuckle.

She scowled at me. "Yes?"

"Nothing, just thinking that you should be full after having dessert for coffee."

Her eyes went wide and I suddenly slapped my forehead. I'd forgotten.

Mindy gave me a huge grin and said, "I know just the place to get a nice lobster dinner."

"But,..."

"No buts," she pointed at me. "You lost."

I got up and shuffled over to the counter to refill my cup with black coffee. When I got there, I gave my order and reflected on my foolishness in betting that I could go an entire day without once teasing her. It was going to cost me.

CHAPTER 26

September 19, 1850
San Francisco

My Darling Catherine,
It seemed somehow fitting that I write you today on our six month anniversary, even though it is almost that long since I last held you in my arms.

We arrived in San Francisco just a few days ago, and have been working to outfit ourselves for the gold fields. Prices here are outrageous. We paid fifty cents for breakfast our first day, and then decided to eat in our room after that. It is a tiny space above a hardware store, and priced dearly, but there are six of us sharing so it is not too bad. There is one bed, big enough for three if nobody moves in the night. It was my turn on the bed last night, so I slept better than I had on the floor, but nearly fell out when Jonathan rolled over sometime in the middle of the night.

I bought a pick, shovel and mining pan yesterday, along with sturdy boots and some overalls made of heavy denim, depleting a fair portion of my remaining cash. I hope to be able to eek out a few months in the gold fields with what I have left, and will hopefully find gold at some point. I have heard that many of the miners do manage to make just enough to be able to continue mining, while waiting for the big strike.

It certainly is not what we were told in the east. We heard of the wealth to be found on the sides of the hills, and in the creeks. But I have talked to several who have tired of the ceaseless work with little or nothing to show for it. Sure, everyone knows someone who has hit a big strike, but when I ask, they just shake their heads. Many more have not done as well. Still, I look about this city, with the fancy carriages carrying men who were just like me a few months ago, and then found gold. They stay in fine hotels and drink only the best liquor. I hope that God will permit me to join them, so that I can hurry home to you, a man of means.

I suppose that if I strike it rich out here, and put you up in style in a big house with a staff of servants, your brothers will have to accept me.

Ah, dreams... I have much work to do first. There is no point in planning how to spend money I do not have.

Still, I am glad to be here and confident of the future.

We head east tomorrow. Many go on the stage, or horseback, but those ways of travel are too expensive for us. We have hired a man with a freight wagon and he will haul us up to the hills for a fraction of the other means. It will be all the better when we return in a fancy coach.

I miss you and think of you constantly, longing for the day when I can again hold you in my arms and express my love. Until then, I keep the locket with your picture close to my heart.

Joel

I folded the letter and handed it to Mindy. Thoughtfully, she put it in her purse next to Catherine's.

"I wonder where they're going?" I said.

She looked at me and shook her head. "Well we suspect that they ended up in Murphys at some point," she mused. "But that was winter of 1852. This letter was written in September of 1850, so where they're going is anybody's guess. Maybe in another letter."

"I've been meaning to ask, how many are left?"

She paused, as if visualizing the pile, and then shrugged her shoulders. "There're quite a few. Half? More than half probably."

I hadn't been with her when she'd organized the letters, so asked now, "And letters from Joel? Were there many?"

She bit her lip thoughtfully and lifted her coffee. "There are still several left. More from Catherine, of course."

"When did the correspondence end?"

She smiled at me. "I'm not sure I'm going to tell you that." Then she giggled at my look of dismay. "Suspense. You can't stand it."

I looked at her nonchalantly. "That's fine. There are plenty of secrets I have. See if you can get them out of me."

At that, she laughed out loud.

"What?"

"You're so easy." She continued to giggle. "You get so excited when you have a secret that you can't possibly keep it!"

"Well that's not true at all." I was offended.

She patted my hand. "Not to worry, it's one of the things I find cute about you."

I grumbled. "I'm not cute. And I can too keep a secret. Name one time I haven't been able to keep a secret from you."

She just laughed again. "Only one?"

I was encouraged. "You can't think of anything, can you?"

She put a serious look on her face and looked up toward the ceiling as if deep in thought. "Well," she started. "Then she suddenly leaned toward me. "That vacation you're supposed to surprise me with? Anywhere? Tell me at the last minute?"

"I haven't told you where we're going." I protested.

"Not exactly, but even though it's months away, you couldn't wait to tell me that it will be a driving vacation or that you had a deal on a place in Palm Springs." She leaned back and smiled.

"Well maybe that's not where we're going," I responded. "Maybe that was a ruse."

She smiled at me and patted my hand again, condescendingly. I pulled away and tried to sit up straight, acting offended. "You don't have any idea where we're going."

"That's true," she said. Then she lifted her cup and drained the last of the coffee. "But I have a pretty good idea. You want to drive. You keep saying that you'll take me someplace warm even though I've been clear that I know you'll keep me warm wherever we go. And it's in March." She licked the last of the caramel carefully around the top of the cup, and put it back on the saucer. "Warm in March, driving distance, and you can get a deal in Palm Springs. Hmmm. You're too easy."

I sat there and looked at her. Two could play this game. I would not be defeated this easily. Let's see how she'd like a trip to the snow country of Utah, or maybe a last minute flight to the Canadian Rockies, or even the Grand Canyon. Hah. See how warm she'd be then! I made a mental note to change the reservations in Palm Springs.

"So?" she asked. "Mr. Secret Keeper. How's that?"

"You don't know," I added. "And besides, that's in the

future. I might be bluffing you." I sat back and folded my arms, trying to look confident.

"You need another example?" she asked.

"You haven't given me the first one yet," I blustered.

She looked down at her cup and was about to pick it up when she remembered that the coffee was gone. She looked at my black coffee and raised her eyebrow. I thought of telling her to go get her own if she was so busy being right, but decided that wouldn't serve my best interests. I nodded in assent and she lifted the cup.

After she swallowed, she grimaced, "How can you drink this stuff?" Then she looked around. "How do you like the decor?"

I decided to play along with her clumsy attempt to change the subject. "It's an interesting place," I said. I pointed to a painting above the counter. "I particularly like that piece. It reminds me of ..." I paused, looking at the painting. It was a stylized oil showing an oak forest in brilliant reds and oranges and yellows and greens. It looked almost surreal the way that everything flowed together.

She turned and studied the painting. "Nice," she said. "It would look good over your fireplace."

I nodded, agreeing. It would indeed fit that place wonderfully. I thought for a moment. I could see the price tag on a 3x5 card to the left of the painting. Doable, a little more than I'd want to spend, but definitely doable. Still, I didn't come in here to buy art. On the other hand...

"The prices tend to be negotiable," she added.

I looked again at the painting. It would definitely look good in my living room, adding a nice splash of color and just the right amount of abstraction. I was about to say something about it when my mind turned back to our previous conversation. "Hey, you were supposed to come up with another example. You couldn't!"

"Me, she asked innocently?"

"Yes, you." I grinned righteously at her. "You can't."

She turned her head, as if in thought and very slowly brought her hand up to the diamond pendant dangling from a chain around her neck. "Hmm, let me think."

I shook my head in disgust. I'd given her the pendant a couple of months ago, had in fact planned out how I was going to give it to her, what I would say and do, how she would react, and the whole bit. Then a couple of days early, I'd just pulled it out and presented it to her. Maybe she was right. Maybe I did have trouble holding a secret. Still, it would be pretty easy to change the Palm Springs reservations. Of course, not being terribly fond of cold myself, I might have to think of another warm location.

She continued to fondle the pendant, and I gave her a mocking bow, conceding the point. I hadn't expected her to be gracious in victory, and she wasn't. "Now let's see, about that lobster dinner." She smiled and batted her eyelashes at me. "Next Saturday?"

CHAPTER 27

Mindy held me to my word, and we did indeed have lobster in the Cannery area of Monterey. I have to admit that it was very good, at least from what I tasted of hers. I'm not a big lobster fan, so had a nice Ahi steak while she feasted on the lobster complete with bib and all the other fanfare. And of course, since it was a bet lost on my part, she added a slice of prime steak to the meal. An expensive wager.

After dinner, we sat savoring our coffee. The sun had set while we were eating, and it was dusk outside the window. It wasn't too dark to make out the bay, but nearly so. As we ate, we'd enjoyed watching the otters frolicking in the water below us, laughing at their antics. Now the first stars were rising, the bay was quiet, and we both felt the contentment of a good meal.

I was looking out the window, pretending to ignore her while I rubbed my foot against her ankle.

She smiled and rubbed back. "I heard from one of my cousins."

I turned and sat up, most thoughts of footsie forgotten. "Really? Any help?"

"I think so. Anyway, she called yesterday. Her name's Marsha, and she lives in Omaha. She and her husband have recently retired, and she's been trying to do some genealogical research of her own. She said she'd compiled quite a bit of data going back into the mid 1700's."

I was all ears. "So did she have anything on Catherine?"

Mindy nodded, her excitement growing. "She did. Evidently,

her great grandmother was also Marie, though she was related through my uncle Frank, not Grandpa Joseph. She promised to send me a copy of her research. In return, I've offered to copy the letters between Joel and Catherine." She smiled.

"Great," I said. "And Joel, did she have anything on him?"

Mindy shook her head. "No. Although she had wondered why she couldn't find any trace of a husband to Catherine. We talked about the wedding that never was, and she mentioned a couple of sources she might look up to see if there was any record. She's going to check them out this week."

"Anything else?" I asked.

"Not much. I suppose I'll hear back from her in a week or so." Then she stopped and grinned. "She did have one thing that was interesting. She e-mailed it to me this morning."

Mindy handed over a piece of paper. Though it was plain copy paper, it was clear that the document was quite old. I scrutinized it. The original had obviously been well worn, wrinkled and torn along one side. The writing on it was cramped, as if the writer was trying to get as much written down as possible. I began to read, slowly, carefully, hesitantly.

"Arnold Lewis, late of Bradford Twp bequeathed his plantation to his son, Thomas Lewis (yeoman), subject to payments to his wife, Jeanie and children, Robert (yeoman), Jonas (cooper), Phillip, and Catherine. The heirs acknowledge payment by current owner Thomas Lewis. Bk 26, Page 419. July 26, 1847."

Mindy cocked her head to one side as I read. I glanced through the draft again, and then looked up at her. She was nodding. "It seems to confer ownership of the farm to Thomas upon their father's death." She paused, "Interesting. I hadn't seen anything about Jonas or Phillip though her mention of brothers seemed to be more than just Thomas and Robert. I suppose that's another angle to research."

I'd taken a sip of coffee. Now I spoke. "It would explain why Thomas seemed to be the boss of the family. He was not only the older brother, he was also the legal owner of the property. Huh. But he had to pay the others to buy out their shares."

Thinking aloud, Mindy continued. "So Thomas was a yeoman, another word for a farmer in those days, I suppose."

"Let me look it up." I pulled out my cell phone and went to the dictionary application. "Yeoman. Here it is, 'in former times was free and cultivated his own land.'" I looked up at her. "That would describe Thomas, since he was certainly free, and was working land given to him by his father." I paused. "What about the others?"

Mindy reached over and took back the paper. She read aloud, "Thomas Lewis (yeoman) Robert (yeoman), Jonas (cooper), and Phillip and Catherine didn't have anything listed after their names."

I thought for a moment. "I remember that Thomas was born in 1818, so he would have been what, twenty-nine then? And Robert was a few years younger, so he was also in his twenties. I would think Jonas was between them. Then there's Phillip. Do you suppose he was younger? In his teens perhaps? Maybe closer to Catherine's age, and she would have been just twelve or thirteen when her father died."

"So young," she said slowly. "It's interesting that there weren't any other children." She looked up at me. "Weren't families larger back then? No birth control and all?"

I thought for a moment, "Stillbirths? Any who died in childhood?"

She shuddered. "I hadn't thought of that. I suppose it could have been. That would explain the gaps in their ages."

"And the range. 1818 to 1833."

She nodded, and then shook herself. "Well on that happy note, are you still interested in walking over to the bakery for a cookie?"

I must have been distracted, because she reached over and took my hand, "Charlie? Cookies?"

"Uh, yeah, that sounds good."

§§§§

Later that night, we went back to Mindy's place. While she poured two glasses of port, I settled on the red sofa. I'd picked up one of her many photo books and was perusing the photos when she called out, "You want to turn on the stereo? There's already a CD in there that I think you'll like."

"All right," I responded. I got up and went to the bookcase where she had a small stereo system. I had to kneel down in order to reach the controls to turn it on. I heard the CD mechanism start, and then the opening of a jazz riff by John Coltrane. I smiled. This wasn't her style, but was one of my favorites.

Since I was up, I wandered out to the kitchen and walked up behind her. Putting my arms around her waist, I drew her back toward me and nuzzled her neck. She shivered, as I knew she would when I hit the sensitive skin right at her hairline, and I grinned silently. "Any letters tonight," I whispered softly into her ear, prompting another shiver.

She spun slowly in my arms then reached her hands behind my neck and pulled me down into a soft kiss, ending by resting her head against my chest. "There's one," she purred.

I'd noticed the cookies on a plate beside the port. Taking the plate and one glass, I led her back into the living room. Once we reached the couch, she settled catlike, knees tucked under her skirt, and rocked forward to the coffee table. Somehow, I hadn't seen the letter, but there it was, held down by one of her blue pressed glass coasters. She picked it up and withdrew a sheet of delicate pink paper from the envelope.

October 14, 1850
Pittsburgh

My Darling Husband,
I have heard no word since your last letter, but suppose that it must take months to deliver the mail from California, so letters will come less frequently. Still, it is worrying to me that I have not heard from you.

I wonder if you have gotten to the gold fields. Have you found anything? If so, are you coming home? One can hope anyway.

I heard from Robert yesterday. With the coming of the cooler weather, he is not needed as much on the farm, so will definitely be coming up to Pittsburgh next week. I do so long to see him. It has been so long since I have seen any of my brothers. I wonder if Tom is still mad at me, and if the others have forgiven me for hiding our secret from them.

He says he has news, and will not share it until we are together. I am so excited to have him coming.

The baby continues to kick and squirm. I am getting positively huge and do wish that you were here to see me. My dresses hardly hide my condition any more and I have had a few unpleasant looks from the more proper ladies in town. I have explained that my husband has gone off to the gold fields, but they just tsk at me and give me disapproving looks. I suppose part of it is because you will not be here to help me with the baby. At least I hope that is all it is.

Ruth is a gem. She tells me to ignore their ignorance. In fact, just yesterday we were at the general store, buying sugar and flour when Mrs. Mabry came over to me with a positively evil glint in her eye and asked if 'the child's father' would be back soon. Ruth stepped right up to her and said, 'Catherine's husband is away right now, trying to earn some money so that he can bring his child up well.' Then she smiled so very sweetly and asked, 'And how is Mary doing? And Peter?' Well Mrs. Mabry turned four shades of scarlet. She tossed her head and could not get away from us fast enough. I asked later what that was all about and Ruth just laughed out loud and said, 'Mary is her daughter. It seems that she got in a family way and her boyfriend spurned her, saying that he was not sure that the child was his.' I was rather shocked, and then she surprised me by saying that Peter was an absolutely delightful child, and we should probably stop by and visit one of these days.

I really never know what to expect from Ruth. We were talking one day about one of problems in town. There is a petition being raised to remove the women from the hotel. I had not known this, but evidently it is a house of ill repute. I was quite taken aback, but not nearly as shocked as when Ruth said that we should not blame the poor girls involved. They were simply fulfilling a demand brought about by the men of the community. She went so far as to suggest that any woman who had ill to say about those girls had better first see to her own husband! I was not sure what to say, but later that night, as I lay in bed waiting for sleep to come, began to think of her comments. She is ever the pragmatist, and I suppose that fits well with her other beliefs. Still, harlots in Pittsburgh! Who would have thought such a thing in such a fine, church going community.

I seem to have wandered greatly in this letter. I do miss you so, and the child growing in me is a constant reminder that I am married, but about to become a mother without a husband's support. Oh, I am not worried about money. Ruth has made it clear that the child will want for nothing, and I have a little money of my own, but I do miss having someone to hold me when I am frightened, and I am frightened now about my future and the future of your son, and of course about your own welfare.

I pray every night that you will come home to me soon, and that we can live as any other family.

With all my love,

Catherine

Mindy folded the letter and put it down on the coffee table, and then took a tiny sip of the port. She leaned against me and said simply, "I need to be held sometimes too."

I folded her into my arms, and stroked her golden locks. I stayed that way for a long time, lost in her softness.

CHAPTER 28

The next morning being Sunday, Mindy and I slept in and then went for a walk down by Santa Cruz Pier where we met some friends for breakfast. The restaurant they'd chosen was small, eclectic, and as it sat out at the end of the pier, blessed with a great view of the bay. We chose outside dining, which was a little breezy, but given the warm autumn weather, very pleasant. I could see up to the lighthouse, and noticed a small cluster of surfers, sitting out on the swells waiting for the next rideable wave.

"Steamer Lane," Randall said. "A favorite of the locals. I used to surf there myself when I was a boy."

I nodded, remembering my own surfing days, but recalled that I'd never taken on Steamer Lane, preferring some of the less challenging breaks. I was impressed. "Where else did you surf around here?"

"Are you familiar with the breaks?"

"I was out at Pleasure Point just a few months ago. My brother still surfs pretty regularly and occasionally he talks me into it."

"Ah, a local." He looked down toward the south and pointed. "Well, Pleasure Point was a favorite. Did you ever surf the Hook?"

I grimaced. "Quite a bit. I remember the climb down."

He laughed. "Easier today. They've put in stairs, but in our day, I can remember scaling that cliff with a surfboard under one arm. Quite a challenge!"

"Big boards then too," I added.

"They call them longboards now." He stirred salsa onto his omelet, and took a bite. "Manresa? I got out there occasionally. And a few of the beaches to the north." He looked toward his wife Sandra, and dropped his voice. "I don't talk about those."

I chuckled. The famous clothing optional beaches. "Well I was more of a recreational surfer. I never got very serious about it, and living over the hill, didn't get over here that often. But it was fun." Then I shivered involuntarily, "And cold as I recall. I didn't have a wetsuit."

He laughed and raised his hand for a high-five. "Nor did I. And you're right about the cold; kept us out of the water in the winter I suppose. Now they surf year round." He looked out at the surfers at Steamer Lane again. One was paddling furiously to catch a wave. As we watched, he rose and began to cut his swath up and down the crest. Long before the wave broke against the cliff face, he'd dropped back and was paddling out for his next challenge.

§§§§

After breakfast, we poked our heads into a couple of gift shops on the pier, bought some English Toffee and another cup of coffee, and then made our way back to Karly's place, a good midway meeting point for all of us. Randall and Sandra said their goodbye's and drove off and Mindy and I were also about to leave when Karly asked Mindy, "How's the research on your family coming along?"

I was mildly surprised that she'd shared the letters with anyone else, but given her close friendship to Karly, it made sense.

Mindy smiled. "Well, Catherine's pregnant, as you know." Karly nodded. "We just read a letter about six months into the pregnancy and all's well there. Joel has arrived in San Francisco and is about to take off for the gold country."

"Any idea where?"

"No. We did run into some information up in Murphys, but it's so vague at this point, that I'm not sure it's really him. It seems promising, but who knows." She reached out and squeezed my arm. "Charlie met a couple up there who helped us out." She looked at me, encouraging me to continue, so I did.

"Um. Let's see. He's the local minister and she's a docent in the museum." I smiled at the memory. "Great people and very helpful."

Mindy snorted and playfully slapped my arm. "As long as you don't touch anything in the museum."

Karly raised her eyebrows and I continued. "Melissa's a little particular about her exhibits." I cast a scowl at Mindy. "How was I supposed to find out what gold panning is like without picking up the pan."

She laughed. "Anyway, we were able to look through some of the old town and church records and may have found Joel and his friends." She laughed conspiratorially, "Our detective work!"

I turned to Karly, "Actually, Mindy doesn't know this yet, but Jim sent me an email last week. He's found something else and asked if we're free next weekend."

"What!" Mindy started, "How long have you known this? Why didn't you say anything to me?"

"Uh," I searched my brain. It seemed like a pretty good set of questions. "Uh. Since Tuesday, I suppose. I figured I'd be seeing you this weekend."

She crossed her arms and stared at me. "Since Tuesday and you said nothing."

I tried my best sheepish grin. "Sorry?"

She was quiet for a moment and then said, "Well, I've got plans, but I suppose I can move them around."

I took a deep breath, which surprised me as I didn't realize I'd been holding it. "So you'll want to know sooner next time, right?"

She stared at me. "You are so hopeless. And in answer to your question, right."

I looked from Mindy to Karly and back. They seemed to be sharing a secret that I knew I'd never be part of. "Sorry. Same place? The B&B?"

She nodded, then reached up and kissed my cheek. "That'll be fine. Then she turned to Karly. "We'd better get going. Are we walking tomorrow?"

Karly nodded. "Why don't we meet at the mall at 9:00." She looked at me and chuckled, then at Mindy, "He doesn't know he's not out of the doghouse yet does he?"

She laughed, "Not a clue."

I figured this was a good time to make my exit, and waved as I turned toward the car.

Mindy followed a few minutes later. Her first words after she fastened her seatbelt were, "Really? Since Tuesday and you said nothing?"

It was a short distance, but a long drive back to her place.

CHAPTER 29

Catherine's letter was uncharacteristically short, and from the handwriting, seemed hastily written. Mindy spread the single page out on her coffee table and started to read.

October 27, 1850
Pittsburgh

My Dearest,
Robert arrived yesterday. I can not tell you how excited I was to see him. I had been waiting for days, and each day that he did not appear was harder than the last. Yesterday though, just in time for supper, guess who should come marching up the front steps but my dear brother.
He had brought me flowers too. Such a thoughtful man. Well he took me by the hands, and twirled me around the living room, just like when I was a girl, but so much more slowly, "I would not want to hurt the baby," he said. And all the while he focused on my expanding middle. I have to admit I was a little embarrassed. And the exercise got the baby going, so I moved his hand onto my stomach. I think I shocked him, but when the baby moved, he grinned so large that it got me and Ruth laughing. It is so good to have him here.
He also brought sad news. Mama has become very quiet and seems more and more forgetful. She rarely leaves her room any more, other than for meals, and spends most of her day knitting. At times, according to Robert, he hears her engaged in one sided conversations with our father. I will pray for her. It seems now that she will never get over his death.
And then there was Robert's surprise. Tom is still Tom. He is angry and I suppose still a little bit hurt even after all this time, but he told Robert to let me know that I was welcome to come home after the baby is born if I wish to. He

is leaving that decision to me. I wish I knew what he was thinking, and how he was feeling. I would love to return home, but want to feel welcome. Is it a genuine offer because he misses his sister? Or does he feel obligated? As wonderful as it is to have Robert here, I wish I could talk with Tom.

I suppose I have a decision to make, but it does not have to be made for a few months, so I am just going to enjoy Robert. This morning he and I went for a long walk, and I showed him parts of Pittsburgh I have come to know. Ruth insisted that the two of us spend some time together, "to get reacquainted," she said, so she stayed at home. Anyway, we ended up downtown, and I took him into the general store. He had never been this far from Bradford, and just kept muttering about how grand everything was. And being with him, it was indeed.

Know that I am well, and that I miss you.
You are in my daily thoughts and prayers.
Your loving wife,

Catherine

Mindy looked over at me and I smiled. "Interesting. Do you suppose that she'll go back to the farm?" Then she shrugged her shoulders. "Time will tell." She pointed to the stack of letters on the table. The next few are all from Catherine. I suppose that his just took so much time to travel across the country..." She sighed. "And then there's the chance that some of them were lost."

"Entirely possible," I said. "It seems that hers just went into a box, since she had no address for him. So we can be fairly certain that we've got all of them. But his..."

She nodded. "He mentioned another one sent from Panama City that we haven't seen yet. It may have gone astray."

I looked over to the stack of letters and then back at Mindy. "Another?"

She started to reach for one and then withdrew her hand. "I don't think so. I'll bring a couple next weekend." She smiled and patted my knee as she gathered the letters. "Melissa will want to hear the next one. But as for this weekend, you're still in trouble."

I sat quietly while she latched the correspondence back into the red cabinet. When she rose, I stood too, took her in my arms and gave her a hug. "Could I make it up to you? Maybe upstairs?" I asked.

She just scowled, "Not likely."

CHAPTER 30

Our trip up to Murphys was uneventful. Well not entirely, I suppose. It rained all the way up, and there was a prediction of snow at the higher elevations, but it was unlikely that there would be snow in Murphys, so I wasn't really concerned. Still, I didn't think we'd be sitting out in the little glade behind the church. Too wet, and even for me, too cold.

Mindy and I had found a winery two or three windy miles out of Murphys, on the old road to Sheep Ranch. There was little else on the road, and the rain and the ancient paving made our trip challenging, if short.

I'd been to the winery several years earlier, and could remember enjoying some fine wines while picnicking on the grass with friends, surrounded by acres of chardonnay grapes. Today, though the picnic grounds were open, the cold, soggy lawn looked much less appealing, so in we went.

We'd noticed a few cars parked in the gravel lot behind the building, but were unprepared for the party atmosphere inside the parlor of the old farmhouse. Several people spilled into the entry where the walls were adorned with photos of the area, dating back into the 1880's and showing the original building, looking much the same, as well as the barn and other outbuildings, and of course, rocky hillsides sprinkled liberally with sheep. Mindy and I had to smile at one. A grizzled old rancher stood in the parlor with his hand on his wife's shoulder, surrounded by several well groomed children. All wore their Sunday best, and glared solemnly for the camera. "I always wondered how they got the children to stand still long enough for those old photos. They took a while to process, you know."

I nodded. "Threats. No child abuse reporting then. I'm sure that they had a woodshed, and that one," I said, pointing to a boy who appeared to have just a hint of a smirk on his face, "looks like he may have been quite familiar with the backside of it."

She moved in closer and scrutinized the photo. Suddenly she squealed with laughter. "Look at this," she said. "You can just see it. He's got his hand around his sister's pigtail."

I looked. There was no doubt. The hand was intertwined in the long hair, but it was there, and her grimace perfectly matched his smirk.

"That devil." She pursed her lips and shook her head disdainfully, and then punched me gently in the shoulder. "He reminds me of you."

"Hey, what's that all about?" I started, but it was too late. She'd turned down the long hall and was making her way to the main tasting room. I looked at a few more pictures, and then followed and discovered the attraction. The room was bathed in warmth from the enormous fireplace. I suppose that it had originally been used for cooking as well as heat, as it was certainly large enough, and had a number of wrought iron hoops protruding from the stonework. Three stout oak logs burned merrily, casting their glow upon the gathering in the room. Mindy had squeezed her way to the front, and turning around so that her backside was facing the fireplace, beckoned me with one finger.

As I stepped beside her, she reached up and kissed my cheek. "An apology," I asked?

She tossed her head. "Hardly." Just thanking you for finding this place. I think I'll just stay right here and let my clothes dry out." She inclined her head toward the tasting bar. "I'll start with a little chardonnay."

I backed up and gave her my best courtly bow, lacking only the sweep of my robe. "At your service madam."

§§§§

It took me a while to work my way to the front, as the room was full of people enjoying the festive atmosphere in this island of warmth on a cold blustery day. The tasting staff gladly poured me two samples of the chardonnay, and when I started to turn, insisted that I take a small piece of cheese to Mindy, as it had been specifically selected by their winemaster to go with that particular wine. I took the cheese and the glasses, and later had to agree that the food pairing had enhanced the flavor of an already tasty wine.

By the time I got back to Mindy, she'd moved away from the flames, and was looking at a display of Christmas ornaments. The steam that rose from her hot, damp coat cast a rosy glow around her, blurring her surroundings but casting her face in a clear light, much as a portrait photographer might manipulate his lenses. I smiled warmly at the way that the soft lighting enhanced the red of her curls and the sparkling blue in her eyes.

§§§§

We met Jim and Melissa for breakfast the following morning. They'd recommended an old western coffee house, a simple place that served bacon and eggs, along with pancakes and the like. In a town that prided itself in its gourmet selections, the sign in the window said it all. "Nothing fancy, just plain good food." And they were right.

Over breakfast, we caught up with one another, laughed, and generally enjoyed our unexpected friendship. Finally, the plates were cleared, and we sat drinking coffee. Jim looked at Melissa, and then said, "I suppose you're wondering what the news is."

Mindy responded first, "Have you any information about Joel?"

"Maybe so; maybe no," Jim responded. "But we might have found a source."

Melissa grinned. "He wants to make this so mysterious. I found a letter. It was in the old museum archives."

"From Joel?"

"No," Jim said. "It was written by Samuel and seems to have been lost when..."

Melissa interrupted him. "Who found the letter?"

He rolled his eyes sheepishly. "You did. Go ahead."

She smiled at Mindy. "He gets a little carried away sometimes and I have to remind him who's boss."

Mindy laughed. "I know exactly what you mean." She

glanced over at me. "Exactly."

"Hey," I started. "What's that all about?"

"Sorry," she said, and patted my hand. I looked over at Jim. He lifted his hands in a silent shrug, acknowledging that there was nothing we could do.

Melissa went on as if there had been no interruption. "I was digging through some old documents that had been donated to the museum several years ago. They came from a number of sources, but had been carefully cataloged when they came in, so I had some idea of their origin. I'd gotten to a box that was donated by Ida Mortenson. It was full of county records as well as several letters. Evidently, her grandfather had been pretty prominent in town back in the thirties. He owned a general store and served a couple of terms as a city councilman." She looked around at us. "It was his ownership of the store that was important."

I interrupted her. "Was the store here back in the 1850's?"

She shook her head. "No, but remember that this was a tiny town back in the thirties. Still, it was the largest in the area, so it had the local post office. People came in from miles around to send and pick up mail."

"And," Jim began, but she silenced him with a look. "And Melissa found something," he smiled.

She laughed, and then paused, as if for effect. "Evidently, Ida's grandfather stored the unclaimed mail in his garage. There was the occasional package from the Sears catalog, or mail that was undeliverable for one reason or another..."

"Undeliverable?" Mindy asked.

"I found one that was addressed to Jimmy Williams, Murphys, California." She scanned our faces. "It was a small town, but not that small, considering that some of the ranches might have been ten miles away, or that many of the hands on the ranches were transient. I suppose some moved on without any forwarding address. And if there was no return address..."

"I see," she nodded. "So there'd be no place to deliver it. But what's that got to do with Joel?"

Melissa smiled and nodded. "I was getting to that. There were a couple of boxes from the old post office. Like I said, they included old parcels as well as the occasional letter." She looked around at us knowingly, and continued. "They got older as I dug deeper into the boxes. Evidently, Ida's grandfather wasn't the first postmaster to throw the undeliverables into a box. There's a letter from Samuel Watkins, dated June of 1853." She pulled a tattered envelope out of her purse. "It belongs to the museum now, a picture into that time. I was thinking of putting it under glass with some of the period photographs and trinkets.

We all craned forward to see the old document. Mindy gasped as she saw it. She looked at me. "Isn't that the same handwriting as the one Catherine had?"

I nodded slowly, analyzing the letters. "It sure looks like it." I thought back to reading that letter. I'd been struck by the distinctive handwriting at that time. Samuel wrote with a backward slant, and though consistent and clear, his letters were boxy and crabbed, almost as if his hand had been broken at some time. "I'd want to compare the two..." I looked up at Melissa, "Can we get a copy of this?"

She nodded.

Looking back at Mindy, I smiled. "I think you've got a match."

"So the question remains," Jim interjected, and looked slowly around the table, "who should read it?"

I looked at Mindy, and she looked back at me. We were interrupted by Melissa, "Jim, would you do us the honors please?"

He puffed up like a peacock and beamed, and I noticed a silent communication pass fleetingly between Melissa and Mindy. As I began to wonder whether I'm as easily manipulated as he evidently had been, he began.

"It's in pretty bad shape," he said. He'd taken the paper and turned it over. "It's pretty clear why it never got delivered." He showed us the back side of the letter. It appeared that the letter had gotten wet at some time, as that side of the paper was stained, and the ink had run in several areas. While Samuel's name and return address, Murphys, California, were clear, the addressee was damaged. All I could make out was Mrs. ...el Wat..., ...al Turnp... Road ...st., and below that, just a single letter in a long smudge, 's.'

He turned the letter over and began to read.

June 16, 1853
Murphys, California

Dear Ma,

Sorry I have not written more often. I can not say we have been busy finding gold, though that is partially true. We have made wages, and a little more. Over these last couple of years, we have found a few small nuggets, and a goodly amount of dust. We go into the local Wells Fargo office every few weeks and deposit our gold with them. They take some on deposit and give us cash for the rest, and some of that goes for food and supplies, and some for other expenses. Still, we have built up a small account that will be of use later.

All in all, I have two good partners. So many of the miners throw their money away on drink and women, that I suppose I am lucky there. All three of us are much the same, raised to keep away from the bottle and loose women.

California is a wondrous place. The weather here can be harsh in the winter, but it is not as bad as it was at home. You would like the summer. It's hot and beautiful and dry, and the hills turn a dusty golden color. Higher up, the pine trees stay green year round.

We are a few miles out of a little place called Murphys, named after a couple of brothers who had enough common sense to quit the mining business and set up a hotel. Our claim is on a creek, so we get plenty of water, and can fish for our dinners. Like I said though, there is not much gold.

I know I said I would come back east when I made my load, but I am thinking of staying out here. Truth is, I have taken up with a gal from Murphys, and am thinking of marrying her. She does not want to be mixed up with a gold miner though, so I need to find another line of work. I hear there is a small store and restaurant combination for sale up in San Andreas and we are planning to ride on up there to check it out. Imagine that, me a shopkeeper. Still, it is gold country there, and I know what miners need, so it should work. I have talked with the fellow who owns the store here in Murphys and he'll help me set up accounts with the suppliers out in San Francisco.

I promise to write again soon.

Your loving son,

Samuel

Jim put down the letter and looked across at us. "Does this help?"

Mindy bit the side of her lip and nodded slowly. "I think so." She thought for a moment and then added, "Let's see what we know." Looking around the table, she said, "Can somebody make a list?"

Melissa reached into her purse and pulled out a small pad and brandished a pen. "Ready."

Nodding resolutely, Mindy continued, "The Samuel Joel met was Samuel Watkins, and so was the writer of the letters."

"And the handwriting seems to be the same," I added.

Mindy nodded, "connecting this letter to Catherine." She smiled and continued, "We still don't have a confirmation that he and Joel were partners."

"But we do know that there were three, and one of them had been ill in Panama."

"And Joel had Yellow Fever there."

She looked around the table, "What else?"

Melissa spoke as she wrote, "Samuel, and presumably Joel, were here from at least January of 1852 until June of 1853." She looked at the rest of us. "Any more?"

"This may be a stretch," I said slowly, "but let me try it. There's no mention in any of Catherine's letters of Joel drinking, or even of her family drinking. So could we conclude that he didn't approve of that?"

Mindy looked thoughtfully at me. "Maybe, and that would match with Samuel's partners, right?

I nodded, still thinking aloud, "And that would have made them rather unusual in the gold country."

Jim laughed. "Very, I'd say."

"Okay, what else?" Melissa looked at us. Nobody said anything, so she added, "Samuel said," she reached for the letter, "I hear there's a small store and restaurant combination for sale up in San Andreas and we're planning to ride on up there to check it out." She paused and then repeated, "We're planning to ride up there."

"You're right," I added. "So who's the 'we?'"

She continued. "It's very unlikely that a young woman in 1853 would have taken off for a week or so with a young man who was not her husband. Plus it was dangerous just to be out on the road, especially for a woman. So,..."

"So it might have been the three partners," Mindy added. "I agree. I get the impression that Samuel's gotten tired of mining, and guess that the others might have too." She smiled. "Excellent. Anything else?"

Jim frowned. "Samuel spent some time in town and came to church from time to time, but the other partners didn't." He thought for a moment, "And he and the pastor became friends." He started tapping his finger on the table, "If he got married in Murphys, I'll bet it's somewhere in those old church records."

"So we might be best off continuing to research Samuel," I added.

Melissa wrote, and then looked up, "More?"

Nobody spoke for a while, so she tore off the sheet of paper and handed it to Mindy. "You mentioned that you were going to bring one of Catherine's letters?"

Mindy nodded and reached for her purse but Jim interrupted her. "I hate to spoil the party, but I've got a meeting with the church council. I need to run."

Melissa checked her watch and her eyes widened. "Oh my, we are running late. Me too. I can just make it to the museum if I hurry. Later?"

I looked at Mindy and she shrugged her shoulders. "I have an urge to drive over to San Andreas. Any idea if it's still there?"

I had picked up the check and gently rebuffed Jim's attempt to give me money. Hearing Mindy, I said absently, "It's up highway 49, about ten miles north of Angels Camp."

Well, you're coming for dinner tonight, so how about then? Seven o'clock at our place. Nothing fancy."

Mindy smiled. "Anything we can bring?"

Melissa had looked out the rain streaked window, and was putting on her coat. "A bottle of wine?" She grinned coyly, "That is, if you've broken your family's aversion to the demon alcohol." As she opened the door, she turned her head back. "And the letter, of course."

"Of course," Mindy acknowledged.

CHAPTER 31

It was raining when we approached the Adams' cottage later that day. We'd hurried to San Andreas, browsed through the local museum, and tried to visit a couple of the old buildings. Unfortunately for us, much of the town had been modernized, so little remained, and what did was closed for the weekend. Still, San Andreas was the county seat, and there was some interest in the local history, so many of the governmental agencies had located in the historic section of town, with a goal of preserving the old structures.

Jim was opening the door when I knocked, startling both us and him. "Oh, Hi," he stammered. "I was just going out to the mailbox. Come on in." He turned and called back into the house, "Melissa, they're here." Then he gestured us toward the sofa in the living room and said, "And if you'll excuse me, I'll just grab that mail before I forget." With that, he brushed past and hurried through the rain to the street.

Melissa came in, wearing a yellow flowered apron and drying her hands on a tea towel. "Good evening." She looked around and frowned.

Mindy smiled. "He's gone to get the mail."

"That man," Melissa said as she rolled her eyes. "Well, have a seat and make yourselves comfortable. Is there anything I can get you? Water? Wine?"

I shook my head, "No. I'm just fine." Then I remembered the bag in my hand and raised it, "We did bring a bottle of cabernet. Maybe you'd like me to open this?"

She smiled. "Sure. Come on into the kitchen. I'll get you a corkscrew."

"Is there anything I can do?" Mindy asked.

Melissa shook her head. "Nothing at all. Dinner's in the oven and the table's set. Have a seat and relax."

While I opened the bottle, Melissa and Mindy chatted amiably in the other room. She'd given me the corkscrew and four wine goblets, so I got right to work. I was just bringing the first two glasses to the ladies in the living room when Jim came back in. Staying in the tiled area of the entry, he absentmindedly shook the rain off of his jacket and then hung it on one of the hooks on the wall, next to Mindy's and mine. He'd been thumbing through his mail as he came through the door, so didn't notice everyone looking his way until he raised his head.

"Your guests?" Melissa asked. "You just left them here?"

He paused for a moment and then said, "I had to get the mail. I told them to make themselves comfortable."

She shook her head and muttered something to Mindy that caused both women to chuckle. I figured it was something to do with the social graces of men, or lack thereof, so I called out to Jim, "I was just pouring some wine. We picked up a bottle at the winery out on Sheepranch Road. Would you like a glass?"

Smiling, he nodded his head. "That sounds wonderful. I'd love it." He dropped the mail into a bowl on a small round table by the door, and walked into the living room. "It's cold out there. Think I'll get the fire going."

I handed each of the ladies a glass of wine and returned to the kitchen for the others. Jim was bent over the wood stove, lighting the fire when I returned. Putting his glass on the coffee table, I said, "I was just thinking of what the old pastor in the tent would think of your house here. A nice roof over your heads, real walls, and a warm fire. Probably not nearly as cold and drafty as his tent."

Jim turned and nodded. The fire was spreading from the paper to the kindling. I could hear it crackling in the background and feel the beginning of the heat. "I'm sure it was an exciting time to be here, starting a new church, tending to the minors and the ah, ladies, and all, but it was probably a lot harder than we can even imagine."

I was about to respond when I heard Melissa clear her throat. "Jim, what's an 'ah' lady?"

He swiveled his head and looked at her curiously. "What's what?"

"You said that he tended to the 'ah' ladies. What's an 'ah'

lady?"

"Well they were prostitutes," he replied.

She stared at him. "So?"

"Uh, so I'm sure that a lot of the people in the community may not have thought of them as ladies."

She continued to stare at him and I could see him begin to squirm. By now, Jim had clearly begun to figure out that he was still in trouble, and he looked at me. I stared down into my wine glass and pretended not to notice the conversation. While I was perfectly willing to take one for the team, he wasn't going to drag me into this mess.

Melissa pulled his attention back to her. "What about the men? Were they 'ah' men, because I'm sure that the prostitutes would have had to look for other work if the men hadn't been flocking to their door."

Jim gritted his teeth. "Perhaps I misspoke," he said softly.

"Perhaps?"

He looked beseechingly at me again and I turned my face away. You dug this hole all by yourself buddy. You're going to have to dig your way out.

"Let me rephrase that," he said. "What I meant to say was that it was a difficult time, and the pastor had a lot of work to do building his church out here in what was essentially a wilderness. Fortunately, he had help from a number of good people, men and women."

She stared at him for a moment over her glasses and then with just the slightest hint of a smile, said, "Ah. That's what I thought you meant." She looked toward Mindy. "So how was your trip to San Andreas?"

I was startled by the sudden shift in topic, but Mindy took it in stride. "It was worth the time. We didn't find much, but there was enough there to make it worth another visit."

"Really?"

Mindy nodded. "The museum had some information, as well as a number of pictures of the old town. In one, you can see the general store, along with a man in white shirt and suspenders sweeping the outside."

Melissa smiled. "Maybe you're related."

I glanced at Jim. He was still looking a bit like a deer caught in the headlights, but was starting to follow the conversation.

Mindy's response took us both by surprise. "I took a picture of the old photo. I plan to enlarge it and see if there's any family resemblance."

"When did you do that?" I asked.

She smiled. "Remember when I sent you to ask the docent if they had any listing of the owners of the old buildings? While she was busy, I snapped several pictures."

I could see Melissa frowning. "We don't permit photos in our museum."

Mindy just shrugged her shoulders. "Neither did they." She gestured toward me. "That's why I had him distract the docent."

She took a sip of her wine as if defying Melissa to comment on that. Evidently Melissa thought better of it, as she just nodded and then said, "So did you find anything else?"

"The store was built in 1848, when the town was founded," I said. "Some of the early pictures show that it was just a tent. It burned down in 1849, and was rebuilt later that year, presumably in another tent. The first permanent wooden structure went up in 1851. The stone building was built a few years later."

"Did you get any ownership records?" Jim asked.

I shook my head. "Not this trip. Evidently they have a pretty thorough archive, but it's in the county offices, and today's Saturday..."

He shook his head. "So they're closed."

I continued. "But they're open during the week, and the docent gave us a contact person as well as a phone number and email information. Mindy's planning to call next week."

"Great. Let me know if we can help in any way."

Melissa nodded and looked over at her husband. "That's right. Maybe we could drive up to San Andreas and do some research for you."

"That'd be great," Mindy said. "I'll think about what we're looking for and let you know."

Jim smiled and held up his wine. "Very good choice. I see you bought local."

"Yeah," I replied and glanced at my glass. "There're so many good wineries around here. I'm not sure why the markets even carry other wines." I stood. "Can I get anyone a refill?"

"How about at the table," Melissa said. "The roast should be just about done. Shall we have dinner?"

The meal was an unqualified success. Melissa had decided that since she had a table of four instead of two, she'd take advantage of the opportunity to make a larger meal. The pot roast had been cooking slowly in the oven all day, and was so tender that the meat fell away from the bones with just a slight pressure from the fork. It was delicious comfort food, and opened the door to our various experiences with childhood dining.

After we all cleared the table and shared in washing the dishes, we settled into the living room with a glass of zinfandel port.

Jim pulled a log from the firewood cradle and poked it into the fire, and then turned to Mindy. "So did you bring that letter you were talking about?"

She nodded. "I did, in my purse."

While she was getting the letter, I asked, "You mentioned that you might have found some more information in the old church records?"

"A little bit," he replied with a smile. "I think it'll be helpful." He settled onto the sofa next to his wife. "Melissa went through more postal records, and I've had a chance to look at more of the old journals. Fascinating reading actually."

Mindy had taken her seat with her letter in hand. "Well, are you going to tell us what you found?"

"After the letter," he responded with a smile. "You first."

"All right." She pulled the delicate stationary out of the envelope and spread it out in front of her.

November 22, 1850
Pittsburgh

My dear husband,
I am huge, and uncomfortable, and anxious to have this baby born. I no longer try to tie my shoes, and have contented myself with some slippers Ruth found for me. I have enough difficulty putting those on. Shoes would be quite impossible to tie as I can no longer reach my feet without a great deal of twisting about. Can you imagine what I look like? Ready or not, the baby is coming soon!

Ruth and I visited with a midwife yesterday. Mrs. Albertson is a wonderful woman, with seven healthy children of her own. We mostly just talked. I expressed my concerns and she assured me that everything would be just fine. It would appear that the troubles I am having are perfectly normal and the result of the baby growing within me. It seems that he is going to be a big child. She measured me around the waist and I certainly am not going to share that figure with you. It is enough to say that even I was shocked, and look as if I have swallowed a watermelon.

I do not mind admitting to you that I am a little frightened. You hear all of the stories about difficult births and babies who are born dead, or mothers who die in childbirth. Oh I know that all will be fine, and everyone tells me not to be worried, but still...

Robert left just a few days ago. He stayed for such a long time and it was so wonderful to have him here. He reminded me of how I have missed my family and even though Ruth has been wonderful, I miss home as well. He and I took to walking every afternoon, and we must have explored every inch of this town. I could tell that some of the old biddies are starting to wonder if he is the father of the child, or even my husband. Think of that! The father of my child, or maybe my husband. They think that I am a fallen woman, but you and I know that is not true. I was upset over something that I overheard one day and tempted to speak out, but thought I had best talk to Ruth first. She told me to hold my tongue and not pay any attention. 'Anyone who does not have skeletons in their closet,' she said, 'either does not have a closet or has not bothered to look.' Anyway, it has been wonderful to have Robert here. I have laughed more with him in these past weeks than in the past six months. Sadly, he did have to go back to the farm, but I know that I will see him again soon.

Ruth surprised me with a baby shower last week. It was wonderful. Many of her friends came, and they did indeed shower me with gifts for the baby. I now have a set of bonnets, and booties, and blankets, and all sorts of wonderful things. This will be the best dressed baby in Pittsburgh, I am sure. Well, we ate cake, and talked and laughed, and generally had a terrific time. I would have wished you were there, but it was really a very feminine affair and you would no doubt have felt very out of place. Still, ...

And now my big news. Tom is here! He arrived last night. When I answered the door I did not know whether to laugh or cry, so I guess that I just did both. I know that he loves me, but he is so stern all the time. But to see him at the door, having come to visit with his little sister. I know how hard the trip from Bradford is, and for him to come just to see me! Oh he said he had some business in town, but I know better. He came to see me.

He seems to be a proud uncle already, and could not help but cluck over my belly. Just like Robert, I put his hand on my stomach while the baby was moving, and when the baby kicked under his hand, he jumped back as he had been bitten by a snake. I laughed so hard I cried. And the next time the baby moved, I placed his hand there again. His eyes got so wide and he smiled so big. Well it made me all warm inside to know that he came to see me.

Tom wanted me to stay in Pittsburgh for the next few months, to be near Ruth in case there were any problems. He is not sure that a household of men would know what to do with an infant, and he does not trust Mama to be of any help. 'After the boy grows a little bit, you can come on back,' he said. Well I guess he had not counted on Ruth. She jumped right in on that and said that she was coming home with me. He hemmed and hawed for a while, but then Ruth said that if he did not like that, she still knew where those willow switches were and he was not too big to swat. Tom turned as red as I have ever seen him. He just said, 'Yes ma'am,' like a little boy and figured he could find an empty room for her to stay in for as long as she liked. It is a whole new side to Tom. He will not take that kind of talk from anyone else, but with Ruth, it is Ma'am this and Ma'am that. She must have ridden herd on him when he was a boy.

So it would seem that I am going back to Bradford. After Ruth established who was boss, she softened a little and agreed with Tom that it might be best if we did stay in Pittsburgh for a while after the baby comes, just to make sure that he was healthy and able to travel. Tom was so funny. He said, 'Well of course, that is what I meant. And having you in the house for a few weeks will be wonderful.' She just winked at me, as if to say that she would be staying until she was good and ready to go, and then told Tom that he was right.

I do miss you so. It has been so long since I have heard from you. Are you alright? Have you found your treasure and are you even as I write, flying home to me? I hope so.

With all my love,

Catherine

Mindy was about to set the letter down when Melissa held out her hand for it. Taking the paper, she scanned the document and then chuckled. "I think I would have liked Ruth."

From what I'd seen of Melissa, I think that she was right. They were cut of the same cloth.

"So the baby's due soon," Mindy said.

Melissa nodded. "Very soon." She handed back the letter.

"And it sounds like she'll have a midwife deliver it. I don't suppose there were many hospital births then. Probably a good idea." She looked at her husband. "Our Michael was almost born at home."

"He was indeed. A very quick labor."

"Thankfully," she said. "But we got to the hospital just in time." She lapsed into silence and Jim rose.

"I promised you some more information."

"Right," I said. "Something you found in the church records?"

He'd gone to a side table by the front window, and now I noticed an old journal laying there. It was like the others, a bit tattered and certainly in need of tender loving care. I could tell that the binding was coming apart from the gentle way that he cradled it in his hands. Bringing it back, he sat and opened to a place he'd marked with a scrap of paper. "There's not much," he said, "but you should find this interesting." He pulled out what appeared to be a yellowed newspaper clipping. "I found this in the journal here. I'll read it."

September 4, 1853

Sunday marked a joyous event here in Murphys. Our own Reverend Meeks took himself a wife. The good reverend has been stepping out with Cindy Smith, a local seamstress, and previously one of the girls at the Murphys Hotel, for the past year or so. Well Sunday they decided to tie the knot. Samuel Watkins traveled down from San Andreas, where he has recently taken over operation of the general store to stand up with the reverend and to be married himself.

The double wedding was performed by Captain Bridger of Angels Camp, and late of the schooner Wildwind, which is still moored in San Francisco. "I can not say I have ever performed a wedding where the deck was not rolling beneath my feet," he quipped.

After the captain had completed his service, it was time for Reverend and Mrs. Meeks to change roles. He took up his vestments and presided over the wedding of his good friend, Samuel Watkins to Laura Davies. Miss Davies has also retired from the Murphys Hotel and taken up work as a school teacher in San Andreas. Several of the girls stood with her. Mr. Watkins was joined by his partners, Jonathan Campbell and Joel Woodward.

Jim looked up from his reading. "It goes on a little bit about dancing and the party, but that's the part I thought you'd be interested in."

We were stunned. Mindy and I looked at one another. Finally, I blurted, "It's huge! It's confirmation! He was here!"

Mindy stayed strangely quiet and I gave her a questioning look.

"It's more than that. It's the first time that his name has been mentioned in anything other than the letters. There was always that tiny nagging doubt in the back of my mind about whether he really existed." She beamed. "He's my ancestor, and he came to California."

She looked around the room and her smile faded. "I guess the question now is whether he ever made it home."

CHAPTER 32

Having confirmed the existence of Mindy's ancestor, and with a trail leading to San Andreas, we figured we were making progress, and then Mindy received a letter from her remote cousin.

We'd planned to drive up to San Francisco for some post-Christmas revelry when an arctic storm descended upon Northern California with as much fury as either of us could remember. Tides were running high, and just the day before, a tourist in Monterey had been knocked off a cliff where he was trying to take a photo. He'd been washed into the ocean, but fortunately, had managed to cling to a rock until rescuers arrived. Sewers throughout Santa Clara Valley were inundated with runoff and debris, making travel just to the market an adventure. Mindy managed the freeway trip from her home to mine, but we decided to hunker down in front of the fire instead of driving up to the city.

I laid out a platter of cheese and crackers and fruit, and poured some warm tea. When I suggested a new Chardonnay, she deferred as it was still early in the day and she was hopeful that we'd get out. We huddled together, enjoyed the warmth of the fire, and watched the wind whip the trees into a frenzy out the back window.

"Sorry about San Francisco," I said.

She shrugged her shoulders. "It can't be helped. I sure don't want to drive in that."

"No. Not right now. Maybe tomorrow."

She leaned against me, both hands wrapped around the warm mug. "Maybe." Then she reached up, kissed my cheek, and said, "I have a couple of letters. Would you be interested?"

"Absolutely," I said. "Joel? Catherine?"

"Alice," she replied.

I cocked my head to the side. "Alice? Who's Alice?"

She rose and went to the entry to get her purse. Over her shoulder, she tossed out, "Remember the letters I wrote to my cousins? I got a response." She fished in the purse, and then came back, letters in hand. "Actually, I got several responses, some glad to hear from me; some glad to know about me; some interested in the quest; and one," she held up a letter between her thumb and forefinger, "with some information."

She settled back down onto the carpet, and I strained to see the letter. "So what is it?"

"It's kind of fun," she said. "It's from a cousin Alice I'd never heard of before." She held out the envelope so that we both could read it. "Hmm. Alice Stanton, Kimberly, Idaho. My how the family has scattered."

I reached out and took the letter from her hand and looked at the postmark. It was legal size, and had been sent nearly two weeks earlier. Alice had obviously enclosed several sheets of paper, as it was a hefty envelope. "What's in it?"

Mindy smiled. "Give me back the envelope please, and I'll share." I handed it to her, and she immediately took out the enclosed papers and spread them out on the floor in front of us. I could see that Alice had taken her time in her response. One sheet was a family tree, drawn out on a sheet of 8 1/2 by 11 inch paper and labeled with names, connections, and dates of birth and death.
Another was a map of the United States, with labels for family members in several different states. There were copies of some sort, which I was determined to look at later, and a page of typewritten text. Mindy picked it up and began to read.

December 14th,

Dear Mindy,
I was so excited to hear from you. From the information that you've sent me, I'd guess that we're third cousins.
First, a little about me. My husband and I moved to Idaho from Cincinnati, Ohio about twenty years ago. We were both educators, just like you,

and were able to retire about four years ago. Bill taught high school math and I worked at the local elementary school. My last assignment was first grade. At first, I missed the kids, so now I go in every Tuesday just to help out. I don't miss lesson planning or grading papers at night and on the weekend at all! Bill started a new business selling novelty gift items through the internet. I'm not sure that he makes any money, but it keeps him busy and happy, and that's good. I help out with the books and we use the barn as a warehouse, so we'll see.

Since I've retired, I've been working on building a family tree of my ancestors, so I was very interested when I got your letter. I've enclosed copies of my work so far, as well as a few documents I've found online that you might find interesting. I'd love to see what you're digging up. Please, please send copies of everything. Maybe we can work together.

From what little you told me, it looks like we have a common great grandmother, Marie Stevens. I've tracked down a little bit of information about her, but not much. You'll find it enclosed. Evidently, she was quite a bit ahead of her time. Her husband, Richard Stevens, was a doctor and hospital administrator. Marie, interestingly, was a doctor as well. I have no idea how many women were doctors at that time, but she must have been a rarity. And without doubt, to have even been admitted to medical school, she must have been extraordinary. She had three sons and two daughters. My grandfather was Frank Stevens. He was born in 1874 and worked for the Proctor & Gamble company in Cincinnati. He married in 1918, to Jennifer Gladys. They had two girls and a boy. My mother, Alice, was the youngest, born in 1927. I've included their information on the other charts.

I haven't really researched Marie's other children very thoroughly, but here's what I have. Frank was the oldest. Robert came along in 1875 and I think he was killed in the First World War. Esther was born in 1876 and your grandfather Joseph in 1878. The youngest child was Anne, who was born in 1880 and evidently lived for just one year. There is some indication that at least one other child was stillborn, but I'm not sure about that.

As I understand it, Marie waited until 1881 to petition to be admitted to The Women's Medical College of Pennsylvania at Drexel University. Her husband evidently had a good job, and they could afford care for their children, so she decided to go back to school. I was able to find her medical license, granted in 1885 and have enclosed a copy for your records. It would appear that she went to college earlier, but I haven't found out where yet, though I would not be surprised to find that it was also Drexel University. I don't have much more about her. I do know that her training was in internal medicine and she was a general practitioner. From what I read, most male physicians at the time were primarily *focused on treating symptoms. She was one of many female physicians who were involved in an emerging preventative care movement back at the turn of the century. It seems that she stayed in the Pittsburgh area.*

As for her parents, I have no record of a Joel Woodward, but will certainly add him to my list. Thanks! I've found some documents showing that the head of Catherine's family at that time was Thomas Lewis, a yeoman farmer, and her brother. I couldn't find a record of Thomas ever marrying. Their parents were Arnold and Jeanie Lewis, also farmers. Since your letter, I've begun to research Ruth Smithson Hamilton (again, thanks). Evidently she owned a house in Pittsburgh from 1842 to 1855, so I can place her there during those years. She sold it, not a trustee, so she was still living at that time. Her husband, Harry Winston, owned the Winston Button Manufactory. He seems to have died from an accident in 1833, and she remarried to Frank Hamilton in 1838. He died in 1842. She sold the button factory in 1850, but from everything I can gather, she ran the company from 1833 until she sold it in 1850, so she must have been a remarkable businesswoman in an age when few women worked outside of the home at all, let alone as the mistress of a factory.

Please send me any other information you have, as I'd love to work with you on this family history project.

Sincerely yours,

Alice Stanton

Mindy put the letter down on the table and turned to me. "That's about it. The rest is address, phone, e-mail, and the like. There's not much new, but the information about Marie is interesting. I suppose we can start looking for Richard Stevens, but I'm not sure that's really related."

"He would have been what, Joel's son-in-law?" I shook my head. "You're probably right." I thought for a moment. "It seems that your family has a reputation for strong, intelligent women."

She looked at me and smiled. "Thank you," she said. "I'll take that as a compliment." She took a sip of tea. "It's not going to get you anything, but thanks for the compliment."

I sputtered. "Uh, uh, I wasn't trying to get anything. I was just stating a fact."

She nodded and patted my cheek as she rolled her eyes. "Thank you. Have you ever considered how transparent you are?"

I started to answer, but could tell that I would just be digging myself into a hole, so bit my tongue and reached for a slice of apple. It was sweet with just a little bit of tartness. I looked down at Mindy and chuckled inwardly at the comparison, and then picked up the family tree. It was similar to the one that Mindy had, with the addition of Frank's family line. The other enclosed documents were Marie's medical license and some of the documentation for the Winston Button Factory.

§§§§

We spent most of the afternoon sitting in front of the fire. I got up several times to add another log, but the weather steadily worsened, as evidenced by the occasional shriek as the wind found a gap in one of the windows. The fireplace was going, along with the furnace and I'd noticed the last time I got wood that with the late afternoon, the temperature outside had fallen to 37 degrees, not cold by many standards, but quite chilly for San Jose. By now, Mindy was cuddled up on one end of the sofa, reading her book, wrapped in my down throw and wearing the fuzzy slippers I'd given her for Christmas. I sat on the other end, absently stroking her feet in my lap as I too worked on a novel. The fire blazed away, sending its warmth out into the room, and the Christmas tree twinkled in the corner. It was altogether, a pleasant way to spend the day.

I'd been focused on my reading, and the next time I looked up, could see that it was dark outside. "I'm going to turn on the Christmas lights. Can I get you anything?"

She put a book dart onto her page. "Dinner?"

"Sure," I said. "What would you like? I've got some salmon in the refrigerator. I could broil that up along with a salad. That okay?"

She nodded. "Need any help?"

I shook my head. "You stay there. You've cooked for me often enough that I owe you. Besides, I'll get a chance to see how my famous salmon marinade works under the broiler."

She looked in my direction and smiled, and then buried her nose back into her book. I noticed that since I'd gotten up, she'd curled her feet under her, catlike and brought the comforter up to her chin. I made a quick check of the thermostat on the wall. Seventy-one degrees. Well I suppose it was a mite chilly for Mindy. I turned it up a notch and then went to the kitchen.

§§§§

The salmon was perfect, as I'd expected. I'd found a citrus based marinade a couple of years ago, and tinkered with it periodically since. One thing I'd never changed was the quarter cup of bourbon. After all, why mess with a perfectly reasonable ingredient. Besides, when people asked what was in it, and I replied, 'bourbon,' they always approved. I'd accompanied that with a fresh green salad and some black cherry flavored balsamic vinegar. That morning, I'd picked up a loaf of sourdough french bread, so we were set. Mindy added a bottle of Pinot Noir that matched perfectly with the fish. All in all, it was a great meal.

After dinner, we returned to the love seat, and as I moved to pick up my book, Mindy said, "Are you sure you want to read that?"

I put the book down. "Did you have something else in mind?"

She laughed. "Not that."

I grinned. "Not what?"

She shook her head. "Not what you were hoping. I just thought..."

"And what do you think I was hoping?" I asked coyly.

She laughed again, and shook her head. "You are all male, aren't you? Don't you think you're getting a little old to be thinking of sex all the time?"

I shrugged my shoulders. I thought better than to ask what else I should think about. Instead, I said, "I was just thinking that you are so lovely, and maybe you'd like to cuddle for a while."

"Not really," she said.

She looked at me, and I looked at her for nearly a minute without speaking before I finally got it. "Oh, right. You have another letter!"

She shook her head disdainfully. "About time." She reached into her purse and when I looked, I could see that there were at least two letters. She withdrew one and offered it to me. "Will you do the honors?"

I was surprised, to say the least. "From Joel?" She nodded and I looked at the envelope. "Well it's about time that boy wrote something. He's been pretty neglectful of his bride."

Mindy smiled and then nestled up against me. I was holding the envelope in both hands, turning it over and over, trying to make out the markings on the outside. She took one of my hands and moved my arm around her shoulders, and then cast her green eyes up to me. "Ready?"

I had to pull her closer to take the paper out of the envelope, but she didn't seem to mind, and before I could transfer the paper to my free hand, she reached up and kissed me on the chin. I tightened my grip around her shoulder and pulled her close. Evidently, there was some passion there, as it was quite an enjoyable kiss. Finally, she broke away, "Ready?"

I was definitely ready, but since I figured she meant to ask if I was ready to read, just nodded and flattened the enclosed paper. "Let's see..." I tried to speak, but my voice was a bit too husky. "Um." I took another look at the envelope, cleared my throat, and gave her a quick squeeze. "Uh."

Mindy giggled softly, and then patted my knee. "I was thinking of taking a hot bath before bed."

She stood and moved toward the bedroom, exaggerating the sway of her hips. As she was about to turn into the hallway, she peeked back at me on the couch. She definitely had my attention, but it must have been clear to her that I was confused, so she laughed and then reached her hand out to me. "I have trouble reaching between my shoulder blades."

Well I may be slow sometimes, but I was off the couch in a flash, following her laughter into the back of the house.

CHAPTER 33

Sonora, California
October 30, 1850

My Dear Catherine,
I have finally arrived in California's gold country. I tell you, it has been a difficult journey. It is hard to imagine that it has been over a month since I have written, and I am truly sorry for that, but I have been out in the countryside for the past six weeks, trying to find any kind of transport to the gold area. There are no towns in central California, or at least none in the area that we traveled, so we have walked.

This is a beautiful land. Here it is, almost November, and scarcely any rain. The weather is starting to turn, but it is still nothing like Pennsylvania. Just two weeks ago, as we tromped through the swamps that seemed to go on forever in the central valley, it was sweltering hot and the mosquitos tried to eat us alive. Today it is cooler, but still quite pleasant. I wear my coat in the evenings when it cools down, but during the day, shirtsleeves are perfect. Imagine that. I think of you, and I wonder if you have finished the harvest and started bundling up for the winter. I like the warm weather, but miss the frost on the ground.

We have been hiking east, hoping to get to the gold fields before it gets cold. We tried hiring a wagon, but the prices were just too dear, and we had already spent much of our remaining funds just to buy shovels and pans and other mining equipment. Ah well, we are young, and a good hike will do us good, so we purchased a wheelbarrow, loaded it up, and set off. I had not planned on the swampy areas though. Evidently the rivers flow heavily in the spring, but in the late fall, there is very little water. As a result, the ground is muddy and spongy.

It has made for slow going.

Samuel and Jonathan have been wonderful companions. I wish that you could meet them. I could not ask for better. Since none of us have much, we have decided to pool our money and assigned Samuel the role of banker. He has not much to work with now, but hopefully in a few months, he will be up to his eyeballs in gold. Ha. I can dream anyway. I was fortunate to join up with two fellows whose beliefs are so similar to my own. None of us drink, so there is no money going out for alcohol. I have heard that many miners squander their earnings in the bars. You need not worry about us.

We arrived in Sonora yesterday after a long trudge through the foothills. I can see the Sierra Nevada ahead of us. The distant mountains are still covered with snow from last winter and I hear that there are peaks of over ten thousand feet. It is truly an intimidating sight. Fortunately, we will not have to cross those mountains in our search for gold. I understand that many people have come overland, and had to endure the snowstorms in the high passes. It makes me glad that we chose to come by sea.

Sonora is what I have learned is called a 'tent city.' Although to call this wide spot in the road a city is laughable. For that matter, to call it a road is pretty much a stretch. There are some shops, mostly housed in tents, and just a few wooden buildings. We saw that the Wells Fargo folks are beginning to build a stone bank, but everything else looks very temporary. Still, this is one of the gateways to the gold country, so we are well on our way. I hear there are good prospects about twenty miles further up the hill. We have been following wagon trails to get here, and have been told that we will still be able to follow some semblance of a trail up into the mountains.

I have learned to make flapjacks. Evidently, someone in San Francisco started the tradition, and it has caught on. They are a kind of a cake, poured flat into a frying pan filled with hot grease, and fried until they turn golden brown on both sides. They are actually pretty good, with a little bacon grease or if we can find it, honey, and they keep us going throughout a long day.

I do not know when this letter will go out. I left it with the local sheriff, who says that the postman comes by about once each week, so hopefully it will go soon. Of course, after he gets it, he will have to make his way down to San Francisco, and then they will send it by boat from there. As it is nearly November now, I hope that you receive it by March. We have decided to ration our funds and buy just the essentials, so I need to hold back on postage, but will write again next month.

I can not tell you how much I long to hold you in my arms and tell you that I love you. It has been a long, hard trip, but I am almost there. I would wish you were with me, but this is certainly no place for a lady. We plan to stay in Sonora for a day or two to regain our strength, and then start up the hill again. Hopefully, we can place our claim in the next couple of weeks. And after that, it is just a matter of working hard together to make the claim pay off.

I love you and I miss you.

Your husband, Joel

Mindy and I were nestled under the covers, and when I put down the letter, she lifted her head off my shoulder to speak. "Where's Sonora?"

"About thirty miles from Murphys. Remember driving through Columbia? Near there."

She nodded and lay her head back down. "So they were close."

"Right." I rubbed her back. It was warm and soft and smooth. "But it's south, so they'd have to cross the Stanislaus River." I paused and mused. "And that would have been quite a challenge with no bridges."

"So where would they go?"

"Well, the first we have of them in Murphys area is January of 1852, so they had probably worked another claim."

She nodded without lifting her head and sighed softly. "Maybe."

She snuggled closer, and when I looked, I could see that her eyes were closed. I wrapped my other arm around her, caressing her back and hugging her body into mine. Then I kissed her forehead and smiled, before laying my head back onto the pillow. As I stroked her back, her regular breathing told me that she was asleep. I held her for a long time, thinking of those miners of so long ago, before I too fell into a deep sleep.

CHAPTER 34

I got up early the next morning. The fire was out, and the cold weather had seeped through the walls and windows into the house. The heater was going, and I could see that it was struggling to reach 58 degrees. I hadn't noticed the cold overnight, but since I knew that Mindy was more sensitive to cold, I snuck back into the bedroom and tucked another blanket around her. She stirred slightly, but then slipped back into her regular breathing. I closed the door when I left, so that she could sleep in quiet and went out to the kitchen.

I had a good French roast in the pantry, and fortunately I'd ground some beans a few days earlier. I loaded up the coffee maker, turned it on, and stepped out to the window, where I wasn't surprised to see that although the storm had passed, it had left quite a wake of debris. No doubt, I'd spend the next couple of days cleaning up the mess in the yard. I'd have to wait for a while though, as everything was covered by a thin layer of white frost. I reflected to myself that this was about as close as San Jose would come to a winter wonderland. Then I thought of the work so many would have shoveling snow in a colder clime, and figured it was just as well.

I'd carried Joel's letter out from the bedroom and left it on the coffee table in the living room. After pouring a cup of coffee, I settled onto the couch and began to review it. It seemed to me that we had another avenue to explore in Sonora, and I smiled at the opportunities we would have to visit the Sierra foothills. Murphys, and then San Andreas, and now Sonora. It would make an interesting few months. As I read on into the letter, I saw Joel's mention of flapjacks, and chuckled to myself. Pancakes would indeed make a good breakfast. I had picked up some blueberry syrup in the mountains, so we were all set. I figured Mindy wouldn't mind too much if we skipped slathering them with bacon fat.

I had just started the second griddle full of pancakes when Mindy walked into the kitchen. She'd evidently taken a shower, as she had a towel tied around her head. She was dressed for the arctic in her thermal tights and leotard, fuzzy slippers, and my terry cloth robe.

I smiled. "Good morning sleepyhead." I stepped back theatrically and took in the outfit. "My but don't you look sexy."

She glared at me. "You want sexy, spend a little money on heat."

I offered my down vest and she just rolled her eyes. Although she'd worn it before, she always complained that any jacket without sleeves was a waste of fabric. I decided to change the subject. "I made flapjacks!" I shrugged. "Well, pancakes anyway." I pointed my spatula toward the pan. "They're just like the miners used to eat. Whole wheat, loaded with blueberries, and I figure we can slice bananas on top. And I've got this syrup that we picked up in Murphys." She turned her back and went for the coffee. I knew exactly how she felt. Sometimes a cup of coffee before dealing with my sparkling wit was just what others seemed to need.

I'd warmed the oven as a holding place for the pancakes when I took them out of the pan, and given the chill in the room, had left the door propped open. Mindy settled with her back to the open oven door, sipped her coffee, and sighed. "Now this is more like it. How cold is it in here anyway?"

"Well, when I got up it was 58. It's probably quite a bit warmer now."

She rolled her eyes. "You mean like 59?"

"Oh I'm sure it's at least 65 or so. You can check the thermostat."

She wandered into the other room and I heard a snide comment, "Sixty three. Practically tropical."

"But set to seventy," I replied with a smile, and went back to my pancakes. "Would you like some juice with breakfast?"

§§§§

Much to Mindy's surprise, and my salvation, the house did warm up fairly quickly. In no time at all, we were basking in a warm seventy degrees. I took off my sweater. Mindy grumbled about the cold and left hers on. Breakfast was a hit though, and once we dug into the warm pancakes, the place seemed to magically heat up. Again, the opinions of the management are not necessarily shared by the guests.

We finished the pancakes, and I was washing dishes when Mindy came and cuddled up against my back. I'd have hugged her back, but was pretty wet and soapy. Still, the hug felt good and I leaned my head onto hers. "Warmer?" I asked.

She nodded, and then gave me a quick squeeze. "I have another letter when you finish."

"Great," I responded. "I thought I saw another one last night. Who's it from?"

She swished out into the living room, at least as much as she could swish wearing an oversized terrycloth robe. "You'll have to come out to see."

"I'm almost done," I said. "Make yourself comfortable. More coffee?"

I heard her call from the other room. "No thanks."

I left the dishes to air dry on a towel, and then wiping my hands, walked out of the kitchen. Mindy was cuddled up on the couch, reading a book. One of Catherine's envelopes was on her lap. Seeing me, she patted the sofa next to her and put the book on the coffee table. I noticed that even as the room warmed, she was nestled in the down throw.

I settled onto the couch and picked up the letter. It was indeed from Catherine, dated January 14th. I raised my eyebrows. "You sure this is the next one? Wasn't the last one written in November?"

She nodded and reached out her hand. "This is it."

I handed her back the letter and lifted her feet into my lap. "Nothing I can get you?" I asked.

Mindy shook her head distractedly, already opening the envelope. She took out two pieces of paper and lay the envelope on the coffee table. She studied the papers for a few seconds and then looked sweetly at me. "No fire today?"

"Ah," I started. Then I jumped up. "I was just about to get a fire going."

Five minutes later, fire started, I sat back on the couch. Mindy smiled, kissed me softly on the cheek, and lay her head against my shoulder. "Always taking good care of me. Thanks."

Kissing me again, she lifted up the letter.

Pittsburgh
January 14, 1851

Dearest Joel,

You are a father. The baby and I are both doing well, though I am still weak as a kitten. It is a good thing that Ruth has been here to care for me, as it was a big baby and a difficult delivery. But that is in the past now. She, did I tell you it was a girl? She has the most beautiful blue eyes and bright red hair. And as big a baby as she seemed, she's absolutely tiny. She was born on the fifth, the first baby born in Pittsburgh in this new year. She is sleeping now, resting in the little basket that Ruth gave me at the shower. And even as I write this to you, I feel the urge to go over and pick her up and just hold her and feel her precious heartbeat.

I know I promised you a boy, and I was certain that this baby was going to be a big healthy boy. Instead, she is a little girl who I am told looks just like her mother. So now you have two of us!

Tom left a few weeks ago, and I promised to write him as soon as the baby came, which I did. Other than that, I have done little but sleep and care for our little girl. I find that she does not sleep much, so I must take advantage of any time she is down. I know it will get better, but I am pretty exhausted right now.

I am sorry I did not write earlier, but it has definitely been a busy few weeks. Mrs. Albertson was wonderful. I do not know what we would have done without her. She was so funny though. When we met, she was so sweet and nice, and gentle. Then when the baby was coming, her whole personality changed so that she reminded me of Tom, barking orders and demanding that everyone jump whenever she spoke. Even Ruth, who certainly put Tom in his place, did not even try to stand up to her. But it was all worth it, as we now have a beautiful, healthy baby girl.

I have named her Marie. Marie Ruth Woodward. What a beautiful name for a beautiful baby. Do I sound like a proud mama?

Think of that. I am a mother, and you are a father. Last January, I was a girl in love with a boy and thinking girlish thoughts. Now though, I must think of this baby first and always. How life changes.

Aunt Ruth has been wonderful. I can not tell you how many times she has come in here in the middle of the night when she has heard the baby crying, and taken her so that I could sleep. I look at her, and can see the strain that this has brought to her as well, but the new lines on her face seem to be happy ones. Some days, we both stand at the edge of the crib and just stare at her with wonder, just watching her sleep. When I told her that I had decided to give the baby the name Marie Ruth, she cried. I did too. She has been so good to me and I am so glad that she will be coming home with me.

Do take care, and write soon. It has been so long since I have heard from you. I hope that you are safe in California now, finding gold, preparing to come home.

Your loving wife and daughter,

Catherine and Marie

Mindy folded the letter and put it back in the envelope. "So she's had the baby, and it's Marie."

I nodded. "Marie Ruth."

"I'll check the family tree when I get home, but I don't recall a middle name on there."

"Or a Woodson. I'm pretty sure it just had a first name." I smiled. "From all we've read though, it seems fitting. Ruth seems to have become more of a mother to her than her mother had been in quite some time."

She sat quietly for a while. "I wonder if Joel ever knew. Do you suppose she was ever able to send a letter to him?"

"Interesting idea." I looked over at her. "Did he ever settle and have an address long enough to write to her and for her to send him mail. There's the question."

"Hmm," she said softly, and nestled up against me. I put my arm around her and we both stared into the fire.

CHAPTER 35

The next time I saw Mindy was almost two weeks later. She'd been busy; I'd been busy; everything seemed to conspire against us getting together. We finally decided to meet for lunch in Los Gatos, about midway between her house and mine.

As always, it was difficult to park in Los Gatos, and I finally found a place about three blocks from the restaurant. I was about to about to take my coat, when I had to smile to myself. Here it was, the middle of January, with temperatures in the high sixties. I was wearing a light sweater, so I left the coat in the car. Only in California. I was whistling lightly to myself as I strolled down the sidewalk into downtown when I heard a voice.

"Hey stranger, wait up!" I turned just in time to see Mindy coming up behind me. "Didn't you see me back there in the parking lot?" I pulled in just as you were getting out of your car.

I took a few steps back and hugged her before giving her a very proper kiss on the cheek. We were in public, after all. "No I didn't," I responded. "I must have been daydreaming. About you, most likely."

She just laughed and punched me lightly on the chest. "Good answer!" Then she turned serious. "So where are we eating?"

"Just down the street here." I wrapped my arm around her shoulder and pulled her close to me. It felt good to feel her against me again. "The brewery."

She wrinkled her nose. "A brewery? Is that because you

know I love beer so much?"

"No," I laughed. "I'm sure you can get your diet Pepsi there. And they do have great sandwiches and an excellent selection of designer pizzas."

Lifting her eyebrows, she shot me a questioning look. "Designer pizzas?"

"Yeah," I hugged her again. "You know. Thai chicken with peanut sauce, or Mexican enchilada pizza, like that." I hugged her again. "I'm glad to see you. It seems like forever."

She smiled and leaned her head against my shoulder. "Me too."

§§§§

We skipped the designer pizzas. Instead, Mindy ordered an oriental chicken salad and I had a light veal marsala. Both were excellent. Mindy did not, however, skip the diet Pepsi. It was delivered just as she liked it, straight up, no ice. I wasn't about to leave a brewery without sampling one of their brews though, so had them bring me a dark ale.

When the drinks came, Mindy tasted the ale, made a face at me, and said, "You can't really like that stuff. How can anybody drink that?"

I fumbled. It was a very good ale. "It must be an acquired taste."

She just snorted. "Well don't ever plan on me acquiring a taste for that. Are you sure it isn't just used dishwater with a little brown coloring mixed in?"

I was insulted. "This is..." And then I saw her smile and paused. "Well if you don't want to share, there'll be more for me."

She laughed and sipped her Pepsi. "I brought something with me."

"A letter?"

She shook her head.

"You've been researching?"

A nod.

"What?"

"Records from San Andreas from the 1850's to 1870's."

"Really! What did you find?"

She reached into her purse. "There's not much, but I copied a few things. I think there's more in what it doesn't say than there is in what it does."

I cocked my head to one side and reached for the first paper. It was a newspaper article from the San Andreas Independent.

"DIED -- at San Andreas, Cal., April 21st, 1856, of a disease of the lungs, Jonathan Campbell, in the 27th year of his age, formerly of Fulton County, New York.

DEATH and BURIAL of a MINER -- In another column of the Independent, the death of Jonathan Campbell, a miner and shopkeeper, and a very worthy and laborious young man, for years a resident of this neighborhood, will be found chronicled.

His disease was bronchial infection, contracted by incessant toil and exposure in the cold weather."

There was more, telling of what a wonderful young man he was, how industrious, and how beloved he had been in the community. There was also a short poem about the fickleness of life at the end of the obituary, but I didn't need to read it. I looked at Mindy. "I didn't see any mention of Joel or Samuel."

"No," she responded. I couldn't find anything about either of them."

I was looking at the article. "I'd guess that he's the right one though. Name, age, place of birth all match."

"And he was a miner and shopkeeper."

"Do you suppose he kept mining after they moved to San Andreas?"

I shrugged my shoulders. "It's possible. They may all have." I looked back at the paper. "A disease of the lungs. They seem to say that it was something caused by working in the creeks in the wintertime. It would have been freezing cold."

She reached over and took back the article, and then folded it and slipped it back into her purse. I took a sip of my beer, not knowing quite what to say.

Mindy solved that. "It's kind of sad. I feel like we knew them."

I nodded. "Jonathan least of all, but still..."

"But still," she agreed, and then pursed her lips and wiped

away a small tear. She repeated herself in a whisper, "But still..."

I reached across the table and took her hand, squeezing it gently. "We talked about next weekend, maybe going down to Paso Robles for some wine tasting. I kind of feel like I'd rather go on up to San Andreas. Maybe see if we can find where he was buried."

She nodded her head, smiling sadly. "I'm sure we'll find wine there too." She looked up at me and took a deep shuddering breath. "I wonder if his mother ever knew what happened to him."

CHAPTER 36

We'd been walking around the old pioneer cemetery in San Andreas for nearly an hour when Mindy finally called out, "I think I've found something."

The place was pretty enough, in a rural sort of way. Mature oaks provided patches of shade throughout the rambling hillside. The day was sunny, and the rain that had fallen in recent weeks had prompted the growth of new green grass, lush enough in some places to nearly cover the stone markers. I ambled slowly over to a small depression between two trees, where Mindy was standing, trying to be careful to walk between the graves.

"Look here," she said. She was hunched down and used her hands to lift a broken stone. We'd long abandoned the ordered rows, and now were searching the perimeter, taking the time to scan both intact and broken markers. As she lifted the stone and brushed the underside, a spider ran off into the brush, and she shuddered, but retained her hold on the weathered granite. I could see where the base of the original marker still stood, its top broken off in a jagged line along an ancient fault. Lichen grew on both halves of the stone, making it difficult to read the writing, but I could clearly make out the name, 'Campbell.' Mindy had a rag in her purse, and used that to brush the dirt off the remainder of the stone. The letters had worn over time, but were still clear enough to read.

Jonathan Campbell
July 1, 1828 - April 21, 1856
Miner, Shopkeeper

Devoted Husband, Father, and Friend
May you rest with the angels

"We found him," I said softly. "You found him."

Mindy looked at me and nodded, and then lifted the stone almost reverently, leaning it against the original base. She used the rag to clean off the mud and debris that had accumulated over the years. After wiping for a few minutes, she said, "I had a water bottle in the car. Will you get that for me please?"

"Sure," I said, and walked down to the car. We'd picked up two bottles of water at the local store, and hardly touched them on our trip up to the cemetery, so I brought both of them. When I returned, Mindy had cleaned off the larger pieces of dirt and settled the stone securely at the base of the original marker. She smiled when I handed her the first of the bottles. "Thanks."

She sprinkled some water on the rag, and then cleaned the last of the soil off the stone. When she was done, the marker, though weathered, was clean, and Jonathan's name and message were clear for all to see.

I'd retrieved her backpack from the car when I went for water and now I handed that to her. She smiled at me and took the bag. She'd bought a bouquet of flowers when we stopped for water and now she took those out and laid them tenderly at the base of the marker. With that done, she stood and looked down at the grave. "He was so young. I hope he had a happy life."

"I hadn't known he'd married," I said.

"Or had children," she said wistfully. "I wonder what became of his family."

I smiled. "Another mystery to solve."

She looked up, smiled, and kissed me on the cheek. "For someone else."

She leaned against me then, and I put my arm over her shoulder, both of us still looking down at the flowers and the gravestone. "Our search for Joel seems to be leading to much more."

She smiled again, and then knelt to rearrange the flowers. Rising, she took my hand and led me back toward the car.

As we came over a small rise and looked out at the road, I could see a man standing by the gate to the cemetery, holding his horse by the bridle. He was older, and well weathered. If I'd had to guess from the sparse grey hair that peeked out from his stained brown cowboy hat and leathery face I'd have said that he was well into his 80's. We walked down toward him and I nodded, "Hi."

"We don't see many folks up in the old cemetery," he responded. "Got family up there?"

Mindy answered. "More like a friend of the family."

He cocked his head, begging more information.

She pointed back toward Jonathan's grave. "It's a long story. He was one of my great great grandfather's partners."

"And you came all the way up here just to put flowers on his grave? This partner of your what? Great great grandfather? Must be some kind of story in that."

She laughed. "Sounds pretty silly, doesn't it. Like I said, it's a long story."

He smiled for the first time, showing a mouth full of yellowed teeth with a gap where one of his canines should have been. "Time I have. I try to keep an eye on this place." He pointed to another corner of the cemetery, surrounded by a short wrought iron fence. I'd noticed it earlier, but decided to search the open areas first.

"Guess I'm the local historian. Most of my family's buried up there. Suppose I'll be up there someday too." He chuckled. "Not too soon, I hope!" Then he inclined his head toward the horse. "This is Callie. If you've got the time, I'd be interested in hearing about the old fellow. I keep a pot of coffee going all day long, and Mamie, she's my wife, bakes the best apricot pie in the county. There's one coolin' in the kitchen window right now. Interested?"

I wasn't quite sure what to say. We didn't really have any plans beyond visiting the cemetery. We'd talked about checking out the local museum again, but were pretty flexible. Mindy solved the problem. She reached out her hand.

"I'm Mindy and this is Charlie. We'd love to take you up on your offer."

The old fellow smiled and stretched out his gloved hand. "Sam." He pointed up the road. "See the barn up there?"

I looked and could just make out the top of a barn about half a mile away. I nodded.

"You two drive on up, and I'll follow behind on Callie. You'll see the driveway on the right." He gave a sharp nod of his head as if to dismiss us, and then turned to mount the horse. I looked at Mindy while Sam and Callie walked off down the road.

CHAPTER 37

"Well, what do you think?" I asked as we drove up the road.

"He seems nice enough, and we don't really have any plans."

I shrugged my shoulders. "Well he caught me with the apricot pie."

She chuckled. "Just like your grandmother used to make?"

"You never know. Could be." I smiled and squeezed her hand. We turned onto a gravel drive that led to a barn, and beyond that, a tidy yellow farmhouse. I pulled to the side to wait for Sam.

He wasn't far behind us. Within a minute or so, he came ambling along, heading for the barn. As he passed us, he pointed toward the house and yelled down, "Park over there, in front of the house. I'll be right over."

Sam left Callie in a corral next to the barn and met us at the front door. "I'll brush her down later. Meantime, let me introduce you to the wife." He opened the front door and yelled out, "Mamie, I've brought company." He motioned toward an old fashioned parlor, furnished in a combination Victorian-western style. I sat down on an antique horsehair sofa, and Mindy sat next to me.

Sam sat at a stool in the doorway and pulled off his boots, replacing them with fleece lined slippers. Mindy and I had changed out of our muddy shoes in the car, but still I felt the need to follow his lead and reached for my shoes. He waved me off. "Don't you worry about that. I've been out mucking out the stalls. Mamie'd have my hide if I came into her living room in those boots. Your shoes are just fine."

He poked his head into the kitchen just as a woman stepped into the doorway. I had to smile. Standing side by side, they were the perfect western couple. The weathered old man, skinny as a rail, and the plump white haired lady in a well worn calico dress, covered by a simple yellow apron. I flashed on my grandparents in their old farmhouse in Merced. And then I smelled the pie. I must have died and gone to heaven.

Mamie gave Sam a look that was half affection and half teasing. "You've picked up some more strays?"

"You betcha," he answered. "I told 'em I'd give them a cup of my coffee and a slice of your pie and they just followed me home." He grinned at us and then back at his wife.

"Well then, I'm Mamie," she sighed. "Make yourselves comfortable. Coffee?" she asked.

Mindy and I had stood when she came into the room, and now I said, "Thank you. Black."

Mindy walked over and said, "Can I help?"

"Absolutely," she said. "You can cut the pie. It should be cool enough."

Sam took a chair across from me. "So who were you checking out up there in the old cemetery?"

"Jonathan Campbell," I responded.

He screwed up his face. "Not sure I remember the name. Where's he planted?"

I smiled at his term. "He was up in the corner, uh, North West, under the old oak tree with the downed branch."

He looked out the window in the direction of the cemetery, as if trying to visualize the spot. "Can't say I remember seein' that stone, and I know that place pretty well. When'd he die?"

"1856," I answered him. "The stone had broken off and was lying facedown in the dirt. It looked like it had been that way for years."

"Well that'd explain it then. 1856. He was an old timer. This place was just gettin' started. My folks came around that time. A pretty wild time to be up in these hills."

"I imagine so. Lots of gold was taken out of this area."

He nodded nostalgically. "Lots of gold."

Just then, Mamie came in with two mugs of coffee. She put mine down on a battered pine table in front of the sofa and handed the other to Sam.

"Thank you," I said. I turned to Sam. "It smells delicious."

"I like my coffee," he said. "Like I said. I keep a pot on all day. You never know who might drop by."

I lifted the mug, cradling it in my hands and saw what seemed to be a look pass between Mamie and Mindy. Thinking nothing of it, I took a sip. It had to be the strongest coffee I had ever tasted in my life. I was pretty sure that if I'd had a spoon, it would have stood straight up in the mug. Trying to hide my grimace, I swallowed and looked again at Sam. "Thanks."

He'd taken a big gulp of the coffee, and when he put down the mug, I could see that it was already half empty. "I hope you don't mind it a little strong. Tastes better that way."

I had the impression he was measuring my manhood with his coffee, so I smiled again. "It tastes just fine to me."

"So who was this fellow you were visiting? Jonathan something?"

"Jonathan Campbell," Mindy responded. She'd sat down next to me with, I noticed now, a cup of weak tea. Mamie had the same.

He screwed up his face, thinking. "There were some Campbells here. Old timers. Moved out," he looked at his wife, "what, fifty years ago?"

She took a sip of her tea. "Probably. I went to school with a couple of them." She thought for a moment. "Jess and Sandy, I think. She nodded. Right. Jess and Sandy. Last I heard, Jess was a plumbing contractor down in Stockton. Sandy married one of the local boys and they settled up in West Point. Jimmy Blake. I was in her wedding. She and I still exchange Christmas cards." She smiled. "Of course, they'd be getting on by now."

"Bah," Sam responded. "You're not old. You're still my sweet young flower."

She looked at him, and then back to Mindy. "His eyes aren't as good as they used to be, but I don't mind too much."

Sam laughed. "So you say this Jonathan Campbell was your great great grandfather's business partner. I'd be interested in hearing how you managed to track him down." He furrowed his brow. "And why you were even interested!"

I looked at Mindy and she launched into the short version of the story. We'd told it often enough by now that it was easy to stick to the most important details.

Mamie and Sam listened attentively, and when Mindy got to the newspaper article about Jonathan's death, he nodded knowingly. "So you think this fellow might help you to find Joel."

Mindy shrugged her shoulders. "He's always been the one we didn't know much about. I don't know whether finding his grave will help the search for Joel, but I think we felt we needed to pay our respects."

Sam smiled and took another mouthful of his coffee. "I'm sure he'd appreciate that." I felt as if we'd passed another test. First the coffee, and now the purpose for our visit to the cemetery.

Mamie added, "That's so sweet. I'll have to mention that to Sandy next time I write. I'm not sure she even knew about his stone up there. Maybe she'll come visit."

"Maybe so," Sam said. "Tell her to bring her brother. Now that I remember him, he still owes me 10 cents for a wager he lost. About time he paid off." He looked at his wife and smiled. "You think that pie's about ready to be served?"

Mamie grinned affectionately at her husband and turned to Mindy. "This man has the worst sweet tooth I've ever seen. Shall we get that pie?"

As the ladies rose, Sam asked me, "You having any luck searching the old records?"

"Some," I said. "The county's been a little difficult, but the local museums have been helpful." I took a sip of my coffee and suppressed a shudder. If I wasn't careful, I'd be wired higher than a kite on the caffeine by the time we left. "You have any suggestions?"

Sam put down his cup and I noticed that the coffee was gone. "Well, like I said, I'm kind of the local historian for that cemetery out there. Have been for the past twenty years or so since I retired." He started to lift the cup, found it empty, and put it back on the magazine that served as a coaster. "I can tell you pretty much everybody who's buried out there, but not too much about any of them. I know my family, of course, back into the 1880's or so, and a few of the neighbors." He reached up and rubbed his chin, thinking. Just then we were interrupted as Mindy and Mamie came back in, each carrying two slices of pie on china plates.

Sam and I each stood and took a slice of pie. I'd been able to smell the aroma of tangy baked apricots since I'd first entered the room, but the intensity of it struck me with almost a physical force and I lifted the plate to my nose and inhaled. The pieces were actually quite small, but they brought a whole range of memories to mind and I sat back down grinning ear to ear.

Mamie giggled. "I hope you like apricot pie."

"I love it," I said. "My grandmother used to bring apricot pies when she visited. Lots of good memories." I sniffed again and said, "I don't remember the aroma being this pungent though."

Sam had taken a piece onto his fork, and before putting it into his mouth, said absently, "Mamie has an old family recipe. Some kind of spice, but she won't even tell me what it is." He grinned.

Mamie smiled at him and then to us. "I hope you like it. Like he says, it's an old family recipe."

I bit into the first piece. It was heavenly. Tart and sweet mixed perfectly with the delightful flavor of fresh apricots. The room went silent as we all ate pie.

Sam was the first to break the silence. He put his plate down and stretched back. "Mmm. That was good. Nothing like apricot pie and a cup of coffee." He looked at Mamie. "Speaking of which, is there more?"

She'd just lifted a tiny piece of pie on her fork. Now she motioned with her head. "There's more in the kitchen if you want it. Why don't you take your mug when you take in the plates." She smiled sweetly.

Sam nodded, his instructions clear. He looked at me, "Can I top off your coffee?"

"I'm good, thanks." He smiled knowingly and picked up our plates.

Everyone had finished except for Mamie, who left about half of her slice. She touched a dainty napkin to her lips and turned to Mindy. "So it sounds like this Joel of yours lived here in San Andreas."

"For a while. We've traced him here in the early 1850's. After that, we don't know anything."

Mamie called out to the kitchen where I could hear Sam rinsing the dishes. "Do you know of any Joel," she turned to Mindy, "Woodward was it?" Mindy nodded so she continued, "Joel

Woodward in the cemetery?"

Sam poked his head through the door, dishcloth in his hand. "No. No Woodwards at all." He looked down at the cloth disgustedly. "Just a moment and I'll be finished here."

I had to smile inwardly. The man who'd tested me with the high octane coffee was stuck washing the dishes.

When he came back in, he was carrying another mug of coffee. He sat and took a swig. Mindy was telling about how the three partners had bought the local general store. Sam listened for a while, and then broke in. "I remember my folks had a store, way back when. I used to have some pictures, could probably find them if you want. As I recall, they sold it some twenty years before I was born, so it's been gone for a while. Whole building's gone now." He scowled. "Put in a strip mall. Progress." He lifted the mug to drink again and added, "That's when they bought the ranch we're on now. Thirty-nine hundred and seventy five acres."

He took a drink and I asked, "Cattle?"

Nodding, he swallowed and put the mug down. "That's right. That and a few horses. My grandsons are in charge now."

I must have looked surprised because he added, "Oh, you won't see them here. They're over at the new section, out beyond the hill out back. This was the original farmhouse, being closer to town. With trucks, they can move around pretty easily, so they built a new metal barn with a concrete floor out near the highway. Not as romantic as the old relic here," he nodded toward the barn out front, "but easier to maintain and a lot more sanitary." He smiled proudly. "Sharp kids. They're making a go of it."

"When did your family come to San Andreas?" I asked.

He shrugged his shoulders. "1850's, I suppose. Just like hers. The first one was a miner, came out from back east. No money in that though." He looked around the room. "The early fellows did okay, but as the creeks got panned out, there wasn't much left. My great grandfather was a sharp man. He could see that the ones gettin' rich was sellin' supplies, so he got into that business."

Mamie spoke up now, "Sam, I think those pictures are in one of the albums in your desk." She looked at us. "If you'd like to see them."

"I'd love to," Mindy said. "Anything to help give us a feel for the time."

I added, "We've been wandering through the museums in the area, and that's helped, but seeing someone's family photos would be great. It would really personalize it much more."

Sam rose. "Just a bunch of old photos, but maybe they'll help you. Like I said earlier. One thing I do have now is time."

While Sam rumbled about in the other room looking for the photo album, Mindy asked Mamie, "So was your family one of the old time families here too?"

"Well, not as long as Sam's. They were among the founders. My folks came about the turn of the century. 1900, that is." She smiled. "Just had another. Imagine that. One hundred years."

"Anyway, my father was a mining engineer. By then, nearly all of the mining operations were pretty big. He helped design the shafts, and rail systems." She smiled fondly, "He always said that without engineers like him, it would be a lot more dangerous than it was."

"Did he work here in San Andreas?"

"Toward the end. Mostly Copper though," she said. "Excuse me, Copperopolis. Copper's what the locals call it."

We'd driven through Copperopolis on the way up the hill. "That's quite a ways."

"Oh yes," she replied. "Especially back then when there weren't many good roads. "We lived there for a while, and then for several years after we moved up here, he used to drive down for the week and back for the weekends. Said he liked life here better."

I nodded. "A long distance commuter before the days of long distance commutes."

Mamie just inclined her head. "My mother was a strong woman."

Suddenly, we heard a voice call out from the back of the house. "Found it."

Sam came back into the living room carrying a dusty old photo album. "I doubt that I've looked into this thing in the past ten years."

He was about to blow the dust off the cover when Mamie caught his eye and handed him a napkin. "I'll get a damp cloth, she said."

When the album was cleaned off, Sam came over to the sofa where he and Mamie squeezed in between us. He laid the album half on his and half on Mamie's lap and opened the front cover. The first several pages were a mixture of photographs and daguerreotypes. Most were stiffly staged, with participants staring seriously at the photographer.

"Do you know when these were taken?" Mindy asked.

Sam shook his head. "My mother had them in a box. A few had labels, but most were blank. I've filled in the names that I know, but quite a few of them are just photos of an earlier time. Nothing more."

I nodded. "Still, it is interesting to see them and think of them as your family album."

Mamie grimaced. "Ugh. To think that we're subjecting strangers to a showing of the family album."

Laughing, Mindy said, "And if you had family movies, it would be that much better. This is fascinating!"

Sam turned a page and pointed to a boy. "That's my grandfather there, and I assume that the man with his hand on his shoulder is my great grandfather." He took out the photo. It was dated, 1871, but that was all. I recognized the two in a few other photos, but again there were no labels. On another page, Sam pointed to a family shot. "I remember this one. It's labeled." He took out the photo and turned it over. "Let's see, where are my..." He frowned, and then walked over to a table by his chair and picked up a set of reading glasses.

Coming back, he said, "SallyAnn, Jonas, Walter, Sam Sr., Sam Jr.," he paused, "he was my grandfather. Sam's a family tradition." Then continuing, "Laura, Annie, Robert, Theodore, Alice, 1875. Whew. A good sized family."

"Are any of them still here?"

"Oh, yeah," he answered. There's a good smattering of cousins all around the area. Quite a few have moved out over the years, but there's still a good gathering at the summer barbecue."

He turned back to the photo album, replacing the photo and turning another page. "Ah. I know this one. My grandfather showed it to me. That was the old general store my great grandfather had."

Mindy gasped and reached out to touch the picture. She looked up at me. "Is that?"

I stared at the photo and nodded.

In a tremulous voice, she said, "I think we've seen this photo before."

Sam looked at her. "It's possible. I made copies for the museum several years ago. Didn't you say you'd been there?"

She nodded, but continued to stare at the photo. Then she said, "Is there anything written on the back of that one?"

Sam took out the photo. "Not much. Grandpa's store, 1857. Looks like my father's handwriting." He put the picture back.

I looked again. It was the same picture we'd seen in the museum, of the man in the white shirt and dark suspenders sweeping the front of a general store, presumably the only general store in San Andreas at the time.

My attention was broken by Mindy. In a voice that still reflected her shock, she said, "I'm sorry. I don't think we ever got your full name."

Sam looked at her. "It's on the mailbox. You must have missed it. Watkins. Samuel Watkins.

CHAPTER 38

Mindy sat, dumbfounded. She started to speak several times, but couldn't. Finally, Mamie reached over and took her hand. "Are you alright?"

She nodded. "It's just..." She shook her head and I answered for her.

"We're a little shocked to say the least. You see, Samuel Watkins was her great great grandfather's partner. They were miners and later bought the store in San Andreas together."

Now it was Sam's turn to be shocked. "You've got to be kidding me." He grinned. "Well if that ain't a kick in the pants." He reached over and shook Mindy's hand. "Partners!" Then he shook his head again, as if just beginning to register what she'd said. "So what was this great great grandpa's name again? Woodward did you say?"

Mindy nodded, still too stunned to speak. When her voice came out, it was quiet and unsure, like a little girl's. "Joel Woodward. They came west together. Joel was from Pennsylvania; Sam was from New York."

"Well you've got my attention now," he said. "When was that?"

"1850."

He nodded. "Sounds about right. From what I was told, Samuel, my great grandfather, that is, he ended up here sometime in the 1850's." He grinned. "It is indeed a small world!"

Mindy nodded, and we were all quiet for a long moment until

finally, Sam rose. "This calls for a celebration." He looked at me. "How do you take your bourbon?"

I hesitated. "Uh, straight up."

He nodded approvingly. "And Mindy?"

She shook her head. "I'm more of a wine drinker myself."

Guffawing, Sam reached into a cabinet beneath his desk. "I'm sure Mamie'll take care of you then." He pulled out a bottle and two glasses and poured a generous portion. "And you'll be staying for dinner. I need to hear more about this Joel of yours. I never heard a word about partners in the store."

Mindy and I exchanged glances as I took my glass. Catching the look in her eye, I nodded and then found my voice. "That's a very generous offer. We'd love to."

Sam looked over at Mindy again and said, "I hope you don't have any of those strange city vegetarian ideas. This is a cattle ranch. We eat beef!"

I chuckled and Mindy, just getting her bearings again, turned to Mamie. "How can I help?"

Dinner was sumptuous. The steaks were well aged, and then grilled perfectly on a big brick barbecue out the back door. Sam presided over the cooking, grilling corn on the cob next to the steaks while he nursed his bourbon. He'd offered to refill my glass more than once, but I declined and he seemed to nod approvingly. It seemed that a toast was one thing, but drinking for the sake of drinking was definitely another.

"I've always liked my bourbon," he said, "but just a little at a time." He'd took a tiny taste, and continued. "My old man wouldn't approve even of this. His folks used to complain that one of the worst mistakes this government ever made was repealing prohibition." Smacking his lips, he said, "but I don't see anything wrong with a little taste of bourbon now and then."

I nodded. "You know, we actually have a letter from Sam, your great grandfather."

"Really? Well how about that! I'd love to see it!"

"I doubt that Mindy's got it here. It's probably back in her place in Santa Cruz. She could send you a copy though."

"A letter from Samuel Watkins," he mused. He looked at me. "From the 1850's?"

"1850 exactly."

"I'll be darned. Musta come for the gold rush."

I grinned. "As I recall, he and his partners pretty much stayed away from alcohol."

He pursed his lips and nodded. "I wouldn't be surprised. No, I wouldn't be surprised by that at all. It's kind of been a family tradition."

He flipped the steaks, tossed a little salt and pepper onto them, and then added, "Any mention of his wife? I'd be interested in finding out about my great grandmother too."

How to get past this one, I thought. "Uh, we found a newspaper article in the Murphys paper about their wedding."

He looked at me, waving the spatula in my direction. "When was that?"

"Mid 1850's. I don't recall the exact date, but we have a copy of the article."

"I imagine it gave her name. I'd love to cross reference it."

"It did. I don't recall offhand though. We were mostly focused on Joel. But then, Mindy does have the article. I'll ask her to send that too."

"Huh," he mused and checked the barbecue. "She from New York too? He send for her after he got his stake?"

"From what I recall, she was local."

He looked at me for a while and then started talking to himself as if trying to figure out where she might have come from. "Now as I recall, the women either came married, or..." He broke into a big grin and started laughing. "Those rascals! It would seem the family bloodline might not be as pure as I was led to believe!" He laughed again, and raised his glass toward me in another toast. "Well good for them."

§§§§

The steaks were better than I'd anticipated, and after dinner, we sat sated in the parlor nursing an after dinner coffee and tea, thankfully prepared by Mamie instead of Sam. At one point, I'd mistakenly called the room a living room and been corrected by Mamie that in a traditional farmhouse, it was still a parlor. As I looked around now, I could see that this room, while supposedly the hub of the household, was in fact a room reserved almost exclusively for guests. The family generally gathered in the kitchen or the dining area in the back of the house.

Sam swallowed a mouthful of coffee, scowled as he found it much too weak for his taste, and said to Mindy, "Charlie tells me you have a letter written by my great grandfather, and an article about his marriage." She nodded and he continued. "I'd love to see them someday, if you can send me copies. I never knew the old man. I think he died about 1910, well before I was born, but I did hear stories about the old days here."

"I've got two letters actually."

I looked at her quizzically. I knew of the letter from Panama, but hadn't seen any others. Seeing my look, she smiled knowingly. "The one that Melissa found, in the museum. To his mother?"

I cocked my head. "Oh. That's right. I was thinking of letters to Catherine."

She patted me on the shoulder and turned to the others. "I'm sorry. Maybe I should explain. We've been reading the letters a couple at a time over the past several months, as we conduct other research. We met some people in Murphys who have been helping. One is a docent in the local museum and she found an undelivered letter to Sam's mother. Evidently the postmaster just threw it in a box"

"I'd sure like to get a copy of that one too!"

"Not a problem," she said. "I'll send copies as soon as we get home."

Sam nodded thoughtfully. "So what can you tell me about the old guy?"

Mindy glanced over at me, sipped at her tea, and said, "Not much more than we already have at this point. They came to California, and we think they mined near Sonora and Murphys before buying the store. Samuel seemed to be the leader. Or if not that, the biggest personality." She paused, glanced at me, and added, "I do have a letter with me if you'd be interested in hearing it. It's one of Joel's"

"Absolutely," he said.

Sonora, California
January 15, 1851

Dearest Catherine,

I know this says Sonora, but that is not really where we are. We have managed to put together three claims on a little creek that feeds into the Tuolumne River. We are actually about eight or ten miles southeast of Sonora, but it is the nearest town, with a population of a couple of hundred hardy souls along with a general store, hotel, and a few places to get a good meal.

It is winter here, as I know it is back home. The weather varies from bitter cold, with wind and rain and even a little snow, to bright and sunny, even comfortable to be outside without a hat and coat and then within days, snow again. It is a strange place.

We managed to get three adjacent claims, so we are working those every day now. Claiming land for mining has been a strange process. Many of the better claims were taken by the first to arrive, so that is why we are some distance up the river. Also, being here, we have gotten more land in our claim. I hear some of the claims in the best areas are a mere eight by eight feet. Imagine that! A man works the creek, stores his equipment, and lives in a tiny space like that, with another man on either side, working their sections of creek. How they avoid fights over gold in such confined quarters I swear I do not know. We have put together three claims of fifteen by fifteen feet, so have a little bit of room.

Initially, we panned for gold, wading out into the creek, filling a metal pan with soil from the bottom, and swirling it around to get the light material to drift up to the top so that we could remove it. At the end, only the heavy soil was left, hopefully laden with gold. We tended to pick up some dust, but not much, and a full day's labor for all three of us would yield only a small amount. It is difficult, back breaking work, standing knee deep in freezing water, bent over at the waist for hours on end, searching for that elusive golden speck.

One thing we have in abundance throughout this area are pine trees, meaning we have firewood to keep warm, and also a good source of lumber. We have just finished building a cradle and rocker. Using it is still hard work, but three men, working together, can sift through much more soil, hopefully increasing the gold yield. Time will tell, as we just put it to work yesterday.

My partners are dedicated working men, and I admit that I struggle at times to keep up with them as I am still weak from my bout with Yellow Fever. Sam has gone up and down the creek, talking with others and learning their techniques, and as I mentioned, he is our banker and set up an account for us at the Wells Fargo office. Jonathan is tireless, often standing in the creek from dawn to dusk, sifting the soil in his search for gold, so it is not surprising that he found our first nugget. It was not much, just about an ounce, but exciting nonetheless.

Finds like that make it easier to dip back into that cold water.

I think of you often, and remembering our short time in the glen back home keeps me going on the hardest days. I have taken to kissing the locket before turning in for the night, imagining that my kiss lands on your lips and that you can feel my touch.

I know how difficult it must be for you to have me so far away, as it is very hard on me, but remind myself that my goal here is to put together a small purse of gold, one that will allow us to get a good start on a piece of land back in Pennsylvania. I am confident that I am on my way to doing that.

By the time you receive this, the weather will have turned here, and I am sure I will be glad to work the cold water on hot days. Hopefully by then, I will also have a good account in the local Wells Fargo office.

You are in my dreams, my hopes, and my prayers. Know that you are loved.

Joel

Mindy put down the letter and looked around. Sam and Mamie seemed to muse quietly for a moment before Sam said, "So he was their banker. Makes sense. Everything I ever heard about the man indicated that he was a leader; an organizer. He was the mayor, councilman. He even ran for state assembly at one time." He rose and walked to an old photograph on the wall. "This was the house Grandpa Watkins grew up in. I can remember playing there occasionally as a child." He lifted the photo off the wall and brought it over to us. He pointed to a child sitting on the front porch. "That little fellow is me. You can see my folks, and back there on the swing, are my grandparents." He turned the photo over and read the back. "Watkins house, 1934." Nodding, he looked back to us. "It was kind of the family homestead. Sat on about five acres on the edge of town. My great grandfather built it and it passed down over the years. My grandparents still lived in it even after they bought the ranch." He smiled. "It had a great big basement where we'd get together for parties. Grandpa liked pool, and he had a pretty substantial pool table down there. A great place for a little tike."

"Is the house still there?" Mindy asked.

"No." He scowled as if the memory was distasteful. They sold it in about 1940. You probably drove by it on the way out here. There's a supermarket there now." He rehung the photo and stood, looking at it. "Oh well. I always preferred the ranch anyway. Too many people in town."

Pausing, he tasted his coffee and then mused, "So you have a letter from the original Sam Watkins. Always wished I'd had a chance to meet the old fellow."

"That letter you just read was 1851?" Mamie asked. Mindy nodded and Mamie continued. There couldn't have been much here then. A handful of ranchos, a few Indians."

"And gold miners," Sam added. "They started coming by the thousands. Called themselves 49ers."

"Still," she said, "It's not like there were family farms, businesses, all that. It was a pretty wild time. I suppose a man out here then would have had to be pretty strong, both physically and mentally."

"Well, a man still has to be strong," Sam muttered. "Especially in the ranching business."

Mamie looked at him over her glasses. "I suppose." Then smiling at Mindy, asked, "Can I get you another glass of tea?"

§§§§

Knowing that the drive to San Andreas would be relatively short, Mindy and I had decided to stay at the same bed and breakfast we'd enjoyed in our past visits to Murphys. Later that night, as we snuggled up in the big featherbed with her head on my shoulder, she commented sleepily, "Imagine finding Sam's relatives!"

I'd been dumbfounded, and replied, "So unlikely."

She had a way of stroking my earlobe that both soothed and aroused me, and she was doing that now. I kissed her brow, and enjoyed the sensation as she mused, "I wonder if we'll find any of Joel's relatives here."

I took a deep breath, considering the possibility. "I suppose we could search for his last name."

She shook her head softly. "I already have. There aren't any here." Pausing for a moment, she snuggled in closer. "Of course, if he married here and had daughters,..."

I nodded. "It's possible, especially if he never thought he'd be going back."

Suddenly, Mindy jumped up. "I almost forgot. I have

another letter from Catherine. I was planning to read it tonight, but then with everything that happened, I completely forgot. Let me get it. She crawled out of bed and ran through the dark to her purse. Leaning over, she fumbled in the bag, then said, "Dang. Can't see a thing." She turned on the little antique table lamp and resumed her search, quickly finding the envelope she was seeking. Turning, she caught my eyes and frowned at me. "Enjoying the view?"

When she'd jumped out of bed, I'd laid back on the pillow, hands behind my head, and watched her search. She'd slipped into bed directly from her shower, taking the time only to roughly towel off before sliding under the covers, and now, breasts swaying in the dim light as she swiveled back toward me, presented a delightful view. I nodded. "Very much so. If you want, you can just keep dancing around over there while I watch." I paused. "Or you could come back to bed." I opened the covers. "It's a lot warmer here next to me, and I know how you like your warmth."

She scowled. "I'm so glad you're willing to make that sacrifice for me."

"Any time, my dear," I replied, grinning. I patted the bed and she hurried back under the covers. Taking the letter from her hand, I put it on the night stand. "Let me warm you up first," I said.

It took a little effort, but after about an hour, she was finally warm again, and I suggested, "Were you planning to read? I've been waiting."

She glared at me and shook her head, muttering about men, and then reached for the letter. As she rolled back onto the bed, letter in hand, I reached over to pull her close but she pushed me away. "I wouldn't want to distract you and keep you waiting again."

I tried mentioning that I only wanted her warm, and made an attempt to reach for her again, but she slapped my hand. "I'll just stay over on this side and read the letter. You keep your hands to yourself over there."

March 27
Bradford, PA

My husband,
Robert came and picked us up last month and I have just been too busy to write. Marie and the farm have consumed all of my energy.

Ruth kept saying that she would simply close up the house in Pittsburgh, and didn't need much, but she certainly filled up Robert's wagon. Much of what she brought though, was her canning, and the storage from her root cellar, so we will all be well fed in the months to come.

According to Robert, Tom wanted to come, but pressing business at the farm was going to keep him there, so he sent Robert. And of course, it was another joyous reunion! Robert packed my meager belongings into just two trunks, one for me and one for the baby, and then tied everything down, and off we went. He only spent one night in Pittsburgh, so it was a quick trip for him, but he needed to get back right away as it is almost planting season. Ruth has a neighbor who will watch over the house, and she has told them to rent the place out if they can find a nice family. I am not sure about the details, as I really was not paying much attention.

Interestingly, when word got out that we were leaving for Bradford, we had a parade of visitors, come to wish us well, and cluck about the baby. Of course, some avoided us. Those ladies, notice that I say, ladies, as they certainly act as if they are everyone's betters, have made a point of staying away or snubbing us whenever we have gone to the general store or even for a walk with Marie in the pram. I suppose that would have bothered me at one time, but after spending time with Ruth, and especially after hearing her share some of their secrets, well I can do without them just fine.

I found out about Tom's important business when we got to Bradford. He had been inquiring about putting Marie into an orphanage. He visited one outside of town, and even went to a judge to get the proper papers. You can imagine that we exchanged words. I will not tell you what I said, because it embarrasses me just to think of it, but I certainly did not comport myself as a proper lady. Tom insisted that it would be for the best, that I could never get on with my life as the mother of a bastard child, and that we certainly could not raise the child in town. "Think of what the neighbors will say," seemed to be his argument. That sent me off the edge and I said some things that I do wish I had held back. But Marie is not a bastard child, as Tom so heartlessly called her, and regardless of what those church folk might say about our minister, I have decided that I am absolutely married to you. That will not change. Anyway, our exchange ended with me in tears and my brothers, except Tom, hiding. And no, they were not a woman's tears. They were tears of fury. In the end, Tom was shocked and backed down. Later on, I looked to Ruth for guidance, but she just smiled at me and went back to her knitting. I do suppose I have picked up some of Aunt Ruth's independence. She told me a couple of days later that Robert and the others have given me a nickname, one they probably will not share with me, or *with Tom for that matter. At first, I was offended, but the more I think about it, the more I like it. They call me 'mama bear.'*

In the past month, Tom and I have made our peace. It was not easy, as we both said things that were hurtful, but he seems to have come to accept us as a part of the household. Still, we tread lightly around one another. I suppose I am a little frightened of him as the older brother and boss of the family still, and now that I have shown my temper, he is a little more careful around me. It is better, but it is not a happy house by any means.

I miss you desperately; your touch, and the nearness of you. I suppose having you absent has forced me to be more outspoken, but it is not a side of my personality that I am comfortable with yet. Maybe if we had both stood up to Tom it would have been better, or maybe worse. I can not be sure. But back in the quiet of our room, I would like to think that we would be a team, and I really do not have anyone who supports me unconditionally now. Well maybe one, Marie. Ruth will always be there for me, but it is not the same.

I long for your voice as much as I do your touch.

Your loving wife, Catherine

Mindy folded the paper and returned it to the envelope on the night stand. "Interesting," she said. "From Pittsburgh to Bradford, and from Tom wanting an orphanage to truce in the house, all in one letter."

"It's been a couple of months," I added.

"True. I imagine she's been pretty busy, moving, taking care of an infant, and all the rest."

She was still against her edge of the bed, wrapped up tight in the down comforter, and I made another effort to sidle up next to her, in part for the contact, and in part because in wrapping herself in the comforter, she'd pulled most of it over to her side, and my backside was freezing in the winter cold. She gave me a warning glance and I stopped. "I thought you might be cold," I tried lamely.

"Just fine thanks." She reached up and turned off the bedside lamp. "Good night."

"It is a little chilly in the room."

"Not for me," she replied, and I could hear the laughter in her voice. "I'm nice and toasty."

"Uh, I thought maybe you'd like to share the comforter. You may not have noticed, but I'm mostly just covered by the sheet."

"It's a good thing then that you don't get cold."

I gritted my teeth. She wasn't making this easy at all. "I don't very often, but I would be grateful if you'd share the comforter with me so that I can keep you warm."

She rolled over. "I'm sorry, I didn't hear that. Did you say something about being cold?"

I could just make her out in the dim light. Still, I focused on her face and said, "You are an evil person!"

I may not have been able to see very well in the dark, but I could feel the bed shiver with her silent laughter. "Me? Is that how you plan to get me to share this nice warm comforter? Calling me evil?" She sighed. "It is very cozy." She rolled over again, pulling more of the comforter around her, leaving me with just the sheet, and not even much of that. "I'm glad that that you don't feel the cold. A night like this could be pretty unpleasant."

I tried pulling part of the comforter toward me, but that didn't work at all, as she just grabbed it tighter around her. I gave up. "Ok. You win. I'm cold. May I please have some of the comforter?"

She rolled back toward me, "Did I hear you say you were cold?"

"Yes. I am cold."

She chuckled. "Well why didn't you say so." She opened the comforter and invited me in. It was delightfully warm. She gave me a kiss, and then rolled over so that I could spoon against her back. "I certainly wouldn't want you to be cold," she said.

CHAPTER 39

Mindy and I spent the next morning searching the local museums and libraries, but found nothing about Joel. Just before lunch however, we did come across an article about the founding of the San Andreas Temperance League in 1856. Among the founding members were Mrs. Samuel Watkins and Mrs. Jonathan Campbell. No first names were given, as I imagine was customary at the time. Still, it was further evidence that they and their husbands had become leading citizens of San Andreas by then.

We stopped for lunch at noon. We'd started early, and not wanting to waste any time, had skipped breakfast, so were both hungry. I'd noticed a little hole in the wall restaurant in the older part of town, 'The Hungry Miner.' I didn't know whether it would be good or not, but it seemed to fit the theme of experiencing the old days.

Picking up the menu, I said, "So what do you think? This place look okay?"

Mindy looked around, scanning walls. They seemed to be built from salvaged barn wood, and were covered with an assortment of vintage mining and farming tools, the rust attesting to their age. She smiled. "Probably not haute cuisine, but it'll be interesting."

A minute later, the waitress came over. She seemed as much a fixture of the restaurant as the tools. Outfitted in a denim dress covered with a clean white apron, her greying hair tied back in a ponytail, she looked as if she might have fit in one of the old photos. "Hi, I"m Sandy. Are you ready?" She had her order pad in one hand

and pen in the other, and I guessed that most people didn't dawdle over their menus. I ordered two iced teas and water and then asked for recommendations.

She smiled. "It depends upon what you like. The Miner's Special is good. Pretty much anything you get that's grilled will be good. That's Willie's specialty. His pulled pork sandwich is a local favorite too." She leaned in and whispered. "I don't know what you like, but I'd stay away from the salads. Pretty much iceberg lettuce and a tiny slice of tomato."

I knew Mindy had been leaning toward a salad. She frowned and pointed to an item on the menu, "How about the trout tacos?"

She nodded. "If you like trout, they're pretty good. Some people don't like trout, and then they're disappointed, but hey, if you don't like trout, don't order it." She shrugged her shoulders. "I take them home for the kids sometimes, and they seem to love 'em. He makes a great salsa to go with 'em. Spicy."

"Well I think I'm ready. I looked at Mindy, questioning. She looked up at Sandy. "I'll try the trout tacos. Does the salsa come on the side?"

Sandy jotted a note and nodded. "Spicy or mild?"

"Definitely mild," Mindy said.

Then she turned to me. "And for you?"

"I'll take a Miner's Special. Can he cook that medium?"

She smiled. "I'll see. Willie's pretty particular. He serves it the way he thinks it'll taste best." I scowled and she laughed. "Don't worry. It'll be good."

"Okay then, can I get you anything else?"

We both shook our heads and she headed up to the window to place our orders. She called back into the kitchen, and a moment later an older man poked his head out. They exchanged a few words, and he came out to our table. The man didn't really fit my image of a restaurant cook. His grey hair was clean, but flowed well down his back, and his full beard must have hung half way down to his navel, partially covering an apron that read, "Don't Mess With The Chef. He's Cooking Your Food!"

He looked at me. "You order the Miner's Special?"

I nodded. "That's right."

"Well here's the deal. I cook my burgers medium rare. It just seems to taste better that way. So that's the way I'm going to cook yours. Okay?"

"Um..."

"But if you don't like it, you let me know. I'll slap it back on the grill for you and ruin it your way."

"Sure," I said.

"All right then." He turned and left. I thought I could make out some muttering about city folk who thought they could have anything their way.

We were city folks, no doubt about it, and that was confirmed to us by our tour of the walls. Mindy recognized a few of the tools and I could place several others, but many were mysteries to us. Worst of all, I couldn't even tell whether some were used for mining or farming, or both, or neither. She pointed to one. It seemed to be a long metal rod, about three feet long. One end flared out a bit while the other was rounded. "What do you suppose that one is?"

"I'm not sure," I said. "Do you suppose it was some sort of pick, and they beat on one end to loosen rocks?"

"Could be," she replied.

There was a rocker and cradle assembly in the corner, and while we waited for our meal, we inspected it. "This must be what they built when they were in Sonora." We looked at it, and I tried to imagine three young men using it. It was essentially a large box, set up on a cradle. Inside the box, screens of different sizes served as sifters of sorts, allowing ever smaller rocks to fall out. One man might be pouring in soil and water, another slowly rocking the contraption back and forth, and a third checking the slurry for signs of gold. "Compared to that pan we saw in Murphys, this would have saved a lot of work."

Mindy had moved on to a collection of photographs on the back wall that showed San Andreas in the early days. I joined her and noticed almost immediately that the old photo of Sam sweeping the front porch of the general store had made its way to this wall as well. I was about to comment when Sandy came out with our lunches.

I had to admit that the Miner's Special was excellent just the way it was cooked. The burger was served open faced on a sourdough roll, and covered in cheese, onions, and peppers. The secret though, seemed to be in the barbecue sauce that Willie later admitted he kept tinkering with. The salad on the side was simple, just as advertised - iceberg lettuce with a tasteless slice of tomato. I was midway through my burger when I first came up for air, and noticed Mindy pouring a little salsa on her trout taco. "How's yours?"

"Good," she said. "I can see why people who don't like trout wouldn't like it because it definitely has that flavor." She favored me with a grin. "But I do like trout, and it's really good, especially with the salsa. You ought to taste it."

I looked at mine. Then I looked at hers. Then back at mine. Then at hers. I could tell that even though I didn't want to mar the taste of my burger, I should maintain peace by tasting the trout so I reluctantly cut off a small slice of mine and took a piece of hers. She was right. It was quite good. Then I went back to the Miner's Special. Mine was better, especially after I got the trout flavor out of my mouth.

We'd finished and I got up to pay the bill when Willie came out again. "Well, will you be sending that back?" He gestured toward my obviously empty plate.

"You were right," I admitted. "It was excellent."

"Glad you liked it," he beamed. "By the way, I noticed you checking out the old rocker and cradle over there. Want it?"

I must have looked confused because he laughed and continued. "It's for sale." He swept his arms around to take in the walls. "Everything in here is for sale." He paused for a moment and smirked. "For the right price."

"Thanks," I said, "but I don't think I've got a place for it."

"Yeah, not too many do. If you're interested though, I've got some old nick-nacks in that box by the register." He turned back toward the kitchen, then looked back. "Sandy'll show you. Enjoy your day."

I watched his retreating figure and thought about the variety of people that one meets. Here was this man, an accomplished cook, working a tiny restaurant, and looking like he'd just come in from panning for gold. Well, cleaner. I shook my head and went to the register.

Sandy took my money and showed us to a small wooden box next to the register. As Willie had said, it was full of nick-nacks, although to be more honest, most of what she had was junk. I motioned for Mindy to come over and look. She left some bills on the table, and then joined me.

"Willie seems to think that we might be interested in some of the treasures in this box.

She wrinkled her nose. "Looks like it's ready for the trash can." She started to signal me to go, but I'd picked up an old broken pocket watch and was checking it out.

"My grandfather had one of these," I said. I pointed to the manufacturer's name. "Look. Waltham. I think that was the brand he had." I could see where the cover had broken off, and the stem was obviously bent. I tried to wind the watch, but it wasn't going to work. "Interesting. I wonder who it belonged to." Looking back up at Mindy, I continued, "Maybe one of the old miners. Probably a story about him too!"

Mindy had found a chipped perfume jar and held it up for my inspection. Its age was given away not only by the wear, but by the multiple air bubbles that had formed in the glass when it was blown. "Probably very nice at one time." She smiled. "And there's likely a story behind this too!"

I chuckled, and then seeing a piece of paper at the bottom, reached down to retrieve it. It turned out to be a simple manila envelope, and I was about to toss it back in, but decided to see what treasures it held. I dumped the contents on the counter, and was rewarded with a variety of receipts, some of which dated back only a few years, along with a paper-clipped bundle of old newspaper ads, "Rolaids for 19¢," and a stack of picture post cards. I started repacking the envelope when Mindy stayed my hand.

"What," I said, turning to her.

She reached out and spread the cards on the counter. Among the color post cards that clearly came from the 50's and 60's, were a few that were sepia tinted, and seemed older. She gingerly picked out one card and lay it in front of us. "That's the store!"

I bent down to inspect the card. It sure seemed to be the same store shown in the photo, but the image was so small that it was hard to be sure. Mindy must have thought the same, because she took the card from me and walked over to the picture of the store on the wall. Holding it up, I could see that she was right. The store looked exactly the same, right down to the angles of the awning and the implements in the window. There were three men standing out front on the porch this time, all dressed alike with aprons over dark pants and white shirts, and all wearing ties. The man in the middle, holding a broom and smiling for the camera looked just like the man sweeping in the photo on the wall.

Mindy beamed, "That's got to be Samuel."

"And the others?"

She took the photo to our table in the front window where the light was better. "I'll bet they're Joel and Jonathan." Now that we'd moved over to the light from the window, we could tell that it was definitely the same store, though the image was much smaller and suffered from the limitations of nineteenth century photo clarity.

"Look at this," she said. "Is that writing?"

She angled the photo to take best advantage of the light, and I could just make out what appeared to be pencil marks at the bottom of the photo. The man in the middle was labeled, "Samuel Watkins." Above and to the left read, "Jonathan Campbell," and to the right was, "Joel Woodward."

Mindy and I stood rooted to the spot, staring at the face in the photo. We'd found her great great grandfather in the most unlikely of places. She turned the photo, bringing it closer to her face. "Do you think we could enlarge it?"

"Probably," I said. "It'll be grainy, but I would think so. If you scan it onto your computer and use some good photo processing software, you might be able to restore it pretty well."

She took the photo and stared at the face of her long lost relative for a while longer. When she tipped it up to the light again, I noticed the back. We'd been so focused on the picture, it had never occurred to us to look at the reverse side. "Hey, look," I said. There's writing here.

Mindy flipped over the postcard and laid it on the table again. The print was very light, again the product of a pencil, but I could make out a few words. Mindy angled the card to the light and stepped up to the window to see it. Suddenly, her eyes went wide. "Look!" she exclaimed.

I stepped behind her and looked over her shoulder. The writing was clearer now in the bright light, and the address was easy to read,

Catherine Woodward
Bradford, Pennsylvania

CHAPTER 40

We walked back to the counter, carrying the card. Mindy picked up the others, scanned the photos in them and compared them with the one we'd just found, and then stuffed them back in the manila envelope. I called out to Sandy. "We'll take this one."

She came over, looked at the card, and said, "I suppose we can let you have that one for, let's say, a dollar. Sound okay?"

"That'd be great," Mindy nodded, and took out her purse. "Would you have any more?"

Sandy shook her head. "Every once in awhile somebody drops off a batch of old junk and Willie buys it. We never know when it's going to happen or what it's going to be." She looked wistfully at the tools on the walls. "Sure you can't use any of those?"

I shook my head as Mindy slid the postcard into her purse. "I wouldn't know what to do with most of them, and I don't want any of them cluttering up my walls."

Sandy nodded then muttered, "Yeah. I know what you mean."

§§§§

We'd passed a park down the street, and Mindy made a beeline to one of the benches. It was in bright sunlight, and as soon as she sat, she took out the card. I slipped down beside her and watched as she turned the card back and forth.

She looked up at me. "I was hoping we could read it in the

sunlight.

"Maybe," I said. She was holding the picture so that it caught the full light, and it was quite a bit easier to read the penciled in names at the bottom. She turned it over. The writing on the back was faint, but we could still see the address clearly. I read,

"Dear Catherine,

No more mining for us. With the gold we banked, we have been able to purchase the general store in San Andreas. You can see us out front. I have labeled everyone so you will know who's who.

I have a business and a home here now, and we both know that there is nothing for me in Pennsylvania. Please come. You can write me in care of the postmaster in San Andreas, California.

Your faithful husband,

Joel

"Wow," I said slowly. "He's asking her to come to him." Mindy nodded, lost in thought, and I continued, thinking aloud. "Is there a date anywhere on the card?"

She turned it over and over. Finally, in the upper left corner above the letter, she found scribbled lightly, "22 August, 1853."

"So he'd been gone for three years."

"And Marie would have been two and a half years old."

She looked at me. "But she never got the letter."

I hadn't been thinking of that and looked quizzically at her. "Um..."

"No stamp," she said. "And it's here. And we can be pretty certain that she never traveled to California."

"You're right." I looked above the address column. From the torn bits of paper sticking there, it was clear that there had been a stamp at one time, but it was gone, and the card had never been postmarked. "I wonder what happened."

She just shook her head. "I'm not sure we'll ever know." Then looking off into the trees ahead, mused aloud, "Why would somebody peel off the stamp?"

CHAPTER 41

We'd scheduled our trip to overlap a Monday, so that we could search the public records, but were unable to find anything new. Disappointed, we drove home and arranged to meet about two weeks later for a picnic at the beach in Asilomar State Park down on the Monterey peninsula.

Even though it was still February, we were experiencing an early spring, with glorious sunny days and temperatures in the high sixties. It was perfect weather for a little tide pool exploration.

We found a parking place right next to the beach, climbed down the gentle cliff face, and hiked across the sand to a tumbled outcropping of rocks. Mindy had organized this adventure, and now, leading me by the hand, pulled me out onto the rocks. "The tide's out right now," she said. "It should be a great time to see what's living out here."

I could see a number of pools, but surprisingly few signs of life in them. As we walked further out, to where the waves were breaking against the rocks, I continued to look into the pools, but was disappointed. Sure, there were quite a few small insects and the like, but few fish or other larger creatures. The last time I'd really been out to the tide pools, I reflected, I'd been much younger, and hiking along the cliffs of San Diego, some five hundred miles to the south. There the pools had been virtually teeming with life, from small fish, to anemone, to the occasional crab scuttling along the bottom. I could even remember the abalone fastened to the side of some of the rocks. Here I saw precious little. Of course, the water was much cooler here, but still.

Finally, Mindy stopped, far enough out on the rocks that they'd definitely catch the wave action. She entwined her arm around my waist and leaned her head against me. Sighing, she said, "You're still in trouble."

I looked down into her face and could see just the glint of a smirk in her eyes. "Still?" I asked.

She nodded.

"How can I get in trouble for what I didn't do? My motives were pure!"

She shook her head, as if dismissing all of the frailties of men.

I'd arrived at her house with flowers and a bottle of Pinot Noir, ready for the adventure at the beach. I rang the bell, and then waited longer than usual for Mindy to answer the door. When it finally crept open, she was hidden behind it, peeking out only her head, while motioning me inside. Curious, I stepped in and walked to the kitchen, careful to remove my shoes before stepping onto her clean carpet. Once there, I put the wine on the table, and then turned and asked, "Do you have a vase for the roses?"

Mindy had closed and stepped out from behind the door by then, and I noticed that she was dressed in an apron, and from the looks of it, only an apron. I stepped over and wrapped my arms around her. Sure enough, I thought, as I hugged her and ran my hands down her back and onto her naked buttocks, only an apron. I stepped back, holding her by the shoulders, and then kissed her forehead. A whole range of thoughts went through my mind. Was this my lucky day, and she had decided upon some kind of strange apron fantasy with the stranger at the door? Or was she cooking and didn't want to get her clothes dirty? Or had she just gotten out of the shower when she heard the doorbell and grabbed the closest piece of clothing, an apron? Or was this really, as I mentioned before, my lucky day? Decisions, decisions.

I continued to hug her while I mulled the possibilities. After all, hugging a half naked woman while trying to solve a dilemma wasn't a terrible way to spend my time, and even if it wasn't my lucky day, at least I'd get in a good voyeuristic hug. Finally, I decided to play it safe. I backed away and smiled. "You lost your pants."

She nodded and I continued. "I'll get the vase, since you probably don't want to be climbing the stepladder with me behind you right now."

I turned back into the kitchen to the flowers, the vase, the scissors, and the water. And that's where the trouble began.

"I meet you at the door wearing nothing but an apron and all you can do is give me a quick pat on the butt and then cut the flowers?"

"Uh,"

She stared at me and I could see that I'd definitely made the wrong choice. I tried back peddling. "I, uh, didn't want to offend you by jumping to conclusions."

"Jumping to conclusions?"

"Uh, just in case you'd just gotten out of the shower or something?"

"And if I'd just gotten out of the shower, why would I put on an apron, which I keep in my kitchen, instead of the robe that hangs in my bathroom?" she stared at me and I began to wilt.

"Or might have been cooking?"

"Of course," she scowled sarcastically, "because you know that I always cook in the nude." As she said it, it seemed to make a lot less sense than it had before.

"Uh, so this was kind of a fantasy thing?" I tried.

"Well you have part of it right," she stated flatly.

I looked at her with a sheepish grin and stepped over to take her back into my arms. Maybe I could still save the day. "Part?"

As soon as I stepped in her direction, she put up her hands and warded me away. "That's right. It was part of a fantasy. It isn't any more." She turned toward the stairs.

"Well now that I understand," I started. I stepped toward her again, and started to follow her upstairs.

She whirled back at me, venom in her voice now. "Don't you dare come up here. There is nothing for you upstairs."

"But..."

"No buts or butts for you." She turned back up the stairs, intentionally wriggling her cute little fanny when she rounded the corner. At the top, she yelled down from the landing outside her bedroom. "I'll be down in a minute, as soon as I'm dressed. Don't you even think of coming up here."

§§§§

Back at the beach, I continued to look out at the waves, crashing against the furthest rocks, and sending water swirling around the low lying pools at our feet. "I'm really still in trouble? What will it take to get out?"

She shook her head as if I was the most clueless man she'd ever met. "I don't know yet. I'll let you know when I think of it."

She knelt down and peered into one of the pools. "I think I saw some hermit crabs." A shell moved and she shot out her arm to point. "There. See it scuttling along?"

I squatted down and looked in just as a few other crabs started to move, and just as a larger wave broke against our rock, showering us with spray. Well that's not entirely accurate. It showered me with spray, but since I was leaning over her shoulder, she was almost entirely protected. I shuddered and jumped up. "Argh," I shouted as I shivered. "Cold!"

She moved a little further inland as protection against the next wave while I stood shocked by the freezing water. I could tell from the heaving of her shoulders that she was almost convulsive with silent laughter. "Okay," she giggled, "That's a start."

I stared at her for a moment before gingerly making my way across the rocks. At least one fair thing had happened. In the warm sunshine, my clothes would dry fairly quickly, and my sneakers were waterproof. I watched her make her way back to the beach, squishing along in her sodden shoes.

CHAPTER 42

Mindy had chosen the restaurant, a continental place on the peninsula with paella as a specialty. Fortunately, we'd each brought a change of clothes, so our sandy, wet beach adventure hadn't left us unfit for fine dining.

She'd raved about this place several times over the past several months, and as I'd never tasted paella, had insisted that we each order a bowlful. I was a little surprised, given that we frequently shared a meal. I had heard that paella was especially rich, so figured that we wouldn't be eating much, but she'd quelled my question by saying, "It's so good that I want to take some home." That made sense, so we settled in to wait for our meal over a couple of glasses of pinot noir.

§§§§

The paella was excellent; the wine calming; and the French country atmosphere of the restaurant enchanting. Still, being a clueless man, I couldn't help but digging my hole a little deeper. The waiter boxed up both plates of paella into a single carton for us to take home, and I sat, pleasantly digesting the paella and swirling the last of the pinot in my glass, when Mindy asked, "So would you get it again?"

"Here?"

"Yes," she answered. "Here."

"I don't know. It was very good, but I might want to try the Oso Buco next time." No sooner had I finished, than I knew that was the wrong answer. I tried to backpedal, but it was too late.

"You didn't like it?"

"Oh, no. It was wonderful."

"But you wouldn't order it again?"

"I'm sure I would."

"But you just said you'd try the Oso Buco."

I hemmed and hawed. "Uh, I figured that anyplace that cooked the paella that well was worth further exploration, and I like Oso Buco."

She swiped at her lips with a napkin and said, "So you didn't like it well enough to get it again."

I could tell by now that there was no right answer. I caved. "If we come here again, I will definitely get the paella."

"Even though you don't like it." She stared at me and continued. "I doubt that I'll waste this place on you again since you didn't like the paella."

Just then, I saw the waiter out of the corner of my eye. "Do you have a dessert menu?"

He was most accommodating, and we quietly shared an almond soufflé.

Later that night, Mindy cuddled against me on the couch. Evidently, time and the sweet soufflé had worked their magic, and I was at least partway out of the dog house. Still, I was careful. I kissed the top of her head and stroked her shoulder. "Friends?" I asked.

She chuckled softly. "Of course." She snuggled in a little closer. "Did I give you a hard time?"

Everything in my being was screaming, "YES!" Cautiously though, I said, "There were a few moments."

From where I was sitting, I could look down at her curls, but couldn't really see her face. Still, I could swear she was grinning. "You mentioned on the phone that you had another letter from Catherine."

"Mm," she whispered. "Two letters actually." She sat upright and reached for the coffee table. The letters were waiting there under one of the coasters. I recognized the envelopes, the same style that she'd used before. And as before, they bore no stamps. I hadn't thought much of that previously, but now we seemed more attuned to the fact that their correspondence was largely one sided. I was surprised then, when Mindy shook out a third letter from between the two. "And one from Joel."

April 29, 1851
Bradford, Pennsylvania
My Dear Husband,
Happy Anniversary!
Is it as difficult for you as it is for me to realize that we have been married for a year now? I suppose that some would say that we are no longer newlyweds. And yet we never even got to be newlyweds. I have thought of you all day, and those thoughts have put a smile on my face while I did the laundry and baked a pie for dinner this afternoon.

Marie is a healthy, happy baby. She has started to coo and is the cutest little thing you could ever imagine.

Tom and Robert and the others have been working long days in the fields, preparing the soil for planting. The snow is just about gone, and it is muddy, but a farmer's work never ends, they say.

Anyway, after eating our mid-day meal a couple of weeks ago, Marie lay in her basket, fussing. I had just fed her, so I knew that was not it, and then Robert picked her up. She immediately quieted, and reached for his beard. I had not thought about it before, but generally Ruth or I have held her, and she has had little contact with the men. And with you in California, she has not even had a father to play with. She had never had the opportunity to play with a beard, so she reached out and grabbed a good handful of whiskers, and then tried to pull them toward her. Robert hollered, and Marie squealed, and pretty soon they had turned it into some kind of game. She would pull, he would shake and growl, and hoot, and then they would both convulse with laughter before beginning the whole thing again. I think at first, she was scared, but with all the rest of us laughing, she could tell that it was all right. He ended up bouncing her on his knee so that she giggled and then raised her arms for more. Finally, Tom spoiled the fun by reminding everyone that the furrows would not cut themselves and sending them back out to the fields.

And then last night, the miracle happened. I call it that anyway. I suppose that is why I am writing today. Raising a baby has been harder than I could have imagined, and now that I am back at the farm, I feel that I have to help out with the chores, whereas in town, Ruth pretty much told me that my only job was Marie. So I have been exhausted. I must admit that the others have told me to back down, and do less, but it is hard, with so much to do. Anyway, I was so tired last night that I can barely remember nursing Marie and falling into bed. I do not know why I woke later; maybe because it was so quiet. I have gotten used to Marie's little cooing noises, and I did not hear anything. At first, I panicked. I jumped out of bed and ran to her cradle but she was not there. So I ran into the hall and could see the flicker of a candle downstairs.

It was Tom. He was rocking back and forth in my mother's old wooden rocker, cradling Marie in his arms. When I got to the parlor, I could see that he had a bowl of warm goat's milk, and was dipping a tea towel in it, feeding her. And that little piglet was suckling on that towel like that was the best meal she had ever had. I went over to take her from him, but he just shook his head with a yawn. "She was fussing and you need your sleep; go back to bed," he whispered. "I will bring her up, by and by." Marie saw me, and I expected her to start to cry for her mama, but she just closed her eyes, cuddled against Tom, and continued to nurse.

I was so tired that I turned around and went back up to bed, and as I was climbing the stairs, I could hear him singing a lullaby. It startled me at first, because I could remember my mother singing that very song and it pulled me back to the days when I was just a little girl. I stopped at the door and listened for a minute, and then I cried, but they were happy tears, because for the first time, I feel that Marie is really a part of the family.

I long to hear from you. It has been so long and you are so far away. I know that the mails are slow, and that any letter you write may not even make it here. Still, I need my husband and Marie needs her father. I pray that you will hurry home.

With all my love,
Catherine

Mindy lay the letter on the table and looked up at me. "Sweet," I said. A picture of family life."

She nodded. "It seems as if Marie has been accepted." She reached over and took a chocolate truffle out of the candy dish, offering it to me, "Would you like one?"

"I'll share one with you."

Lowering her eyes, she placed the truffle between her lips, and then raised her face to mine.

I could take a hint. Evidently I was forgiven, at least part way. I cupped my hand behind her head and pulled her forward, letting my lips meet hers, the truffle in between. It was delicious.

Later that evening, Mindy handed Joel's letter to me. "Your turn."

March 2, 1851
Murphys, California

My Dearest Catherine,
As you might have noticed from the address, we have moved. It is not far, about thirty miles as the crow flies, but it took some time, as we had to trudge through the mountains and across a pretty good sized river. The area around Sonora seemed to have been largely mined out, and we were working awfully hard to find almost nothing. Of course, standing in ice water all day and looking for gold may have been part of the problem, but we did not want to admit to that, even if it was winter. Anyway, we did what so many others have done, packed up our bags and moved along to another claim.

We are about eight miles outside of Murphys now. Our claim is quite a bit larger than before, and it is more of a wilderness area. There are fewer men here, as Murphys is just a tent shanty compared with Sonora.

Jonathan found a good sized nugget yesterday, and that helped to confirm to us that this was going to be a lucky place. It was round, and about half the size of his thumb, so it should make a good addition to our savings at the Wells Fargo. I can tell you, after we all had a good look at it, that water seemed to get a lot warmer.

He and Samuel remain good partners and friends. I am amazed at times at my luck in finding the two of them so early in my journey. They are even tempered, and both seem to be able to shake off the evils that tempt other men here in the mountains. I am fortunate indeed.

I hope that you and your family are well. I think of you often, and when I am discouraged, the image in my mind of your laugh, with those deep blue eyes, and your golden ringlets always lifts my spirits. I know that I am far away, but somehow, can feel you next to me when I roll out my bedroll at night. And the warmth of your touch and the beat of your heart lull me to sleep after even the hardest of days.

I am forever,
Your loving husband,

Joel

Thoughtfully, I folded the letter and placed it gently back in the old envelope. Mindy was sitting silently next to me, presumably thinking of what we had just read. I sat back on the sofa and put my arm around her shoulders, drawing her closer to me. She leaned into my shoulder and I reached down to her chin, lifting it so that I could gaze onto her face. She smiled and I said, "Me too."

She twisted her visage, looking up at me questioningly.

"I agree with Joel," I said.

Still confused, she paused.

I smiled and tapped her lightly on the nose, then leaned back and mused. "Sometimes, late at night, when you're here and I'm at my place, I have trouble sleeping." I gave her a little squeeze with a chuckle. "And then I imagine those blue eyes, and the copper hair, and I draw a mental picture of your laugh." I reached down and kissed her softly on the forehead. "And it's as if I can feel the warmth from your body, and the beating of your heart." I paused and looked down into her eyes. "And then all is right with the world and sleep comes more willingly." She reached her lips up and I brushed them with a kiss. "So I agree with Joel. Me too."

We sat quietly for a couple of minutes before she whispered, "Okay. I suppose that makes up for before."

CHAPTER 43

I woke early the next morning and slipping carefully out of the warmth of the bed, managed to disentangle myself from Mindy without waking her. I was restless, so I dressed quickly and tiptoed down the stairs. There was a pad by her phone, and I wrote a quick note.

"Gone for a walk, back soon. Charlie"

I left the note on the kitchen table, where she'd be sure to see it, and slipped quietly out the door.

The early spring that we'd enjoyed so much had turned to a chilly drizzle, so I tightened the raincoat about me and set myself in motion. Mindy lived not too far from a strip mall large enough to have not just one, but two good sized coffee houses. One was a national chain, and predictable, and the other a little spot favored by the locals for its iconic blends. I figured it was a good morning to hang out with the locals.

The rain was light, and the puddles that would make the return trip more challenging hadn't yet formed, and within about twenty minutes, I was giving an order for coffee. The girl behind the counter laughed when I gave her my order. "That's it?"

I shrugged my shoulders. "I like coffee," I said. "I'm not much into the fancy stuff and I'm a bit too old for the full leaded stuff, so yeah. A small decaf will be great."

She shook her head, as if disappointed at my simplicity. "No problem."

She poured my coffee in a real ceramic mug, and as I always

do, I confirmed that it was indeed decaf, confiding in her conspiratorially, "You really don't want to see me after a cup of regular coffee. I can't sit still."

Now she laughed and handed my the cup. "My brother's the same." I laughed with her and turned as I heard her say to the woman behind me, "And what can I get for you?"

I looked around the place. It was definitely not one of the national chains, with their modern lines and piped in jazz. The chairs and sofas were old and patched. Bits of newspaper were scattered on small garage sale tables, and best of all, a man sat in the corner playing an acoustic guitar. I looked at my watch. It was 7:30 in the morning, and the musician was already at work. I noticed the coins and bills scattered across the bottom of his guitar case and made a mental note to add a few of my own.

The coffee was good. Did I say that clearly enough? It was really good. Despite the fact that I'd skipped the Cappuccinos and Lattes and Mochas, I had still had quite a selection of the local blends. I'd selected a mountain grown Costa Rican that promised to include hints of clove and cinnamon. And it did. As I took the first few sips, I could tell that my only mistake had been in getting a small cup. Ah well. Refills were only fifty cents.

I chose a comfortable chair in the window where I could watch the rain, and took out Joel's letter. I felt a little bit guilty about spiriting it out of the house without Mindy's permission, but not enough to bother me overly much. I took my time, reading the letter again, and imagining his experience in the California gold country in March. I'd spent enough time in that area to have a pretty good idea of the weather. In a word, unpredictable. I could remember being snowed in one Easter on the fifth of April. And I could clearly remember skinny dipping with my brother in the Stanislaus River, no later than mid-April. It had been so hot that day that it had seemed like a great idea until we jumped into the snow melt. The sun had heated the granite banks though, and we basked like a couple of lizards later on.

I was about to put the letter in my pocket when I felt someone looking at me. I turned and noticed a fellow whose wrinkled face and grey fringe told me he was about my age, or possibly a little older. I nodded and he nodded back. I'd noticed him earlier sipping on his coffee as he surfed the net on his laptop. "Your friend's behind the times," he said. Noticing my confusion, he tapped his computer. "Email."

I chuckled. "My friend didn't have email. Just snail mail. And in this case, very slow snail mail." Now it was his turn to be confused and I continued, "The letter was written in 1851."

He furrowed his brow. "You a researcher?"

"Of a sort," I said. "This letter actually belongs to a friend of mine. It was written by her great, great grandfather. We read it for the first time last night."

"Really!" He looked around and motioned to the empty chair across from me. "Mind if I join you?"

"Not at all," I shrugged.

He picked up his computer, transferred it to my table, and was about to sit when he noticed my empty cup. "Get you a refill?"

"Sounds good," I said, reaching for my wallet.

He waved me off and took my mug. "Costa Rican?"

I nodded and he took the two cups to the counter, dropped a dollar into the bowl there, and filled both. When he returned, he handed me my cup and sat, and then reached out his hand. "Call me Bill."

I took his hand. His grip was firm, but secure, like he was confident enough not to have to crush me, but wanted me to know that he was serious about the introduction. I liked that. He looked over at the letter and asked, "May I?"

I inclined my head and he gingerly picked up the old parchment. I watched and noted that his lips moved as he read, as if he was trying to give voice to Joel. Finally, he handed back the letter. "Interesting," he said. He raised his eyebrow. "You say he was her great grandpa?"

"Great, great," I responded.

He nodded. "A different time," he said, and then continued, thinking aloud. "Letters, gold miners. As I recall my history, they didn't pay much attention to the families left behind."

I shook my head. "No. It was pretty much about the glorious, brave men who traveled west to find their fortunes."

He laughed. "Glorious. There's a good term." He looked up at me. "You ever do any mining?" I shook my head and he continued. "Hard work! Really hard work," he emphasized.

"So you did some mining?"

He shook his head. "Not really. Played at it. Thought there must still be some gold out there for a boy who wanted to look for it." He chuckled. "Looking back, it was mostly an excuse not to go out and get a job when I got out of college."

I smiled. "You find any?"

"Oh sure," he said seriously. "Just about everyone finds a little." He took a sip of coffee. "It's like gambling though. You find just enough to keep you coming back, and don't notice that you're slowly going broke." He looked at me. "I kept it up for a few months; found a few ounces; but you can't live on that. Then I figured out that a real job wouldn't be nearly as hard." He snorted. "And I didn't even touch winter. I was strictly a fair weather miner."

As he reached for his coffee again, I asked, "So what did you end up doing?"

His cup was just about to his lips and he stopped it. "Went back to school. Got my masters and eventually my doctorate. History."

"From the mines to the classroom," I said.

He nodded. "Researcher mostly. My specialty was ancient Greece."

"Was?"

He nodded. "I retired last spring." He raised his cup. "Spend my time enjoying life now. Hanging out in the coffee houses and pontificating on whatever tickles my fancy." He laughed, and I had to join him.

"So how'd she come across this letter?"

I gave him the brief story, and he smiled. "A mystery man."

"He was," I added. "We're not quite sure what happened to him, but we've been able to track him to California, and we know he was here until at least 1853."

"Mind if I ask how you've run down all this information?" He asked, and then added, "as an old researcher."

Unconsciously, I raised my hand and began ticking ideas off on my fingers. "Well, there're the letters, and we've met a few folks who've been able to help." I looked up at him. His head was bobbing up and down as I spoke. "We've been to several museums, searched county documents, asked some family members, and let's see," I paused. "Oh, and we've found some newspaper articles." I picked up my coffee and took in some of the warm spice. "Any suggestions?"

Bill looked out the window for a moment, then said, "Ok, you've got museums, public records, family, newspapers." He looked at me, "Online searches?" I nodded and he continued. "You search public records in Pennsylvania?" I shook my head and he said, "Well you can probably do most of that online." He paused and then said, "How about churches. They keep some pretty detailed records of births, deaths, baptisms, that sort of thing."

I nodded. "We found a minister in Murphys who helped quite a bit."

"Well then you've hit most of the big sources," he said. "It's kind of like tracking down a mystery. You have to be willing to follow each little piece of evidence, no matter how vague." He picked up his coffee, drank some, and then tapped his finger on the table. "I don't know whether this'll do you any good, but it's worth a try. If you know what you're looking for, sometimes the antique stores up in the gold country can be a good source." He snorted. "Most of what they have is junk, but there is the occasional treasure."

I grinned at that and he looked at me. "You found something."

"We did," I nodded. "An old postcard in a restaurant in San Andreas. It had their pictures on it."

He jolted, surprised. "Outstanding." Then he turned serious. "Well keep it up. You never know what you'll find."

He took out his wallet and extracted a card. "If you need help, give me a call. I'd love to be of use." Then he looked at me conspiratorially and added, "It'll give me something to do, and I'm sure my wife'll be happy to have me out of the house." He grinned.

I looked at the card. It was simple.

William Islington
Historian - Retired
historybug@sqcc.edu

"You still work at the college?" I asked.

"Not officially, but keeping the e-mail and being able to use the facility were a couple of the retirement perks. I also volunteer two days a week." He shook his head. "So many of the kids can't put two sentences together to save their lives. I help with writing One on one tutorial makes a difference."

I nodded. "Good for you."

"Anyway," he said as he stood, "If I can help, drop me a note. I'd love to be of assistance. Like I said, I've got the time." He looked out the window. "And now I'd better go. My wife's probably finished at the market." He winked at me. "I'm not allowed to join her there. Seems I buy too much junk." He waved as he went out the door. "You hang on to that card."

And then he was gone. I sat, looking at his business card. Interesting man. And his idea about the antique stores sounded kind of interesting, but on reflection, finding something related to Joel would be like looking for a needle in a haystack. And just how many antique stores were there in that part of the gold country? A couple of hundred? More?

I took a last sip of my coffee, bussed the cups up to the counter, and decided that I should head back. Mindy was sure to be up by now, and would be wondering where I was.

CHAPTER 44

July 8, 1851
Bradford, Pennsylvania

My Wonderful Husband!
I got your letter yesterday! After so many months, it was wonderful to
hear from you. I was so bubbly and excited that I could hardly sit still.
Everyone wondered what it was, but I did not say, just beamed. I am sure that
Ruth knew, but she held her tongue.

By now I have read it at least a hundred times, and committed it to
memory. It is such a wonderful letter that I can not help smiling whenever I think
of it. Thank you! Thank you! Thank you!

You will have to tell me where Murphys and Sonora are. While I was
in Pittsburgh, I went to the library and looked at a map of California, but there
were almost no cities identified there. I found San Francisco. I also found
Sacramento City, San Jose, and Monterey, though the librarian told me that he
thinks that some of those are just Spanish mission settlements. He was very nice
though, and allowed me to trace a copy of the map onto a sheet of paper, so that I
can refer to it as I get your wonderful letters.

You said you had gone east from San Francisco. Would you have gone
toward the Stanislas River? Is that one that you crossed? From what I could tell
on the map, it comes out of the mountains east of San Francisco. Is California
big? It is so hard to tell, not having a way of comparing with Pennsylvania. You
mentioned how long it takes to travel from place to place and I wonder if it is
because of the distances, or the lack of good roads. I know so little and need to
know more so that I can figure out where you are. Please write to me soon.
Better yet, tell me where I can write you!

Congratulations on finding your nugget. I pray that you are all successful so that you can hurry home to me.

Marie is my angel. She is cute as a button, and doing more every day. She has been trying to push herself up onto her hands and knees lately, so no doubt she will begin crawling soon. Part of me can not wait, and part of me is scared to death. Once she starts to move about on her own, I will not be able to keep anything away from her. But what a joy she is. Even Tom has taken to playing with her now. He bounces her on his knee, and chews on her fingers and she giggles and giggles until he can not help himself and lets go with great big belly laughs. They have seemed to come up with some kind of secret language all their own, and even though she still loves the attention from all my brothers, it is clear that Tom is her favorite, and she is definitely his. He has a way of looking at her that sets her squealing with laughter. And she can do the same to him. I have heard of little girls wrapping their daddies around their little fingers. Well, with you in California, she has turned her wiles on Tom and it is clear that in his eyes, she can do no wrong.

And now my big news. Robert is engaged to be married. Do you remember Josie Matthews? Her family has a farm a couple of miles from here. We all were in school together, and she was just a quiet little thing who always sat in the back row and almost never spoke up. I hardly ever even noticed her, but evidently Robert was paying attention. It seems he has been courting her for the better part of a year now. Of course, I was in Pittsburgh for much of that time, and then had a new baby to deal with, but still, I never knew until he invited her family to dinner a few weeks ago. Well, it was clear from the looks that they shared across the table that they were more than just friends. And after supper, just as I thought that they were about to go, Robert said that he had an announcement to make. He had already spoken with Josie's father and asked for her hand. And John had welcomed him to the family. Just like that. When I looked around the table, I could see that I was the only one who was surprised. From what I found out later, Robert and Tom had discussed the matter at some length, and after a while, Tom had also given his blessing. So I am to have a sister. Imagine that. I have never had a girl in the family other than Mama and Ruth, but Ruth is so much older, and Mama, well you know about her troubles. Josie made her way around the table hugging all of my brothers and commenting on how wonderful it would be for her, one of nine girls, to have brothers at this late date. When she got to Mama, she hugged her, but Mama said, "Catherine, what is the big fuss?" And it was clear that she thought Josie was me. Ah well, a little sadness with all the joy. She gets so confused.

They plan to marry in August, and after that, Robert will move in with the Matthews while they build a cabin for the two of them. John said that he was looking forward to welcoming Robert into the family and taking him in as a partner in the farm. So it will be a busy summer. I am to be a bridesmaid, and Tom will be best man. With all the work we will be doing together, it looks like I will pick up an entire family of sisters, not just the one.

You are in my thoughts every day. Be careful. Be safe. Be joyous for you have a wife who loves you and a darling daughter who can not wait to meet her father.

And most of all, come back to me. I do not care about the gold and I am sure now that even Tom will welcome you back into the family.

With all my love,

Catherine

Mindy put the letter down on the night table. She'd still been asleep when I returned, so I quietly slipped off my clothes and crawled back into bed with her. Unfortunately for her? me? both? I hadn't anticipated how cold my body was when I snuggled up against her. I only thought she was asleep. She was somewhere in that half sleep, between waking and still dreaming, and when she felt my cold body against hers, and while it felt heavenly for me, it was icy for her and she howled and shoved me away. It took a while before I was allowed to touch her, and even then, I felt guilty.

Oh well. I apologized; she got over the initial shock; and we got back to nesting together under the covers when my body heat increased to acceptable levels.

"So where did you go to get so cold?" she asked.

"I went out for a cup of coffee."

She raised her eyebrows. "You were gone that long? And I didn't even notice? I must have really been tired."

"I guess. Anyway, I went out to Jerry's Java. They have a really nice Costa Rican blend."

"Cinnamon and cloves?"

"So you've had it?

She nodded. "One of my favorites."

"I met an interesting guy there." I explained about Bill, and about his suggestion that we check the antique stores.

She looked at me skeptically. "How many stores do you suppose there are in that area?"

"I know. A lot."

She snuggled against me. "Oh well, it'll give us something to do."

I enjoyed the warmth, stroking the back of her head and kissing her forehead. She was running her finger up and down my spine so lightly that I'm sure all she was touching were the fine hairs. She knew that I was ticklish there, and that it drove me crazy, but I just gritted my teeth and continued to hold her. I'd learned early on, that while I could be ticklish over virtually my entire body, Mindy seemed immune, and actually preferred that light touch that had me squirming in agony. Life wasn't fair.

"I had a strange dream," she said.

"You did?"

"Um hm,"

"What was it?"

"Actually I'm not sure it was a dream. It seemed so real. But so strange."

I backed onto one elbow so that I could see her face and she looked up at me. "Like I was really awake, but like a dream too."

"Well?" I asked, "What was it?"

"I dreamed that I got up in the middle of the night and went downstairs to the kitchen."

"Okay," I started.

"And then I got out the leftover dessert from last night and ate it."

"The soufflé?"

"Right."

"Strange dream. Were you hungry?"

She laughed. "Not that I recall." She looked up at me. "What do you think? Did you notice me leave?"

"No. I don't think so." I thought. "No, not at all."

She shrugged. "It was a strange dream, but seemed so real."

"Spooky," I said. "Do you have any history of sleepwalking?"

"No. Not since I was a kid. And besides, this was like a dream but it was so real. You know what I mean? Everything was like it really is, no strangeness except getting up for the soufflé."

"Probably just a dream then," I said.

And that's when she decided to read Catherine's letter. And

while she did, I drifted my fingers up and down her body, tryig to tickle her. At one point, she started to shiver and put down the letter, and I thought/hoped that I'd been successful. "I know what you're trying to do, and it's not bothering me at all. As far as I'm concerned, those light strokes are heavenly, not ticklish, so if you want me glowing, keep it up."

Well, I suppose that glowing was just exactly the way that I wanted her, so she read while I stroked, trying to touch nothing but the finest hairs, and she read some more, and when I lightened my touch even further, she started to purr.

§§§§

Later, we went downstairs for breakfast. There were soufflé crumbs on the counter, a dirty fork in the sink, and when we looked, a small piece missing from the container in the refrigerator.

CHAPTER 45

The rains continued for the next week, overwhelming the coastal sewer systems and dumping several feet of snow in the Sierras. Mindy and I both had to work anyway, so it didn't matter much, but we had planned another trip to the gold country to continue looking for clues about Joel. But since neither one of us was terribly keen about driving on icy roads, we decided to wait.

Instead, we turned to the internet in our search for information about Joel and Catherine. I was at my place one evening when Mindy called. She'd found another trace, and wanted me to know that she was emailing me a copy.

"So what did you find?"

"I'm not sure," she said. "It might be something, or nothing."

"Sounds intriguing. Where did you find it?"

"Take a look at it first, and then I'll tell you."

I carried the phone into the other room, and booted up my computer. Mindy meantime, continued to chat about her day, her walk down to the village with her friend Gena, and her upcoming dinner with friends. After what seemed a long time, I was able to open her email. "Okay, I've got it."

"Fine," she said. "You read it and see what you think."

There were two copies of the document. The first was a well worn, brown paper letter that had been scanned into someone's database. The second was a verbatim copy, this time typed out complete with misspellings and other errors.

December 12, 1853
San Francisco, California

Mr. Joel Woodward,
Sir, I thank you for contacting me, but know of no employment oportunities in the banking industry of San Francisco at this time. If you will send me your particurlars however, I will be most happy to circulate them around the local businesses to see if I can secure you an appointment
You indicate that you are presently a co-owner of a general store in San Andreas. Have you considered a trade position in San Francisco? There are ofen openings with the importers, as they frequenly lose their help to the gold fields. I would be happy to arrange apointments with some of the larger houses if you so desire.
Please inform me of how I may be of further help.
Sincerely yours,

Robert Perkins, Esquire
Attorney at Law

I was fascinated. "Mindy, where did you find this one?"

"Online. I did a search for Woodward and letters and 1850's. I also searched for Catherine's letters but didn't find anything."

"Amazing. Well it seems to place him in California in December of 1853, if nothing else."

"And evidently he was interested in returning to San Francisco, but not necessarily to Pennsylvania. Do you suppose there was some kind of falling out between the partners?"

I thought about that. From what we knew, the three had started the store, but later on, it was clear that it was Samuel's. Jonathan died in 1856. What happened to Joel? Why wasn't he still mentioned as a partner? "I suppose it was possible," I said. "But they always spoke so highly of one another that it seems unlikely."

She seemed to hesitate on her end. Finally, she said slowly, "But possible."

"Oh yeah. Absolutely. They were together for almost four years by then? It's possible that they started to have different goals. They'd grown up together, but maybe the store was mostly Samuel's idea of a future."

"It sounded like Jonathan was still mining."

"True. Interesting." I paused, thinking. "I feel like we're working on peeling an onion. Each time we read a letter or do a search, we find one more tiny clue, but never enough."

She laughed. "Well in that case, it's a good thing you're at your place and I'm at mine. I don't need your onion breath!"

"Hey! What do you mean, onion breath."

She just laughed. "So do you still want to go up to Murphys this weekend?"

"I think so. The weather's clearing so it should be beautiful. I understand that it'll be pretty warm, highs in the 50's."

"Ah yes. Toasty. I'll bring my down jacket!"

"You don't trust me to keep you warm?"

"Always. But I'll still be bringing my down jacket."

I laughed, and we decided on a good meeting place and time. I wasn't necessarily looking forward to beginning a search of antique shops, but it would be an interesting diversion. Besides, Jim and Melissa told us to call the next time we were in town so that we could get together for dinner. And with Monday being President's Day, it should be a good long weekend.

§§§§

The weather in Murphys was glorious, with clear skies punctuated by puffy white clouds. The January warm spell had prompted the growing season, and the hills were covered with new grasses that sprouted with the recent rains. Even the flowering peaches in downtown Murphys were covered with blossoms, and the occasional yellow daffodils were starting to pop up all along the roadsides. Spring was definitely coming to the Sierra foothills. Mindy leaned against my arm as we walked along, "It's always so pretty after it rains."

"You warm enough?" I asked.

"Thanks for asking. I'm fine." She looked into my face and giggled. "Let's stay on this side of the street for now though, in the sunshine."

"No problem. You tired of antique shopping yet?"

She groaned and I had my answer. "Past tired." We'd spent most of the day browsing antique shops for relics from the 1850's, starting in San Andreas, and working our way through Angel's Camp and up the hill to Murphys. "If I see another Cameo brooch I might just scream."

I laughed. "I'm with you." Let's call it a day and drop by the Adams' a little early." I looked at my watch. We were scheduled to meet them at 6:30, and it was almost 6:00. "Sound okay?"

Mindy shook her head. "Not a chance. They're expecting us at 6:30. All we'll do by showing up early is throw off their preparation for dinner."

I'd noticed her meticulous attention to manners, and the convenience of others many times in the past. Once, when I'd suggested dropping in on my brother, she'd been appalled at the thought, saying that it was rude to even think of arriving at someone's home without a prior appointment. So it didn't surprise me that she was now opposed to showing up thirty minutes early for dinner. Oh well.

"There's another shop just up the street. Let's see if they're still open."

I groaned. "If you must."

She smiled and squeezed my arm. "Maybe we'll find something interesting."

"Harrumph." I grumbled. "Not likely."

So up the street we went, into Mabel's Trinkets, our ninety-fifth antique shop of the day, well maybe it wasn't exactly our ninety-fifth, but it felt that way. Mindy took the lead when we entered, going up to the counter.

The white haired woman at the counter looked at her, smiled, and said, "Just a sec, dear." She finished bagging a woman's purchase, gave her a wonderfully warm smile, and said, "I hope you like this vase. I've always thought it was lovely."

"Thank you ever so much," the woman replied, "I can't wait to get it home. I know just where it's going to go."

"Well you enjoy it." With a final smile, she turned to Mindy, "Hi, thanks for waiting. What can I do for you today?"

Mindy flashed her friendliest smile and started, "Hi, I'm Mindy and your name is?"

"I'm Mabel. Just like the store." She grinned, and in that moment, she reminded me of my grandmother. I was startled. They looked similar, but not identical. Whereas my grandmother had been slight, this woman was more rounded, not heavy, but not thin either. And her hair, though in a similar bun, was entirely white, not the salt and pepper that I remembered. It was her eyes, I decided. The twinkle, the sparkle, and the warmth were all there.

She and Mindy had been talking while I was lost in my head for a few seconds, and now she turned to me, "and you?" she asked.

"Uh," I looked at Mindy.

She shook her head and rolled her eyes before turning back to Mabel. "His name is Charlie. And he doesn't always listen terribly well."

I was about to respond when Mabel said, "I know just what you mean. My husband has a little case of selective hearing himself." They both laughed and looked at me like indulgent mothers at a spoiled child. I smiled weakly.

"So what can I get you?" Mabel asked.

Mindy had perfected her spiel by now. "We're trying to trace a relative of mine who was here in the 1850's. Would you have anything that might date from that time?"

Mabel thought for a moment. "I probably do. Come along over here." She took us into a back room where there was an assortment of old dishes, bottles, perfume jars, and other novelties. She looked at Mindy, "Would this be what you're looking for?"

Mindy frowned, "I was hoping more to find a letter, or something like that."

"Wow. Really specific. And I suppose not just any letter but one from your old relative."

"Ideally."

"Well. I'm not sure I can help you there. We deal mostly in trinkets, you know," she smiled, "the type of thing people can use to decorate their homes."

She started back out to the main room and looked around the shop. I followed her gaze. I could see clothing in the back, enough to outfit a nice theater group in an early twentieth century revue. There was a section that held some furniture, mostly tables with marble tops along with a few lamps, and of course, dishware everywhere. I even saw a few toys that I remembered from my own childhood. Finally, Mabel clicked her fingers and said, "We have a little nineteenth century jewelry. Would you like to see that? It's a long shot, but some of it is engraved."

She turned to a glass display case. Mindy and I followed. When we got there, I could see that she had a small collection of watches, lockets, bracelets, and the like. And of course, the ubiquitous cameo. There was one necklace with a simple gold charm that caught my eye, but it seemed much newer than 1850.

She pulled out several of the pieces and put them onto a velvet pad. "Maybe one of these?" she asked. "They should be around that time period."

Mindy picked up a pocket watch, opened the face, and was startled to see a man's name engraved in the cover. "Joseph Warren," she read. "1884." I'd noticed a man's ring, and turned it to see if the inside had been engraved. It had been, but the writing was so worn down that it was difficult to read. Besides, I couldn't imagine that a penniless boy from Pennsylvania would have carried such a nice piece of jewelry. We took a quick look at the other pieces, but nothing stood out for us. Finally, Mindy turned to Mabel. "I don't see anything here, but thank you for your time. You've been most helpful."

"That's my goal," she said as she moved the items back to the display case and locked the doors. She turned toward the front, and then stopped. "You're looking for letters?"

Mindy nodded. "Or cards, documents, something like that. We found one, and hoped that there might be more."

"You might try Arnold. He tries to specialize in the gold rush era." She looked under her counter. "I think I have one of his cards here." She pulled out a stack of business cards and began thumbing through them as she talked. "He keeps a little place down toward Sonora. Let's see..." She turned over another card, and then grinned triumphantly. "Here it is." She lay his card on the counter.

I leaned over to look. "California Gold, Arnold Sampson, Sole Proprietor." I looked at Mindy. "What do you think?"

"Jamestown?" she asked. "Where's that?"

Mabel answered. "About twenty miles, toward Sonora. It's easy to find." She picked up the card. "Here, let me copy his information for you." She hurried back behind a curtain into her office space.

While we waited, I said, "You think it's worth it?"

"I don't know," she answered. "If it's just more of what we've already seen, probably not."

I looked at my watch. "Almost 6:30. We should probably get on to the Adams' place."

"And now we'll be right on time," she added with a coy smile.

"Yes we will." I grinned. "You do such a good job of keeping me proper."

"An ongoing challenge to be sure," she replied and reached up to kiss my cheek. "Let's see how we feel tomorrow. I'm about antiqued out for today."

Mabel came back. She'd made a copy of the card which she handed to us. "Is there anything else I can get for you?" She reached out with her hand to point around the store. "A nice Tiffany lamp? New 30's hat for the lady? Spats for the gentleman?"

Mindy laughed. "This card will be perfect. Thanks for everything."

"Good luck then," Mabel said. "Sounds like an interesting quest."

I looked back. "It has been that."

§§§§

Melissa had insisted that we dine in an older Irish restaurant on the main street in Murphys. The food was wonderful, and the decor, set in a nineteenth century Victorian house had put us in the mood to continue our discussion of Joel and Catherine.

After dinner, Jim suggested that we try one of the local ports, served in what had originally been the parlor of the home, and now swirled his unconsciously while he listened to our update. "So Samuel Watkins ended up settling in San Andreas."

I nodded. "And his family still lives there."

"Ranchers now though."

"I had the impression that they're involved in more than just ranching, but that's their main business." I looked across at Mindy, who was deep in another conversation with Melissa. "In any event, they retained ownership of the general store for many years after the three men bought it in the '50's."

"Any record of Joel?"

"Not much. The letter from the San Francisco attorney is the last word we have. And that was pretty vague."

Jim took a sip of the port and set his glass on a side table. "How many letters do you still have to read?"

I looked again at Mindy and she smiled across at me, but continued her conversation. "I'm not sure. Not too many. Mindy's been holding them pretty close, parceling them out just a couple at a time. She'll know."

He nodded, pressing his fingertips together in a meditative pose. "I've looked occasionally here, but haven't found anything else. Melissa found a little. I'll let her fill you in on that. It may be helpful."

"So I understand," I said enthusiastically. "Has she shared this with you?"

He chuckled. "Yes, but I'm sworn to secrecy." He touched his finger to his lips and crossed his heart. "Can't speak on penalty of who knows what."

Now I laughed. "Understood." I looked over at Mindy again, and she interrupted her conversation.

"What are you two laughing about?"

Jim shook his head. "Nothing."

I laughed again and she bored in with her eyes. After a few seconds, I squirmed and added, "I too am sworn to secrecy."

She pursed her lips and turned back to Melissa. "Men," she said.

I laughed and turned our conversation to sports. The San Francisco Giants had started spring training, and hopes were high that they'd have a good team, with a couple of young prospects who showed remarkable ability.

Later that evening, Mindy pulled out two envelopes and laid them on the marble topped coffee table. "I only have a few left," she said, "and was hoping I'd be able to share another with you two. You've been so helpful."

Melissa picked up what appeared to be a letter from Catherine and smiled. "She was faithful, wasn't she."

Mindy scowled. "Remarkably so, considering that her man ran off in search of gold and didn't write very regularly."

She opened the letter. "This one is written in September of 1851." She paused, and then added, "Even hers seem to have become less frequent as time went by."

"She's busy," Melissa mused. "And she hears from him so

infrequently that she may forget from time to time."

Mindy cocked her head to the side, thinking. "Still, since none of these was actually delivered, they're more of a diary than anything else." She looked down at the letter and then back at Melissa. "Now there's an interesting thought. I think she did mention a diary. Maybe she just wrote letters when she was lonely. Wouldn't that be interesting to read. Hmm." She turned back to the letter. "Unlikely we'll ever find that."

September 29, 1851
Bradford, Pennsylvania

Dearest Joel,
I hope that you continue your good fortune in Murphys, so that you may come home soon. Both Marie and I miss you sorely.
Ruth announced yesterday that she intended to pack up and return to Pittsburgh in the next few weeks, after the harvest is complete. She wants to get back before the weather turns cold again. I tried to talk her into staying, but she just laughed and said that she is not needed here any more, now that the baby is getting along well and I have taken over the household. Besides, she needs to get back to attend to her interests in Pittsburgh. I had not known that she had interests there, but evidently she has invested in some of the local businesses and worries about whether her money is being properly cared for in her absence. Anyway, Robert offered to take her back. I must admit that I will miss her. I have grown accustomed to having a woman around the house. Well, Mother is here, but you know what I mean. And her wise counsel has helped me through many a thorny issue with Tom and the others.
Robert and Josie's wedding was a wonderful thing. People came from all around to help celebrate. She wore a beautiful white dress, along with flowers in her hair. I must admit that I was a little jealous, given our hurried and secret wedding. Still, I have no complaints about my husband aside from the fact that he has been away for far too long.
Having sisters is wonderful! I try to find some excuse to travel over to the Matthews place at least once each week. Lately, I have been taking the buckboard over every Tuesday so that I can join the ladies there in a quilting bee. We sew, we laugh, and we talk about all of the gossip around the town. I have been asked a few times about you, and always say that you have promised to return after you have your stake to buy a farm here. I am afraid sometimes that my loneliness shows through my brave front, but there is really nothing to be done.

You will be back when you can and not before.

I do have fun there though. Mary Alice and a couple of the other girls in the community have joined us on occasion. It is good to be in the company of others and leave my cares behind. Little Marie loves our trips there. She coos and giggles and seems to relish the attention of all of the women. I find that everyone wants to hold her, and play with her, and it is nice to get some time free from attending to her.

Tom is very focused on the harvest this year. The cold spell that we had at the beginning of this month damaged some of the crops, and he is determined to get everything else in and taken care of before any more cold weather. He is worried that the almanac has predicted a harsh winter. I think he is worrying over nothing, as the almanac is frequently wrong, but that is his nature and I suppose it is good that someone is that serious about protecting our livelihood.

Marie continues to grow. She is pulling herself up now, holding on to anything she can get her hands on. Yesterday evening we were all settled around the fire, reading and repairing equipment, when Marie tried to pull herself up against Tom's old spaniel, Jake. She got to her feet, and was so proud of herself that she just beamed. That evidently was enough for Jake though, as he stood up and walked over to Tom. Poor Marie took a tumble and landed on her bottom. No harm was done, just hurt pride, but she cried and I had to pick her up and calm her. The men laughed and Jake just settled back down in front of the fire. When I put her back down, she scooted back over to Jake and stood up again, then proceeded to bounce up and down as if she had conquered some kind of mountain. We laughed and she laughed and Jake just snorted and went to sleep.

I do miss you and wish that you could be here to enjoy your daughter. She is a wonder. Hurry back.

I send you my love every day.

Catherine

Mindy put down the letter and turned to the rest of us, awaiting our responses. Melissa was the first to speak.

"Is it just me, or does anyone else seem to think that maybe she's moving on without him?"

"I had the same impression," Jim added softly. "She's finding a home for herself in Bradford." He paused, breathing deeply. "In some of the early letters, she sounded so forlorn, but now..."

"She's making a life for herself." Melissa smiled. "I'm glad. How many miners actually returned?" She looked around at us. "It couldn't have been many. It was such a long, dangerous journey."

I looked over at Mindy. She was staring out into space, as if trying to imagine Catherine's feelings. "Mindy?" I asked.

She looked at me and smiled sadly. "I think they're right. Do you suppose he'll have a place if he ever does come back?"

I shook my head. "I don't know." Then I inclined my head toward the other letter. "Are you planning to read that one?"

She handed it across to me. "You do the honors," she said.

November 14, 1851
Murphys, California

My Darling,

Our decision to move to Murphys has turned out to be a good one. No, we're not rich, not anything near rich, but we're making a living, and not having to rely on our meager savings. Each of us has now found at least one nugget, though Jonathan is proving to be the one who has a nose for gold. We have been banking our gold with Wells Fargo, and are beginning to show a modest account.

The weather is still warm here, but we can tell that winter is on its way. We have had our first rainfall of the season. Did I mention that it rarely rains during the summer here? We had no rain at all from May through July, and only a light sprinkle in August and no more until late October. The hills are dry and golden, and it looks more like the end of summer than fall. It is so very different from home. I miss the rainfall and I miss the humidity. It is so dry here.

Mostly, I miss you.

There are precious few women in town, and none up here at the mining sites. I find that I miss the clear joyous laughter of women as well as their gentle nature. Men can be hard, and in a place like this, we must rely upon our fellows while being distrustful of strangers. There are those who are wonderful gentlemen, working all day, yet always available to help another. And then there are others always looking for ways to cheat and come by riches through theft or even murder. Sadly for them, justice in the gold fields is quick and harsh.

But I digress. How long has it been since we were together? Too long. I carry memories of our courtship, and our evening in that glade so far away, and those must sustain me on the lonely nights. I do miss you and long for us to be reunited. Rest assured that I am doing what I can to build that stake we talked about so long ago so that we can purchase a small farm and live independently.

Since it looks like we will be here for a while, I have an address. You may reach me through the local sheriff. He is also the postmaster, and will hold letters for miners until they come into town, if he is unable to deliver them on his regular rounds about the camps. He is a good man, and I have written his address for you.

Rick Miller, Sheriff
Murphys, California
Please write, as I long to hear from you and know that you are well.
Your loving husband,

Joel

I looked around at the others. "That's it."

Mindy was smiling. "So he's settled, and he finally has an address."

"I wonder if she ever sent any letters to him in Murphys?" Melissa asked.

I could tell that the museum docent in her was getting interested in this, so I asked, "Might there be any that you haven't found?"

She shook her head. "I wouldn't think so." She looked across at us. "Besides, men aren't nearly as sentimental as women. He'd have been less likely to save her letters."

Jim started to object, but seemed to think better of it. Finally, he added, "Still, he has an address."

"He does," I said. I looked at Mindy. "How many are left?"

"Not many. A handful. I haven't counted." She sighed. "We've read most of them."

We all paused thoughtfully for a while until Melissa said, "I hate to do this, but we do need to be going." She looked over at her husband. "Jim has an early service and Sundays are very busy days for us. Will you be coming?"

I looked over at Mindy. She nodded almost imperceptibly. "Of course. What time?"

§§§§

We hadn't been able to get our usual room at the bed and breakfast, so the proprietor took us to a large suite. "Since you're regulars and I don't have anyone else staying here tonight, I'll rent it to you for the same rate." He showed us around. In addition to two bedrooms and bathrooms, it had a large kitchen and living room, as well as a small laundry room. "We use it mostly for families," he said. "Sometimes, two families will rent it for the weekend. It's a great place for kids, or even just for a group of adults.

I had to agree. The space was the size of a large apartment. To get it for the same price as our little room was a fantastic deal. I agreed to his two night minimum without blinking. After all, we planned to spend Saturday and Sunday nights anyway.

After our dinner with the Adams, we talked over hot cocoa until after midnight. The idea that Joel had sent Mindy an address, and that she'd obviously received it, since the letter was in her cache, opened up a whole new realm of possibilities. Had she written him? If so, had he received her letters? How had it changed his plans knowing that he had a daughter? And finally, now that she had an address, had she saved copies of any of her letters to him? There was a lot to think about.

Finally, Mindy looked at the clock and said, "Oh my. It's late, and you promised to get to church tomorrow by 9:00."

"I did, didn't I." I stood and stretched. It was going to be an early morning.

Mindy was well cocooned in a down comforter we'd found in the closet. Unfortunately, our big new suite hadn't been modernized like the others, and the windows didn't quite seal. The temperature was predicted to drop into the 30's overnight, and despite the fire, the room was drafty and cold. But then, as I said, Mindy was wrapped in the down comforter, cozy warm, and evidently not thrilled about getting up despite the late hour.

Finally, she rose, discarded the comforter, and shivered, "Brr. I think I'm going to take a shower before bed."

She practically ran to the bathroom. Within seconds, I heard the shower running. Knowing that there was no shortage of hot water, I figured she'd be there for some time. Time enough for a surprise anyway.

When Mindy emerged from her shower, I was waiting. One of the perks of the suite was a set of terry cloth robes, embroidered with the name of the bed and breakfast. Another was a washer/dryer combination. I set the dryer to high, tossed in one of the robes, and in just a few minutes, was waiting for Mindy with a toasty robe when she stepped out of her shower. Before she could even begin to complain about the cold room, I wrapped it around her. The ear to ear grin that she rewarded me with was all the evidence that I needed that I'd made a good decision.

"You are my knight in shining armor," she said, and favored me with a nice long kiss. "This is wonderful." She purred as I led her to bed. I'd doubled up the down comforter on her side, just to keep her warm through the night.

"But how are you going to stay warm?" she asked.

"I plan to stay close to you."

"Ah," she sighed, and then she whispered in my ear. "And I have a feeling you may get really lucky tonight."

§§§§

It turned out that Jim was just my kind of minister. The congregation was surprisingly large, filling the tiny church. He led them through a series of hymns and other songs, talked a bit about the needs of the local food pantry, and their duty to help the poor, and had us out the door before 10:00.

I noticed people dressed in a wide variety of clothing, from the traditional Sunday Best, down to one old fellow who wore torn jeans and a flannel shirt. Their common element though, was enthusiasm, especially when singing. Melissa played the organ, and Jim directed a small choir, who led the rest. The door had been left open despite the cool weather, for air circulation, and I'm sure that they heard us in downtown Murphys, two blocks away.

After the service, Mindy and I talked quietly, occasionally exchanging a greeting with others there, while Jim and Melissa met with their congregation. As I saw the crowd at the front of the church dwindle down to just a few, we made our way over to our friends.

Jim shook a last hand and turned to me. "Well, what do you think. Do we do it right in the small churches?"

"Looked good to me," I said. "And interestingly, it could have been a sermon given back during the gold rush."

He cocked his head in reflection for a moment before agreeing. "I'm not sure they had a food pantry then, but certainly there were those who were down on their luck."

Melissa joined us at about that time. "It's finally starting to come together," she said to her husband.

He nodded and Mindy looked at her questioningly.

"Oh, I'm sorry. I've been talking with the chairwoman for the spring festival. It's one of our big events of the year. They're getting pretty well organized."

"So what do you do?" Mindy asked.

"Oh, it's fun," she said. "You should try to come. We'll have a big barbecue, games for the kids, live music, and this year we're going to tie it in with an arts and crafts faire."

"Sounds like quite an undertaking."

Melissa smiled. "Piece of cake. Especially if you have lots of volunteers."

Jim turned to Mindy. "You're both right. It's a big job, and Melissa's role is to organize the volunteers. She puts on some of the best festivals in the area. That's why she was able to talk the arts group into coming. They know there'll be a crowd."

"So this is all tied in with the church?" I asked.

"There are three churches involved this year." I must have looked surprised, because he continued, "I told you. It's a big festival!"

"Is this a fundraiser as well?"

"Of course." He pointed to a gazebo in a forested area at the back of the lot. "2008."

"And don't forget the roofing job done the next year," Melissa added.

"That's right," he said. "After we split the proceeds, each of the churches has a pretty good take. Then we pull out a generous donation and send that off to some of the other charitable causes in the area."

"The food pantry," Mindy said.

He looked at her. "Right. Among others. So, you coming? It'll be the weekend of May 20th. Hope for warm weather."

Mindy looked at me and I shrugged my shoulders. She rolled her eyes and said, "I don't know about Mr. Undecided, but I can probably be here."

"Great," said Melissa. "Any jobs you want?"

I laughed but Mindy glared at me and said, "We'd be glad to help. Anything we can do from the bay area?"

"Phone calls," Melissa said. "I'll get you a list. We're looking for donations for the silent auction."

Mindy gave me another long look. "I'm sure that Charlie would love to make phone calls for you. And I'd be glad to help too."

I smiled at her. "Sure."

Jim patted me on the back. "Thanks for the help. You folks like a cup of coffee? Melissa would love to share that surprise with you."

I'd forgotten. Melissa had found something and sworn Jim to secrecy. "Sounds good."

"Great," he said. He looked at his wife and she patted her purse. "Okay then. How about Mountain Coffee on main street. They make a good breakfast too."

§§§§

The coffee was overshadowed by an outstanding fresh Mexican omelet. After I'd used my toast to scrape the last of the salsa off of the plate, leaving it almost clean enough to use again, Mindy asked, "Hungry?"

"I guess, and it was very good."

She passed me a knowing smile and squeezed my thigh under the table. I reached down and patted her hand. I suppose I'd worked up quite an appetite the night before. I turned to Melissa, "So what did you find?"

"You're going to like this," she said. She pulled out a sheet of paper and held it out for us to see. It was clear that it was a copy of something. The paper was dark and the original had obviously been stained in places. "Occasionally, someone will give us a box of old stuff, hoping it can be of value to the museum. Usually it's junk, but sometimes, it's a treasure. This," she patted the paper, "is a copy of a document we got several years ago."

"Several years?" Mindy asked.

"Right. We're all volunteers, and frankly, the workload can be overwhelming. This has been sitting in a crate full of assorted records in the storeroom in back of the museum. Nobody even knew it was there until just last month. There are a few of us who poke through the old stuff whenever we have a chance, but frankly, it can be a challenging task, sifting the gold from the rocks, so to speak. Anyway, I was going to call, but then you mentioned that you were coming up, so I decided to wait."

Mindy nodded. "So you found this?"

Shaking her head, Melissa continued. "Not me. I mentioned your quest to the others at the museum, and posted a note in the office just in case anyone came across anything related to your three young men. One of the other ladies found this one."

She smiled and said, "I'll read it to you. Bear with me. It's handwritten."

I, Joel Woodward, being of sound mind and body, in the Town of Murphys in the County of Calaveras, in the State of California, do by this Last Will and Testament, give and bequeath to my dear wife Catherine Woodward, everything of which I may die possessed, or which may be hereafter due to me, subject to the following gifts. To my two business partners and fine friends, Jonathan Campbell and Samuel Watkins, I bequeath $100 each. Should Catherine Woodward predecease me, I give and bequeath all of my possessions to my daughter, Marie Ruth Woodward, subject to the same gifts enumerated above.

I do assign my good friend Samuel Watkins as the executor of this will. For his services, he may deduct his expenses, not to exceed $25.

Signed this fourteenth day of July, 1853
Joel Woodward

Witnessed by:
Samuel Watkins, 14 July 1853
Robert Perkins, Attorney at Law, 14 July 1853

After Melissa read the document, she passed it to Mindy. As she and I read it, I was impressed that she'd gotten through it so easily, given the obviously deteriorated condition of the paper.

"Where did you find this?" Mindy asked.

Melissa smiled. "Got your attention didn't it." She leaned over. "Like I said, it was in an old box of stuff. Evidently one of the packets was from the files of one of the first lawyers in Murphys." She referred to the letter, "Robert Perkins. He kept copies of all of the wills that he witnessed, and stored them. These came from his attic. Some folks were remodeling an old house on Main Street, and found these when they were running some new wiring."

"Amazing," I said. And then something jogged in my memory. "Perkins," I said. Have we come across that name before?"

Mindy looked at me, curiously. "I don't think so." She hesitated. "Wait. Not the letters, but I think there was something."

I looked over at Melissa and Jim. They looked interested, but lost. And then I had it. "The lawyer Joel wrote to in San Francisco."

Mindy smiled and Jim frowned. She turned to him. "We came across an old letter online written by a lawyer in San Francisco to a Joel Woodward. Evidently, Joel was seeking employment in the city."

"When was that?" he asked.

She laughed. You mean, when did he write it or when did we find it?"

"Okay, both, I guess."

"Well I found it online. I was looking for nineteenth century letters that might include Joel's name, and it popped up. As for when it was written, ..." She looked at me. "1853 or four?"

I nodded. "I think so." I tried to explain to the Adams. "It seemed curious, more than important, but now that he had a prior contact in 1853, who knows."

"It explains how they knew one another, if nothing else," Mindy added.

"So what do you make of the will?" Melissa asked.

"Interesting," I said. "But where does this leave us?"

Mindy looked at me, her eyes glowing. "I can tell you one thing. We haven't seen any letters confirming it yet, but we know now that he knew about Marie!"

I smiled. "She must have gotten a letter to him."

She looked at Melissa. "Did you find any documents for the other two men?

"No," Melissa added. "We were looking primarily for Joel, so something else might have slipped through, but nobody mentioned anything." She sipped from her coffee cup. "We'll keep looking though. Does this help?"

Mindy beamed. "It's wonderful! I can't thank you enough!"

Jim broke into the conversation at that point. "Oh, I'm sure you can. Just make those phone calls. The church needs money."

CHAPTER 46

For some reason, finding out that Joel knew about Marie seemed to change our feelings about him. Before, he'd been a man who had run away from difficulties in Pennsylvania, leaving his bride of one day behind to go in search of gold in California. Now he was a man who had a child in Pennsylvania, and more importantly, knew about that child. Our search suddenly became a matter of determining not only what had happened to Joel, but what we could find out about his character.

Or so our conversation went the following day. We decided that we just couldn't face the thought of prospecting, my term, not hers, through one more antique store. Other than sore feet, our search had yielded nothing. In fact, the stores seemed to have very little interest in even carrying the type of material we were looking for. So we decided to drive home.

I delivered Mindy to her front door after a long and interesting drive, during which we discussed most of what we had discovered so far, and determined that we had more than accomplished our original goal. We knew beyond doubt that Joel Woodward, though erased from Mindy's family records, did in fact exist. Why he'd been forgotten, we could only guess, and would likely never know for sure. Mindy vowed to spend some more time over the next days scouring the internet for clues.

In the meantime, we arranged to meet at my place the following Saturday. I hinted that I had a special surprise in store, one that I thought she'd enjoy. Mindy was curious, but distracted by her thoughts about Joel, so she didn't pursue the secret as thoroughly as I might have expected. But I could wait. She wouldn't be patient forever, especially when I started dropping clues as the week progressed.

§§§§

I told Mindy to dress semi formally the following Saturday, as we'd be going to a theatrical event. She showed up, looking fit for an evening out, in a black dress and heels. She'd done her hair before leaving home, and commented that if it rained and ruined her work, she'd be blaming me. Fortunately, the weather was predicted to be fair.

I escorted her into my car, and off we went. It took nearly an hour to reach our destination in Palo Alto, where I'd managed to secure two tickets to a dance ensemble. Although the prospect of watching dancers didn't particularly excite me, I knew that she and her family loved everything to do with dancing.

I was surprised when we arrived to find the auditorium filled with families with children. I reviewed the advertisement I'd taken from the newspaper. It was definitely listed as a professional dance ensemble. Mindy however, knew exactly what was going on. She looked at the flyer and then said, "They are a professional dance troupe, but they're also instructors. We're going to be watching a dance recital by kids." She looked around. "I'll bet that just about everyone in the audience has kids in the show."

I looked around. "Not everybody," I groaned.

She patted my knee and kissed my cheek. "It'll be fun."

The first act confirmed her suspicion. The performers were probably 3 or 4 years old, and they were delightful. They danced for about two minutes, checking occasionally with unseen leaders behind the curtains, but generally remembering their routine and moving with a joy only a small child can show.

Over the course of the next hour, we watched as adult and child performers regaled the audience with a variety of steps, some remarkably complex. We cheered the Russian men with their strength and power, looked in awe at the grace of women who seemed to glide across the stage without ever moving their legs, and laughed as children corrected one another while maintaining concentration on their own steps. Mindy particularly liked the seven year old girl who reached up, grasped a boy by the back of the head, and turned his face so that he was pointing in the same direction as the others, all without missing a step.

We left, light hearted, and chatting gayly about how charming the performance had been. I had to admit that I'd thoroughly enjoyed it, and that the children had stolen the show from the professionals.

I'd planned dinner in an Italian place nearby, so we drove there. When we entered, Mindy looked around, skeptically. "Not too many people here."

I checked my watch. "It's early still, not yet 6:00. Don't worry," I said. "You'll like it. I promise."

She smiled and squeezed my arm. "I trust you." She looked around at the empty tables again, and I knew that trust might be conditional. Just then the host came and escorted us to a nice table in the back. I suppose one of the benefits to arriving early was the wide choice of tables.

He seated Mindy, placed napkins on our laps, and suggested a glass of house wine, which was quickly delivered. As we took our first sips, Mindy started to revise her opinion of the place. "Well the wine is pretty good for a house brand, and the menu looks promising." I just smiled.

We decided to share a Caesar salad and Chicken Piccata served in a fresh fig sauce. As I handed my menu to the waiter, Mindy said, "I've been researching Bradford again."

"Did you find something new?"

"More something different." She took a sip of her wine, and then putting down her glass, continued. "I decided to go after the old land records. You remember when Sam Watkins told us that the spot of the old general store was now a strip mall? Well I wondered what had become of the Lewis farm."

"Did you find it?"

"Oh yeah. It's amazing how complete some of those records are, even after what," she paused, thinking, "160 years! Anyway, I did find the old homestead, if you can call it that."

"And?"

"And it's still there!"

I was stunned. "Really? You've got to be kidding. The town didn't expand over it?"

She shook her head, and then smiled. "It did." I must have looked confused, because she laughed. "Let me explain. The house is still there, but it sits on just three acres. Most of the farm is gone."

"So the town did expand."

She nodded. "I'd love to visit it though. Evidently the house and grounds were donated to the city by an Angela Lewis Jacobson. I looked on my family tree, but her name wasn't there. She seems to be part of another branch that I didn't know about."

"I wonder who her parents were? Robert's line through his new wife?"

She shrugged her shoulders. "I don't know. That's a whole different search, and not one I'm ready to take on just yet." She reached for the wine, sipped, and said again, "This is a really good wine for house and it seems to be getting better and better."

I drank from mine and nodded. It was impressive. Whoever selected their wine must have chosen carefully. "So how did she get the farm?"

"No idea. Again, that's another search." She paused for a moment. "What I do know, is that the old farmhouse has been restored. It's a museum now, and the barn is also being maintained. They're open to school groups and the general public. They even have a small restaurant and an vintage store there."

I was stunned. "How did you find out all of this?"

"It wasn't that hard," she said smugly, and reached into her purse. "Once I found their web page." She pulled out a sheet of paper. On top, it said, 'Living History at the Lewis Family Farm.'

I took the offered page and scanned it. "Fascinating! Your family home is now a museum!"

She nodded. "I read the original deed signed by Mayor Williams when he accepted the gift from my ancestor. It stipulates that the city is to maintain the farmhouse and grounds in a condition similar to their present state, and open it up to the public as a park and a piece of living history."

"It must cost them a tidy sum."

"I'm sure it does, but it seems that she left a trust fund to pay for that."

"I wonder how much she left."

Mindy smiled again. "You don't trust me to do my homework?" I grimaced and she laughed. "I wrote it on the back of that paper."

I turned the paper over. "Twelve thousand, eight hundred and twenty six dollars." I looked up. "It doesn't seem like much."

She reached for the paper and slid it back into her purse. "Not by today's dollars, but it was probably pretty substantial in 1907, and invested in some kind of annuity over the years..."

"So your family's farmhouse has been a city park for the past hundred years." I shook my head in wonder. "It'd be fascinating to go there. To walk through Catherine's room and maybe see the desk where she penned her letters, to see her kitchen, or the chair that Tom sat in when he rocked Marie. Wow!"

"Someday," she said. "Maybe this summer? Can you get time off?"

I was about to answer when the waiter showed up with our salad, or salads. He'd divided the salad onto two plates, and each looked like a full offering. We were both hungry, so focused on our food for the next few minutes. When Mindy spoke next, it was to gesture with her fork toward her plate. "Okay. This is one of the best Caesars I've ever had."

I just smiled.

The Chicken Picatta was equally good, and the dessert, a lemon tart covered with raspberry glaze was the perfect ending to the meal. We were relaxing over a cup of coffee when Mindy reached into her purse again. "I have another letter from Catherine, if you're interested."

I just chuckled. "Of course."

November 20, 1851
Bradford, Pennsylvania

My Dearest Joel,
I apologize for not writing. I noticed that it has been nearly two months. I have been so busy, and it has been so long since I have heard from you, that I have just been putting it off, thinking I will write tomorrow. Well it is finally tomorrow, and I am taking the time to write.
Ruth left two weeks ago and the house seems very lonely without her cheery presence. We are all invited up to Pittsburgh whenever we can find time, and I am determined to go visit, maybe when the roads clear next spring. She has helped me so much, not just by taking care of me, but by helping me to grow up

and to stand up to my brothers. It is something I was never really able to do in the past. Now, well now it is like I am a different person. Of course, being a mother has something to do with that as well.

Marie is the love of my life. Of course, I still love you, but that is different. She is starting to talk. Her first word was not mama or papa, as I had hoped. It was Jake. Well, 'J' anyway. You remember Tom's old hunting hound? Well ever since she has been crawling, she has chased that dog all through the house. They have become best friends, and more than once, I have found him curled up, sound asleep under her crib. I have had to draw the line on her sucking on his ears or his tail, though he is so indulgent with her that I am sure that he would not mind even if she was to bite him. Speaking of which, she has three teeth now, and they are sharp. The teething has been hard, and I finally took Ruth's advice when Marie was fussing one night and rubbed a little whisky on her gums. It stopped her fussing, but I hope she does not develop a taste for it. Where Ruth got the whisky I do not care to know. It certainly did not come from this house.

Marie has started to walk around furniture, holding on, and Tom has been walking with her, though sometimes her feet just can not keep up and she ends up dangling and falling, and they laugh and he picks her up and tosses her up into the air, eliciting even more giggles. They are inseparable. She's started to call his name too, though she can not get out much more than Ta at this point. And yes, she has finally called me mama. She is a smart girl, your daughter, talking, and about to start walking. I moved things up when she started to crawl, and again when she started to pull herself up. And now it is time to move them again. I suppose it will not be long until she is climbing everything she can reach and it will not matter where I put things.

She remains a loving child though, and some of my favorite moments are in the evenings, after she has been fed, when she cuddles up against me. I have begun to read to her, stories from the bible mostly, and she seems to follow along well, often wanting to turn the page. It does not take long though, before she is sound asleep. I tend to follow not too long after.

We are getting ready for Thanksgiving dinner. Robert and his new wife have invited our entire family to their home, and though Tom grumbled a bit about breaking the tradition here, we finally accepted. I will join the ladies in the kitchen, and look forward to the laughter and camaraderie there. I suppose the men will settle into the parlor, or go out to the barn to check out the new equipment and talk about next year's planting. It's too bad it's 1851 and we don't have a television, as I'm sure they'd enjoy a football game.

How will you spend Thanksgiving? Do they celebrate in California, or do you continue to look for gold? Will you be having a Thanksgiving feast? I hope so.

I think of you often, even if I have been remiss in writing. I pray that you are safe and well, and that you return to me soon. I need you here.

Your loving wife,

Catherine

Mindy put the letter down, folded it, and returned it to her purse.

"Interesting," I said.

"Did you like it?"

"I especially enjoyed the part about football."

She laughed. "You looked like you might be dozing off, so I threw that part in."

"You thought I was dozing?"

At that she opened her mouth with a big guffaw. "Please!" she scowled.

"Me?"

Giving me her best innocent look, she mimicked, "Me?" She rolled her eyes and said, "Actually, you shouldn't be tired at all, considering the nap you got during the dance recital."

"I wasn't..." I started to answer, but she feigned a snoring sound, so I just sputtered a bit, and then stared at her. The light from the candle on the table danced off her eyes, and by their sparkle, I could tell that she was silently having a wonderful time at my expense. "Any other changes you made?"

"In what?" she asked.

I stared at her. "The letter."

She shook her head slowly, side to side, then smirked, "Would I tell you if there were?"

Chuckling, I took her hand and kissed her fingertips, slowly working my way up to her palm and along the inside of her wrist until she squirmed and pulled it back. "Probably not." I said, and called for the check.

CHAPTER 47

Mindy had always been so careful about putting the letters back into her folder, and hiding the actual number of documents from me, that I was surprised later that evening to see them laying on her coffee table. She was upstairs, and I was curious but didn't really want to break her confidence. Still, they were in two piles, one much larger than the other. Interesting. I settled on the sofa and opened my book to read while I waited for her.

As soon as Mindy came downstairs, I motioned toward the letters. "You'd better put those away. I've been resisting the temptation to go through the last ones, but my will power can only last so long."

She gave me a hard look, and I raised my hand defensively. "I've been good, but I admit that I'm curious." Turning my head away from the letters, I continued. "Please put them away now."

Laughing, she picked up the packet and wrapped the letters inside. I watched out of the corner of my eye. Her body language said that she trusted me. Maybe. As soon as she'd put them back into the red cabinet, I relaxed. "Thank you."

"So you wouldn't take them out of there?" She scowled. "You have that much will power?"

"Out of sight; out of mind," I said.

"I see." She sat next to me and I put my arm around her shoulders. She slid closer and we nuzzled together like that for a few minutes. Her scent was enchanting. She'd bathed while she was upstairs, and used the body wash I'd given her. I closed my eyes and luxuriated in her feel, her smell, and her warmth. It wasn't long before I was dozing.

After a few minutes, Mindy said, "You seem to be far away. Tired?"

I nodded. "It's been a long day. Bed sounds good."

She stood and reached out her hand to pull me up. "Me too."

§§§§

The following day dawned warm and sunny. It appeared that spring was definitely in the air, so we decided to take advantage of the weather with a trip up the coast to Año Nuevo State Park.

Mindy wanted to drive, so I agreed to navigate. It also gave me the opportunity to sightsee along the way, something that I miss when driving.

It was a glorious morning. As we slipped up the coast, I was impressed with the contrast of the verdant hills on the right and the sparkling blue of the ocean on the left. It was definitely God's country. I commented on a few hearty surfers out in the water. Spring had arrived, but the water was still pretty nippy. Only the diehards would jump in there, even with a good wetsuit. On the other hand, the waves looked good, and maybe the lack of competition played a part in attracting them to the water.

I hadn't been to Año Nuevo in several years, and had to smile as we maneuvered into the tiny gravel parking lot. Little had changed. It was not a widely used park. True, there was one small swimming beach there, as well as a sheltered spread of white sand that attracted a group of people whose beachwear preferences were most commonly described as clothing optional. I hinted on the way up that maybe Mindy would like to lay out au natural and enjoy an all over tan. She assured me that she'd be appropriately dressed for the beach. If I was interested in naked sunbathing on the other hand, I was welcome to do so, and she'd certainly enjoy applying sunburn lotion to my sorry little pink bottom. After a good laugh, we both opted for a hike instead.

Anyway, we crunched across the gravel into a parking space and climbed out of the car. We'd packed a picnic before leaving the house, and now I shouldered the backpack that held our water, fruit, and sandwiches. Even though it was a warm day, in anticipation of the offshore breeze we'd probably face at the point, I threw two jackets on top of the food, and off we went.

The start of the main trail was marked by a weathered sign. The trail itself ran through beach scrub, that was made up of a good wall of mixed blackberry and poison oak bushes. We kept to the middle of the trail. Fortunately, the blackberries were just beginning to flower, and it would be a few months before we might be tempted to chance the thorns and poison oak for the occasional berry.

"Have you been here before?" she asked.

I continued walking, holding her hand, and answered. "Several times, but it's been a few years."

"Do you suppose we'll see seals?"

"I'd expect so," I answered. Año Nuevo was known as one of the primary breeding areas for the elephant seal, and we would be visiting just in time for pupping season. "Have you been here?"

"No. Strange isn't it. It's not that far away." She squeezed my hand and we continued down the trail.

About five minutes into the park, we came to a side trail, and I said, "Here's your chance. That one goes down to the beach."

She scowled at me. "I didn't bring a suit."

"Neither did I, but that's the point. They're optional here."

She just inclined her head toward the trail. "Keep walking."

And so we did. We walked for about a mile before our cliff top trail turned inland and we saw the first elephant seals. The going was harder in deep sand, and we both felt a little claustrophobic, as the dunes lifted as high as twenty feet on either side. Still, we relied on the occasional marker and trudged ahead. As we came to the top of a small rise, I could make out an island beyond the point, whose main feature was a crumpling lighthouse. And then, with a few more steps, the beach spread out in front of us. We were still a couple of hundred yards away, but I could definitely tell that we'd entered elephant seal territory. There were hundreds of them. By and large, they looked like big brown slugs, sunbathing in the sand. Every once in awhile, one would raise its head, snarl or bark, and then settle back down. I was about to go forward, when Mindy gripped my hand and held me back. Not fifty feet from us, off to the right side of the trail in one of the dune valleys, was an enormous seal. I'd have thought he was asleep, but his eyes were open, tracking us. Periodically, he smacked a flipper at the sand flies who buzzed about him.

Ahead of us, stood a park ranger, directing the few tourists who'd come to the park, and keeping everyone far away from the local seal. "Let's go up there," I said.

Mindy looked over at the seal, who lifted his head as we approached, showing off his prominent tusks. "Is it safe?"

I smiled. "It should be. He's off a ways." Holding her hand, I led us slowly up to the park ranger.

As we approached, she smiled and said, "Go on over there. We've got a good viewing area. You'll be able to see most of the action on the beach."

The viewing area was pretty simple, a broad spot on the sand, at the top of a dune. There were only a couple of others there, so we were able to get a good spot.

We were closer now, and were able to look down on much of the beach. We watched for a while before Mindy said, "Can you see the pattern?"

I frowned at her. "Pattern?"

She nodded slowly. "They overlap a lot, but there seem to be some clusters down there."

I looked again, and sure enough, there were a few definable concentrations, where the population of elephant seals seemed denser than others. And then there were others areas where there were just a few scattered seals, all males from the looks of their trunks. A second ranger was pointing to one particularly large group. I could see a number of pups there, mixed in with several females. A larger seal seemed to be wallowing his way toward one edge of the group. "Do you see that one?" she asked. We all nodded and she continued. Now if you look into the middle of the group, toward the water, you'll see a massive male."

Mindy grabbed my arm and pointed. "See him? He's huge."

The ranger nodded. "That's one of our dominant males, and this is his harem. The one sneaking up is a younger male, and he's going to try to cut out a couple of the females."

Mindy watched while he continued. "He's reached an age where he's wants to start his own harem." Suddenly the old male raised his head and bellowed. "Ah," the ranger said with a smile. "He's noticed that he's got competition." The big bull rose higher, and continued to roar. The other, seeing that he'd been discovered, stopped, but held his ground.

"So what happens now?" I asked.

"Probably nothing. He's been spotted. They'll likely shout back and forth a bit, and then the younger one will back off.

Mindy and I watched for a while, as the younger male elephant seal settled into the sand, on the edge of the harem. The old bull watched for a while, and then lowered down himself. Just when we thought that the excitement was over, the younger male rose and scooted toward one of the females, obviously attempting to cut her out of the harem. With a loud roar, the old bull shot up into the air, towering over the other seals around him, and romped toward the interloper heedless of the females and pups in his path. The young male, seeing the old bull, lifted his body, barking his own challenge.

The two met with a thud audible to us on the bluff a hundred yards away. Even from our vantage point, the size of the animals was impressive. Both had risen to their full height so that when they slashed at one another with their tusks, their heads were easily six to eight feet above the ground.

"Look," Mindy cried, and tightly squeezed my arm. "He's hurt."

The ranger spoke without turning toward her. "Don't worry. You see the darker spot on their chests? That's a thick leathery patch, almost like a shield. If you could see them up close, you'd see that most of the males are pretty well scarred."

Indeed, above the clamor of the battle, I saw several other bulls rise up, looking over at the fighters, displaying the crisscross pattern of scars across their own breasts.

The ranger continued, "It's got everybody's attention now. Look there." She pointed to another male who'd turned toward the combatants. Unbeknownst to him, another of the young males had taken the opportunity to romp into his harem. He nuzzled against a female, she squealed, and her bull turned instantly, bellowing and slogging toward the interloper. The young male backed off, snarling but cowed under the aggressive eye of the old bull.

I turned my head back to the main battle. Blood streaked down the fronts of both bulls, as they rocked back and forth, seeking an advantage. And then suddenly, as quickly as it had begun, the fight was over. The young bull pivoted, faster than I might have imagined, and sprinted, elephant seal style, toward an open piece of sand by the water. While we watched, he slid into the ocean, no doubt, to soothe his wounds. His opponent roared again, and returned to his own spot in the middle of his harem. He settled slowly, obviously a little sore, but fully aware that for today at least, he was still king.

Mindy was shivering. "That was amazing!"

I nodded, grinning in excitement. "Does this happen often?" I asked the ranger.

She just smiled. "Sure. Several times a day." She paused for a moment. "Did you notice the seal in the sand when you came up the trail?"

I motioned with my hand. "Back there?"

"That's the one. He lost his harem a couple of days ago." She shrugged. "The law of the wild," she said wryly. "One day, you're on top of the world, and all the ladies want your attention. The next day," she tilted his head toward the lone seal, "you're sleeping alone at the bottom of a dune."

I looked at Mindy and she said, "Don't worry. I won't make you sleep out here alone in the dunes."

I wasn't sure how to reply, so said, "Is that because I'm your stud muffin or because I keep you warm."

She just smiled a mysterious smile, took my hand, and said, "How about some lunch? We can sit up on the cliff back there and watch the seals."

We turned and headed back down the trail. I did notice that she didn't answer my question.

§§§§

We settled on a small bluff, just a short walk off the main trail. From there, we could see the action down on the beach, but were well removed from any of the seals. Better yet, we were sheltered from the breeze that blew down the coast from the northwest, and could fully enjoy the delightful warmth of the sun.

Mindy had packed the picnic, and all she'd told me was that we were having sandwiches. I expected something like peanut butter and jelly, something that would survive a day out of the refrigerator. I was pleasantly surprised then, when I opened the bag and found an ice pack wrapped around a nice slice of smoked salmon. "Looks good!" I said as I raised my eyebrows toward her.

"Thought you'd like it," she replied. "Cajun okay? You like a little spice, don't you?"

I grinned and leaned over to kiss her. "It's perfect."

She'd also brought a sourdough baguette along with sliced pear, and to my great surprise, a small plastic container of balsamic vinegar and olive oil. I looked up at her again, raising my eyebrows in surprise and she said smugly, "We may be primitive out here, but that doesn't mean that we can't eat well."

"Of course," I replied.

We continued to watch the seals while we ate. There were a couple more minor skirmishes, but usually it was a much younger and smaller male just trying to see if the old bull was paying attention. They always were, and the youngster would back off quickly. Ah, the hazards of sexual frustration.

The sun had baked the sand, and we luxuriated in its warmth, chatting easily about what we watched for over an hour. Finally, Mindy withdrew an envelope from the front pocket of the backpack. "I didn't think it would be a good idea to bring an original to the beach," she said softly, so I made a copy." She unfolded the paper and handed it to me. "It's from Joel."

Murphys, California
April 16, 1852
My darling wife,

It is hard to believe that I have been gone two years. The time has slipped by without my really noticing it. We have been very busy working the new claim, but it still does not seem like a very good excuse for my absence. I miss you and think of you often.

Murphys is a good place to be. We have been fortunate enough to make several good deposits with the Wells Fargo bankers, and our account is growing. Unlike some others, they have a good reputation in the gold country here for honesty and reliability. And that has served them well as they have many customers. I was talking with one of our neighbors, a fellow who is mining a strip just a couple of hundred feet upstream from ours, and he told me that he had deposited a good sized nugget with another outfit last year, only to have the banker skip out of town with everybody's gold. The rumor is that he caught one of the packet ships back to Panama, and intended to return to New York from there.

He had better. I can just imagine what would happen to him if some of his customers found him here.

I always enjoy a trip into town to the local office. What a contrast we must appear to them. The clerks are always dressed in freshly cleaned and pressed clothing, with their green eyeshades. We, on the other hand, wear the same clothes days or sometimes weeks at a time, washing them only in the creek, or occasionally at the Chinese laundry.

Today though, I feel good. We have been tied to the claim pretty much day and night for the past months, and decided to take a little break, so we rented a room in the Murphys Hotel for three nights, and splurged on baths and meals. Samuel even got a shave and a haircut. It was hard to recognize him, and as you might expect, Jonathan and I gave him a good ribbing. I was not quite so profligate, and settled for a simple trim, but I will tell you, I feel like a new man. It had been so long since I had dipped into a warm bath that I had forgotten how good it could feel.

We have made a number of friends here and up in the gold fields. There are certainly a good mix of scoundrels here, but also many good men who like us, hope to find enough gold to return home with a stake for the future.

The longer I stay here, the more I like California, and I have begun to think that we could make a home here. The land is cheap and plentiful, and with water, rich for the growing of crops or ranching. I have met a number of men who have decided to settle here, usually with women they have met since arriving in California. Others have sent for wives and girlfriends that they left back east. A couple have even returned to their old homes with plans to bring the family back here. As the trails across the country improve, I understand that many of the challenges of travel are fading away.

I know that it would be a hardship for you to leave your family behind in Pennsylvania, possibly never to see them again. I suppose that I have the advantage there. Having grown up in the orphanage, I never got to know any of my family. I know from my talks with you and others how wonderful it is to have a loving family, and certainly have regrets. On the other hand though, I have nothing but you binding me to Pennsylvania.

I find that I am rambling, but putting pen to paper with you is like pressing you to my breast in many ways, and I do wish that you could be here. Perhaps one of your brothers has an urge to see California. Or perhaps I should return to bring you out here. I feel that my future is here in California and want to start that future with you at my side.

Write me when you receive this letter and let me know of your plans. If you will not leave Pennsylvania, I will certainly be disappointed, but after an absence of two years, will understand. If one of your brothers will escort you across the country, I will do my best to help set him up once he arrives. As I said above, we have been able to save a little bit of money and I would willingly share my good fortune with him. And if you wish me to come back, and to bring you out here myself, I will fly to your side.

I am sending again, as I've sent in my last several letters, my contact information. Sheriff Miller and I have become good friends, and you may direct my mail in care of him.

  Rick Miller, Sheriff
  Murphys, California
  You are my love and my future.

Joel

I was breathing heavily as I put down the letter. "Wow. Interesting."

Mindy nodded enthusiastically. "So he's sent for her."

"Yeah. He mentioned sending several letters. Do you suppose she didn't get them?"

"I don't know. Maybe. I'm sure mail between the east and west coasts was pretty uncertain back then."

"And she never went."

She shook her head slowly. "Not that I know of." Then she gave me a startled look. "Do you suppose..." she began tremulously.

"What?"

"He gave her three choices."

I reflected on the letter, and then opened it up. One choice jumped out at me and I re-read it aloud. "If you will not leave Pennsylvania, I will certainly be disappointed, but after an absence of two years, will understand." I looked up at her. Her face was waxen, and she looked on the verge of tears.

"She stayed behind." Her voice was almost a cry.

I reached for her and took her into my arms. Stroking her back, I said softly, "We don't know that."

We rocked that way for a couple of minutes until she leaned back and I saw that her cheeks were streaked with tears. Taking the hem of my shirt, I gently wiped them away as she sniffled.

Mindy shook her head slowly from side to side. "But we do," she moaned. "We do. She never left Pennsylvania. We know that."

CHAPTER 48

Our drive back to Soquel was quiet, with both of us lost in our own thoughts. Mindy's face was set and firm, reflecting a sadness I hadn't seen in her before. I reached over and squeezed her hand, and then held it all the way back to her place.

We'd planned to go out to dinner that evening, a kind of impromptu celebration of the year we'd been dating, but somehow the mood was broken. I suggested that we get ready to eat, but she was listless, and I couldn't move her to take a shower. Finally, I took her to the couch, sat her next to me, and held her close. "I think that maybe we should read another letter."

They were definitely Mindy's letters, and I'd always followed her lead regarding when and what we should read. She looked up at me. "I'm afraid of what we'll find," she said. Then she sat up straight. "Maybe that's why his name doesn't show up in the family tree, why Marie wasn't listed as Woodward. Maybe..." She leaned into me again and sighed.

I thought for a while. She may be right. It could be that we'd read all of these letters and become invested in this relationship only to find that distance killed it. Somehow though, I didn't think so. If that had been the case, why would she have saved the letters? Why would Marie?

I spoke carefully. "We're imagining the worst. If that's the case, then we already know it. We may find that something else happened."

Mindy shuddered, "And what might that be?" Then she rose

and walked to the red cupboard. She withdrew the packet of letters and put it on the coffee table before spreading them and taking out a letter from Catherine. "I'm going to open a bottle of '5'," she said, pointing to one of her favorite wines. "Would you like some?"

I nodded, and as she rose, looked down at the stack. Her choice of wine, though coincidental, was ominous. The way that the letters were spread it was clear to see that after this letter, there would be just a handful left.

May 12, 1852
Bradford, Pennsylvania

To my sweetest, most darling husband,

I received your letter yesterday and was so happy, after two long years, to have an address so that I can write to you. The idea that you will someday read the words that I pen here today gives me more joy than you can possibly imagine.

Marie continues to be my little darling. She walks now, and is into everything. I put my sewing basket on the table the other day to go check on something. When I came back, she had everything scattered across the floor and was playing with the spools of thread. I wanted to be cross, I really did, but she was only curious. So I picked it up and put it away, though not without a healthy bawl from her when I took away her toys. Or at least I thought I had picked up everything. Evidently I missed a needle, but Tom found it later with his bare toe. Fortunately, he was not hurt much.

Speaking of Tom, he is back to his old high and mighty behavior over the past several weeks. I suppose it has to do with the long winter we have had. It has kept him indoors far too often, and he is anxious to get out and start planting. The ground finally started to thaw, but is still a muddy swamp. It has been sunny the past few days, and he is hoping to get out and plow next week. He has sharpened and re-sharpened his tools several times, just to keep busy. He tried to give me instructions in my kitchen yesterday. In my kitchen! Well you can imagine that I set him straight about that. The way he shot out of the room, you would have thought he was a whipped puppy with his tail between his legs.

Oh well. Maybe we are all a little testy. Like I said, it has been a long cold winter and we are truly grateful to see the sun at long last.

Your sheriff sounds like a busy man, rounding up criminals, delivering mail, and riding all over the countryside. Does he have any help or is he all alone? How many people live in Murphys? Are you close in or far away?

Josie came over last week. The roads were clear, though muddy, so she was able to bring the wagon out by herself. She is expecting a baby sometime in the fall. We spent the day chatting and sewing baby clothes. It was so much fun. Now that I have been getting together with Josie and her sisters, I can not imagine being without sisters as a child. Of course, if the baby is a girl, she will be using some of the clothes that Marie has outgrown. I suppose that many would be suitable even if it is a boy. It will be exciting to have a sister with a baby. Marie is so cute. I am not sure she really understands, but still, she points to Josie's stomach and says, "baby?" We both laugh and say, "Yes, baby." Then she wonders why she can not see the baby right now. I wish you could be here too. Then my happiness would be complete.

Tom took me into town last week and we did some shopping. Of course, our little general store is pretty tiny compared to the grand emporium in Pittsburgh, but still, it was nice to get out. I stocked up on flour and canning supplies and other staples, and even bought some fabric for a new frock. Tom splurged and bought himself a new pair of overalls. The fabric is thick cotton, and should be very durable, even with his hard farming work. They called it denim, and I hear that it started out in California in the gold mining areas. Have you heard of that?

Did I tell you that I have been saving all of your letters? I read them and read them again, until some are starting to fray. I have written several letters to you, but not having an address, have just packed them away with yours. I suppose that I should make a copy of this one, and add it to my collection. That way, I can read it again later and laugh at my foolishness. Maybe I will save them for Marie. It gives me something to do, anyway.

I miss you more than I can say. Be safe, and hurry home.

Your loving wife, Catherine

Mindy put the letter down. "Well?" she asked.

I shook my head. "I don't know what to think. Obviously she hasn't gotten his other letter, but then it's only been a month, so it wouldn't have traveled across the country yet." I thought for a moment and then asked, "The last one he sent, the one where he included the sheriff's address. When was that written?"

She sorted through the stack and found the letter. She opened the envelope and looked inside. "November 14th, 1851," she said.

Her answer was toneless, and I could tell that she was still upset. "So it took six months to get across the country."

She nodded. "Or to come by sea." I looked at the other letters on the coffee table. She saw my look and shook her head slowly from side to side. "No," she said and smiled at me. "Not tonight. I need to let these letters settle in a bit before I read anything else."

"Okay," I said.

She lifted her glass of wine and said, "To Catherine, whatever she decides," then smiled, "decided." I clinked my glass against her and drank. It was definitely a good wine.

She leaned back against the couch and closed her eyes for a moment. Then, without opening them said, "What was that bit about an orphanage?"

That startled me. "You're right. We were so focused on him asking her to come west that we completely forgot that." I looked over at her. She was sitting up now, alert. "Do you suppose that might be one of the reasons why her brothers didn't want them together?"

"Could be," she said. "It would certainly explain his apparent lack of background."

"Hm," I mused, and we both settled back against the red sofa, lost in thoughts about possibilities.

After a few minutes, she took a last sip of wine and then stood. "How about a movie?"

I looked at her. The pain, though masked, was still plain on her face so I grimaced and said, "Sure. One of your dance movies?"

She laughed and picked up my empty glass. "Do I look that pathetic that you would be willing to sit through a dance movie?"

"Well if you want something else," I murmured.

She just chuckled and headed for the kitchen with the wine glasses. Tossing a look back over her shoulder, she grinned. "I like your idea. Too late to change your mind now. I know just the one."

Oh well, I thought. A night of dance. It could be worse. Surgery? Dental work? I shrugged. It was good to see her smile again.

CHAPTER 49

The revelation that Joel had invited Catherine to California, while expected in some ways, still caught us both off guard, and it took some time to digest it and move forward. I hadn't realized how much Mindy had invested in the research into her ancestors until we read that letter. For that matter, I hadn't really considered how much I cared about two people from the nineteenth century. As hard as it might have been, and despite increasing evidence to the contrary, we had always assumed that they would find a way to come together again. Now though, we really began to doubt that outcome.

So when we met for dinner a couple of weeks later, I didn't really know what to expect. What I got was a cheerful Mindy who evidently had put the disappointment of the previous letters behind her. "I started thinking," she said. "And the bottom line is that they lived and died a century ago. There's nothing I can do to change what happened. My role is just to uncover it, and I'm more determined than ever to continue that."

We had prime seats in one of Santa Cruz' finest eateries, and were looking out on a choppy sea in the Monterey Bay. Winter had returned with a vengeance, unleashing several days of rain and high winds throughout the area. We'd even had a touch of snowfall in the mountains surrounding the bay area. So nobody was surfing, or even boating, for that matter. Still, despite the rain that lashed the windows, the view of the ocean was exceptional, and we both felt lucky to be able to share it.

We'd been commenting on a few hardy gulls braving the

wind when Mindy made her announcement.

"I've gone back to the internet," she said. "And I think you'll be surprised by what I've found."

"You found more?"

She nodded. "I suspect, that if I keep looking, and have the patience and creativity to keep going in different directions, I'll find more still."

I had to agree. "It makes sense. I suppose there's a finite amount of material available, but until you find it all, you won't know."

She fumbled in her purse for a moment, and then pulled out a small envelope. "I downloaded this a few days ago." She handed it across to me. I extracted the paper and was about to unfold it when our waiter arrived.

"What can I get you tonight?" she asked.

In some ways, this was a special meal for us, a return to the restaurant where we'd eaten on our first date, and in the past Mindy had indicated that she liked it when I ordered for her, so I said, "She'll have the salmon with dill sauce and a glass of your house chardonnay. I'm going to have the lamb with a glass of the house zinfandel."

I had gathered the menus and offered them to the waitress when she continued, "Would you like salads?"

I looked at Mindy and decided. "We'll share a Caesar."

"Very good." She looked questioningly at Mindy who smiled at her, and then added, "All right. I'll be back in a minute with your wine."

After she's left, Mindy started to laugh. "I don't think she approved."

"Of what?" I asked. "Of me ordering for you?"

"You're in Santa Cruz. This is definitely an area where women have staked out their independence from men. She probably thinks that you're a prehistoric chauvinist." Then she leaned forward and said conspiratorially, "I hope she doesn't spit on your lamb!"

"She wouldn't do that," I stammered.

Mindy just shrugged. "You've insulted the independence of women. Who knows what she'll do." She could see the shocked concern on my face and added, "Probably not though. She seems like a sweet girl. Probably one of the university students working part time." She swirled her water and took a sip. "Still..."

"Waiters don't do that," I said. "It's just an urban legend."

"Oh I agree," Mindy said quietly. "Might make the lamb taste better though." Seeing the outrage on my face, she burst into new paroxysms of laughter. "You look so sweet when you're upset." She reached over and patted my hand. "But I still think lamb wouldn't likely suffer from a little saliva." She grimaced and shuddered a bit. "Don't know why anyone would want to eat that stuff in the first place." She squeezed my hand then let go and sat back. "Go ahead, open the letter."

I snorted. "Sure, now that you've ruined my dinner, you want me to open the letter."

She started laughing again and this time, as much as she wanted, she couldn't stop. Pretty soon, she'd infected me and I was laughing too. Every time one of us tried to stop, a glance at the other would start the giggling again. Finally, I turned to look out the window and catch my breath. Teeth clenched against the convulsions that still threatened to take me, I shook my head. "You are an evil person," I hissed.

"Me?" she asked. "I'm not the one who's making them kill a little baby lamb just so I can stuff my face with it."

I started to answer, but this time it was she who turned her head, wrapping her arm around her face in an attempt to quell the laughter. Fortunately, that's when the waitress came with our wine. We both held it together while she put it down on the table. It wasn't easy, but we did it.

As she stood again, she said, "Your salad should be up in a minute. Is there anything else I can get for you?"

I shook my head. "No thanks."

She turned to Mindy, who winked at me and added, "We're just fine, thanks."

She started to turn when I opened my mouth again. "I do have a question though."

"All right," she answered, turning back to me. "What can I do for you?"

"Mindy," I gestured toward her, "She seems to think that I may have offended you by ordering for both of us."

Our waitress turned to Mindy and I could see some kind of silent communication pass between them even though Mindy was shaking her head as if I was truly clueless.

She looked back at me, having received Mindy's message. "Uh," she said, "Not at all. Happens all the time."

"Good," I said. "No offense was intended." She smiled and I added, glancing out of the corner of my eye at Mindy, "So you wouldn't really spit on my lamb, would you?"

The look on Mindy's face told me that I was now in real trouble for sharing that little tidbit, but the waitress saved the day. She looked at Mindy, and then back at me. "Absolutely not," she said straight faced. Then she grinned at Mindy, "Interesting idea though."

And with that, Mindy lost it. Every time she looked at me for the next few minutes, she burst into a new set of giggles. My only satisfaction came when she finally started to settle down and took a sip of wine, only to snort it out through her nose. Finally, she wiped the tears out of her eyes and shook her head slowly from side to side. "You are sweet," she said, "But what makes you think that you can out duel two women." She rose and kissed me lightly on the cheek. I had enough common sense to keep my mouth shut. Nothing I could say would do me any good at that point.

§§§§

Later, over dessert, I opened her envelope. Inside was a simple record from. It took me a moment to figure out what it was. There were a number of notations, some longer than others, but one had been highlighted, and I focused in on that. "Tax records?" I asked.

She nodded.

I looked back at the paper in front of me. It was a listing by address of people's tax liability in Bradford, Pennsylvania for the year, 1866. One line read:

47 Amm Street Catherine Lewis $28.59

That was all, but it told us a lot. "This was her house?"

Mindy nodded. "It would appear so. And note the name. Not Woodward, but Lewis."

I mused slowly, looking at the document, "Her maiden

name." I thought for a moment. "So as of 1866, she was not married."

"And she owned property."

"Right," I tapped the paper, repeating aloud. "And she owned property. Marie would have been what, fifteen?"

"I hadn't thought of that," Mindy said. "She would. I suppose they both lived there." She said it in a way that left it anything but clear whether she was sure, but then everything was becoming a little more vague at the same time that we were learning more.

"Interesting," I said. "Interesting."

Mindy had moved next to me to share the dessert, and now she smiled up at me. "Thank you for dinner. It was fun." I rolled my eyes and she chuckled again and patted my hand. "I have another letter at home if you're interested."

§§§§

Back at Mindy's house, we settled down onto the red sofa. The wind and the rain had picked up, and gusts periodically rattled the windows. Mindy had taken out the letter and was beginning to read when a particularly violent gust slammed a tree branch against the front window and seemed to shake the entire house. Startled, I jumped at the noise, and then nervously settled back onto the couch. "Windy," I said sheepishly.

Mindy was about to reply when we lost power. We sat silently for a minute or so, waiting for the lights to flicker back on, but as time stretched out, came to the realization that we may have a power outage. I looked around the living room. Daylight was entirely gone, and the cloudy skies pretty well blocked out any moonlight that might have helped us. And without streetlights, it was dark, really dark. I could hear Mindy shuffling about at the end of the couch, but couldn't see her.

"Mindy?" I questioned.

"Stay there," she said. "I've got some candles in the kitchen."

I looked toward the kitchen. Nothing. It was no more or less black than the rest of the house. I thought of navigating through her living room in the dark, past the various pieces of furniture, the artwork displayed on cabinets and walls, and decided my best bet was to sit still. "No problem," I replied. "Need any help?"

"No." I listened to her passage through the living room, and except for one small, "ouch," could detect no problems.

"You okay?"

"Stubbed my toe on a dining room chair. I'm fine." I waited for the rattle of a cabinet, but instead heard the singsong melody of her computer turning on, and recalled that we'd been looking at a video of African animals before heading out for dinner. A few seconds later, the screen powered up, throwing a dim light throughout the room.

"Good idea," I said. She didn't respond, but presently lit a flashlight, and came back with two candles and a book of matches.

"This should do," she said, lighting one of the candles. She'd picked up a pair of small candlestick holders in the kitchen, and settled the lit candles into them on the coffee table in front of us. Then she turned off the flashlight. "Remind me tomorrow. I need to buy more candles. I only have five left."

"This happens often?"

"Not really, but still, it's nice to be prepared."

"And your toe?"

She smiled. "You're sweet to ask. It's fine. Somebody forgot to push in their chair this afternoon."

It was good that it was dark. I'm not sure she saw my grimace. I had been sitting on the chair in question. "Oops."

She reached over and kissed my cheek. "Not a problem. I'm fine." Then she picked up the letter and held it up toward the light. "Now where were we?"

I frowned. "Can you read by candlelight?"

"Not very well." She handed the letter to me. "But I've noticed that you read pretty well in the dim light upstairs."

I took the letter, and in trying to find the best light, decided to settle on the floor with my back to the sofa. Mindy followed suit, sort of, with her back leaning against me. Just as well.

October 29, 1852
Bradford, Pennsylvania

My darling husband,
I received your April letter last month. Ever since, I have been

wondering how to respond.

Marie continues to grow, and play, and laugh. She brings joy to everyone around her. She is almost two, and starting to run in her own way, complete with stumbles and falls, and then a quick look to see if an adult has noticed to determine whether her fall warrants a cry. She is so funny. Last week, we took her into town and Tom insisted on buying her a penny candy stick at the general store. Evidently, she liked her first taste of sugar, as the look on her face was absolutely rhapsodic.

The harvest was good this year. Tom and the others worked to exhaustion day after long day to get it in, but now, with nearly all of the work done, and the cellars and barns full, we can rest assured that there will be plenty of food and money for the coming year.

Josie's baby was born on October 6th, a healthy baby boy. They are calling him Robbie, though his full name is Robert Anderson Lewis Junior. We skipped a couple of quilting sessions, while Josie convalesced after the birth, but then she insisted that we all come over last week, in part because she needed adult company, and in part to show off her new son. He is so tiny. I had forgotten just how small our little Marie was when she was first born. I held him for a while, but I could tell that he was confused that I look different from his mother, as he started fretting for her after a few minutes and I had to hand him back to her. Robert came in from the fields at lunchtime with some of the other men and immediately went to his son. He is the picture of the proud papa, showing off what his boy can do, even at this tender age and speculating on what he will become in the future. Watching the three of them made me a bit melancholy. They are such a happy family, and I am so pleased for them, and yet I miss you dreadfully, and know that Marie needs her daddy.

Speaking of Marie, she is fascinated by Robbie. Her language is growing by leaps and bounds, but she is still stuck for words to express what she feels around him. She wanted to know when he would be ready to play with her, and why he sleeps so much, and why he can not walk. I tried to explain, and I think she grasped some of what I told her. At least, I could tell by her questions that she was trying to make sense of this loud, tiny thing that has come crashing into her world. It was funny, when on the way back home in the buggy, she wanted to know when she would see him again. When I told her that we would be going over the next Tuesday, she wanted to know if he would be a big kid like her by then.

Until yesterday, the fall has been dry and warm, but the nights have been getting colder, and I find myself snuggling up under an extra comforter these days. I need you to keep me warm at night. Yesterday it rained all day, and gave us an indication that old man winter is on his way. It is a good thing that the harvest is finished, allowing the men to stay dry in the barn, building new bins for food storage and repairing broken stalls. I baked bread, and the fire from the oven kept the kitchen nice and warm all day long. Tom made Marie a straw doll, and she played with that and later slept on a blanket in front of the hearth while I took out needle and thread and tended to my mending. Come lunchtime, I was able to serve a fresh loaf with melted butter, a slab of ham, and fresh picked apples. So despite the rain, it was a delightful day.

And now I come to the part I have been dreading. I have been round and round in my mind over this, and tried to think of what to tell you about your suggestion that I join you in California. I desperately want to be with you, and Marie needs her father, just as I understand that you want your family with you. But to leave my family and never see them again, while I travel to California. I am not sure that I can do that. Despite all of the problems that I have had with Tom over the years, we have become remarkably close since Marie was born. She has brought out a tender side of him that I never knew was there. There is so much uncertainty for me in a journey to California. The trip would be too difficult if we were to travel alone, and I am not sure that I can ask one of my brothers to make the sacrifice necessary to take me to you. At best, they would be leaving here for a year or more just to escort me. At worst, well it is an extremely dangerous trip that only the hearty take on. I do thank you for your generous offer to help set them up in a business there, but must decline. So I am left with the other options. Go by myself, stay here, or wait for you to come to escort me.

Please understand how I have agonized over this decision. I know the hardship and disruption that this will cause you, and hesitate to even write it down, but here is my decision. Although it will pain me to leave my family behind, in the end, I am your wife and will do what you want. I have just one requirement. Marie and I cannot make that journey alone, so I need you to come and get us. There, it is said. And now that I have committed it to paper, I feel almost giddy. I am to go to California with you, to really start my married life as your full time wife, and to introduce you to your little girl.

Write to me soon, and let me know of your plans. I shall count the minutes until we are re-united and can begin our grand adventure together.

With all my love,

Catherine

I finished the last line and looked down at Mindy. She still leaned against me, but had lowered her head, and I could just see that she was wiping a tear from her eye. "Are you alright?" I asked.

She nodded and spoke in a husky voice. "I didn't think she was going to go. I..."

I squeezed her to me and held her for several minutes. Finally, I managed to say, "Me too."

We sat there, lost in thought. The sound of the storm in the background and the candlelight dancing on the walls seemed to take us to Pennsylvania, that stormy day so long ago. I wondered what it must have been like, sitting by firelight on a cold night. Would they be chatting cheerily in front of the warm fire, dreading the moment that they'd have to dash back to their cold beds? They read, I suppose, and likely read the bible, the one book every family seemed to have. I imagine that they read aloud, but couldn't be sure. Maybe each read something different. Marie would have played, and they probably played with her. I wondered if any of the men played a musical instrument, remembering that playing and singing were fairly common on those long winter nights. Catherine never mentioned either a piano or a fiddle, so they probably didn't have one. Finally, Mindy interrupted my musing when she straightened herself up and rose, holding her hand out.

I looked up and could see the candlelight flickering off her eyes and casting her hair into a golden halo. "Time for bed," she said.

I looked at my watch. It was after ten, and normally, in the world of light, we'd have watched a movie or played a game.

I took her hand and she pulled me up. When I came to my feet, I took her in my arms, stroking her back as I gave her a long hug and kiss. Breaking it off and leading her toward the stairs, candelabra in hand, I said, "I agree."

CHAPTER 50

We woke up the next morning to blue skies. The storm had blown through, and though there was quite a bit of debris scattered about, the community seemed to have weathered the worst of the winds with little damage. Power was restored overnight, so before taking off for the day, we reset all of the clocks.

"Remember that I want to get some candles on the way back," she said as we closed the front door.

"Right," I said. "Along with the salmon and broccoli for dinner."

She smiled. "You don't really have to cook, you know."

Hand in hand, we started down the hill toward Capitola Village. I replied, "I know. Just thought it would be nice to have a barbecue tonight."

"I have leftovers. We could get into them."

I'd seen her leftovers. "That's okay. I'm looking forward to cooking. Really."

Since her house was only a little over a mile from the beach, we decided to have breakfast at one of the coffee houses there. It was a pleasant walk, bright and sunny. The birds were out again, after having gone into hiding during the storm, and with spring flowers all around us, it couldn't have been more pleasant. Almost before we knew it, we'd arrived.

Mindy pointed to an upstairs coffee house. "How about this one. They'll have a nice view of the bay."

I shrugged my shoulders. "Sounds good. I'm getting

hungry." I looked for a menu on the wall, but seeing nothing, asked, "What kind of food do they have?"

"Oh, they're mostly just coffee, but they have some scones and muffins too."

I nodded and we climbed the stairs.

I should have known what to expect, this being Capitola, but was a little surprised when we entered the place. Sure, the aroma of coffee was intense, and pretty wonderful after our walk. And they did indeed have a wide assortment of pastries. And there were several people sitting around enjoying a cup of coffee along with a newspaper, or a magazine, or a laptop. Some even talked with friends. What caught my attention though, was the decor of the place. The walls throughout the restaurant were painted a deep royal blue, and dotted with golden stars and planets. A cone shaped hat that matched the decor sat on the counter next to the cash register, and the ferns in the windows nearly blocked out the light. I felt as if I'd stepped right into Merlin's world.

I stopped suddenly enough when I entered the restaurant that the couple behind us on the stairs stumbled into our backs. With a turn of my head, and an uttered "Excuse me," from all four of us, we proceeded, and I made my way to the counter.

Five minutes later, I had a small decaf in one hand and a vegan blueberry scone, whatever that meant, in the other. Mindy had opted for a chilled coffee with milk and a scoop of ice cream (soy, of course). "A milkshake?" I asked. "Isn't it a little early for dessert?"

"It's a coffee beverage," she informed me. "Just like yours."

I could tell that pursuing that conversation would be foolish, so gestured toward the far wall. "I see an empty table in the corner there."

She was ahead of me, and the others who had also seen the table. Of course, this was the type of restaurant where tables were large and sitting with others was not only possible, it was encouraged. She turned to the couple we had bumped into at the front door. "Would you like to join us?"

And so we met Alice and Frank, a couple just a few years older than we were, who had decided only last year to spend their children's inheritance on a beach house in Capitola.

I pulled out Mindy's chair for her as I made the introductions. It seemed that Alice and Frank had met at one of the

Silicon Valley start-ups several years earlier and taken minimal pay in exchange for stock options.

"Life was pretty lean for a long time," said Frank, "but when the company went public, it paid off."

"So now you're living the easy life in Capitola Village, walking the beach, and relaxing over coffee at the Mystic Cup," Mindy reflected.

Alice smiled. "Well, not every day. We still consult one day a week..."

"And Wednesdays are pretty much dedicated to golf," Frank added.

"Oh, stop!" I laughed. "Golf, beach, work one day a week. Sounds like retirement is good!"

Frank raised his mug and tapped his wife's glass. "I've got no complaints." He looked across at us. "What about you two? You get in here often?"

I shook my head and Mindy answered. "Not really. Usually if I want coffee, I walk down to the local coffee house. They roast their own and serve a pretty good blend." At Frank's raised eyebrow, she continued. "It's a little hole in the wall a few blocks from my place over on Soquel Avenue."

And so we sat, passing small talk over the next half hour until Alice suddenly looked at her watch and tapped Frank's sleeve. He glanced at her and she said, "It's almost eleven and I've got an appointment." She turned to Mindy. "It was very nice meeting you. Hopefully we'll see you again."

Frank rose. "We're here pretty much every Monday morning after our walk. Look us up."

And as quickly as that, they bussed their mugs, waved, and were gone.

"Interesting people," Mindy mused. "Sounds like retirement's agreeing with them."

I nodded. "Soon. Another couple of years."

She took a sip of her coffee, or milkshake, whatever it really was, and then said, "I brought another letter. Interested?"

"Always." I responded. "Whose?"

She reached into her purse and handed me an envelope. "It's from Joel."

January 16, 1853
Murphys, California

My Darling,
    I suppose that I should say Happy New Year 1853. But I have been separated from you now for nearly three years, and that takes much of the joy out of a new year. I have missed you more than usual over the past couple of months, and hope you received my earlier letter inviting you out to California to be by my side.
    Winter has been harsh this year, but we have plodded on, not wanting to waste a day. It has been especially hard on Jonathan. He seems to want to stay in the icy waters the longest, yet has the least tolerance for it. Just before Christmas, he caught cold, and Sam and I were worried for his life. He recovered, but was weakened. The doctor thought he might have slipped into pneumonia had we not taken him into town where he could stay warm and dry while he recovered. He is back here now, but we have kept him out of the water as much as possible. Each day he feels a little stronger, and I can tell that we will have quite a fight on our hands soon, but are determined to limit his work. Anyway, it has been cold and wet, intermixed with snow. We had nearly three feet in our little claim for a few weeks. It is mostly melted now, but still the constant rain and near freezing temperatures have made for a difficult winter.
    Do not worry about me though. I have a healthy constitution and have been able to shake off the chills more easily than many.
    We have some exciting news. Sam and I were running a load of silt through the rocker the other day and came across a pretty good sized nugget. When we got it down to the local Wells Fargo office, they weighed it in an just over twenty-one ounces. It is the biggest strike we have had, and with all the rest we have saved, has given us a pretty good bank balance.
    You would think that we could not wait to get back out there and dig for more gold, and maybe last year that is exactly what we would have done, but not this year. Sam and I began to talk, and then we went to visit Jonathan in the hotel. We have decided to get out of the mining business. It is just too hard, and too uncertain. Now that we have a some money, we have decided to look for something to invest in. It seems that the ones who are really making the money are the shopkeepers who sell mining supplies in the mountains. Anyway, we have contacted a local lawyer and asked him to check and see if there are any businesses for sale. Together, I am sure we can make a go of it.
    You would be proud of me. Last Sunday we all went into town for church of all things. There is a small church in Murphys. The minister is a

young fellow, and seems to have a way about him that makes you just want to come visit. Anyway, it is not much of a church, just a canvas tent with some benches and candles inside, but he keeps it mostly dry and warm and I suppose that is a lot of the reason he gets folks in there. He and Sam have become fast friends, and he has been after me to come visit. Anyway, after church, we went over to the hotel and had a root beer. Sam's sweet on one of the girls there, and they get together after church on Sundays. I suppose that is a good part of his reason for heading off to church every week. Also, since he stayed there the last few weeks, it seems Jonathan has made a couple of lady friends too. Not me though. I am waiting for you. I have the best already, and do not need to mess with the rest.

Well, just writing this letter has cheered me up. Seems that thoughts of you have a way of doing that. I will have to spend more time just thinking of you.

It seems like a long time since I invited you to come out here. It was probably April or May, and I wrote again a couple of times last summer, but just in case those letters did not get through and this one does, I am asking you to come out to California and make a life with me here. As I said before, I will come to you if you want, and bring you back with me, or if one of your brothers wants to make the trip, that would be grand too.

Anyway, write in care of Rick Miller, the sheriff in Murphys, and he will see to it that I get your letter.

Last week, I dreamt that I was lying with you on a warm spring day in a field of flowers. We talked, and we laughed, and we watched butterflies flit from blossom to blossom. Suddenly, a gentle breeze rustled through the garden, carrying a delightful fragrance. I asked you what it was and you said, "they're sweet peas." And now, when I think of you, I think of my sweet pea, waiting for me, as I wait for her.

Your loving husband,

Joel

I looked at Mindy as I read the end of the letter, and she leaned over and kissed me. "How cute. His sweet pea." She gave me a serious look. "Do you have any special names for me?"

I folded the letter as I thought. Handing it to her, I reached over and snuck a kiss. "How about if we stay with the family tradition. Alright, Sweet Pea?"

She laughed. "Nice save." Then looking down at our empty mugs, she said, "Are you interested in a walk on the beach?"

§§§§

Driving home that evening, I started thinking. It seemed that Joel and Catherine were both ready and indeed anxious to get back together, but as of the winter of 1853, he still didn't know either that he had a daughter or that Catherine had decided to move to California. That in itself spoke volumes about the whirlwind communication world of the 21st century. Whereas they were reliant upon written correspondence, often taking three to six months to be delivered, we could communicate instantly, virtually anywhere in the world. Wow.

I reviewed my recollections in my head. His will was dated in the summer of 1854, so Catherine's letter or letters must have finally reached him by then. Also, he was present at Samuel's wedding, in the summer of 1853, so he hadn't yet left the gold fields. And somewhere about that time, he sought employment in San Francisco. I rubbed my chin as I drove, thinking some more. Jonathan died in the winter of 1856, and though there'd been mention of his partner Samuel, I couldn't remember anything about Joel. Interesting. Had he left by then? And if so, what happened to him?

And then there was Catherine. We had no indication that she ever went to California. And from what we knew, she never stopped using her maiden name. What was that all about? Hmm. It seemed that the more we learned, the more mysterious it became.

I drove on, trying to puzzle my way through Mindy's curious family tree. It was only when I saw my exit coming up on the freeway that I decided to try and figure out how he would have tried to travel back to Pennsylvania.

CHAPTER 51

I did a little research over the next week, and found that transportation to and from California in 1855 was still a serious challenge. Railroads wouldn't be completed for another decade, and even stage lines were in their infancy. Simply put, there was no expeditious public transportation system. There was no getting around the fact that in the days before super highways, railroads, and air travel, three thousand miles was an enormous distance.

Hopefully, the answer would be in a forthcoming letter.

§§§§

Mindy and I met in Santa Cruz the next Saturday for dinner.

"I've been wanting to come here for ages," she said as she picked up her menu. "They're supposed to have outstanding lobster."

I smiled. She did love her lobster, but personally, I could take it or leave it. Was it tasty? Certainly. Was it worth a special trip or a big price tag? Not to me. But if it made her happy, we'd go for the great lobster. Anyway, I was dining with her and that was good enough for me. And the restaurant was one of those that sat partway up the hillside with an incredible view of the bay. I could tell already that the sunset was going to be stunning.

"So what looks good?" I asked, knowing full well that it would ultimately include lobster.

She grinned. "You know what I want, but you decide." I scanned the menu. One lobster entree.

"You want to split the prime rib?" I asked cautiously. I could be evil if that's what she wanted. "Or the surf and turf? Steak and Scampi?" I looked up at her, hoping to see her reaction. There was none. Well, maybe just a minor hardening of her smile. " Did you want to share?"

"Of course."

"Salad?"

"That sounds good." She looked at the menu. "Hearts of palm?"

I reached over and patted her hand. "Just what I was thinking."

Just then the waiter approached. "Good evening. Can I get you something to drink?"

Mindy looked at me and I said, "Actually, I think we're ready to order."

He stood still as a statue, hands clasped behind his back. Obviously in this restaurant the waiters were expected to memorize the orders, not write them down. I was always impressed by the fact that a waitress with a pad and paper occasionally confused the orders, but these highly trained memory experts always got them right.

Well, down to business. The way that Mindy was looking at me, it appeared to by my decision what we'd eat. Of course, I knew what that meant. She'd claim not to care what I ordered, but no doubt I'd hear about it if it wasn't lobster.

"Tell me about the lobster."

"An excellent choice. We fly them in from Maine and then serve them very simply. A little seasoning; a little drawn butter; some lemon. They're served on a rice pilaf along with fresh seasonal vegetables."

I nodded. "We'll be sharing a meal, so we'll take one lobster dinner." I checked the menu. "We'd also like to share the Sirloin Tips appetizer and a Hearts of Palm salad."

"Very good choices," he said. "And to drink?"

"I noticed you serve a Monterey Vineyards Chardonnay. We'll take a bottle of that."

"Excellent. I'll place your orders and be right back with your wine." He picked up the menus, and for some reason I've never fully understood, took the wine glasses from the table. I mean, if they plan to take them back and then bring you new ones when they bring the wine, why bother putting them out in the first place. A friend who worked in a dinner house in college explained to me that they wanted them out for display purposes, but they got dusty, so they removed them so that the customer would have a new one. But they poured water in the same glasses that sat on the table before we arrived, so that couldn't be it. I suppose I could add that to the mysteries of the universe.

I was still wondering about that when Mindy interrupted my thinking. "A full bottle of wine?"

"It's a really good Chardonnay. I thought it would go well with the lobster."

"But a full bottle?" She shook her head.

"What?" I asked.

"Are you trying to get me drunk and loose so that you can take advantage of me?"

Hmmm. Good idea. "I hadn't thought about that. In that case, I'll have a small glass and you can have the rest."

She laughed and threw her napkin at me. I was about to hand it back when I felt her toes sliding up my leg. Should be a good night.

§§§§

I had to admit later that the lobster was good. Actually, it was very good. In fact, it was probably the best lobster I'd ever had, what little I got of it. It was a good thing I'd ordered that sirloin appetizer. On the other hand, given that I rarely ordered lobster, it may have been rather pedestrian. But then there was the rapturous look on Mindy's face as she sucked down the tender white meat. So I guess it was as good as I thought. Maybe all of that first class treatment they got on the flight out from New England helped. I wonder if lobsters are served a meal during their flight, and if so, do they wear lobster bibs?

Anyway, we finished, took off our bibs, and sat back glowing with contentment, and probably a little wine. I turned to Mindy. "So you're the lobster fan around here. What's the point to the bib?"

"It can be messy."

"Spaghetti's a lot messier than this, but you don't get a bib." I stared at her. Let's see her come up with something to beat that.

"And the ambience." Okay, so she beat it. I shrugged my shoulders. If I ever serve lobster at home, I'll need to remember to lay in a supply of bibs.

"Were you planning to get dessert?" she asked.

"I'll share if you like. I picked dinner. You pick dessert." That was at least partially true. I picked the appetizer. And placed the order.

She looked at the dessert menu and then at me. "Chocolate lava cake with raspberry sauce?"

"That is definitely a winner."

She smiled. "It's their signature dessert."

"You've had it before?"

"No, but friends have told me not to skip it."

"Well if friends have told you not to skip the lava cake, we can't very well disappoint them, now can we."

Laughing, she set down the menu and reached into her purse. "I brought another letter."

At the sound of that, my ears perked up. "Whose?"

"Joel again." She handed it over to me just as the waiter came to take our dessert order.

§§§§

I tried to read while we ate dessert, but it was just impossible, so I handed back the letter for further inspection later. Her friends were right. The lava cake was outstanding. In fact, I was tempted to order another to go, but remembering that after we read the letter, Mindy was expecting me to take advantage of her, I held off. After all, we didn't want to be uncomfortably full. On the other hand, it would make a very nice breakfast...

May 16, 1853
Murphys, California

I got your letter! I was so excited I was dancing all around the sheriff's office. I got your letter!

It's been so long since I've heard from you, and your news has stunned me. I have a daughter! Oh how I wish I had been there to see her as an infant, to hold her, to share her first days.

And even better news. You want to come to California to be with me. Of course I will return to Pennsylvania to bring you out. It will take some time, but I will get there. I have already started to think about how to travel. The overland journey is very hard, and very long, so I plan to travel by sea again. I know I got ill in Panama, but am told that it is rare for one to succumb to Yellow Fever more than once. So I will plan to travel that way. It should be faster and safer overall. As far as our return, I have not decided. It is very tempting to load up a wagon with goods not available in the west, but there is still that hard journey. I plan to talk with shipping agents in San Francisco to see if I can ship goods here. Maybe the best would be to send them around the horn, and meet the load in San Francisco. You should be thinking about what you might want to bring.

You are going to love my partners. As I have written you, Samuel and Jonathan are fine upstanding men. We have had many a rough scrape in the mountains here, and I can think of no others I would rather entrust with my life and my fortune.

I mentioned in a previous letter that we are retiring from the gold prospecting business. It is very hard work for uncertain returns. We are purchasing a general store in San Andreas and hope to make our fortunes there. I have spoken with Samuel and Jonathan about going to bring you back, and they agree that it is the right thing to do. They will mind the store while I return to Pennsylvania.

And now the hard part. It will take planning to prepare for my trip to Pennsylvania. Oh, I know, I rushed off three years ago. Has it really been that long! But I must plan my return and book my passage more carefully. If nothing else, it is much more difficult to return to the east from California. Many of the crews abandon their responsibilities on the ships and run up to the gold fields. So I must find a responsible captain and crew to carry me back. Who knows, I may have to work as a sailor during the voyage.

Also, I must stay here to help my partners to start our new venture. There is much to do to get the store on a solid footing financially. The previous owner spent so much time prospecting for gold, that his business did poorly, and he allowed the building to go into disrepair. We hope to rebuild both the building and the business. So I guess what I am trying to say is that I can not return this summer. I have started to make inquiries, and find it would be best to leave next spring.

I plan to move down to San Francisco in about March. I should be able to gain employment there, and will then be able to take advantage of immediate offers of passage east. Samuel and I talked about this at length, and he agrees that if I can stay until then to help with the store, they should be able to do without me after that, so long as I promise to return.

Write again, as I cherish this letter from you. Tell me more about little Marie. I wish to know everything that she does and says. Tell her that her daddy is coming to see her soon!

I will sleep tonight with a happy heart knowing that I will soon be reunited with my love.

Joel

I looked up over the letter as I finished. Mindy's coffee lay untouched on the table and her eyes were shining. "Wow!" was all she could say. And "Wow!" again. And again.

I smiled. So one of our questions had been answered. Joel planned to return in the spring of 1854, and he planned to return by the same route that he used on the way out. The last few letters should be interesting.

I was about to hand Mindy back her letter when I felt her toes crawling up my leg again. I'd already paid for dinner, so decided it was time to make our way back to her place. I stood and reached out my hand for Mindy. After all, she had expectations of me.

CHAPTER 52

Breakfast was simple the next morning, toast and fruit, and after the rich lobster of the night before, a perfect starter.

"So what did you have in mind for today?" I asked as I slathered my toast with blueberry jam. We were sitting in Mindy's dining room, enjoying the early glow of the sunshine. I'd given her an array of daffodils the night before, and they now sat on the dining room table, as well as the coffee table in the living room, and her nightstand upstairs. Several had opened over night, adding a touch of dainty yellow cheeriness that warmed the room.

"Did you remember your clubs?" she asked.

"I did. A few. You mentioned the driving range."

Mindy nodded. "There's a nice little course just up the road." She was looking out the window. "It should be a grand day out." Indeed, the sky was blue and the birds were singing. A mild breeze blew in through the open screen door, rustling the blinds. It was a tempting hint of summer.

"So I finally get a chance to see you hit a golf ball," I started.

Her response was quick and definite. "And you'll keep your comments to yourself!" She glared at me. I'd been trying for months to get her out onto the golf course, but she'd steadfastly refused, worried that I might editorialize about her swing.

"My lips are sealed," I smiled and took a bite of toast.

She just rolled her eyes. "We'll see."

§§§§

Urban golf had generally been my pattern. I hit around buildings or alongside freeways. Mindy's range was a thing of beauty, surrounded on three sides by redwood trees. Looking out over the green expanse, I almost lost my urge to hit golf balls and was tempted instead to suggest a hike. Almost. I looked out at Mindy, stretching before her start. An afternoon hike might be fun. Still…

We got a couple of buckets of balls, found two spots to hit from, and began. And we seemed to be pretty well matched. Whereas I could hit the ball farther, her shots usually flew straighter. I could tell that if we were actually on the course, she'd march determinedly up the middle of the fairway while I'd be trudging through the rough. So a three hundred yard hole to her would be what, three hundred yards? And for me? Maybe four-fifty? Of course, I could console myself with the thought that I'd get to see more of the course and have the opportunity to hit out of more interesting lies. Hah.

I stopped at one point and stepped back to watch. Mindy eyed me a she addressed the ball, smiled, and swung her five iron. Her ball flew off the tee high, straight, and true; a thing of beauty.

"Nicely done," I said.

She grinned. "Thanks. It's always better when you hit it well with an observer."

I could only nod. I had to agree with that.

Fifteen minutes later, we finished our buckets and packed up. I headed toward the car when Mindy pointed, "They have a putting green over there."

"Sounds good. I have a putter in the car."

§§§§

Later, although we hadn't really played a round of golf, it seemed that a trip to the nineteenth hole was in order. I ordered a beer for myself and a Diet Pepsi for Mindy. She disliked beer and had toyed with the idea of wine until she saw that their selection included three of the best wines money could buy, so long as they came in a box. Wrinkling her nose, she shook her head. "I'll leave those for somebody else. Bad wine tends to give me a headache."

I laughed. "You never know. They might be great wines in disguise."

She looked back at the taps sticking out of the wall. Red, White, Rose. "Right."

What the clubhouse lacked for wine, it more than made up for in ambience. True, the carpet was an indoor/outdoor affair that had obviously struggled through years of golf spikes and spills, and the tables were 70's laminate, but that didn't matter. The windows on the west wall were expansive, angling up some twenty feet to a point at the ridge-line of the roof. The foreground was all grass, and sand, and golf course. Beyond that, the redwood forest stood tall and stately. And best of all, in the distance we had a wonderful ocean view. I sipped my beer and stared in amazement. Why hadn't someone found this place, decorated it, and turned it into a fine dinner house? With decent food, it could be packed every night.

Mindy must have been reading my mind, as she said, "Nice view."

"Amazing," I replied.

"One of our hidden treasures. I thought you might like it." She reached over and touched her soda to my beer in a silent toast. "Thanks for keeping your mouth shut."

I smiled. And decided to keep it shut a little longer.

She evidently didn't notice, as she continued. "They actually serve a pretty good steak here if you're interested."

I looked at my watch. It was a little after five, and we hadn't eaten since breakfast. Well, we'd snacked a bit, but I was starting to get hungry. "That sounds good." I looked around the room.

"No waiters," she said. "You order at the bar, right where you got your beer."

I shrugged and took another sip of my beer. It was an amber lager, just to my liking. I offered Mindy a sip and she screwed up her face in disgust. I had to laugh. "More for me then!"

"Do they have a menu?"

She pointed to the whiteboard above the counter. Fancy. It was actually dated. Let's see. Chicken sandwich, hot dog, grilled cheese, hamburger, cheeseburger, a couple of omelets, nachos, and the ribeye. An easy choice. I looked back at Mindy, "One or two?"

"They're big," she said, "and they come with plenty of other stuff. Let's split one unless you're starving."

I got up and ordered. One ribeye dinner, $12.99. What a deal. I couldn't wait to taste it. Hopefully it wouldn't have the texture of shoe leather.

Twenty minutes later, the steak was sizzling at our table. Of course, I'd had to go to the counter to pick it up, but had I waited for the waitress to deliver it, I'd still be sitting there, and sitting, and sitting. So I went up to pick up the steak, and figuring that it would be best to save a return trip, ordered another of their fine amber lagers and a refill of the Diet Pepsi. While the cashier poured my beer, I tasted the sweet potato French fries. They were hot and nicely seasoned, so I figured I might as well taste a few more. When I returned to the table, Mindy had set us up with napkins and flatware, and we were ready to go.

"Smells good," she said. "But what happened to the fries? There appears to be a big hole in the middle of the plate."

I looked back at the counter, then up at the ceiling. Shrugging my shoulders, I replied, "You've got me."

She leaned over the table and puckered up for a kiss. I responded. It was nice but short and I tried for more but she'd returned to her seat. "Just as I suspected. French Fry breath." Laughing, she picked up one of the fries. "I suppose the rest are mine?"

I sputtered a bit, "Uh," and tried reaching out to take one of the fries. She slapped my hand away and then turned away and began to shake. It was that laugh she gets when she's trying her hardest not to laugh, but isn't going to make it so she just shakes for a while, starting with her shoulders, then her arms, and finally has to lift her hand to her mouth to try to hold it all in. It's not really a giggle, and not really a laugh, and it's kind of like trying to hold back a sneeze, and eventually, it sets her whole body quivering, from the tips of her toes to the tops of her ears. The more she tries to contain it, the bigger it will be when it finally comes.

There were several other groups in the restaurant, and they all turned to see what was causing the commotion. All they saw was Mindy practically doubled up with laughter as she wagged a French fry in front of me, like the school teacher she was, scolding a naughty little boy. Did I mention it was contagious? I tried to sit stoically, waiting for her to finish, but finally, I lost my self control as well. Like I said, they probably wondered what was so funny. Well if either of us had been capable of a coherent sentence, we could have told them. It was the French fries.

Some time later, while we worked on our steak, which was, by the way, very good, and surprisingly tender, and as I ate salad while watching Mindy devour the French fries, she said, "I thought we might read another letter tonight."

"Interesting," I said and reached for a fry, trying to be nonchalant. She darted her hand out and brushed mine to the side. "Uh uh," she smiled.

I gave her my best sad puppy look, causing her to begin laughing again, though not with the wild abandon of earlier. "Oh, all right," she said and picked up a couple of fries. She held them out as if she wanted to feed me. I reached in, opened my mouth, closed my eyes, and...nothing. I opened them again just in time to see her take her fingers from her mouth, obviously chewing my fries. The look on her face and the sparkle in her eyes were absolutely devilish.

"You will get yours," I sulked.

She just laughed and motioned toward the plate, "I already have mine."

I went back to the steak, thinking of strategies for revenge and wondering how I could have been so easily had.

April 29, 1853
Bradford, Pennsylvania

My Darling Joel,
I suppose by now, that you must have my letter. Just in case though, I have written three more repeating my enthusiasm to join you in California. I can not wait for you to come and sweep me off my feet, and then carry me away with you to our new home.

Marie turned two a couple of months ago and I have begun to understand what others mean when they call it the "terrible twos." Do not get me wrong, she is still delightful and sweet, and lovable and wonderful. Still, she has her moments. She has become a master of a new word, and she uses it several times each and every day. Whenever she does not want to do something, she simply says, "No." And then sometimes she stamps her little foot as if to add emphasis. If it was not so frustrating at times, it would be absolutely darling.
She pulled it on Tom the other day. He had been out in the fields with the new plantings all day, and when he came in, he was dog tired, and dirty, and hungry. I had cooked up some chicken along with greens and bread, so dinner was ready, and after washing up, he was definitely anxious to sit down and eat. Marie was

playing with her doll on the floor, and he told her to put it away and join us at the table. He had built a little booster chair for her over the winter, and had it out and ready. She just looked at him and said, "No!" and resumed playing. Now you have to understand. Usually, when Tom talks to Marie, they're playing, and she talks and giggles, and runs about. I do not think she had ever turned her full personality on him. He was taken aback and said, "Marie, I said it was time for dinner. Put your doll away." Well, she looked at him again, shook her head, and continued to play. When he got up to go over to her, she looked up, and then stood, crossed her arms across her tiny chest, stamped her foot, and said vehemently, "NO!" I'm not sure Tom knew quite what to do. He looked over at me as if to ask for suggestions, but I just lowered my head and worked on bringing dinner to the table, but I could still see out of the corner of my eye. My great big brother was completely flummoxed by teeny tiny little Marie. It was all I could do not to laugh. Finally, he just shrugged his shoulders. "All right then, you go ahead and play. The rest of us are going to eat." Then he went over and sat in his chair and proceeded to heap food onto his plate. Well, we all sat, and we all started dinner, and finally, Marie decided that she wanted some too. She went over to Tom, raised her hands, and asked him to lift her up to her chair.

He ignored her, but I could tell it was killing him. She tried a couple of the others, but they just looked at Tom and ignored her too. Finally she went and got her doll and put it in her toy box, then came back to Tom. He picked her up, thanked her for putting the doll away, and offered her some chicken, all the time holding her on his lap and hand feeding her. I was not sure who had won, but it will be interesting to watch the battle as it plays out over the months to come. Did I mention that she has got him wrapped around her little finger?

Yesterday, we had a big surprise. Ruth came back. I had not seen her in over a year, so to hear that she had come and planned to stay for a month was wonderful news. Evidently, she had written to Tom, and they had agreed to surprise me. Well, they certainly did. She is as strong willed as ever, and it is fun to watch the boys, all grown men, tiptoeing around in her presence. As we reminisced about our adventures in Pittsburgh, I also began to wonder whether her influence on Marie in the womb helped to form some of that little headstrong temperament.

I have begun planning for my trip west. I still have not told anyone here. As far as they are concerned, I have not had any communication with you since you left three years ago. I have not decided exactly how or when I will bring you up with them, or how I plan to tell them that I will be leaving for California with you. It will be a fight, of that I can be sure, but as your wife, I belong with you.

One of the things that might help with the others is another decision I have made. You do not know this, as I have never been able to send you a letter until now. Reverend Peterson was not authorized to marry us. It is a long story, and I do not plan to tell you about it here. As far as I am concerned, I am married, and you are my husband. Nonetheless, in the eyes of our community, the marriage does not exist. While to you, and to me, I am Mrs. Catherine Lewis Woodward, to the people here, I remain simply Catherine Lewis. If it was only for the people in California, who would no doubt accept our description of our relationship, I would not worry. I would change my name, and be done with it. But I must get acceptance from my family, so have decided we must remarry. I am sure that once you understand what happened here, you will be in accord with my wishes. As for Tom and my brothers, I have no doubt that now that we are older and more stable, and can explain what happened, they will be willing to bless our marriage.

Write soon and tell me of your plans. I pray every night for your safe return and look forward, my husband, to hugging you to my breast.

Your loving wife,

Catherine

I looked down at Mindy as she finished. Evidently, I couldn't keep the smirk off my face, and she asked, "What?"

"It's everything she said about two year olds. They are as cute as can be, but they are definitely a challenge!"

We were back at the house, sitting on the red sofa. Mindy had nestled against me while she read the letter, and I had one arm around her, holding her tight. "Would you like some dessert?" I whispered into her ear.

"Mmm."

We'd picked up her favorite raspberry napoleon at the bakery on the way back from the driving range. I had been plotting my revenge for her French fry attack all evening.

CHAPTER 53

Mindy's birthday had fallen in January, and I'd offered at that time to take her someplace special, but we'd both had difficulty juggling our schedules, so now, in the middle of May, still hadn't really celebrated. I'd been frustrated for a while, having had several ideas that she had dismissed either because of other commitments or simply because she wasn't interested. Finally though, I decided to try subterfuge. I suggested that we spend the weekend up in the north bay, wine tasting in Sonoma County, eating at the variety of fine restaurants there, and hiking along Stinson Beach and Bodega Bay. She hadn't really explored the area, so was enthusiastic about going.

"Have you hiked through the Muir Woods?" I asked.

She looked at me. "I don't think so. Where is that?"

"Marin County. Not too far from Mount Tamalpias."

Shook her head. "No. Funny, isn't it. I've traveled all over the world, but not there."

So I started planning our adventure. I found a nice little bed and breakfast, checked the menus of a couple of restaurants, and told her to reserve an upcoming weekend.

When the time came, we took off, driving up Highway One. It was a beautiful trip, and except for the section crossing San Francisco, a great time for relaxing along the coastline. We arrived at Muir Woods just after midday.

I parked the car and took out my backpack. She looked at me and I shrugged. "Lunch."

The park didn't look like much from the parking lot, but as

we started walking, it became clear that we were in one of California's special places.

"It's so peaceful," she said, awed by the towering trees.

I nodded. We were completely surrounded by old growth forest, walking down a pathway that snaked its way back and forth across a small creek. The crowd was small, and we'd managed to find a gap between groups. The dampening effect of the bed of needles that covered the forest floor silenced people's voices so well that it seemed that we were all alone. Mindy and I noticed a bench, somewhat hidden off to one side, up a side trail. I pointed toward it and she smiled. Whereas the main trail through the park was largely boardwalk, this one was a simple dirt path. We walked off the boardwalk and back into a small circle of redwood trees. The bench was old but comfortable, carved out of a stump, and both the seat and the back had been polished smooth by generations of people resting while enjoying the quiet of the forest.

Mindy smiled, "This was the mother tree."

I nodded. Redwoods often rose from the roots of older trees. Over the years, old trees died and decayed, returning to the forest, but the young sprouts, some of them hundreds of years old themselves, remained, forming a circle around the perimeter of the old stump. When we sat on the bench, we sat on the remainder of that old mother tree.

I leaned back and looked up. The trees towered straight up, hundreds of feet above us, a mixture of reddish bark and dark green fronds. The first branches were probably fifty feet high, so we were literally in a forest of redwood pillars. Mindy settled against me, and we sat for several minutes, enjoying the silence, awed by the grandeur of the forest.

Finally, she spoke. "I've hiked the forests around Santa Cruz several times, so I thought I knew what a redwood forest was like."

I closed my eyes and smiled. Nearly all of the forest around Santa Cruz had been harvested at one time or another. There was nothing like an old growth forest to bring out primordial spirits. I had one arm draped over her shoulders and squeezed her. "Pretty amazing, isn't it."

I could feel her head bob against my chest. We sat for a few more minutes and then I said, "Are you hungry?"

She laughed. "Starving actually. I guess the fruit didn't last."

"I offered you some of my toast this morning."

She ignored my comment and reached for the backpack. "So shall I see what you brought?"

"Go ahead," I said.

She opened the bag, and began pulling out various things and putting them on the bench between us, "Let's see. Bottled water. Good. French bread and cheese. Ooh, more cheese." She smiled. "Ah, cheddar for you and stinky cheese for me?" She reached in again. "Apricots and one more little package at the bottom." She pulled it out. "Chocolate sauce." She smiled. "For me?"

"For the apricots," I said as I reached for my knife to slice the cheese.

"Oh," she pouted.

"You didn't want it on your apricots?" I asked.

Smiling, she said, "I thought you might have something else in mind."

I just shook my head. "You are incorrigible." I'd brought some clean wipes, so washed the forest off our hands and then opened the jar and dipped my finger into the chocolate. "A taste?" She opened her mouth and I dabbed a tiny morsel onto her tongue.

"Mmm," she smiled. Then she picked up the jar and looked at the label. "Interesting. Chocolate apricot with cabernet."

"I thought it was appropriate." I dipped my finger in again, and she looked up at me, opening her mouth as she closed her eyes. I rubbed my fingers together and then quickly painted two stripes down each cheek.

She jumped back. "Hey, what was that for?"

"I thought that's what you had in mind."

She scowled. "Now I'm going to be all sticky."

I shrugged my shoulders and leaned over to lick off the chocolate. It was delicious. Chocolate, apricots, cabernet, and Mindy all blended together.

"Well?" she said.

"Very good." I hesitated.

"But?"

"A little dusty and just a tad bit salty."

She leaned back. "You take me on a hike through the forest. What do you expect?"

"Umm..."

"Exactly. Umm." She turned away, but I could see the hint of a devilish look on her face. What I didn't notice was that she'd taken the jar of chocolate. When she turned back, she had a big glob on one finger. "Lean over," she said. When I hesitated, she smirked. "What, a double standard?"

I closed my eyes and grimaced as I leaned in. She painted my face far more elaborately than I had done with hers, getting my cheeks, my forehead, my chin, and a little in my hair. And she was right. It was sticky. Fortunately, she was hungry and the creek was nearby.

§§§§

Later that night, showered, clean, and far less sticky, we cuddled beneath a warm down comforter in the bed and breakfast. We'd ended up hiking several miles before eating a light dinner, and I was drowsy and looking forward to a good night's sleep, when Mindy reached over to the nightstand and picked up a letter. "Another one from Joel."

December 2, 1853
San Andreas, California

My darling wife,
I hope all is well with you and our little Marie. I think of you often and look forward to the day when we are reunited.

We have been working hard to rebuild the store. In fact, that has become more than enough of a job to keep one of us busy while the others tend to customers. We sell a wide variety of goods, from flour and beans for cooking to bolts of cloth and clothing, to picks and shovels. And our business, while slow at first, has been picking up. Evidently the word has gotten out to the far flung mining camps that we have reopened with fair prices and a good supply of needed goods.

The store is good sized for a town the size of San Andreas, and we have no difficulty between the four of us stocking it and serving our customers. Initially, we invested nearly all of our savings in the store and an opening inventory as well as bulk orders for some of the food supplies and other goods that we hoped would sell quickly. Now that we have been in operation for a couple of months, we have had to re-order more than once and are getting an idea of what merchandise to carry. More importantly, we are already making deposits back into the bank and building up our savings. It seems that our new business venture will be successful.

There are two small apartments upstairs. As I mentioned in an earlier letter, Samuel married Laura Davies back in August, so they have taken one of the apartments while Jonathan and I share the other. Laura has been a great help in the store, understanding the needs of a growing population of women in ways that we men certainly do not. In fact, her small ladies section is one of the more profitable areas of the store.

It is a great luxury after years of rolling out my bedroll on the ground, to be sleeping on a bed again. And I am definitely looking forward to being inside and out of the rain this winter. Having you with me in a few months will make it even better.

Samuel and I both worry about Jonathan. He has kept the claim in Murphys and insists on spending several days each month mining for gold. He takes a little, but certainly not enough to justify his effort or the long days he spends wading the icy water. The fall has been mild, but he plans to continue through the snow season this winter, and I am especially worried as he has not yet completely recovered from his illness last year. They talk about gold fever, and it appears that Jonathan has it. I am certain that if it were not for his sense of responsibility toward Samuel and me, he would return to the gold fields full time.

I am planning to leave for San Francisco on the first of March, and hope to find employment there while I wait for a ship down to Panama. I have been in touch with an agent who informs me that while there are a few making the passage back and forth, their schedules are irregular. Nonetheless, I should be able to start my journey no later than the first of May. If all goes well, that will deliver me back to Pennsylvania sometime next summer.

I am not sure that I quite understand what you were saying about our marriage not being real, but will do what I can to make everything right upon my return. Everything seemed so real to me at the time, but if the reverend was not qualified, we will find one who is.

I must be thinking of you quite a bit, as I dreamed of you again last night. You were sitting on a red and green striped blanket in the shade of a big elm tree. I recognized the spot, as it was one that we picnicked in so long ago. The day was sunny, and the meadow was filled with a rainbow of summer blossoms. Little Marie was by your side, head down, watching as you helped her to tie a bonnet onto her doll. I wanted to reach out and hold you both, but whenever I tried, you slipped through my arms, as if you were no more substantial than smoke. I woke, then smiled at the thought that soon my dream will come to life and I will be able to hold you both in my very real arms.

Your loving husband,

Joel

Mindy smiled. "What a sweet letter! I loved the part about his dream."

She'd lain her head on my shoulder while I read, and after a minute or two said, "Do you ever dream about me?"

"Uh..."

She lifted herself up onto one elbow. "Well? Joel dreams about holding her. It's so romantic."

I hesitated. "I've never been very good at remembering dreams." I smiled. "Probably."

"Hmm," she said. She took back the letter and folded it into the envelope and lay back down. I noticed that her head went back to her pillow.

I reached over and stroked her forehead, then kissed her on the cheek. She murmured softly, "Good night."

"Am I in trouble?" I asked.

She rolled over and kissed me. "Of course not. Good night."

It was a pretty perfunctory kiss, and I lay back down just as she rolled her back toward me. Guess I'd better work on my dream remembering skills. Of course, if I told her tomorrow about a wonderful dream I had about her tonight, she'd probably think I'd just made it up, which would probably be true. Hmm. What to do. What to do.

I was laying there on my back, staring up at the ceiling wondering how to solve my dilemma when Mindy turned over and snuggled up against me. Her body was warm and soft and forgiving. She kissed my neck and nestled into my shoulder. I closed my eyes and we both drifted off into sleep.

CHAPTER 54

Evidently I was tired, because when I awoke the next morning it was already bright and sunny out. In my half dream state, I rolled to Mindy's side of the bed, reaching for her warmth, but the bed was empty and the mattress already cold. I opened my eyes, yawned, and looked at the clock. Hmm. 9:15. Guess I'd slept in.

Our room was actually a tiny suite, situated in an upstairs corner of the building, with a bedroom and adjoining sitting area. I opened the door, and found Mindy there. She was nestled into the rocking chair, legs tucked under her, and wrapped in a downy woven afghan. Just like a cat, she'd found a comfortable spot, where the sunlight cast its warm glow. Evidently, she had been reading and listening to music through her ear buds, but now the book was laying face down on her lap and her eyes were closed.

I tiptoed back into the bedroom and decided to let her sleep while I cleaned up and got ready for the day. When I next emerged from the bedroom, she had returned to her book. She looked up as I opened the door. "Morning sleepy head," she said with a smile.

I thought of pointing out that she'd been sound asleep when I first came out, but decided to kiss her instead, so knelt by her side. It was long and gentle and left me wanting more, but evidently that was not her intent. She broke away, she put down her book, and asked, "Hungry?"

"For you?" I asked. "Always."

She rolled her eyes and removed my hand from her shoulder. "My randy sixteen year old boyfriend. How did I get so lucky?" She started to rise, "Actually I was referring to breakfast in the dining room. Remember, they close at 10:00."

"Ah. Well if we must."

She chuckled and patted me on the head. "Maybe after breakfast. You'll have more energy."

I was feeling pretty energetic right then, but figured maybe she was projecting her needs onto me. Maybe she needed to eat breakfast to have more energy. That being the case, I decided to join her.

§§§§

Over eggs and bacon and pancakes and blueberry syrup and pots and pots of coffee, we planned our day. I had already planned to take her out to Tomales Bay, so guided the conversation in that direction. "It's pretty bleak, but beautiful in its own way. I was thinking maybe a hike through the park there, and then there's a pretty good restaurant where we can have dinner." When I mentioned the hike, her eyes sparkled. Ah, my Mindy, always up for a good walk. It was sunny and warm outside, but I knew that Tomales Bay could be cool even on the warmest of days, so added, "I'll put our coats in the backpack just in case."

§§§§

The road out to Tomales Bay wound across the ridge line of the little coastal range with commanding views out over the Pacific. As we descended, we passed through a small eucalyptus forest before arriving finally at the park entrance. The sunshine we'd seen earlier was gone, hidden behind high fog, but the view across the bay was clear, and we could see several other hikers already on the trails.

I parked the car, and we loaded up the backpacks. That done, I turned to her, "Ready?"

She nodded and we set out. The bay was long and narrow, opening to the ocean at the northern end, and the trail that I'd chosen wrapped around the southern tip and then out onto the peninsula to the west. Our walk skirted between the marshlands just inland from the water, and the remainder of the forest. As I had expected, the soil was damp and spongy, with frequent signs of wildlife.

We'd been walking for about an hour, and had traversed the southern end of the bay, when we came out of a small copse of trees into a broad open meadow. I noticed movement at the far end, and froze. Mindy sidled up next to me and I clutched her arm. "Look," I said, raising my arm to point. There ahead of us, on the far side of the meadow was the herd I'd hoped to see.

She gasped and smiled. "Deer. They're big."

I shook my head slightly. "Not deer, elk. This park is known for its herds of elk."

I was carrying binoculars, and took them out now. The elk grazed some three hundred yards ahead of us so we shared the binoculars back and forth and remarked on their markings and behaviors. "They're so noble," she said. "Big and powerful, and yet so graceful."

I nodded. I couldn't have said it better if I'd tried. After a while, I saw her gaze drift up the trail and said, "Shall we go on?"

Taking my hand, she led me up and away from the meadow. The trail meandered through the forest, constantly switching back and forth as it climbed the hill. We stopped periodically to inspect a wildflower, or to look out at the vista. During one stop, Mindy said, "It's so different! It's hard to believe we're only a couple of hours from home."

"You like it?"

She grinned. "Yes. No. I don't know. A great place to visit, but I wouldn't want to live here. Too cold. To damp."

We'd both put our coats on some time before, but the persistent fog laid down a sheen of moisture that left them wet to the touch. I'd been wearing a cotton hat when we'd started out, and it was as wet now as if I'd been caught in a downpour. She looked to the east and shivered. "Imagine. Just a few miles inland, it's a warm, sunny day."

I hugged her to my side. "You getting cold? Want to turn back?"

She shook her head. "I'm okay for now. What's over the ridge?"

I just shrugged my shoulders. "I've never been up this trail before. Shall we check it out?"

Taking my hand again, she led the way.

The trees gave way to rolling grassland, their leaves bent with the weight of the dew, as we approached the top of our little mountain. The trail widened but continued to climb steadily upward, more gently and more in a straight line now than before. A cluster of boulders, worn by the wind and the weather, guarded the top of the trail. We worked our way through them as through a maze, and suddenly emerged.

The view was breathtaking. Laid out far below us, waves rolled over submerged boulders and crashed onto the rocky coastline. It seemed that we had been walking forever through fog, but everything to the west was crystal clear, and we could see for miles up and down the coast, from the white capped chop that seemed to stretch for miles out to sea, to the narrow strips of beach, inviting, but nearly abandoned on this seemingly warm, sunny day.

The reason was clear. The wind was vicious, tearing at our clothing and threatening to send my hat far down the hillside.

Mindy spoke, and I leaned in to hear her, but could make out only patches of speech through the buffeting gale. "Back here," I yelled, and pulled her back into the relative quiet of the boulders.

"I was just going to say that it's gorgeous, but so windy!" She shivered again and shook her head. Her beautiful red locks had stood straight out out behind her when we'd looked out over the sea. Now they puffed around her head, a sodden, tangled mess that mocked the effort she'd put into dressing them earlier in the day. "It's too bad. I'd like to hike down further, but not today."

I squeezed her hand. "I hate to tell you, but this is actually a pretty good day. It's clear and it's not raining."

"But the wind!" she exclaimed.

"It's always windy here." She looked to the south, where a number of houses dotted the hillside, facing out toward the wrath of the storm. "I couldn't live here. How do they manage the wind?"

"I'm with you," I said. "I'll take warm tropical breezes any time." She shivered again, and I wrapped her in my arms, hoping to transfer some of my warmth. "Time to head back?"

She nodded and kissed my cheek. "I think the wind drove all that dampness right through my jacket and into my skin."

I couldn't resist. "We have that Jacuzzi tub back at the B&B. Space enough for two in a nice warm bath."

She grinned wickedly, "Sounds good. Since you don't get cold, I'll go first. You can open the wine."

And then she was off, skipping down the trail, taunting me to follow.

§§§§

A couple of hours later, I pulled off the road into a small parking lot. We'd come across the ridge line, and down into a sheltered crescent bay. Our room was a few miles further along, fronting the bay, but sheltered from the weather. "I thought we were going back to the B&B," Mindy protested.

"I wanted to stop here first," I said. She looked across at me and rolled her eyes. The heater and her seat warmer had been pumping out the heat ever since we'd left Tomales Bay, so I knew she wasn't cold. Of course, her pants were probably still damp, and she'd talked about combing out the tangles in her hair. But it was late afternoon, and we were both getting hungry.

"I'm sure you'll like the place."

She looked out her window. It was anything but impressive. Henry's Fish House had been around for decades, and in all that time, I'm not sure that it had ever been painted. Weathered brown wood was the motif of choice here. Even the sign was worn. Impressive? Certainly not. It was a dismal looking place, set up against one of the piers that jutted out into what was definitely a working fisherman's wharf. It looked very much like what it had started out to be, a bar, a place for fishermen to share a beer and a few tall tales after a day out on the ocean. But I knew different.

"Come on," I said. I parked the car and, and immediately ran around to her side to open her door. I reached in for her hand, "You'll like it."

The look on her face didn't admit any possibility of 'liking it.' Instead, I could definitely read on her face that she was indulging me, and that I would absolutely pay later. We'd see about that. I'd planned this birthday trip with care, and this was just one of many surprise adventures.

We walked across the lot, Mindy huddled against me for warmth. We were back on the coast, so any protection we'd gotten from the fog earlier was gone. It was definitely cold and clammy out.

And then we entered Henry's. The restrooms were located on either side of the door as we entered the long hallway that led to the restaurant, and Mindy immediately excused herself and made her way into the ladies room. Several minutes later, she emerged, cleaner certainly, and with hair that she'd at least attempted to tame.

I held out my arm and she took it. "Feeling better?"

"Much. Thank you." She looked down the hallway. "You sure you want to stay here?"

"I think you'll like it."

Now you have to understand. Had Henry's just been a bar, catering to fishermen, It probably could have survived over the years. Barely. But Henry, or whoever ran the place now, knew that their days of thriving off of fishermen alone, were numbered. And so while it remained the same on the outside, the inside had been upgraded. Don't get me wrong. There was no glitz and polish in Henry's. No brass or chrome. No fancy paintings on the walls. It still retained much of the same character that it had carried over from the old days. But despite the simple furnishings and weathered wooden walls, Henry's was a gem. They were rumored to have the best chowder on the west coast of the United States. In addition to that, they had expanded their beer menu to include several excellent local microbrews as well as the old standbys. They were located on the edge of the wine country, and had a carefully selected assortment of wines, many of which were available by the glass. And best of all, they knew that even on a warm summer day, hikers from Tomales Bay, vacationers who had dared walk through the wind at the beach, and even the local fishermen, would be looking for ways to shrug off the cold and damp by the time they showed up, so in the middle of the restaurant, they'd built a huge stone fireplace. I'd never been there when it wasn't blazing cheerily away.

We walked down the hall, toward the cheery voices in the bar. As we turned the corner, I glanced down at Mindy. Her eyes widened as she took in the place. Or shall I say, the fireplace. We'd arrived before 4:00, so the restaurant wasn't nearly as busy as I knew it would become. There were two open tables right next to the fireplace. She looked up at me and I just nodded.

When we got to the table, I pulled out her chair and seated her. We had a prime spot, with a great view of the bay, plenty of elbow room, and of course, the fire.

I grinned smugly, "Will this work?"

She looked around. "Yes."

"You didn't seem so sure in the car."

"It's not much to look at on the outside."

"But..."

She smiled and patted my hand. "You're right. It's very nice inside."

"And..." I stared at her.

She got the message. "And I should never have doubted you." She squeezed my hand this time. "You take very good care of me."

I smiled. "Yes I do." I didn't for a minute think that she would never doubt me again in the future, but it was nice to be proven right, if only for the moment.

The waitress arrived with our menus and asked to take our drink orders. I forestalled her, looked at Mindy, and then decided to take advantage of her never doubt me line. "We're ready to order now."

Mindy cocked her head at me in surprise. Evidently she did want to see the menu. Oh well, too late.

"We'd each like a cup of the Manhattan Clam Chowder. After that, we'll split a Caesar Salad and a Grilled Seafood Platter." She wrote and I looked at Mindy. She seemed to be taking this in stride. "And I saw a bottle of the North Coast Cellars Pinot Noir on the counter. We'd like that."

The waitress smiled. "Very good. Anything else?"

"I think that's enough. We may need to save room for dessert."

After she left, Mindy looked across at me. "A full bottle again?"

"I figure what we don't finish tonight we can drink tomorrow night."

"Hmm. So, the seafood platter. What's that?" She seemed to try to stare through me. "Somehow I didn't even get to see a menu."

I just chuckled. "You warm enough?"

"I'm getting there. What's the seafood platter?"

"I'm glad you're warming up. I know you don't like being cold."

She just glared at me.

"It's a surprise, but I think you'll like it." I directed her attention out to the bay. "Oh look, see the otters out there?"

She held her stare for a moment, and then reached across and slapped me gently on the forehead. "It better be. Don't even let me see the menu." She shook her head sadly from side to side. "You'll get yours."

I just smiled and continued to watch the otters. I guess that the 'never doubt me' line had expired more quickly than I'd expected. On the other hand, there were possibilities still available in the rest. I wondered what she really meant by, 'you'll get yours.'

§§§§

Dinner was excellent. Dessert if anything, was better, and we finished the wine back at the bed and breakfast, luxuriating together amongst the bubbles in the Jacuzzi tub. Later, as we rested drowsily under the down comforter, Mindy nuzzled my ear. "Would you be interested in listening to a letter from Catherine? Or are you too tired?"

That roused me. "I can probably stay awake for a letter."

January 5, 1854
Bradford, Pennsylvania

My Dear Husband,
Another year has come and gone. Hopefully, by January of 1855, we will be together.

You will be happy to know that we are all well here, though it is turning out to be a bitterly cold winter. Fortunately, we had a good harvest, and have put away a plentiful supply of food for ourselves and our livestock. We were also able to sell a good portion of our harvest so have some much needed cash to purchase other necessities.

Last fall, Tom installed a pot bellied stove in the living room. He had been skeptical at first, but a few of the neighbors had them and raved about how much more effective they were at heating the house than the fireplace had been. It sits right out in front of the fireplace, in the main room, and vents out through the flue, and they were right. It does produce more heat while using less wood.

Anyway, he was so pleased with it that he immediately ordered another one for the workshop out in the barn. It arrived yesterday, and he and the others are working on setting it up now. They do spend quite a bit of time out there this time of year, repairing tack, sharpening farm tools, and doing other chores that they are just too busy to do in the warm weather. Often, they have come in chilled to the bone after a winter's day in the barn. I am sure that they will appreciate the warmth from the new stove once they get it working. Meantime, the house is very cozy inside despite the brutal cold outside.

Marie has been talking to beat the band. She is so curious and wants to know every little thing. She has so many questions, and for many of them, I simply do not have any answers. "Why is ice so cold?" she asked yesterday. "I told her it was because it is frozen water and she wanted to know why. I told her it was because it was winter and the air was cold and she wanted to know why. She keeps asking until I run out of answers and still asks more. She is definitely a smart and curious little girl.

For Christmas, we all traveled over to see Robert and his family. The boys had converted the buckboard into a sleigh for the winter, and we glided almost effortlessly down the lanes. Marie and I bundled up tightly with our heavy coats and extra blankets and woolen mittens, and it made for a wonderful trip. The sky was such a brilliant blue, and the air was crisp and cold, but we were snug and warm under our wraps. On the way over, a tree fell with such a loud snap that it startled poor little Marie, who thought that it had been a gunshot. Tom assured her that everything was perfectly safe, and though he had the reins, she climbed into his lap for the remainder of the trip. She seems to know that gruff as he might be, he is a big man who will protect her and keep her safe.

Once we got there, Marie and Robbie had a wonderful time. It is hard sometimes to imagine that he is over one year old now. He is definitely at the age where he can get around and gets into everything. I enjoy watching him toddle, so uncertain on his feet sometimes, especially when he is trying to keep up with a running Marie. He reminds me of her when she was that age. The two of them run and run and run until they drop, exhausted and then just lie there panting and giggling, and after catching their breath, get up to run some more. They have become very good friends, and though Marie still wonders when he will be a big kid like her, he has grown to the point where they can play together.

I received your letter from May in early December and have been so busy preparing for the holidays and with everything else that I have not been able to respond.

I am so glad that you have been able to stop mining. It seemed like such dangerous work, wading the creeks for a little sparkle of gold. So you are to be a merchant, and I am to be a merchant's wife. How exciting. You must tell me all about San Andreas. Is it a large town like Pittsburgh or is it more like our Bradford? What kinds of crops do the farmers grow there? Is there a good school *nearby for Marie?*

I cut the new 1854 calendar out of the almanac and am keeping it in my dresser drawer. You might think this silly, but I circled March first, the day that you may be leaving the gold country for San Francisco, and September first, a time that I imagine that your ship might arrive in Philadelphia. And I have begun to cross off the days one by one, to show that you are coming ever closer to me.

You remain always in my thoughts and my heart. Come to me on wing of angels my love.

Catherine

Mindy folded the letter. After putting it back in the envelope, she nestled down into my arms. I kissed her hair, clean and smelling of her new Sweet Pea shampoo.

"I was wondering," I said, "How many more letters are there?"

She sighed and I wondered if she'd heard me. Finally, she answered sleepily, "Just a few. He's almost home."

We lay there for a while and soon I could tell by her rhythmic breathing, that she'd fallen asleep. A long day, a hike through the forest, a good meal, and a warm bath had all combined to make me drowsy as well. I closed my eyes and joined her.

CHAPTER 55

"Yesterday is just a memory and tomorrow only a promise. Only today is real," I read. "Interesting outlook on life." I turned to Mindy but she wasn't really paying any attention. We'd spent much of the day wandering through gift shops in Carmel, and had finally arrived at one of my favorites. It was a nautical shop, devoted to clothing and equipment for the wanna be yachtsman. While I'd been perusing a display of plaques, Mindy was trying on jackets. I wandered over in time to help her into one.

"Hi," she smiled.

"Comfortable?"

"Well I know you're not going to believe this, but it's too hot!"

I laughed. "You're right. I'm not going to believe it." I lifted another jacket on the rack. "Hmm... It says here that it's guaranteed to keep you warm and dry in the worst ocean weather. Should be great for a spring day in Santa Cruz."

She stuck her tongue out at me but I barely noticed. "I thought this other number might be a code but it could be the price." I held it out for her to see. She scowled and immediately removed the coat. "No charge for looking, I'm sure."

"I'm not taking any chances." She carefully returned the coat to the hanger. "Might be nice in the winter though."

I had to agree. The coat looked warm. Of course, for that price, it should keep her warm in Antarctica on a cold winter day. Carmel, a wonderful place to shop but an expensive place to buy.

"Do you want to try the bakery down the street?" I asked.

"Sure." She looked around at the variety of clothing, model boats, and other novelties. "There's a nice display of hats over there." She grinned, knowing that she'd found one of my weak points. I was a sucker for a good hat.

"Well..."

"Come on," she laughed and took my hand, leading me to the hat display.

I tried on a few and mugged for the mirror. Mindy laughed until I found a beautiful red bonnet with a huge purple rose on one side and a veil that came down over the wearer's face. "It's you!" I claimed and placed it on her head.

She took a quick peek into the mirror and then with a look of horror, ripped the hat from her head. "I don't think so," she stated flatly. I had to agree. The hat was hideous on the stand. On her head, the clash between the red of her hair and the colors of the hat were almost too painful to behold.

"The bakery?" I asked again.

"Much better than the hats," she replied. Then taking my hand, she led me out of the store.

I had a black and white cookie, one of my favorites. Actually, I knew the bakery and knew their product line, having visited a few times before. Now if you've never had a black and white cookie, you've missed one of the great pleasures of life. I'm not sure how other bakeries do it, but this one has the process down. They start with an exceptional butter cookie, large and thick, shaped like a heart, the kind that just melts in your mouth. Then they dip one side of the heart into dark chocolate and voila, a black and white.

We walked up the street to the park and found a bench where we shared the black and white along with coffee. Mindy insisted in dipping her part in the coffee, but that just goes to show that she was a black and white cookie virgin, not knowing how to truly savor just the cookie itself. I thought of scolding her for that, but figured if she wanted to ruin both her cookie and her coffee, that was up to her. She did try once to dip my half of the cookie into the coffee, just so that I could taste it, but I quickly interceded before she could violate either.

I took a last sip of coffee. "Shall we walk down to the beach?"

I'd caught her with a mouthful of cookie, so she just smiled and nodded. Standing, I pulled her up, tossed my coffee cup into the garbage, and asked, "Any ideas for dinner?"

We talked while we walked, and finally decided that barbecued hamburgers and a salad at her place would be best.

I have always been intrigued by Carmel Village. Nobody lives in a house. Everyone has a cottage. The streets wind and twist and bend and roll with the tree roots. It is as much a lifestyle as it is a place to live. As we walked down to the beach, we saw a few of the locals, working in their gardens or enjoying the sun on a semi-private patio. We waved, and many waved back, before resuming their work.

The beach at the end of Ocean Street has always been one of my favorites. I'm not sure why. We'd spent a week there once when I was a child, so maybe I had a collection of good memories, or maybe it was the sense of seclusion, or the Monterey Cypress that surrounded the sandy shore, like wind blown sentinels guarding their domain. But it was beautiful, and though the water still wore its winter chill, I insisted on shucking my shoes and wading barefoot into the surf. Mindy watched, also barefooted, from the dry sand while I splashed up to my knees. Later, she took my hand and we walked side by side at the water line, but every time a larger wave came in, she'd break away, to watch as it washed over my feet and toes, only to return when it had gone.

"I feel sorry for the people who live in Kansas," I said suddenly.

She looked at me quizzically.

"They don't have an ocean."

"Ah," she nodded. "We didn't have much of an ocean in Ohio either."

"But you had the Great Lakes there, right?" She nodded skeptically, so I continued. "How do you live without being able to return to the water occasionally. It's restorative." I smiled at her.

She could tell that I was in a weird mood. "You're not planning to swim are you?"

I shook my head. "Too old for that." I gestured toward the water. "And way too cold!" I stared out at the sea for a minute, then reached for her. She came tentatively, avoiding the swirling foam. "But I'll never outgrow a walk on the beach with my Sweet Pea!"

She gave me a playful shove just as a new wave came in, and

then turned and ran to the dry sand. I'd been a little off balance when she'd pushed, and it was all I could do not to go tumbling into the surf. Still, I kicked up quite a bit of water as I danced around trying to keep my balance and splashed droplets all the way up onto my shirt.

I turned and looked at her. Her shoulders were quivering with silent laughter. My initial thought was to go and get her, pick her up, and dump her into the ocean, and then I looked down. My clothes were spotted, but not really wet, and the image in my mind was too delightful to spoil, so I began to laugh as well.

§§§§

Mindy had a couple of burgers in the freezer, so we tossed those onto the grill and cooked them up for dinner. As expected, they were excellent. She'd kneaded in an assortment of cheeses and spices before freezing the meat, wanting them to be quick, ready meals. And they were. Just before the burgers were done, I added four slices of focaccia bread to the grill. Everything finished at the same time, including Mindy, who had whisked upstairs for a quick shower and emerged smelling of sugar and spice and everything nice.

"Would you like to read another letter after dinner?" she asked.

"Of course. I'm always up for that."

"I have two written just about the same time, one from Joel and one from Catherine."

"How about both?"

"We'll see," she demurred. "Maybe. There are only a couple left. I'm a little reluctant to read the last ones."

I nodded. I understood. So much mystery remained, and yet the source of the explanation was starting to dry up. Anxious as I was to read more, I still wanted to extend the experience.

"Whatever you decide," I said quietly and kissed her on the back of her neck. She smelled delicious, and as I traced my tongue along her spine, she quivered and turned into my arms.

"We'd better eat dinner while it's hot," she said, but her voice was husky, and I could tell that she was torn.

March 22, 1854

San Andreas, California

My Dear Catherine,

I arrived in San Francisco a few weeks ago and decided to send you this letter. I am working temporarily in a factory near the waterfront. My work in the store as well as my experience in the gold country were an excellent reference. The owners of this warehouse are a group of brothers who spent some time digging gold themselves, before returning to San Francisco to go into trade. They saw the need for heavy duty clothing, and have hired seamstresses and others to make pants and bib overalls out of heavy canvas cloth. I saw some of the clothing when I was up in the mountains. Indeed, we sold several pair of the pants in our store. They were bulky and stiff, and not quite as comfortable as lightweight cotton clothing, at least initially, but were quite durable, and popular among the miners. To simplify matters, they are produced in dark blue only. The color eventually fades, but the pants wear and wear and wear. I handle some of the bookkeeping, and also work as a salesman to the commercial houses that have grown here to support the stores in the gold country. It is interesting work, and will keep me until I can arrange passage to Panama. In addition, I have been told that the chances are good that I will be able to return to my job when I come back to San Francisco. We will see. That may be an interesting option, but will be at least one year away.

There is a ship leaving the day after tomorrow, which is part of the reason why I am writing you today. This letter will go on in their mail bag. It is far more efficient than mailing through Sheriff Miller in Murphys, and relying on itinerant mail carriers.

Our store is becoming very successful. Part of my role here initially, was to buy merchandise to replace our dwindling supplies. I came down with Jonathan and a couple of other men we hired to help. They left yesterday, and will carry the supplies back up to San Andreas. They will be traveling in a caravan with some other merchants along with hired guards for safety, as parts of California are still wild and lawless.

I hear that there is a coastal packet due in next week. They make a regular run down to Panama every couple of months. I have already spoken with their factor in San Francisco and arranged passage. Hopefully, that will put me in Panama by the middle of May. From there, I will engage passage home.

It is hard to put my feelings into words right now. Going to meet you seems almost impossible, but I know that by coming to San Francisco, I have taken the first step in that long journey. I am excited, and anxious, and more than a little bit nervous. And yet I am strangely calm because I know in my

heart that it is the right thing to do.
I will love you always,

Joel

I smiled at Mindy after I read the last lines. "It doesn't seem real, does it?"

She shook her head. "So he's finally on his way home."

"He is." I nodded. "And he seems ready." I laughed. "No more gold fever."

"No. He's healed, but I don't think that his was ever a serious case."

"No." I turned to her. We were cuddled up on the red sofa, and she was leaning into me. I reached down and cupped her chin to give her a kiss. Brushing her lips, I said, "No. Just Catherine fever. I suspect it's hereditary."

She looked at me curiously.

"Well I have Mindy fever." I reached in for another kiss, but she shrank away, pursing her lips as if she'd tasted something sour.

"Oh, what in the world could you possibly think you'd get with that line?"

I tried for another kiss, but she rose and stood looking down at me, shaking her head. I tried to rise a couple of times, but she just warded me off with her hand. Finally, she reached down and drew me up. "Come on, you slick talker you. There's another letter upstairs."

As she turned the corner to go up the stairs, I danced a quiet little jig. It may have been a bad line, but we were on our way upstairs.

§§§§

Some time later, nestled together under the covers, Mindy unfolded Catherine's letter.

August 5, 1854
Bradford, Pennsylvania

My Dear Joel,

I received your March letter just yesterday. I was surprised that it came so quickly, but suppose that you were right. Mailing it directly from San Francisco saved considerable time.

I am writing this letter and posting it to the small box into which I have put so many, not knowing where to send them, but still feeling an overwhelming desire to write you.

Mindy reached over to her night stand for the envelope. "No address, just Joel Woodward. Another one for the box."

"A hidden one, most likely, since she didn't want anyone else to know." I took the envelope from her hand. It was the same stationary we had seen many times before. I handed it back. "So what else does she have to say?"

It is hard for me to imagine that you may even now be sailing up the coast toward Philadelphia. Shall we meet again in days? Weeks? A month? I am also anxious, and nervous, and very, very excited.

I think back to our courtship and marriage. I was in many ways, a little girl then, in love with a wonderful boy, headstrong and defiant, but terribly intimidated by my brother, Tom. I am not that little girl any more, as you will soon find out. I am a grown woman, and a mother. I yield to Tom when he is right, or when it is not worth the battle, but I have no difficulty standing up to him when he is wrong. Strangely, I believe that he respects me all the more for that. I suppose that I learned much of that backbone from Ruth. The more I know of her, the more I am impressed by her strength of character.

It hardly seems possible that Marie will be nearly four years old when you first meet her. She has grown into a delightful little girl with a strong personality of her own. She is wise well beyond her years, and I watch with amazement as she seems to effortlessly bend her uncles to her will. I am sure that a part of it is their indulgent nature with her, but at times, I see her manipulating them and can tell that they have no idea what is going on. I admit to having suppressed many a chuckle. And then I wonder, is she doing the same to me?

I have read from the bible to her since she was an infant, and as she grows older, her fascination with some of the stories there has grown. She has her favorites, and asks for them from time to time, later wanting me to elaborate, adding details and characters to the words that are written there. It has turned into kind of a game for us. Recently, she has started picking out words on her own, and has at times, been able to read entire sentences with little or no prompting. At first, I was sure that she had simply memorized parts of the passages from my frequent readings, but now I am not so sure. She sits in my lap and screws up her little face, and then copies me, pointing to the words one by one so that she seems to really be reading them. I am sure that part of this comes from being a proud mother, but another part of me thinks that she is very young to be reading anything at all.

We approach another harvest, and again are looking for great bounty, as the summer weather has been perfect for growing with warm days punctuated by frequent light showers. Tom has proven to be a good farmer and others have noticed that his yields are generally among the best in the area. Consequently, his advice is frequently sought by other farmers in the community and I know that is a source of pride for him.

Speaking of Tom, the strangest thing has happened. For so many years, he concentrated only on the farm, rarely ever visiting others and I do not remember him ever courting at all. Lately though, he has been spending time with Sarah Johnson. You may remember her from school. She was a few years older. Anyway, she married Bill Nevins and they had three children, two boys and a girl. Two years ago, Bill was working on clearing a new piece of land when he was thrown from his horse and one of the stumps dragged across his leg. It festered, and he died a few weeks later, leaving her a widow. Several of the men in the community helped her to keep the farm going, plowing, planting, and harvesting, so that she and her children would keep their livelihood. Evidently some sort of a spark must have developed between Sarah and Tom, as he began to talk of her more and more. And now he is courting her. It is a strange and wonderful thing, and has softened him some.

I could go on, but Marie has wakened from her nap and is pulling on my skirt, seeking attention. Know that my heart is bursting with excitement and love for you. I long to be in your arms again.

Catherine

She looked at me as she read the last words. "Interesting."

"Which part?" I asked.

Smiling, she tapped the letter. "The part about Tom." Then she hesitated and added, "And the part about Marie reading. She's what at this point, three and a half?"

I did a quick calculation in my head based upon Joel's departure. April of 1850? "Yeah. About that. Precocious."

"She did become a doctor in the 19th century." She paused for a moment. "A woman doctor. That's saying something. She must have been brilliant just to get into medical school."

"So there you go. Reading at three." I shifted gears. "I don't remember anything about Tom having a family. Was there anything on your family tree?"

Mindy looked at me skeptically. "You want me to get out of this nice warm bed to go dig around my office for the family tree? It's cold out there."

I lifted the cover on my side. Probably still 72 degrees. But that was relative. I pulled her close. "How about in the morning. That better?" Then I nuzzled against that spot on the back of her neck. "And that?"

She shuddered and I felt those goose bumps pop out. Evidently I'd hit the right spot. She turned to kiss me. "Morning would be good."

§§§§

The next morning, we pulled out the family tree. There was no mention of Tom marrying, but then there was no mention of Joel at all, so who knew. It might be an interesting course to pursue some day, but wasn't really related to our primary goal of searching out Mindy's direct ancestry.

"How many letters are left?"

Mindy looked toward the bundle, but didn't move to count them. "Four," she said.

"Wow. End of a journey." I thought for a moment. "Well maybe there will be more information there."

She nodded. "Maybe."

CHAPTER 56

We'd planned to go back up to Murphys for a weekend in June, so I called the Adams' to ensure that they'd be there and booked a room at the same Bed and Breakfast we'd stayed in earlier.

Most of Saturday, we spent wandering around the countryside, getting out to Sheep Ranch, population 32, of all places. It wasn't much, a few houses clustered in a small oak forest. I had to laugh when we drove by the post office. It reminded me of Joel's letters and his comments about Murphys in the 1850's. Someone had cut a door into the side of their garage and put an official United States Post Office sign up above. Actually it was the only sign of employment in the community. I suppose anyone living in Sheep Ranch enjoyed small town living. Or would you call it a village?

Mindy was handling the map while I drove. This area wasn't listed on any GPS. Too remote, I suppose. "I think that if we stay on this road, it should take us out to Highway 49," she said.

"Are there other options?"

"Well," she grinned at me, "We could turn around and go back the way we came in. I don't see any side roads."

I looked ahead. The road, as she called it, was pretty rough, stretches of gravel intermixed with asphalt. "We just passed one back there."

She checked the map. "Not here," she said. "Try it if you want, but I'm not sure where it goes."

I turned around and winked, "A little adventure?" There was no asphalt on the new road. It was all gravel, except for the patches of dusty dirt. I drove down about a mile, past a few small ranches with smaller houses until it dead ended. Ahead of us was the most amazing sight in all of Sheep Ranch, so I parked the car. "Want to get out?"

We'd been driving for over an hour, so it seemed like as good a time as any to stop. I opened my door and stepped out, and then remembering, ran around to Mindy's side and let her out as well. "Thanks," she smiled and favored me with a kiss. "Always my gentleman."

I took her hand and we walked up to a white picket fence. Behind it was a large rambling farmhouse, showing years of neglect, but impressive nonetheless. I looked around. No cars, no people. For that matter, no real signs of life anywhere. "What do you suppose it was," I asked.

Mindy stepped toward the gate and looked back. "I don't know," she said. "I'd thought it was a house, but it's much too big. Hotel?"

I scanned the building. It was certainly big enough. At one time, it had been painted white, with green trim. The deck, or I suppose it was called a veranda, was covered, about twelve feet wide, and wrapped around the entire building. There were at least a dozen windows just in the front, just on the bottom floor, with more up above as the building rose up two full floors. Half was built up to a third floor, and the rest was a large railed terrace. Interesting what you might find if you just poked around a little bit.

It had an abandoned air, but Mindy was not to be put off. "Shall we?" she asked, and reached out her hand.

"Shall we what?"

"Knock on the door."

"Uh."

"Oh, come on. It won't bite you. Maybe somebody's home. I'd love to find out what this place is doing out here." She looked around. The lot was overgrown, interspersed with trees, but it appeared that there had once been a spacious lawn area surrounding the house.

I checked out the stairs leading up to the porch. They looked a little rickety. Interesting yes, as long as we didn't fall through. What the heck. You only live once. "Sure."

I joined her and opened the gate. It swung with a

pronounced squeak. "Needs Oil," I muttered. There was a flagstone path of sorts leading up to the house. At one time, it had probably been very nice. Now though, many of the stones were broken and the whole thing was grown through with weeds and grass. When we got to the front stairs, I insisted on going first, and figuring that the structure was probably strongest at the edges, made my way up the extreme right side, holding onto the handrail. It flexed a little bit, but seemed firm enough. I looked back. Mindy was right behind me.

The veranda was raised about five feet, and we hadn't been able to see the decking from the roadway. There were several holes, but the section leading up to the doorway seemed newer, and looked sturdy enough. Looking for a line of nails that would give away a solid joist, I made my way to the front door. I was right. That part was solid.

I knocked, and a hollow sound echoed through the house. We waited a few seconds and I knocked again. I was pretty sure I'd hear anyone coming, but there was nothing.

Mindy, meantime, had stepped to the side and was brushing the dirt off of one of the windows. "Boy are you going to be embarrassed if somebody really is in there."

She looked at me and shrugged. "If anybody should be embarrassed, it's whoever should have been washing these windows."

I had to laugh. "A little dirty?" I knocked once more, louder this time, but still had no response.

She waved me over. You need to look in here. This place was impressive."

I walked gingerly over to where she was. Clearly this part of the porch had been repaired several years ago, and still felt sound. I brushed another spot clean and looked in. "Wow." We were looking into a spacious entry. A wide central staircase wound its way up to the second floor. Though needing repair, it had clearly been built to impress. I could see a large drawing room off to the right, and made out what appeared to be a carved marble fireplace. There was no furniture to be seen. I suppose it had been removed at one time or another. "So what do you think," I asked. "Farmhouse? Mansion? Hotel?"

She shook her head, still spying through the window. "I don't know." She started to the right. "Let's take a look down there. There's a closed door and I can't see into that room."

I shook my head. "I don't think so. This patchwork repair doesn't go very far. I'm afraid you'll fall through."

She scowled at me and started off again, but I grabbed her arm. "No. I don't want you to go out there. I fell through a deck that I was repairing once. I was lucky not to have broken my leg. As it was, I was pretty badly cut up. I don't look forward to running you down to the emergency room from here." I pointed. Just beyond where she wanted to go was a sizable hole in the deck. The wooden ends were jagged and I could see more than a few rusty nails sticking out.

She frowned at me and I figured I should lighten the mood. "Besides, I really don't want to get arrested as a peeping tom." I inclined my head. "Let's take a look out back."

Mindy hesitated, but finally agreed and we made our way carefully back down the front stairs. The flagstone walkway wrapped around the entire building, so we followed it. The back was pretty much the same as the front. There was a good looking back door, but the steps were in far worse shape than the front. I climbed up a foot or so and looked over the top. Much of the decking had rotted away. I shook my head. "No going up there."

The real treasure out back was an octagonal gazebo, about twenty feet in diameter. Like the rest of the buildings, it was old, but seemed to have been kept up more recently, as the steps and the flooring were solid. We climbed up and surveyed the property. A small creek ran behind the gazebo, cutting diagonally through the back end of the grassy expanse. I could see what appeared to be a pair of overgrown horseshoe pits off in the distance.

"I put my arm around Mindy's waist. "So what do you think?"

She smiled up at me. "I'm glad we came down this road. Interesting place." She cocked her head to one side. "I was just imagining this in its heyday." She spread her hands out to encompass the gazebo and started thinking aloud. "It's a bright sunny day. Midsummer, and hot. The band would have played here. People would have been scattered across the lawn, picnicking, women with parasols; men wearing jackets and ties; little boys in short pants chasing little girls in frilly dresses, or maybe trying to catch frogs in the creek." She looked back at the house. "They'd have served lemonade, nothing stronger, though I suppose some of the men might have fortified it from a flask."

I laughed and joined in. "And the rails would have been decorated with bunting, red, white, and blue bunting." I looked at her. "Fourth of July?"

She smiled, nodding her head, and then leaned against me. "They'd have set up a big barbecue and served steaks, and beans..."

"And ice cream."

Laughing, she continued. "That's right. Ice cream." Then she took my hand and led me down from the gazebo. "All this talk of food is making me hungry. I don't think we've eaten since breakfast and it's what, 4:00?"

I snuck a look at my watch. 3:45. Close enough. "What were you thinking of?"

"Let's drive out the old road and see what we find."

"Sounds good," I said. "But first..."

She looked at me. "First?"

I nodded, thinking. "Let's stop at the post office. Maybe they know something about this place."

"You never know."

§§§§

The postwoman was dressed in overalls. The door had been locked when we arrived, so I knocked. It took a while, and we were just about to leave when we heard the latch turn. "What can I do for you? Letter to mail? Just put it in the slot there."

Mindy gave her best smile. "Hi, I'm Mindy and this is Charlie. And you're?" She extended her hand.

The woman looked at her skeptically, evidently leery of strangers in her very small town. Then she smiled and took Mindy's hand. "Mary Forster, Postmistress."

Mindy shook her hand. "Actually Mary, we were just looking at the old house down the road and wondered if you could tell us anything about it."

She scratched her head. "Huh. The old Randolph place?"

I shrugged my shoulders. "I guess. Down at the end of the street there? Big old white house, run down."

She nodded. "Yeah, that's the Randolph place. Hasn't been anybody living there for years."

"So it's a house?" Mindy asked.

"That used to be the Sheep Ranch. Big spread at one time, hundred years ago or so."

"What is it now?"

"Don't know," she shrugged. "Try to sell it every once in awhile. No takers." She scanned the buildings around her. "It's not like this is a very big town."

"So who owns it?"

"I don't know. Some folks in San Francisco. Bought it about fifteen years ago. Thought they'd turn it into a hotel I guess." She scowled. "Never really got off the ground."

That explained the repairs to the veranda and the gazebo. They looked like they might be about that old.

Mindy wasn't finished yet. "Is it for sale now?"

I looked at her and mouthed, "What?"

She ignored me and Mary said, "Could be." She looked back into the post office. "I might have one of the old flyers. Let me check." She went inside, and I peeked in the door. The office was tiny, as I suppose should be expected in a community of thirty-two. She had a stack of papers on the counter, and after blowing the dust off the top, fingered through them. A few seconds later, she said, "Ah, here it is. Want a copy?"

"Sure," Mindy replied. The woman loosened a paper clip at the top of what appeared to be half a dozen sheets. She handed one to Mindy, who took it and smiled one of those dazzling smiles again. "Thanks, Mary. We'll get out of your hair now." She turned toward the door. The woman nodded and proceeded to put the stack of papers back on the corner of the counter. We seemed to have been forgotten.

I walked back out to the car. Before I was half way, I heard the door close and the bolt lock. Smiling, I went to Mindy's side and opened the door for her. She got in, looking at the pictures of the house. I could see them over her shoulder. They were black and white and grainy, but definitely showed the house and grounds. The price tag seemed a little high for a place in need of a lot of repair, but what did I know about real estate in the greater Sheep Ranch market. Did they even have a realty office?

"Still hungry?" I asked.

She nodded absently.

"All right then.

§§§§

We'd agreed to meet the Adams at a local bistro for lunch the next day, so knowing that we'd be eating later, we skipped the breakfast offered at the B&B.

Mindy and I did some window shopping while we waited. The warm summer weather was definitely here, and I could tell that the afternoon in Murphys would be hot. On the other hand, noon was still pretty nice, with temperatures in the mid-eighties. By the time Jim and Melissa arrived, I'd secured a nice table on the restaurant patio. We were sitting comfortably, talking about Sheep Ranch when Mindy saw them coming up the street. She waved, and Melissa waved back.

"Long time no see," Jim said as he sat across from me. "How've you been?"

"Good," I said. "We've been exploring the area and actually drove out to Sheep Ranch yesterday."

He chuckled. "I sometimes think Murphys is small. Why Sheep Ranch?"

"Well," I looked at Mindy. She was lost in conversation with Melissa. "We were just driving back roads, getting a feel for the area, and saw a sign and a left turn arrow. Six miles later, and no chance to turn off, we were there."

He nodded. "Pretty remote."

"Interesting town."

"I haven't been out there in years. Anything new?"

"What qualifies as new?"

He laughed. "In Sheep Ranch, I guess anything built in the last ten years or so."

"Well in that case, you'd recognize just about everything there."

§§§§

Lunch was good, and we enjoyed getting reacquainted. As we were sitting over iced tea later, Jim said to Mindy, "We were glad to hear you'd called. We haven't really found anything new, but figured it would be interesting to get the latest news from you."

It had been a couple of months since we'd last seen them, and we'd read several letters, so Mindy brought them up to date. She then opened her purse and brought out another letter. "There are only four left. Should I read it?"

Melissa leaned forward. "That'd be wonderful. So he's going home?"

Mindy nodded. "So it would seem." She showed the envelope. "Look at the postmark."

I leaned over. "Aspinwall, Panama." I looked up at her. "Where's that?"

She shook her head. "Panama somewhere." She took out her phone and looked it up. "Here it is. Aspinwall was founded by Americans working on a trans Panama railroad. The city's name was changed to Colon in 1890."

Melissa was looking over her shoulder while she read. "Amazing. An encyclopedia in your purse."

Mindy grinned. I knew she loved her technology, and the immediate access she had to information.

"So," Jim said. "If I remember my visit to Panama, that's on the Caribbean side."

I was impressed. "Good. I knew Panama, but that's about all. East coast then. So he's gotten through the jungle."

Mindy handed me the letter. "It's from Joel. You want to read?"

"I thought you'd never ask." I smiled as I took the letter.

August 15, 1854
Aspinwall, Panama

Dear Catherine,
The hike through the jungle was more brutal than I recalled, but then I was ill for much of the previous journey. Still, I am here, in Aspinwall, looking out over the Caribbean Sea, ready to rejoin you. You will be happy to know that I had no problems with illness or injury during the hike across this narrow isthmus. I am actually fortunate that I have been working so hard in the gold fields, for I was very strong before beginning the trek.
It is hot here in the tropics, but it is beautiful as well, and I am sure that if we choose this route back, you will appreciate the variety of flowers that seem to

grow on every bush. It has rained every afternoon since we landed in Panama City, and I suppose that accounts for the many lakes and rivers we had to cross, and for the constant dampness in the air.

This letter will go out with the mail packet on Friday, and hopefully you will receive it in a few weeks. I have booked passage on the SS Central America. The ship runs a regular freight service between the US east coast and Central America, and always carries passengers as well. I feel fortunate to have gotten passage as most are still going to California, not returning. I understand that she is a new steamship, with a paddle wheel along one side to power her when the winds are light. I well remember the days we spent on our journey to California, when there was little or no wind crossing the Caribbean Sea, when we seemed to drift with the current. I will be glad not to suffer again from that problem. The ship is not in port now, so I can only imagine what she looks like. The agent expects her to arrive to take on cargo and passengers next week.

I am anxious to see you again, and to meet my daughter for the first time. Does she know that I am coming? Can she even imagine that she has a father who is not there?

I have thought about where we should live. I definitely want to return to California. It is such an interesting land, and a place so filled with opportunity for a man who is willing to work hard. I believe that we will be very happy there. I do feel a strong pull to San Andreas, and to my partners and the store there, but you may not wish to live and raise our daughter and any other children in such a rough and primitive environment. I was assured by my employers in San Francisco that they will re-hire me upon my return, so we have that option as well. There is also a third option that I have been considering lately. I might want to set up a freight line, to move goods from the great port of San Francisco up to the growing communities in the interior, and to provide transportation back. I believe that could be a very successful venture. My savings and the small income I receive from the store will give us the opportunity to decide which path to pursue.

You are ever more in my daily thoughts, and I can not wait to be with you again.

Your loving husband, Joel

I folded the letter and looked at the others. "Well, what do you think?"

Jim was the first to respond. "It sounds from this and from what you've told us, that you really did find a long lost relative. It's still curious to me that he wasn't on the family tree."

"It doesn't appear that they ever moved to California," Mindy said. "Did I mention that she owned property in Pennsylvania in her own name several years later? Her maiden name."

"Well isn't that interesting," Melissa added. "That must have been rather unusual. Where'd you find that?"

I looked toward Mindy and she continued, "I found an old tax record in Bradford, 1865 or so. She had a house."

"And Joel wasn't on the title?"

"That's the thing," she said. "There's no record of him in Pennsylvania at all. I can't even find anything about him before he left."

"But he was here in California."

"Absolutely. We can prove that. Otherwise, it might almost seem as if she'd made him up."

"And how many more letters did you say are left?" Melissa asked.

"Three?" I asked.

Mindy replied. "That's right. Just the three."

Melissa nodded thoughtfully. "Do you mind if I ask who they're from?"

Mindy smiled. "One from Joel. Two from Catherine."

Jim stared at her for a moment, and then he smiled. "I don't suppose you brought another one, did you?"

She reached back into her purse and gave him a coquettish grin. "As a matter of fact, I do have another, but was thinking of waiting for this evening."

"Ah. As you wish."

Then she smiled. "We had hoped to do a little wine tasting this afternoon. Would you like to join us? And then a letter later on?"

Melissa looked at Jim questioningly and he replied. "A little maybe. Not very much. The community doesn't expect me to be entirely dry, but they do want me to be sober."

I laughed. "Understood." I looked across at Mindy. "Where did you have in mind?"

"I don't really care. There are so many places in Murphys. Or we could drive somewhere." She patted Jim on the shoulder. "It seems we have a designated driver!"

§§§§

It turned out that we did elect to go out of town, and ended up about twenty miles away in Jamestown. It appeared that the three main features in Jamestown were the variety of touristy antique shops, the restaurants, and the railroad. And the railroad was primarily a tourist venue, offering history and rides around the local area.

Three small wineries had opened a joint tasting room in one of the 19th century stone buildings and that's where we ended up, and interestingly, how we met Frank. It turned out he was a co-owner of the tasting room, owner of a very small winery, and a retired chemist who'd worked for a major Silicon Valley technology company.

When I asked him, tongue in cheek, what he recommended, he brought out his label, showed a zinfandel, and offered a pour. I couldn't help but taunt him a bit, "I see you have three zinfandels. What about the other ones?"

He looked at the others on the shelf. "They're good too, but I think you'll like this one best." Then he chuckled. "Of course, if you had come yesterday, you'd have met Randy, and he'd have told you mine was okay, but his is better." He paused for a moment, mid pour. "Bottom line is drink what you like." He winked at Mindy, who'd been following our exchange. "But try this one first."

It was a busy Sunday, so we weren't able to talk much more, but he did offer his card, and said he'd be happy to take us up to his winery if we came back and gave him some notice. "I do tours once a month, by appointment, and I'd love to have you."

So we tried his zinfandel, which I didn't particularly care for, and then a Cabernet that was okay, and finally his petite syrah. That one I liked. In fact, I ended up buying a bottle, partly because he'd been so gracious that I didn't want to leave without buying something and partly because, well, it was a very good wine. Who knew. A retired chemist. Where was the long history of family involvement stomping grapes in the wine industry?

So we wandered through Jamestown, skipping the train ride but trying a couple of wines, and finally ended up in the park, sitting in the gazebo, and listening to Mindy.

September 7, 1854

Bradford, Pennsylvania

Dearest Joel,
I received your letter from Panama this afternoon, and had to sit down to write to you right away. After all, if I wait even until tomorrow, you may already be here.

I am so excited about seeing you. It seems that I have prayed every night that we might be reunited and now my prayers are about to come true. Hurry home!

I am glad that you were able to make the trip through Panama without any difficulties this time. Despite all of the flowers you described, it sounds like an absolutely wretched place. I am sure that I will be very unpleasantly hot if we do decide to return to California that way. But I will be with you, and I am sure you will take good care of me regardless of how we travel.

Marie is asleep right now. She had a big day, filled with excitement. Tom has ridden with her on Old Belle, his horse, several times since she was just a toddler, but today he decided that she was big enough to ride by herself. Of course, he walked on one side and I on the other just to be sure that she did not fall off, but it was not necessary. She held the reins and sat up straight in the saddle just like an old pro. I have sometimes wondered at the phrase, 'ear to ear smile.' Well she certainly had one! We were all very proud, and Marie was just bursting and could not talk of anything else for the rest of the day. I wish that you could have seen her. She was so excited about being grown up enough to ride a horse by herself. At one point, she wanted us to let her make a circuit of the corral by herself, without our help, but I certainly was not going to allow that for my three year old daughter, farm girl or not.

Tom has been funny about his courtship. He really does not want to talk about it, and my brothers tease him mercilessly. Still, I am glad for him. Sarah is one of the women who joins us for quilting. She is a good, strong, compassionate woman, and makes a good match for Tom. As headstrong and domineering as he tries to be with everyone else, he has been as meek as a little lamb the few times I have seen him with her.

Well, this letter will be short, as you will be here very soon, and it is growing late. I have much to do tomorrow and Marie will be wanting my attention at first light. I wish you well, my love.
Your loving wife,
Catherine

Mindy smiled as she folded the paper and put it back into the envelope. "It was short."

Melissa asked, "Is Tom her brother?"

She nodded. "Evidently, he was my great great, who knows how many greats, uncle. He seems to have taken on a father role with Marie."

"Ah," she sighed. "So how does he feel about Joel coming back?"

"At this point, I don't think he knows."

Jim chortled. "Oh, to have been a fly on that wall when Joel came walking in. There must have been some real fireworks!"

That stopped us for a moment, all wondering what that would be like. After all, Tom was, to a great extent, the only father Marie had known. Finally, I asked, "Was there an address on this one?"

Mindy shook her head and Jim looked curiously. "Address?"

She turned to him. "Many of Catherine's letters don't show an address on the envelope. It's as if she was writing to a diary."

He cocked his head, but Melissa nodded slowly. "She wrote, but couldn't deliver the letters because she didn't know where he was."

"Ah," said Jim. "So she just saved them." He gestured toward the letter she'd just read. "For you."

"I suppose you're right," she said, looking at the envelope she still held in her hand. "Just for me."

I looked at her and smiled, all the time thinking, and then there were two. How would this end?

CHAPTER 57

Summer had come to Santa Cruz, meaning that the beaches were blanketed with early morning fog, which generally burned off by about 11:00 leaving glorious warm days. Further inland, where Mindy lived, the days began warm and sunny and stayed that way - what my father used to call barbecue weather. She and I chose one of those days to walk from Natural Bridges along the coast into Santa Cruz.

I had never walked through there before, and Mindy was anxious to show me that part of her extended neighborhood. She directed me to an entrance road, alongside the Natural Bridges State Park and from there, we quickly made our way out to West Cliff Drive. We crossed, and found a pedestrian pathway that hugged the cliffs into town.

I stopped for a moment when we reached the pathway, and Mindy asked if I was all right.

"Just enjoying the view," I said. "It is spectacular here." There was just enough breeze to stir the air. We carried light jackets just in case, but even Mindy had hers tied around her waist. I pulled her close and we leaned against the fence. Just beyond us, the cliff face fell fifty feet into foaming waves that swirled and crashed incessantly against the rocks. "So where do we go from here?"

"Lunch at the wharf," she said. "A couple of miles."

"And all like this?"

"Pretty much."

I pulled away from the fence. "In that case, lead on."

while we walked, we talked about a number of things, but I

357

found that walking in that area required pretty close attention to our surroundings. We were in no danger of stepping off a cliff; the railings protected against that; but we were hardly the only ones there. Bicycle riders came from both directions, frequently ringing bells and calling out from behind, "on your left," before whizzing past. The trail was also populated by joggers, walkers, and rollerbladers. One family came by with a golden retriever on a leash, a child in a stroller, and another small child winding along the trail on a tiny bicycle. Clearly, this was a busy place.

And yet, with nothing to our right but ocean and the occasional cluster of surfers, it seemed at times, as if we were the only ones there.

We'd walked about a mile when I saw a house that jutted out across the street, taking advantage of a corner in the cliff to capture views both to the north and south. "Look at that place," I said as I pointed.

Mindy nodded. "The rock house."

I looked at her. "It has a name?"

"I'm not sure if it really has a name, but it's known as the rock house."

"It makes sense." The entire outside of the house was covered with rocks. It sat on a narrow lot, but one that jutted all the way out to the end of a little peninsula, and as we approached, we could actually see through huge plate glass windows on one side, out the windows on the other, and then past the neighbor's house to the ocean beyond. "Amazing location."

"And they have a yard."

I hadn't really been paying close attention, but now that she mentioned it, that was true. Most of the old cottages had small yards out front, a little grass and some native shrubbery. The newer mega homes were in many cases, built nearly out to the property line, saving just enough room out front for a small patio. This place was special. It must have originally sat on two lots, and was set back behind a beautiful grassy meadow surrounded by rosebushes. It seemed that a front yard patio with barbecue was a requirement in the area, and who could complain with the spectacular views of the ocean. This one was fenced with planter boxes and more flowers.

I smiled. "Quite a place!"

She squeezed my arm. "One of my favorites."

It was an older house, and as I turned back to the ocean, I could definitely see why the original owners would have chosen this location. From where we were standing across the street, the cliffs fell off to either side, almost giving the impression of standing on an island.

I looked down and was surprised to see a large rock, seemingly floating a few hundred feet off shore. Several harbor seals had appropriated space on the rock, toasting in the warm sun. As I watched, one old grizzled male slipped rather effortlessly into the water and swam out a way. Mindy had been watching too, and just smiled when I said, "Too warm? Time to cool off?"

"Maybe, or he could just be hungry, or in the mood for a swim," she responded and we continued our walk.

I had been able to see the lighthouse in the distance for some time, when finally we arrived at another open park. Passing through, we dodged groups of young university students chasing Frisbees and waved to families gathered on blankets for a picnic. The fog that had hovered a little way off the coast when we started our walk was largely gone now, leaving a warm, if breezy day at the beach.

§§§§

Some time later, we walked out onto the pier. Mindy had suggested getting sandwiches in the restaurant out at the end. We made our way up the pier, past gift shops, restaurants, wine bars, and of course, seafood markets. Normally, the restaurant patio was protected by glass walls to shield diners from the cool wind that often buffeted the area. Today though, the windows were open, to allow breezes to pass through. I couldn't have imagined a better place to spend the afternoon. And so we sat, drinking iced tea and sharing a delicious rockfish sandwich.

Once we finished, Mindy reached into her purse and pulled out one of the familiar envelopes. "I brought a letter from Joel," she said, and handed it across to me.

I looked at the postmark on the envelope. This one had been posted from Havana. I looked up at Mindy, "So Joel is making good progress."

"It would seem so," she said.

"His last letter?"

She nodded. "The last we have anyway."
I nodded and opened the envelope.

August 27, 1854
Havana, Cuba

My dear wife,
We have stopped here in Havana for a few days to unload and load again. As I've watched the slaves doing their work, I've been amazed at the hundreds of tons of sugar we must be carrying. And more mountains of the stuff fill the docks.

Not too far away, is another mountain. This one though, is made of wooden casks that I am told are filled with rum. The volume held in those casks must be enough to keep every man in Pennsylvania in a drunken state for an entire year.

You might wonder why I've written you from here. The fact is, we will be stopped for several days taking on cargo and awaiting some passengers. There is a mail packet leaving tomorrow though, so I decided to take the opportunity to send you another letter. If all goes well, I should follow the letter into your arms by just a week or so.

This ship is far larger than the one we sailed down to Panama in four years ago. I have been told that there are over five hundred passengers and crew on board, and can certainly believe that, as it seems that wherever I go, I am surrounded by people. As before, I am sharing a cabin with other men. One, Michael, is returning to Virginia from California. Unlike me though, he had little or no success in the gold fields. I suspect that a part of his misfortune may have been his addiction to strong drink, as I have rarely seen him sober. When I think of him, I am reminded of how fortunate I was to have met Jonathan and Samuel. They helped turn what could have been a disastrous adventure into a successful one. Aaron is my other bunk mate. He is returning to Boston from Colombia. It seems that he has spent the past few years there studying the natural history of the jungle. He is an interesting man when he speaks, but often keeps to himself, writing in his journals.

The paddlewheel is a wonder. We passed through an area of calm seas shortly after leaving Panama. Whereas we drifted, hoping for wind on the journey south, in this case, the captain powered up the giant wheel and we continued on our way, if anything, faster than when powered by wind. I am told that one of the reasons that the ship is so large is because one of the holds must be devoted entirely to coal to power the monster wheel. Indeed, we do leave a stream of black smoke that is probably visible for miles behind us.

Earlier today, I went ashore and purchased a bolt of colorful cloth for you. It is interesting to compare the dour colors that are worn in Pennsylvania with the vibrant reds and yellows and greens that one sees everywhere here. I hope that it brings you pleasure.

I have reached the point where I am counting the hours until we are reunited again. It is difficult to imagine that in only a few short days, I will not only meet my daughter, but will also be able to take both of you into my arms.

With all my love,

Joel

"So," Mindy said. "Havana. He seems to have come almost full circle."

"He's almost home." I did some quick calculations in my head. "They probably travel at a speed of eight to ten knots, so cover say two hundred miles in a day. I suppose they'll reach Philadelphia in a week or ten days at most."

"Depending upon their stops," she said.

"True. They probably have several stops up the coast." I paused. "So maybe two to three weeks."

"And then a week crossing the state."

I nodded. "So he'll probably arrive sometime around the end of September."

"If all goes well."

I smiled. "Of course. If all goes well."

§§§§

That night, Mindy had planned a surprise. I had anticipated a barbecue at her place, and had even pulled into the parking lot at the market on the way back when she interrupted my driving.

"We're going out tonight."

"Out? I thought we were going to barbecue."

"Nope," she said. "I have reservations at Jason's on the Strand."

I'd parked the car, and now I looked across at her. I don't recall you mentioning that."

She smiled enigmatically. "I didn't. Hope you're hungry."

I reflected on that. We'd walked four miles into Santa Cruz, two to three miles around town, and four miles back to the car. In the meantime, I'd had half of a fish sandwich and a cookie. "I can eat," I said. "Someplace good?"

"I think you'll like it. It's different."

§§§§

And so at 7:00, we pulled into the parking lot at Jason's. Mindy had pointed out that it was only a mile or so from her place and suggested we walk but I'd reminded her that the fog was back with a vengeance, and it was already chilly. "Your choice," I said, knowing the answer. "Cold walk back up the hill or seat warmers and a heater." I smiled. "Either is fine with me." And so we drove.

The restaurant had a large patio outside, and I could see several couples huddled under the gas heat lamps. In addition to being a bit chilly, it was damp, and it seemed that some regretted eating in the open air. Mindy had reservations for an inside table, not far from the fireplace. I smiled. I should have guessed that.

The hostess sat us, and then left without even referring to a menu. I looked across at Mindy. "Menus?" I asked.

"It's buffet night."

And she was right. Across the main dining room, I could see a buffet table with salads and a number of warmers. I'd noticed it on the way in, but figured that it probably provided appetizers for the happy hour at the bar. And maybe it did, but evidently that was where we were to get our dinner.

She looked at me, smiled, and stood. "Shall we?"

And so we walked over to the buffet. It certainly wasn't like the buffet meals I had experienced in the past. We had a choice of a spinach salad with hot bacon dressing or a Caesar with freshly shaved parmesan cheese, and that was just the beginning. I ended up having the Caesar, fresh grilled lamb served over rice pilaf, and just for fun, a little tilapia in lemon butter sauce along with steamed spring vegetables. It smelled as good as it looked and even better than it sounded. Mindy skipped the lamb, choosing instead the herb roasted chicken. When we got back to the table, I was all ready to dig into my dinner when what did I find, but a fresh shellfish appetizer and a glass of Chardonnay. Very nice.

"What do you think," Mindy asked as we sat. "Satisfactory?"

"I'm impressed." I raised my glass. "I like the wine. Did you sneak an order in when I wasn't looking?"

She laughed and shook her head. "Actually, they feature a winery on every buffet night. It's great advertising for everyone." She sampled the wine and smiled. "There's a new wine with each course." She glanced over to the corner where I could see a waiter ensconced with an array of bottles. "Usually, they'll have the appetizer wine, your choice of dinner wines, and a dessert wine." She swirled the wine in her glass. "Good legs."

I couldn't resist. "I agree. It's from all your walking."

She giggled and slapped my hand lightly. "I mean the wine."

"Oh," I said, feigning surprise, and looked at the wine. "That too."

§§§§

If anything, the food tasted even better than it had smelled. And so we ate, and ate, and returned to the buffet table and selected some more, and ate some more. And it seemed that every time our wine glasses dropped below the halfway point, the waiter was waiting with a new offering, but for some reason, maybe it was the vigorous walking during the day, or the sumptuous food, or just the joy of being together, I never felt as if I'd had too much.

Finally, I looked across at Mindy's plate. Aside from a few kernels of rice, it was pretty well scraped clean. Mine didn't even show traces of the rice. I smiled at her, "I think we both qualify for dessert." I gestured at the dishes. "We're both members of the clean plate club."

"Clean plate club?"

"Didn't you have to belong to the clean plate club when you were growing up?"

"Ah," she sighed. "But I'm not sure where I'd put dessert. I'm full."

"Me too, but that won't stop me from at least finding out what it is."

And magically, the waiter was at my side, first to pour some port into a tiny cordial glass, and then to offer us the dessert menu. The chocolate torte was a unanimous choice.

§§§§

Later that night, Mindy and I snuggled up on the couch. We'd chosen to walk home from the restaurant and pick up the car the following morning. It seemed when I stood up, I'd had more wine than I had suspected earlier. A mile walk in brisk, foggy weather took care of that. My head was clear and I felt completely sober by the time we reached Mindy's front door. Of course, with the chilly weather, we'd walked quickly too, but not quickly enough for Mindy. And that's what led us to the red sofa. She sat, folding her legs under her, and melded against me, wrapped in a warm knit afghan, and we stayed like that for quite some time, quietly listening to soft jazz.

After a while, I noticed her toes sticking out, so I began to rub her feet. They were icy. Evidently her sandals hadn't provided any protection against the cold. So I took them into my lap and tried to massage some warmth back into them. She purred, and soon we were laughing. She slid back a little bit, and still wrapped in the afghan, pushed her bare feet against my chest. It seemed almost like a challenge, as if to say, "Even you can't warm these toes." But she was wrong. I pulled up my shirt, and brought her feet inside against my bare skin, continuing the massage. Initially, she tried to pull away, but I held her tight, and as the warmth of my chest began to work its way into her feet, she closed her eyes and sighed.

Soon, her feet were warm, my chest had a couple of cold spots that I knew would soon dissipate, and we decided to settle closer together. I kissed her on top of the head and whispered, "My turn?"

She looked questioningly at me. I reached down to take off my socks. "Go ahead, open your blouse. Time to warm my toes."

She stared for just a few seconds before responding, "you'll notice that I kept my toes perfectly still, right."

"You did it your way; I'll do it mine," I said as I lifted one leg. "My toes like to wander."

I pushed one foot against her chest, hmm, very soft, and said, "Aren't you going to let them in?"

She just shook her head and laughed. "You are awful!"

I tried my most innocent puppy dog look. It didn't work.

She very deliberately removed my foot, and then stood up and said, "you might as well put your socks back on. Otherwise your feet will get even colder." Then heading toward the stairs, she said, "I'm going upstairs to get Catherine's letter. If you can convince those feet to behave, you may join me."

Well, she didn't say anything about my hands or any other parts, so I figured I was in pretty good shape. "Absolutely," I said, as I bounced off the couch to join her. Then looking down at my feet, whispered, "Good job guys!"

§§§§

Some time later, Mindy opened the last letter. We were lying closely entwined in her bed, very warm, and very cozy. "This is it," she said. She straightened the page, and then instead of looking at it, looked over at me. "A part of me is desperate to find out what's in it, but a part really doesn't want to know." She paused and took several long, deep breaths. And then she began.

November 19, 1854
Bradford, Pennsylvania

Dearest Joel,
I received your news yesterday. A part of me knew, and a part of me was desperately hoping that it could not be true. These past weeks have been very difficult; waiting, frantic for news, anxious, terrified.
I do believe that we could have had a wonderful life together, whether here in Pennsylvania, or in California. And now that will never come to pass. Nor will Marie get to spend long days in the loving embrace of her father. You would have loved her as I do. She is a dear child.
I feel that I have lost more than a husband. I feel the loss of my best friend, my confidant, and to a great extent, my dreams of the future. But I have learned to be strong, and will weather this storm, change my dreams, and go on to be a good mother to our daughter.
I have been without you for so long that I have become very independent. Still, I will miss you so. During difficult times, writing to you or anticipating your letters has helped to keep me going. And so as I sit at my table tonight, pen in hand, I wonder if you will mind if I continue to write to you, telling you about my day, and about our daughter, and sharing my dreams of a future with you.

You will always be my beloved husband,
Catherine

Mindy's voice broke when she read the last words in a barely audible whisper. I looked over at her. Tears rolled steadily down her cheeks, and as she wiped her eyes, I saw that one had stained the page, blurring the ink. It was only one of several spots on the parchment, the others older, dried, and sadly mixed into the story behind the words.

I took the page, carefully folded it, and lay it on her night stand before taking her and holding her in my arms. We stayed like that, pressed together, unsleeping, long into the night.

CHAPTER 58

Lethargy ruled the following morning. Neither Mindy nor I could really get started. We stumbled around her house, silently pouring coffee, uncommunicative, almost unfeeling. A part of me was really surprised by how deeply we had invested in the relationship between Catherine and Joel, two people who had died long before either of us was born. For Mindy, they were family, her ancestors. More important than that though, they felt like family, and for whatever reason, we were mourning. And the worst part about it was that we didn't even know why.

Finally, sitting at the table, listlessly sipping my coffee, I asked, "So what do you think happened?"

Mindy just shook her head. "I don't know." She took a taste of her coffee. "Maybe the whole idea of getting back together, of having a family, all that just overwhelmed him. After all, he'd been on his own for four years." She sat silently for a while. "I just don't know."

I absorbed that, thinking of what information we did have. "It explains the tax record in Bradford, showing her ownership of the house in her maiden name."

Mindy nodded. "If he never came back, and she moved on, well in that case, he wouldn't have had his name on the property Maybe it was a blessing in disguise that their marriage didn't really exist."

"It's possible." I thought for a moment, "She did have money from the original transfer of the house to Tom. I seem to recall that from one of the articles we looked up." I drummed my fingers on the table. "So she likely could have afforded the house."

"I've always wondered why she didn't take his name. I suppose this explains that too."

We sat quietly for a long time before she finally said, "But none of that explains what happened to him."

I got up. "Is the letter still on your night stand?"

She looked vacantly at me before finally inclining her head. "I think so."

I climbed the stairs, noting that I'd raced up them only the night before, and now seemed to find it difficult just to lift one foot after the other. Intellectually, this made no sense, and yet emotionally...

When I came back, Mindy's position was unchanged. I put the letter on the table and then positioned myself behind her, massaging her back and neck. I kept at it for several minutes, until I could feel the knots leaving. She groaned and dipped her head. "Thanks. I needed that."

I continued for a while before stopping and kissing the top of her head, "Right," I said as I sat next to her. "Let's take another look at that letter."

I picked it up and held it so that we could both scan it. As I did so, I noted again the stain left by Mindy's tear. The spot was still damp, and the ink had run just a bit. "Look here," I said, pointing.

She shook her head. "I'm so sorry. I couldn't help it. I just lost it for a while."

"No, not that." I held the letter under the light. "look at the other spots. Yours aren't the first tears."

She took the letter and brought it close. She studied it for a moment before putting it down. "I'm willing to bet that they're Catherine's. She'd lost her husband." She looked up at me. "She must have known why."

I nodded slowly. "I'm sure she did. It seems that she was uncertain for a while."

"He was late," she said. "He'd written from Havana in August and this letter is dated what," she looked at the top again, "November 19th."

"Almost three months."

"How long do you suppose it would take to travel from

Havana to Bradford?"

I shook my head. "I don't know. I suppose it would depend on their stops. The ship seems to have been a coastal steamer." I pondered for a moment. "I can't imagine that the sea part would have lasted more than a few weeks though, and then a week at most to travel inland."

"So he was almost two months late."

I picked up the letter and re-read the first line aloud, "I received your news yesterday. A part of me knew, and a part of me was desperately hoping that it could not be true." I put it back down. "No hints there."

"We never found anything online about a Joel Woodward in Pennsylvania."

"No. California yes, but not Pennsylvania."

She was thinking aloud now, and I could see the life returning to her cheeks along with the renewed search. "And nothing after he left California."

I shook my head.

She looked up at me, "So what happened to him?"

I was about to say something, when Mindy rose and got a paper and pencil. "No sense moping around. Let's see if we can figure this out." She wrote on the top of the paper in bold letters, 'Joel Woodward.' Under that, she wrote, 'Disappeared sometime between August 27 and November 19, 1854.' Then she wrote, 'Kidnapped.'

"Kidnapped?" I asked. "Really?"

She looked at me. It was nice to see the drive coming back into her face. "I'm listing all of the possibilities."

I laughed. "Okay, how's this?" I took her pen and wrote, "Eaten by a shark."

She scowled. "Now that one is just ridiculous."

"You never know. Coastal Florida is known for its shark attacks. Maybe they stopped and he decided to go body surfing."

She rolled her eyes and continued to write. I noticed that she drew a line through my idea. Okay, this was to be her list. 'Changed his mind and disappeared. Killed by robbers in Pennsylvania, or elsewhere. Shipwrecked.'

Now it was my turn. "Oh, come on. How likely is that in a coastal steamer. They were never that far off shore."

She turned and glared at me. "This from the man who wanted to include, 'eaten by sharks.'"

"Well," I started. I was imagining Joel hanging out with his sidekick Friday on an island in the Bahamas. Of course, maybe his sidekick was really named Angelina and she was a hot Caribbean babe, and he decided to stay lost. Hmm. Nothing to be gained there. Maybe I shouldn't mention that. "Okay, maybe he was marooned somewhere after a shipwreck."

She continued. "Problems in Cuba. Returned to California. Pirates."

"Anything else?"

"Met someone else."

She wrote it down. "Did he have any family in the area?"

I shook my head. "I don't think we ever saw evidence of that, and didn't he mention in one of his letters that he'd grown up in an orphanage?"

"You're right," she said. "I remember that too. So that wouldn't have been it."

After a thinking for a moment, I added, "But there must have been somebody somewhere who at least knew of him. Even if he was in an orphanage, somebody cared for him at some point. Could he have gone to them?"

"Maybe they convinced him not to take off with a woman he'd only known for a short time."

It sounded possible. "A woman with a small child no less. And..."

She looked at me. I squirmed. "And what?"

"Well," I said slowly, "Uh..."

"What?" she demanded.

"Well, they may have convinced him not to run off with a woman of low moral character." I could see the fire in her eyes. "I mean, she did have a baby, and no permission to marry." There, I'd said it. I flinched, waiting for her response.

"And it wasn't his child too?"

"This was 1854," I said cautiously. "Attitudes were different then. A woman who got pregnant was considered a slut. A man..."

"And that's changed so much now!" she replied, dripping sarcasm. "Boys can play but girls had better be virginal."

"Uh," I paused, knowing that there was absolutely nothing

that I could say that would be right. Finally, I decided to concede that I was a part of the problem. "Certainly a wrong attitude purveyed by men throughout history. I take no pride in being masculine."

She gave me a withering stare. "Nor should you." Then she moved on, thankfully. "Ok, given the attitude of male dinosaurs, it's possible they might have convinced him that the child wasn't his." She started writing again. 'Relatives.' "I know it seems wrong, but Catherine didn't take his name, and neither did Marie. Maybe he denied that Marie was his child."

"I hadn't thought of that, but if he showed up in Bradford and questioned whether Marie was his child, it certainly would have killed the romance." I thought for a moment. "They were together for just one night. It might have seemed impossible that Catherine could have conceived from their one night together in the glade. He might not have shown up at all."

"And so you think he might have left her."

I nodded. It seemed to make sense, especially if his relations, whoever they might have been, were as antagonistic toward her as her family had been toward him. "And it would explain this other part." I picked up the letter again and read, "I wonder if you will mind if I continue to write to you." Laying the paper down. "She may have written that initially, when she still wanted him, but as her anger set in, decided not to write."

Mindy was nodding, as if it made some sense. "And if he did hurt Catherine, I'm pretty certain from what we know about Tom, that he would have done his best to keep them apart." She wrote some more. "Okay, another possibility."

She put her pencil down. "I think we have enough ideas." We both stared at the list for a moment. "It's how we go about proving them that will be the hard part."

I rose and reached for her hand. The sun had come up and the fog was pretty well gone. "How about a walk down to the village. You want to try lunch in that little coffee house up the stairs?"

She smiled for the first time that day, "That sounds heavenly."

§§§§

And so it went. We decided to rank the possibilities, and then concentrate our search based upon the rankings. It seemed that the likeliest possibility was some kind of communication or maybe no communication at all, that Joel had decided that he was just overwhelmed by the idea of having an instant family. His whole married experience, after all, consisted of one night of passion, hardly a foundation that might prepare him for a long term relationship complete with the stresses of marriage and parenthood. It seemed entirely possible that as he got closer to Pennsylvania, he would have become increasingly nervous, and once he worked his way past the romantic idea of getting back together with Catherine, he'd have come face to face with the prospect of adulthood in a way he hadn't considered before. After all, this was a man who'd spent the previous four years living a rough life with men in a wild west mining community, and prior to that, he'd been a boy. But how could we check that out? We'd spent countless hours already searching the internet and other records for a Joel Woodward, and found nothing after 1854. Over the next few weeks, both Mindy and I continued the search, with no success.

A few days later, Mindy found another reference to Catherine Lewis that confirmed her purchase of the house in Bradford in 1864. It was interesting that as a single, presumably unmarried woman in the mid-19th century, she had owned property, a little like her Aunt Ruth before her. But there was no reference to Joel.

For a while, I pursued the idea that Marie must have listed parents when she was attending the university working on her medical degree. I was able to find her college records, and she did list family members, but that also came up short. Her emergency contact was her mother. A secondary contact was Tom. Again, there was no mention of Joel.

Both Mindy and I had also spent some time researching records in San Andreas, Calaveras County, and even San Francisco to see what we could find of Joel. We knew that record keeping was scant at that time, and that in the tremendous turmoil that was early California, any records may have been lost anyway. We found no mention of his name after 1854.

So we had no record of Joel returning to California, and no record of him in Pennsylvania. It was possible that he might have moved elsewhere, but the chance of finding anything in an unfocused search seemed pretty unlikely. Still, I spent several hours researching the name Joel Woodward, and while I did find a few by that name who were living in the 1850's, their ages were wrong, so I counted that as another dead end.

Our second avenue to search was one that we'd considered earlier, but never really pursued. If he'd really grown up in an orphanage, there should have been records somewhere. Figuring that he was probably a year or two older than Catherine, we focused in on orphanages that were in operation in about 1840. And again, found very little. Yes, there were orphanages, but records were thin and most had operated for a few years and then shut down. One thing that we did confirm was that children left at orphanages were frequently children of immigrants, who were extremely poor. Because of their poverty and removal from cultural supports in the US or abroad, they experienced a high rate of illegitimate births. We also found that frequently, infants or small children were left anonymously, or with only a Christian name. Some babies were simply dropped on the doorstep. In many cases, the administrator of the orphanage had no idea of the child's background and simply assigned a name. So we might have looked right over Joel's records without any way of knowing it was him. Again, we came up with nothing.

§§§§

"So what's next?" I asked as I sipped my coffee. Mindy had come to my place the night before and we'd had a wonderful dinner followed by a night at the theater. Now we were sitting on the balcony, enjoying the early morning sun and watching golfers on the course beneath us. "Do you want me to check out shark attacks in the nineteenth century?"

Her rolled eyes registered her disgust. "If you must."

"Leave no stone unturned," I chirped merrily. I'll look for shipwreck survivors too. Maybe he was marooned on a deserted island. A kind of Robinson Crusoe story?"

She looked into her coffee, and then took a graceful taste. "No doubt, you'll find a message in a bottle."

I brightened. "Now there's an idea. I hadn't thought of that one." I imagined the process. "Let's see. Joel gets shipwrecked, finds a bottle, writes a message, probably on bark, and then caps the bottle and flings it into the sea." I smiled and she again shook her head. My humor evidently wasn't working as well this morning as I'd hoped.

"Unless you have a better idea," I said.

She was toying with the strawberries on her plate. I assumed that she meant to eat them eventually, but could see that she was thinking.

"As unlikely as it might seem, you may have an idea."

I grinned. Validation at last! "I'm not sure we'll be able to find out if he was really eaten by a shark though."

Fortunately, I was able to dodge quickly, as she flung one of the strawberries at me. I looked back just in time to see it go flying off the side of the balcony. I turned back. The second strawberry struck me square on the chin.

"Such violence," I said, feigning an appalled look. "And here I thought you had better control."

But it didn't matter. She had begun to laugh. It built from the familiar quiver that seemed to take over her entire body, and worked to a sputtering as she tried to giggle silently, but couldn't quite hold it in. Finally, the laughter rolled out, an unquenchable tide that took over her entire being. I tried to look serious, to appear to be the adult among us, but that just exacerbated her shuddering.

So I picked up the strawberry from my lap, tossed it over the rail, and wiped my chin, all the time trying to maintain my aura of dignity.

Finally able to begin to speak again, she pointed. "You have whipped cream on your cheeks. And then she convulsed again.

Still dignified, but cracking, I wiped my cheeks. Looking at the napkin, I could see that there was in fact, a fair amount of whipped cream on my face. And I finally lost it, joining her. I must admit at this point, that I took little pleasure in smearing that whipped cream soaked napkin across her face. It was simply payback.

§§§§

Later, clean, calm, and settled back onto the balcony, I continued. "So you're not really thrilled with my shark approach."

"If you must..." she said.

"Ah." I knew what that meant. Only a fool would try to research that idea. "How do you suggest we proceed?"

"Maybe he died."

"Possible," I said, "But we didn't find any record of his death."

"Maybe there was none."

I squinted at her. "And that would be because?"

"Maybe they didn't know who he was."

I thought for a moment. It made sense. "So if he was murdered in Cuba?"

"No drivers licenses," she said. "Did they carry any ID at all?"

"They must have had something." I shrugged my shoulders. "But I'm not sure what. I've heard of men carrying business cards with their names on them, but I think those were more likely to be wealthy. Joel... probably nothing, so that's an idea, especially when you consider that he was traveling alone. If he simply disappeared, it's possible that nobody even noticed. What would we look for? Unknown deaths? Havana and Philadelphia would be the most likely. Pennsylvania? Any of the other cities along the coast?" I grimaced. It could be an exhausting search and what would it prove? That someone unknown had died violently? "Even if we found something, how would we link it to Joel?"

She'd gotten her notepad and wrote down the idea, putting a question mark after it. "How about if we start with the ship. Do we know that it made it to Philadelphia?"

I cocked my head to one side as I considered that. Sure, there were shipwrecks, but this was a coastal steamer. Even if they got into trouble, they'd have run to shore. "Okay. It's a possibility."

She made a note. "Do you remember the name of the ship?"

I shook my head. "We'll have to check the letter. You don't have them with you by any chance, do you?"

This time it was her turn to demure. "No. Copies yes. Letters no."

"You brought copies?"

"How can we research without them?" She smiled, then tapped the side of her head. "Not just another pretty face."

"Not indeed," I smiled, "smart and pleasing to the eye. What a dazzling combination!"

She rose and lifted my coffee cup. "Finished?" When I nodded, she reached over and kissed my cheek. "I'm not sure that was intended as a compliment, or was just more of your sass, but I'll take it."

I did my best to look offended. "Sass? Me? You?"

She rolled her eyes and sashayed back inside. When she came back, she reached into her backpack and took out a stack of papers, obviously copies of the letters. "It was one of Joel's last letters," she said, thumbing through the pile. "Here's one. Aspinwall, Panama." She handed it to me. "Check it out. I'll see if there are any others."

I scanned the letter and quickly reached my hand over to hers to stop her. "This was it. The Central America." I rose and she looked at me questioningly. "Do you have your iPad?"

She nodded and pulled it out, turning it on as she handed it to me. While we waited for it to boot up, I asked, "So any other ideas?"

She referred to the initial list. "Well, it's possible that he changed his name, but that would definitely be a dead end. She tossed her head. "We don't even know his date or place of birth."

"Just an estimate," I replied.

"So we can't search that either."

The computer chimed at us and I opened the browser. Once there, I typed in a search for 'central america.'

"Hmm," Mindy said slowly as she scanned down the list. "Maps, history, Panama, Honduras." She looked at me. "You're going to have to be a little more specific. Here, let me." She typed in 'ship' after central america and hit search.

The first entry we got was SS Central America. "I'll bet that's it," I said. I read the description aloud, "SS Central America, sometimes called the Ship of Gold, was a 280-foot (85 m) sidewheel steamer that operated between Central America and the eastern coast of the United States during the 1850's." I clicked on the link. The fourth line down was sobering.

"Oh my God!" Mindy exclaimed. She read aloud, "The ship sank in a hurricane in September of 1854, killing over 400 passengers and crew and taking a load of 30,000 pounds of California gold to the bottom."

She slumped back in her chair, staring at the screen. Without thinking, I reached over and took her hand. We sat that way, stunned, for the next several minutes.

Finally, she whispered, "She must have gotten news of the sinking in November." I looked at her, but she was lost in her thoughts and I doubt that she even saw me. Still, she had a tight grip on my hand. "He didn't show up. She worried, and each day it got worse until she was panicked."

"And then the news reached Bradford," I added.

She nodded so softly that had I not been watching her, I probably wouldn't have noticed it. "That's probably what it was, a news report. She wouldn't have been listed as next of kin."

"If there even was a passenger manifest, it probably sank with the ship."

"He died nameless," she shuddered. "My great, great grandfather died and nobody even knew."

Somehow, I had expected tears, but wasn't surprised when there were none. Perhaps it was just too sad, or perhaps we already knew. He hadn't returned. There had to be a reason.

I reached over to the iPad and tried a few more reports on the ship. Finally, I came to one that looked interesting. It was a newspaper article, dated in September of 1854. I scanned it until I came to the gist of what had happened, and then started to read aloud.

"On September 9th the SS Central America was caught up in a Category 2 hurricane while off the coast of the Carolinas. By September 11th, the 105 mph winds and heavy surf had shredded her sails, she was taking on water, and her boiler was threatening to go out. A leak in one of the seals to the paddle wheels sealed her fate, and, at noon that day, her boiler could no longer maintain fire. Steam pressure dropped, shutting down both the pumps keeping the water at bay and the paddle wheels that kept her pointed into the wind as the ship settled by the stern. The passengers and crew flew the ship's flag upside down (a universal sign of distress) to try to signal a passing ship while they gallantly manned manual pumps. No one came. Estimates of survivors range from 50-100, while up to 600 perished."

There were a number of other articles, but most of them dealt with the recovery of the ship by treasure hunters in the 1980's.

"Well, do you suppose he was one of the survivors?" I asked.

She shook her head. "If he'd survived, there would be some evidence of it." She stared out into space for a while, before finally wiping away a silent tear. "I guess that's why we never found him."

I stood and lifted Mindy to her feet. Wrapping my arms around her, I held her for some time, stroking her back. Finally, I kissed her forehead and said, "How about a walk?"

CHAPTER 59

Discovering that Joel had likely perished in a shipwreck, though not unexpected, had indeed sobered both of us. We never really discussed it, but seemed to be of accord that we needed to put our research into Mindy's ancestry on indefinite hold. Joel's death seemed too close somehow, to allow us to continue. I suppose that we both, and Mindy in particular, needed a break.

And so over the next few months, we played some golf, ate some fine meals, and did a little traveling. I missed the letters, but had to admit that I enjoyed the respite.

Mindy had written to Jim and Melissa to tell them the results of our research, and Melissa had actually sent a very considerate sympathy card. I suspect that she knew just how invested we had both become in our journey into Mindy's past. And then the following winter, we received an invitation to Jim's 60th birthday party. I'm not sure about Mindy, but I know that I was surprised. We knew them casually, but hadn't formed a close or long term relationship. Still, it sounded like fun, and would be a good excuse to take off for the Sierras again.

The party was scheduled for a Saturday in mid-May. Since we had a pretty good advance notice, we had decided to take a week to relax and resume our exploration of the area. I called the bed and breakfast, and was able to get our usual room at a pretty good rate. It seemed that they didn't have too many week long guests. Mindy had been shopping for birthday presents despite the "no gifts please" note on the bottom of the invitation. I started to question her on that, but she just gave me a look that convinced me that buying a gift was a pretty good idea.

As the date came closer, Mindy and I were sitting in one of the ocean front restaurants we enjoyed in Santa Cruz. She looked at me, and out of the blue said, "Do you remember the winemaker we met in Jamestown? Didn't he mention that he gave tours?"

"Winemaker?"

"You remember. They had what, three or four wineries represented in one tasting room."

I searched my brain. It sounded familiar. Finally, I had it. "He'd been a chemist, hadn't he? Interesting guy." I thought for a moment. "I think you're right. You want to try a tour while we're there?"

"If we can get in. It'd be interesting."

I nodded. It would be. "I may have his business card at home. I remember him handing it to me. If not, it was a small town. I don't suppose they have too many wineries."

She smiled and I cocked my head. "Or," she said, "You could just look on the bottle of wine. Do you still have it?"

I hadn't thought of that. I was sure we hadn't drunk it yet. "I do. It's on the wine rack."

Grinning, she reached over and kissed my cheek. "Why don't you let me know when you get home. I'll call for reservations."

I toasted her with my coffee. "Will do."

"You won't forget?" she asked.

"Oh, I probably will, but I'm sure you'll remind me."

§§§§

And so, in the middle of May, we found ourselves back in Murphys. The weather was glorious, past the snow and chill of the winter, but not yet hot enough to melt the soles of our shoes. Melissa had recruited a number of ladies from the church to decorate the open space behind the building, and they responded by festooning the trees with balloons, streamers, and the like. One large banner hung high between two trees read, "Happy 60th, Reverend Jim!" As I looked around, I decided that it had some of the air of a church social, but when I looked at the arriving guests, that could be understood, as they had obviously invited the congregation as well as Mindy and me, and several other outside friends.

The horseshoe pits had already attracted a crown by the time we arrived, and I noticed a several men gathered around a cluster of barbecues. I left Mindy with a group of women and wandered over. The grills featured chicken, ribs, and burgers. Jim was dressed up in his best barbecue apron, and appeared to be holding court, waving a spatula and tongs while he spoke. As I made my way into the group, he stopped and grinned, "Charlie, glad you could make it." Looking back at the others, he said, "Charlie and Mindy are from the bay area. They were looking up one of her relatives when we met." He frowned then. "Speaking of Mindy, where is she?"

I turned and pointed. "I left her with the ladies."

"Ah," he smiled. "I see she's found Melissa. I'm sure she'll blend right in." He motioned to a group of coolers. "We've beer and soda and water over there."

I looked at the others. Most had sodas, though a few had grabbed one of the local beers. I rummaged through the ice until I found a bottled water. It was a little early yet, and was going to be a long day with the sun already turning hot. The beer looked good, but I figured I'd wait until later; best to keep my head clear. The men were talking sports, mostly commenting on the local high school baseball games, and prospects for football in the fall, along with the occasional grousing about the poor showings of the northern California pro teams. I listened for a while and drank some water before joining in.

§§§§

We drove over to Jamestown for our winery tour a couple of days later. The party had been a big success, and we stayed late with several others to help with the cleanup. They celebrated Jim's birthday on Saturday, and then he was back in the pulpit the following morning, looking no worse for wear, and I noticed that the happy birthday banner was now inside of the tiny church.

Mindy had scheduled our visit to Jamestown for late Tuesday morning, so we had had ample time to recover.

As I drove across the Stanislaus River, she reached over and squeezed my knee. "Thanks," she said, then sat back.

I gave her a quizzical look. "Thanks for what?"

She waved her hands around her. "For this."

I obviously looked confused, so she continued. "I'd never really been up here before. In its own way, it's quite beautiful."

I looked up and down the valley. The road had come roaring down the hill, crossing a bridge that perched a good hundred feet above the river. The sun shone on the water below us, and I could see the sides of the canyon reflected on the surface. It was a glorious sight. "It's not the ocean."

"No, it's not. And I do prefer that. But like I said, there's a different kind of beauty here."

We drove on in silence. The road that climbed the south side of the pass was just as steep as the one on the north, but whereas that one came down the hill in a relatively straight shot, this one snaked along the cliff face, offering breathtaking vistas across the valley along with overlooks that fell several hundred feet to the water. Fortunately, we were on the inside lane of the roadway. I could remember riding on the passenger side of the car going in the opposite direction. I'd had to lean my head all the way out the window to be able to see any road surface beneath the tires on the right side. Finally, the road turned inland, and I was able to relax.

"So are you looking forward to the winery tour?"

"I am," she said. "I've done them before, but it's always interesting. And the growing conditions are so different here than they are on the coast. I'm sure that makes a difference."

Some thirty minutes later, we pulled into the winery. The building itself, was perched on the top of a knoll, and looked down through vineyards that rolled up and down with the contours of the hill. Well to the east, we could see up into the high sierra, and Mindy marveled that there was still a pretty significant snow pack. Down here though, at a much lower elevation, the temperature had peaked just below ninety degrees.

We'd been told to meet our guide in the tasting room, so I parked the car off to the side of the gravel lot and we got out. "So what do you think?" I asked.

Mindy looked around. "It really doesn't look like much."

I laughed. "He's a former chemist. I doubt if his family has been snatching up parcels of land for wine growing over the past half century."

"True," she said. We were both facing the main building. It was modern looking, but seemed more than anything else, like a large barn. A sign above one of the doors said simply, 'Tasting Room.'

I inclined my head in that direction, and said, "I think that's where we're supposed to go."

Mindy took my hand and we walked over.

Frank was working the crowd inside. I turned to Mindy, "This was a chemist?"

He was doing almost a stand-up comedy routine with a bottle of red wine in one hand and two glasses in the other. When he saw us come in, he waved the wine bottle and said, "Ah, come in, come in." Then he winked at one of the ladies in front of him. "What do you suppose we should pour for them."

He turned to us. "You here for the tour?" When I nodded and answered yes, he surprised me by asking, "And how much do you know about wine?"

"Um, not a lot," I hesitated. "I know some."

"Excellent," he shouted to the group. He poured a taste into each of the glasses. "For you ladies, the good stuff. Since they don't know much about wine, I think I'll go find one of the old bulk jugs out back." And to a chorus of cheers, he darted out the back door.

A young woman motioned us to the bar. "Don't mind Frank. He's in one of his moods today." She set two glasses in front of us and referred us to a tasting list. "What can I pour for you? Or would you rather work your way down the list?"

I was about to answer when Frank came bouncing back into the tasting room, carrying an actual gallon jug filled halfway with some kind of red liquid. He waved heartily to the woman who was serving us. "Hold on, they don't know anything about wine. Don't waste the good stuff on them!"

And with that, he took our glasses away from us and replaced them with juice glasses. I glanced sideways at Mindy. She had a look of mixed confusion, horror, and annoyance on her face. I figured I'd best save the day, or at least my day. "Uh," I stammered as he started to unscrew the top from the jug, "She does know her wine."

He looked up at Mindy. "Then why are you hanging around with him?"

She laughed and replied, "I wonder that myself, sometimes!"

"Ah," he exclaimed. "She's slumming!" He poured my glass from the jug and then screwed the top back on. Then he retrieved one of what I was now beginning to look upon as beautiful stemmed wine glasses. He placed it gently on a coaster in front of Mindy and then leaned against the bar. "While he drinks his swill, what can I get for the lovely lady?"

It was all theater, pure and simple, and in spite of being the goat, I was really loving it. Of course, I hadn't tasted the wine yet. I was a little nervous about that, but figured he wouldn't really pour bad wine for a customer. At least I didn't think he would.

Mindy batted her eyelashes and said, "I think I'd like to start with your reserve Chardonnay."

And that's when he surprised her by reaching out, taking her hand, and kissing her fingers. I saw Mindy's eyes go wide, before she snuck a glance at me and started to laugh.

"What," he said, as he looked around at his audience. "I'm pouring her a free glass of wine. I don't deserve a kiss?"

He reached down for a bottle of white wine, poured her a taste, and then leaned over toward her to whisper, "Wait until we get to the Cabernet." He tapped the side of his face with his index finger and winked at her. Mindy, laughing at his antics, played along, kissing him on the cheek.

Feigning a swoon, he cried, "Ah, it's love!" Then he put the bottle back, looked at me, and said, "And the swill? How is it?"

I'd been so busy watching what was going on, that I hadn't tasted anything yet. Quickly I swirled the wine in my juice glass, and raised it to my lips. I tasted tentatively, but then opened my eyes wide and took a bit more. It was good. Really, really good. But I could play his game. "Passable," I said. I smacked my lips and did my best to imitate a wine snob. "It must be the glass. Might be a little better than the box I drank last week."

Everyone was watching him, and as they started to laugh, he grabbed at his heart. "Oh, I'm wounded." He glared at me. "The box he drank last week!" Then with a devilish look on his face, he snatched back my glass. "No more for him! Anybody who drinks his wine from a box won't be drinking mine." He looked at Mindy. "Don't you share with him sweetheart, or I'll take yours too!"

And with that, he picked up his jug and danced a pretty good impression of a jig out the back of the tasting room to the applause and cheers of the patrons.

The man who came back a few minutes later looked exactly like Frank except that he was wearing a hat with the winery emblem on front. And he was all business. "Okay," he said, "Who's here for the tour?"

Mindy and I raised our hands, as did about half of the other people there. He gathered us into a group and announced that he would be starting in the vineyard. "Come with me," he said, "We'll start by looking at dirt."

And then, just to let everyone know that he was still in a playful mood, he added to me, "Even my dirt probably tastes better than what you're used to drinking, but not to worry. I consider educating riffraff like you to be a part of my job, impossible though it may be at times." Then he rolled his eyes and took Mindy's hand and led her out to his grapevine. She looked back at me, and seeing the startled look on my face, just laughed. I could hear him say to her, "Why are you hanging around with him when you could obviously do so much better?"

They were moving quickly enough that I didn't hear her response. Then they both laughed and skipped ahead of the rest of us.

§§§§

And so began an amazing day in the vineyard. Frank must have had elves running around as he moved us from the vineyard, to the crushing area, to the enormous stainless steel fermentation tanks, to the barrel storage area hidden in caves deep under the barn, and finally to the bottling room, as no matter where we went, after he'd given his talk, he was able to produce a perfectly chilled bottle of the wine that he had just described. The one that amazed me most, was the bottle of Sauvignon Blanc that he pulled out from behind one of the grape vines. I hadn't seen anybody there, and yet here came a bottle of wine, cool and tasty, and just sitting in the dirt on a hot day. It was a lot of theater. Fortunately, as a part of my education, something that I was teased frequently about during the tour, I was allowed to taste the wines as we went along. I was told that there would be a test for the novice.

In each area, he described the process, paying special attention to the chemical changes taking place in the wine at that juncture in its development. It turned out that he used the highest quality bacteria for his fermentation, and that he carefully measured the sugar content of the wine frequently during the entire procedure to get just the right flavors. I had known some of what went into making wine, but had never thought of the process as basically an enormous chemistry experiment. It was fascinating. And tasty.

When we got back to the tasting room, Mindy and I bought several bottles of wine, looking forward to sharing our newfound winemaking expertise with friends. I also asked Frank about the jug red he had served. He just laughed and pulled up a bottle of his Reserve Cabernet. "I pour a bottle in here on tour days. They've probably already rebottled the rest and served it in the tasting room. Always good fun."

More fun for some than others, I suppose, but still we had enjoyed the day and in the end, I laughed as I shook his hand and thanked him for the tour.

He did collect another kiss from Mindy when he poured her the Cabernet. Interestingly, I don't think he realized that he'd spent much of the day with red lipstick on his cheek.

§§§§

We got back to Jamestown at about two in the afternoon, and over a late lunch, decided to explore the antique stores and galleries.

"There's not much here," I said. "Where would you like to start?"

"The museum?" she asked.

"Sure," I responded. I'd always enjoyed a good railroad museum, and while this one was small, it should be interesting. I had noticed on their brochure that they featured some of the early trains that had run through the area, as well as an assortment of mining cars salvaged from the various mines that dotted the hillsides.

It turned out that the railroad museum was very small. One engine and two passenger cars along with two ore cars were just about it. The train still ran on weekends, ferrying tourists in a circle from Jamestown to Sonora and back, but this was Tuesday, so it sat quietly in the railroad yard. Still, we were able to climb aboard, sit in the seats, and imagine ourselves on a nineteenth century railroad journey. I think Mindy said it best. The cars were beautifully restored, but the seats were hard, and not very comfortable. Nonetheless, they probably beat the stagecoach.

Later, we wandered among the small shops. I found a painting that I particularly liked in one of the galleries, and tried unsuccessfully to haggle over its price. It was a watercolor of Mosquito Lake done so well that it looked almost like a photograph, except that the colors in the painting absolutely glowed with life. In the end, I left it there, and I think that pleased Mindy, as her tastes tend to run more to abstract art, and away from landscapes.

"So where should we go next?" I asked. "Candy store?"

She laughed and chided me. "You and your candy!"

"Hey," I said. "I ate all my lunch. I'm deserving." Then I winked at her. "Maybe they'll have some Graeters in there."

She just rolled her eyes. "No doubt the best ice cream, but all the way here from Cincinnati? Doubtful," she said.

"But we should look."

She shook her head. "If you wish."

And so I took her hand and led her in. As it turned out, they did not have Graeters Ice Cream, but did have a nice local selection. I debated for a while, and finally ended up with tart raspberry sorbet. Mindy broke down and had some french vanilla. When I asked her how it was, she just said, "It's good, but it's definitely not Graeters."

We'd ordered cups, so that we could sit on the plank sidewalk and watch others go by. They had little tiny tables and chairs with wire heart shaped backs. I kept squirming to try to find a comfortable angle for my back and Mindy laughed. I looked at her. "Have you ever wondered why ice cream shops always have these awful chairs?"

She tried to stay straight faced. "Tradition."

"Harrumph." I squirmed some more. "Who would have started a tradition like that. Why buy uncomfortable chairs?"

She reached across and took my free hand. "It's so that you don't stay too long."

Probably true, I thought. I looked down at my sorbet. It was nearly gone. Mindy was about half finished, but was already wiping her mouth with a napkin. "Did you want more?" I asked. She shook her head and rose. I took a last mouthful of my sorbet, savoring the tart flavor, and joined her. "Where next?"

"I think we've done most of the town. It's not very big."

I looked at my watch. It was after four thirty in the afternoon, and I couldn't imagine that the shops would stay open past five o'clock. "There are a couple more just up the street here. How about if we try those and then head on back to Murphys."

Mindy nodded, and hand in hand, we walked on.

The first shop was a gallery, and we saw all we needed to see from the front window. The paintings tended to be water colors painted of local Jamestown scenes. I didn't see any that stood out for me, and Mindy was definitely not interested, so we walked on. The antique store next door, on the other hand, was more interesting. Sure, most of what they had was junk, but it was well displayed, and the owner seemed to have selected material with some care, as nearly everything came from the late nineteenth and early twentieth century.

Mindy and I were looking at a particularly nice marble topped dresser when the owner approached us.

"Pretty, isn't it?"

I nodded and smiled at her. "My grandparents collected antiques. I remember that they had one similar to this in their bedroom, but I don't think the drawers had a burl wood finish."

"It's not common," she said. "Most were plain wood."

I ran my fingers along the front of one of the drawers. "Beautiful. Walnut?"

"Very good," she answered. "You know your woods."

"My grandfather's business was repairing antiques, so they were always around, and he loved to talk about how they were built." I smiled. "He used to complain that I wasn't a very good listener, but evidently some of it sunk in."

"So he complained about that too?" Mindy asked innocently.

I turned back to the owner. "Evidently a lifelong problem."

She and Mindy both laughed and I asked, "Actually, I was wondering if you had any gold rush era artifacts."

She shook her head. "No, I'm sorry."

Mindy had turned to me in surprise, and I said, "Another interesting period."

"Oh, very much so, but I can't compete with Arnold. That's his life."

"Arnold?" Mindy cocked her head and looked at me, "Do you suppose he's the one we heard about in Murphys?"

"He's upstairs." She pointed to the front. "Just out the front door and to the right. You'll see the stairs."

I saw Mindy's eyes widen and she said, "Somehow I assumed

that the upstairs were just offices and apartments."

The woman smiled, "Most of them are. Arnold's a little different. His shop's not much bigger than an office. Give it a try. You might find something you like." Then she glanced back at her counter. "But you'd better hurry. He closes at five."

I looked at my watch. It was 4:48. "Thank you," I said, looking at Mindy, "Shall we?"

We walked out, and there were indeed, stairs just to the right, along the outside wall. Two small signs, one saying 'California Gold,' and another, simply a hand pointing up the stairs, told us where to go.

And so we walked up the stairs. When we got to the top, Mindy pushed open the door, and we met Arnold. He was a big man, no an enormous one, standing at least six and a half feet tall, but it wasn't his height that made him so big, it was his girth. And yet, he wasn't fat. He was just, well, for want of another word, huge. Mindy had stopped at the doorstep, and I looked over her to see him. "Good afternoon," he called out in a loud, deep voice. "Come on in, I don't bite."

So we entered. "I like your outfit," I finally managed to say.

He looked down. "Work clothes. Wanna fit the image." And he did. He was wearing a worn pair of denim overalls over a long sleeved formerly white shirt. A floppy hat completed the image, covering what was left of stringy silver grey hair that matched the beard that curled down to the middle of his chest.

With an effort, I dragged my eyes away from the proprietor and looked about the room. It was a small space, but full of gold rush era relics. In one corner, I could see an assortment of pans, their dings and rust showing them to have been well used. Photos and other mining equipment decorated the walls. I could tell that we had arrived far too late to really explore this shop, tiny as it might be.

"How long have you been here," I asked.

"About thirty years," he answered. "Anything in particular you're looking for?"

I shook my head, "No. Just looking."

"Well, let me know if you need any help then." He returned to his counter where he seemed to be assembling the day's receipts. Almost as an afterthought, he threw over his shoulder, "If you're looking for something for the lady, I've got a nice selection of jewelry in the display case over there."

I made eye contact with Mindy. She was grinning at me, or just at this enormous man. I knew that her tastes definitely did not run to antique jewelry, but still said, "Thanks, we'll take a look."

While Arnold worked on his receipts, Mindy and I took a look in the case. Actually, Mindy looked. I was far too interested in everything else. "I'd love to come back here, when we have time to really look," I said. "It's the gold rush museum we've been looking for!"

She smiled at me. "Except that it's all for sale." She hugged my arm and said, "Maybe later this week."

I shrugged my shoulders and whispered. "I'm not really interested in buying anything, but it is fun to look at."

I scanned the room, and then looked back at the case. Front and center, he'd placed a display of coins from the 1850's. As one who dabbles in coin collecting, I have always been fascinated by old coins, and coins from that era are somewhat rare. Most of what he had was quite worn, but there were a few real treasures. I identified one Liberty Seated half dollar in excellent condition from 1852. Hmm. Priced at nearly a thousand dollars. Expensive. Next to that was a quarter eagle gold piece dated 1857. I looked more closely. The mint mark was 'S,' meaning San Francisco. Interesting. California gold from the gold rush. The coin was in reasonable condition, and I imagined what it would be like to own a coin that may have been held in the pocket of an old gold miner. I looked at the price. It was actually doable at about $400. On the other hand, I'd want to check prices before I invested in a little tiny shop in Jamestown. His prices might be right, or they might be sky high.

Meantime, Mindy had been looking at some old silver pieces toward the bottom of the case. Suddenly, I felt her stiffen. "Charlie," she said tentatively, "Look at this."

I looked down. There was a wide assortment of pieces, from old pocket watches, to money clips, to rings. Those weren't what had her attention though.

"What is it? Did you find something you like?"

She looked up at me and shook her head, and then pointed. I followed her finger, then squatting down, looked at the piece she had identified.

It was a locket, simple, round, and probably inexpensive. The silver was heavily tarnished, and there were clear dents and scratches where it had bumped against something. Both sides had evidently been set up to hold pictures, but one was empty now. There wasn't much to it, a worn chain and a clamshell that opened or closed on a hinge. As a piece of jewelry, nothing special. What had caught her attention, and what certainly caught mine, was that it was open. On the left was sepia tinted daguerreotype. I had seen a very similar picture of Mindy as a young woman hanging in her hallway. As small as the picture was, the woman in it could have been her twin.

I looked at Mindy. She was staring fixedly at the locket.

"Ah, excuse me," I said. "I think we'd like to look at something here."

Arnold turned toward us. "No problem." He slid a set of papers into a folder and lumbered over to us. "What'll it be?"

"That locket," Mindy said. "The one on the bottom shelf?" She pointed to her picture.

"All right," he responded and unlocked the case. "I've got some others if you want to see those too." He took the locket from the case and frowned. "Little better shape than this one."

Mindy shook her head absently, still staring at the locket. "No. This is the one."

Arnold straightened up and relocked the case. "Come on over here. I've got better light." He took us to the counter and pulled out a velvet pad, setting the locket in the center.

Mindy and I stared at it. I was right. Twins. She reached out a trembling hand and picked it up, turning it to look at it from all angles. Then she looked at me, "Do you think..."

"Could be," I said, "but so unlikely."

She was still staring at the locket. "You're probably right."

We'd piqued Arnold's curiosity, as he said, "You looking for something in particular?"

Mindy looked up at the big man. "This picture looks just like me at that age. I was wondering if maybe..." She paused, as if afraid to say more.

He was gentle with her. "Did you have relatives here back then?"

She nodded. "My great great grandfather."

He reached out and with surprising delicacy for a man so large, inspected the locket, turning it over and over. "I don't see any engraving," he said eventually. He picked up a small magnifying glass and handed it to Mindy, "Care to look?"

She took the glass and spent a couple of minutes, inspecting every surface. Finally, she looked sadly at me and shook her head. "Nothing."

"Did you want to get it?" I asked.

She shook her head, "I'm not sure. It seems right, but..."

"Just a second," Arnold said, and bent down to reach under his counter. When he came up, he was holding a small toolbox. He opened it and rummaged around until he'd taken out a tiny set of needle nosed pliers.

"Sometimes," he said as he slipped a tiny piece of cotton between the blades, "just sometimes..." He reached out his hand, "May I?"

Mindy handed him the locket and he set it on the pad. Looking up at her, he said, "Will you hold the magnifier for me?"

She held it over the locket. "That okay?"

"Perfect," he said, as he bend down to get the right clarity. He deftly used the pliers to lift up the daguerreotype. It resisted at first, but with a little maneuvering, he was able to gently lift it from its perch. The back of the locket was filled with dark red soil, compacted over the years to be almost a part of the jewelry itself. Setting the daguerreotype aside, he reached back beneath his counter and pulled out a pair of cotton swabs and some water. Wetting one, he gently wiped it across the dirt. Within a couple of minutes, he had cleaned out nearly all of the red soil, leaving a darkly tarnished shell. He rubbed a last bit of dirt out of the locket and handed it over to Mindy.

She took it hesitantly, and then held the magnifying glass over the opening so that she could look inside. And then she started to tremble all over again.

"You all right?" I asked.

She looked up at me. Her eyes brimmed with tears, but she was smiling. "Here." She offered me the magnifying glass.

I peered inside. At first, I didn't see anything, and I looked back at her. She was beaming. I looked again, raising the glass up and down until I had a clear focus. Crudely etched onto the back of the locket was a heart. Inside the heart, I could read:

CLW + JW

EPILOGUE

Our tires crunched over gravel as we rolled into the parking lot. The light drizzle that had been with us all morning continued, and when I looked up at the sky, I saw nothing but grey, nothing to convince me that we could wait out this particular storm. Oh well. We'd carried raincoats. I guess we'd be using them.

I turned to Mindy. "Ready?"

She nodded silently, clutching the door handle, but making no move to exit the car. I took her other hand, and squeezed it. She turned and favored me with a melancholy smile. "I suppose."

"Well then," I said, as I got out. The drizzle wasn't bad, just annoying. I slipped on my raincoat and trudged around to the other side of the car. As I opened the door, I reached in for Mindy. She took my hand and I pulled her out, and then maneuvered the door shut. The car was a cheap rental, and we'd already found that the doors weren't hung quite straight. They needed a little coaxing to close. On a day like today, I definitely didn't want one left ajar.

After I finished, I looked back at Mindy. She was looking up the hill, as if dreading what she was about to do. I reached up and massaged her shoulders through the light coat. She reached her head around and kissed my cheek. "I'm okay," she said. "I guess the emotions just got to me a little bit this morning. Funny how that works." Then she smiled and added, "Let's go find her."

Nearly two years had passed since the day we'd found the locket in Jamestown. In that time, we had talked frequently about what had happened with Catherine and Joel, and their hopes and dreams. In the end, we always came back to the same result. Their greatest dream had been the same that every parent has, that their child, in this case Marie, would lead a happy and fulfilling life. And we had no indication that her life had been anything but happy and fulfilling. She'd been a medical doctor, wife, mother, and leader in her community. Her children had gone on to marry and have their own children, following in her footsteps by helping others in their various home towns. I was certain that Joel and Catherine would have been proud.

So I hadn't been surprised when Mindy told me one night as we lay in bed that she needed a sense of closure to the adventure that had been our search into her ancestry. And that had led us to Bradford, Pennsylvania on a rainy day in October.

This was the old cemetery, the public cemetery, and most important of all, the former Lewis family burial ground. Marie had actually been the one who gave the land to the city several years after Catherine's death. We'd seen the grant document. It included a paragraph that reflected on the importance of the City of Bradford in the lives of the Lewis family, and an invitation to all to bury their dead in this beautiful place.

The cemetery flowed up a hill very different from those I had become accustomed to in California. The grass was green all year long, or at least when it wasn't covered with snow, and the graves were shaded by the many trees that made up the deciduous forests of western Pennsylvania. Though the wildflowers were pretty well gone by now, it was still a gorgeous spot, surrounded by low stone walls that seemed to send a message to all visitors that this was sacred ground, and should be treated with quiet respect.

I opened the wrought iron gate and ushered Mindy through. She looked at the headstones that marched in irregular rows up the shallow hillside and pointed to the top. "They get older as they go up," she said. "I imagine that the family was buried on the crest of the hill. The rest was probably used as farmland."

I nodded my agreement, and hand in hand, we made our way to a pathway dappled with the colors of fallen leaves. It seemed that the cemetery had grown in multiple directions, bulging out here, or contracting there, as people selected prime spots for family plots. And so the pathways wound haphazardly through the forest.

I looked down at Mindy and she smiled. "It's so pretty here;

so quiet. If it wasn't for the stones, I'd think we were in a park." She paused for a moment and we continued along the pathway. Then she squeezed my hand. "I'm glad."

Gradually, we made our way to the top of the hill. And then we were there. At the summit lay a simple plot surrounded by a stone border too tall to miss, but certainly not tall enough to be considered any kind of wall. I had to wonder if the original family had wanted to be separate from the town, but not by much. We stood outside and looked at the array of simple headstones. I could tell by their design and wear, without even looking at the markings on them, that some were relatively new while others were possibly hundreds of years old. Indeed, when we wandered about later, we found that the oldest dated from 1779. The Lewis clan definitely had a long history in Bradford.

This being her family, I was determined to follow Mindy's lead in this particular part of our journey, so I stood side by side with her as we looked out on her family's ancestral plot. Several minutes passed, with naught but the sounds of our breathing and the gently falling rain to disturb the quiet of the forest. Finally, she stepped gingerly over the short wall, and into the Lewis family cemetery. Kneeling before one of the stones, she said, "Frank Stevens, my great uncle, 1879-1962." She moved over a bit. "Annabelle Stevens," she looked back at me. "I never met her. 1883-1896. She died as a child."

I'd stepped over the fence and went to stand next to her. She selected another and gasped. "Jonas Lewis. He was one of the brothers. Born 1822. Died 1863 in the great victory at Gettysburg." She looked over at me and shook her head sadly. "He died in the Civil War." She continued along and suddenly dropped to one knee. I looked at the stone as she spoke. "Thomas Lewis. 1818-1874. Huh. He died so young." She patted the ground around his grave and pulled out a few weeds. "I feel like I knew him."

She stood again and we continued our stroll, passing stones that read Frank Hamilton and next to him Ruth Smithson Hamilton, and then Jeanie Lewis, who we now knew had died tormented in 1855.

Mindy led me quietly around a corner where another row of graves awaited us. Some of these headstones seemed newer, and a quick glance told me that many dated from the twentieth century although some of the first ones we'd seen had been relatively recent burials as well. Evidently the Lewis family descendants were not laid out in chronological order. She lay her hand on one. "Here's Marie," she cried. "My great grandmother." She knelt again so that she could read the inscription, "Here lie the mortal remains of Marie Stevens, Doctor, Philanthropist, and Inspiration To All. Born 1851. Died 1925." She turned to me and smiled. "I like that. "Inspiration To All. What a wonderful epitaph." She patted the stone and stood again.

We moved along and read a few more before Mindy stopped and dropped to her knees once more time. "Here she is," she whispered. She reached up to the headstone and brushed away some leaves and other debris. The message on the stone was simple.

*"Here lies
Catherine Alison Lewis
Faithful Sister
Loving Mother
Born June 27, 1833
Died January 16, 1916"*

I stood behind Mindy, one hand on her shoulder, while she cleaned the stone and straightened up debris on the grave. After she had finished, she turned to me and held out her hand. We'd brought a bouquet of flowers in her backpack and she took these now and laid them carefully at the top of the grave.

We stayed that way, motionless for a moment until she rose. "Can I have my backpack please."

I had intended to carry it back to the car, and said, "That's fine, I've got it."

"No," she said. "I need it."

Puzzled, I handed it over to her. She reached into a side pocket and pulled out a small box. I recognized it as the one that Arnold had put the locket into back in Jamestown.

She looked at me and smiled, and then bent down and using her hands, dug a small hole up against the grave marker. She opened the box and took out the locket, turning it over and over in her hands, and gently caressing the daguerreotype, before wrapping everything back in its holder again. Still smiling, she reverently placed the box at the bottom of the hole, and then, with the greatest of care, covered it over. Within a minute, even I couldn't tell that the ground had ever been disturbed.

She stood, and then leaned back against me. I folded my arms around her and rocked her back and forth for several minutes as we looked down on Catherine's grave. While I held her, I could hear her whispering, "Welcome back Joel. You've had a long strange journey, but you're home at last."

Then she turned and I slipped my arm around her shoulders. I kissed her on the top of the forehead, and then turned to go. The path ahead was glowing with the colors of the rainbow that shone between the patchy blue clouds overhead.

The following is a sample from The Ruby Crown, a new book just published in December of 2017.

THE RUBY CROWN
By Stephen T Gilbert

Prologue
June 24th

It was the event of the season, and Quinn felt fortunate to have been able to acquire a seat this close to the stage. Of course, having connections had played a big part in his attendance. On his own merit, he'd still be begging at the door. He looked around the room. The decor was muted, modern, and stylish. Nonetheless, everything in the room spoke of money, from the priceless paintings hanging on the walls, to the quality of the furnishings. He smiled to himself. New York society definitely knew how to put on a show.

Squirming in his seat, he looked around the room. He recognized a few of his fellows, and nodded casually in the direction of one. The man arched his eyebrow on noticing Quinn, then nodded in response and returned to his companion, a young woman likely brought more as arm candy than for her knowledge. Quinn chuckled. Harry had always been a ladies man, specifically one who preferred them much younger. Well, more power to him. Likely as not, if Quinn was to come back the following day, Harry would be accompanied by a different ornament.

As he continued to survey the room, he settled on a familiar figure. Her back was turned, but the familiarity of her mannerisms and the smooth contour of her naked spine caught his attention. Sensing his gaze, she turned curiously and scanned the room. Allison, he thought. There were some good times. Her eyes settled on him, and her face turned cold. He inclined his head and she scowled and turned away. Evidently his memories were more favorable than hers. Oh well.

He picked up the catalog. A number of items were listed in the order of presentation. He scanned down. The big draw was well down the page, and he looked at his watch, a Rolex Oyster he'd worn as a part of today's costume, along with the fine Italian suit and powder blue tie. It was a little before ten o'clock. With luck, the necklace would come up sometime in the early afternoon. He thought of leaving, but knew he'd never be able to reclaim his seat, so he settled in to wait.

At precisely ten, the lights in the room dimmed, and the auctioneer walked across the stage and into the spotlight at the podium. He shuffled some papers for a few moments, undoubtedly conscious of the fact that all eyes in the room had turned to him, and enjoying the ability he had to command the attention and the time of some of the wealthiest and most powerful people in the world, if only for a moment. And then, seemingly organized, he turned to the crowd. "Welcome to today's auction. Let me remind everyone, that each item to be viewed today is listed by number in the catalog. If you need a catalog or any other materials, please raise your hand and one of the attendants will be glad to assist you.

He then turned to his right and signaled an assistant behind the curtain. A young woman in a black leotard and slacks came out carrying a bronze statue and placed it on a table next to him. "Our first item today will be lot number 356, a french bronze figure of a young man entitled, 'Vigor.' This piece dates from the late nineteenth century, after Eutrope Bouret." He pointed to features on the statue. "Note the applied inscription plaque and cast signature, 'Bouret,' as well as the foundry seal inscribed 'Garanti Au Titre, Paris.' This piece stands 26 inches high."

Quinn looked around the room and noticed the bored interest of the spectators, and then up at the screen over the auctioneer's head. The camera operator had zoomed in on the sculpture, so that everyone could see the fine workmanship as well as the identification plaque.

"Bidding will start on this item at $2000. Do I hear an offer?"

A plump woman of about sixty years two rows in front of him raised her paddle. The auctioneer nodded his head, "The lady up front bids $2000. Do I hear $2100?"

Someone behind him evidently raised another paddle, as the auctioneer recognized the man and continued on. Bidding continued for the next minute or so, finally settling at $4300. The woman ahead of him shook her head and turned to her partner. "I was interested, but not for that!"

"I agree dear. Someone definitely overpaid!"

Quinn chuckled softly. Who knew. It was an auction. He looked around the room. The whole process here was very carefully calculated to get the juices flowing and extract the last possible dollar on every sale.

Meantime, the girl had taken the statue backstage and Quinn smiled as a pair of muscular young men dressed in black pants and t-shirts brought out the next item. Evidently the theme for the assistants today was to wear black, so as not to compete with the artwork. Clever. "Our next item is lot number 402, a pair of carved wood radiator covers..." Quinn glanced up at the picture on the screen. Did anyone even have an old steam radiator anymore? These were interesting, if nothing else, hand carved and ornate, in an art deco style. Still, while he could imagine placing the bronze on the mantle, these would be hideous anywhere in the house. To each his own. He looked at his watch again. Ten minutes past ten. It was going to be a long day. He could only hope that the bidding would go quickly.

Lunchtime came and went. Quinn placed his paddle on his seat, hoping that nobody would have the poor grace to move it and take his empty spot, but knowing from his study of humankind, that someone just might. Still, he needed to make a last call, so he waited for the room to empty, and then made his way carefully out to one of the gallery rooms.

He dialed and waited for a response before saying. "Your item will come up fourth this afternoon, so we should be bidding by 2:00. I just wanted to confirm my instructions." He listened quietly. He had, on one occasion forgotten to make the call, and then bid and won a rather small but erotic Japanese print, only to find that his employer had changed his mind. Quinn liked the print, and it did add a certain flair to his bedroom, or so he was told, but it had been an expensive reminder to always check his instructions. "It's a go then. And if the bidding goes over your ceiling do you want a call?"

He stood, carefully noting his instructions before ending the call. "I'll call when the bidding's over. Let's wish you luck." He slipped the phone into the left inner pocket of his suit coat and turned toward the cafeteria. He wasn't really hungry, but coffee would be good.

At exactly 1:48, Quinn's item came up for bid. Two men that he hadn't seen before walked out now, accompanied by a stunningly beautiful young woman. Her long blonde hair had seemingly been tossed causally over one bare shoulder, but everyone there knew that it had been expertly coiffed just for this occasion. She wore a simple strapless cocktail dress; a black sheath that hugged her curves, topped by a sheer satin scarf through which Quinn detected the hint of a deep V neckline. As she settled into the chair that had been provided for her, the two men positioned themselves at either side, and about five feet behind her. Bodyguards? Part of the decor? It was hard to tell. Certainly, security was at high alert today, and he had no doubt that several of the ushers were armed.

The auctioneer took his place at the podium. He scanned the audience and said, "I am certain that this is what many of you came to see today. We at Jonathan's are proud to have been selected to offer one of the world's most exquisite diamonds, the Ruby Crown." He nodded his head toward the lighting booth, and the stage lights dimmed so that all that remained was a tightly focused spotlight on the young woman seated in the chair.

Recognizing her moment, she reached up and unfastened the scarf, dropping it carelessly to the floor. the response of the audience was a collective gasp as her neck blazed with a thousand points of fire.

Quinn had visited the necklace before in the auction house's vault, but had been unable to really scrutinize it, as, for security reasons, the line of viewers was never allowed to completely stop moving. He looked from the girl now, to the screen above. The effect was dazzling. The necklace itself was studded with diamonds, ranging from very small pieces at the top, down to significant stones as it flowed together into her cleavage. The ruby, as it was called, was actually a deep red diamond, set into a cluster of smaller stones.

Quinn was hardly aware of the passing of time, as he examined the amazing piece of jewelry, and just occasionally, the exquisite girl who wore it. His mind drifted over what a thrill it must be for her to wear this amazing decoration, and then briefly, on how much fun he might have helping her to remove it.

And then the auctioneer stepped back up to the podium and cued the lights. He turned to the girl and reached his arms in her direction. "I present to you, the Ruby Crown."

He paused for a smattering of applause as he reviewed his notes, and then continued. "The Ruby Crown is reputed to be the gift that the Hindu ruler, Ballai Sen of the Sen dynasty, gave to his wife Ramdevi at the time of their marriage in 1163. The diamond itself is a flawless, pear shaped 21.3 carats, making it one of the largest red diamonds every cut. The pendant surrounding the stone is made up of twenty-eight perfect round quarter carat diamonds, and the chain, as you can see, is studded with more diamonds ranging from ten to just over one hundred points in carat weight, each of them flawless and brilliantly white. The total weight of this masterpiece is a stunning 63 carats. This is truly one of the most magnificent pieces of jewelry ever produced."

He looked back over at the girl, and the technician lowered the lights so that the spot focused in on her upper body. Quinn looked back up at the video screen, and noticed as he did, several people with hands raised, seemingly pointing at features in the necklace.

After a minute or so, the lights flickered back up and the auctioneer continued. "The entire provenance of The Ruby Crown is unknown, but I can fill a few things." He looked down at his notes, and then up again. From 1153 through 1226, the necklace was thought to have been in the possession of Ramdevi, and upon her death, her son, Lakshman. Whether he gifted his wife with the piece is not known. The necklace then disappeared for some five hundred years, reappearing as a gift to the British Raj in 1762. We know that George III, the new King of England expressed interest in the necklace, but was unable to pry it loose from Roger Hammersmith, one of the founding directors of the East India Company. Members of his family have worn it occasionally, mostly to formal banquets, weddings, and state dinners, over the past couple of centuries. It has been listed today by Roger Hammersmith's heirs. He looked back at the girl, and the lights dimmed once more.

Unlike the other items, which had been offered, described, and bid upon in just a matter of minutes, the Ruby Crown was left on display for nearly thirty minutes, so that men could wonder at it, and women could imagine how it might feel gracing their own necks. Quinn stood. He was tempted to move to the front by the stage, so that he could get a better look at the actual necklace, instead of peering up at the monitor, but noticed that a security guard stood at the front of each aisle. Evidently they were taking no chances with this piece. As he sat back down, he glanced at the woman who had bid on the sculpture earlier. She was ogling the necklace and he thought wryly, that as beautiful as it might be on its own, few could wear it with the elan of the stunning blonde on the stage.

Finally, the auctioneer signaled the lights back on and proceeded with the auction. He gave people a moment to settle, and then said, "We've set a floor on this item of three million, five hundred thousand dollars. Do I have an opening bid?"

Quinn looked about him. His instructions were clear. Enter at seven million, or if bidding stopped earlier. The auctioneer pointed to a paddle in the back of the room. "I have three and one half million dollars. Do I have three and three quarters?" Another paddle shot up and he nodded, and then another and another. As the bidding hit seven million, the pace slowed, and Quinn raised his own paddle. He was just a moment late, as the auctioneer recognized another bidder in the back of the room at seven million, and then him at seven and one quarter. The man in the back raised his paddle again and Quinn responded. It seemed that the bidding had gotten too steep for the others. He waited, and the man cautiously lifted his paddle into the air once more. Quinn immediately overbid him at eight and one quarter million and then looked back, along with everyone else. The man started to rise one more time, and then shaking his head, ruefully dropped the paddle into his lap. Quinn looked forward.

The auctioneer continued on. "I have eight and one quarter million. Do I have eight and one half?" He looked around the room and Quinn started to smile. "Going once. I have eight and one quarter million. Do I have eight and one half?" The room was silent now, many turning to Quinn, wondering who he was. "Going twice. I have eight and one quarter million. Do I have eight and one half?" Quinn waited. He knew to be patient, having been outbid at the last minute before. The auctioneer spoke again, "Going three times. I have eight and one quarter million. Do I hear eight and one half?" He looked out at the audience, and then with a rap of his gavel, said loudly for all to hear. "Sold, for eight and one quarter million dollars, to the man in the dark suit, bidder number 73."

Quinn beamed. Not only had he brought home the Ruby Crown, but his share of this little venture would not be unsubstantial. He and several others started to rise. After all, this had been the event they had all come to see. Seeing the motion, the auctioneer said into the microphone, "We are going to take a ten minute break, and then we will continue with lot 512, Dalius' Sunlight on the Pond."

Just as he turned toward the aisle, the lights were killed and the room erupted in the sound of automatic weapon fire. Quinn's military training took hold, and he dropped instantly to the floor.

The burst of fire had been brief, and when it stopped, the room seemed to be supernaturally quiet, so quiet that he could hear his own breathing, and that of the woman next to him, who somehow had fallen on top of him. A new voice came over the loudspeaker. "That's right. Stay on the floor and don't move, and you won't get hurt. Let me repeat that for anyone who was thinking of being a hero. We will shoot anyone who moves, so stay on the floor and stay still if you want to live until dinnertime."

The loudspeaker went quiet, and now Quinn could hear the sounds of muffled sobbing all around him. One man growled, "Ouch, watch where you're pushing," and then went silent again. He was tempted to raise his head, to see what was happening on the stage, but just as he figured it was safe to do so, the air was rent with another gunshot and a shriek. The voice came back over the microphone, above the screams. He sounded agitated this time, "Perhaps I wasn't clear before. If you move, we will shoot you. Do not rely on the dark. We can see you quite well!"

For the next several minutes, the only sounds Quinn heard were the whimpers of the terrified guests. The woman on top of him was one of the worst, and he did his best to comfort her, but she wasn't listening. Worse, she seemed to gain weight with every passing second, and had steadfastly refused to move her knee out of his groin.

When he figured ten minutes had passed, and surely the bandits had gone, he tried to push his way up, only to be met with her flailing arms and a muffled shriek to stay still. Frustrated, he relaxed down again, angrily pushing her knee to the side. And then the lights went on. Quinn blinked his eyes against the brightness, took a deep breath, and started to untangle himself.

When he had lifted his head over the level of the seats in front of him, he could see four men in police uniforms running down to the stage. One of them reached the front and jumped up onto the platform where he reached forward to the microphone. "Everyone take your seats." He repeated himself. "We have sealed the auction hall. Everyone take your seats. You will not be allowed to leave at this time. Make yourselves comfortable." A number of people had bolted for the back of the hall as soon as the lights went on, but they were rebuffed at the back by a swarm of police, guarding the closed, and presumably locked exit doors. The officer repeated into the microphone. "Take your seats everyone. You are safe now, but I have to ask you to be calm."

Quinn reached down and helped up a few of his older neighbors, motioning them to their seats before he sat. Looking at his chair, he noticed that the handle to his paddle was broken and the number torn, but he didn't think that he'd need it any more. It was going to be a long afternoon, and that bonus he thought he'd earned was probably gone.

As he settled into his seat, he looked up to the stage. The officer at the microphone was speaking into his chest mike and motioning toward one of the side doors. As Quinn looked in that direction, he saw two other officers leave the group at the back and run over there. Several others were on the stage now, grouped around the bodies of the model and the auctioneer. Quinn craned his neck to see over the crowd and then gasped in dismay. The auctioneer was lying face up, moaning in pain. A spreading red stain on his shoulder told him who had been shot. The blond, the beautiful young woman he'd so recently been fantasizing about, was trying to rise to her knees. She looked out toward the audience, and for a moment, Quinn imagined that they made eye contact before she slumped back down, the hair at her temple entwined in a gory mess. The Ruby Crown was gone.

ABOUT THE AUTHOR

Stephen T Gilbert is a retired businessman, teacher, and elementary school principal. He is the father of one daughter and the grandfather of two delightful grandchildren. In the years since he retired, he has taken up an old love of writing, and has published six books.

His titles include the following:

Adult books:

The Ruby Crown, the first chapter of which is included here.

The Prompter is an adult time travel, adventure story that ultimately becomes a love story. Evan works for an agency that travels back in time to help ancient civilizations to advance technologically. When he is sent back to ancient Sumeria to introduce copper technology, all goes well until he falls in love.

Children's books:

The Ruby Ring series, Casting the Die and Seizing the Crown are the best sellers. Robert, his twin sister Marie, and their friend, Johnny embark upon an quest in a medieval kingdom after Robert is given a magical ring of kingship by his mother. The books, written at a 5-6 grade level, are filled with magic, intrigue, and adventure.

Uncle Albert is the story of a sixth grade boy who suddenly becomes the principal of his school. As might be imagined, his problems only begin on that first day. He has to face angry parents, stubborn teachers, and gleeful students. Ultimately, he is forced to find solutions with the help of his friends. The book is written at a 4-5 grade level.

The Santa Hat is a novelette written at a 2-3 grade level about an eight year old boy who moves with his mother to a new community. It tells of the challenges he faces and the people he meets.

Made in the USA
Monee, IL
25 January 2024

52357474R00226